THE HOUSE WHERE IT HAPPENED

MARTINA DEVLIN

WARD
RIVER
PRESS

Published 2015
by Poolbeg Press Ltd
123 Grange Hill, Baldoyle
Dublin 13, Ireland
www.wardriverpress.com

A catalogue record for this book is available from the British Library.

ISBN 978-1-78199-930-1

Printed by CPI Group (UK) Ltd, Croydon, CR0 4YY

www.poolbeg.com

ABOUT THE AUTHOR

Martina Devlin is an Omagh-born author and journalist. Her prizes include a Hennessy Literary Award, and the Royal Society of Literature's VS Pritchett Prize. A current affairs commentator for the *Irish Independent*, she has been named columnist of the year by the National Newspapers of Ireland.

More information is available at www.martinadevlin.com

To all of us Devlins who were there. Everyone was true:
Frank, Niall, Tonia, Cathal, Conor, and especially Celsus

CONTENTS

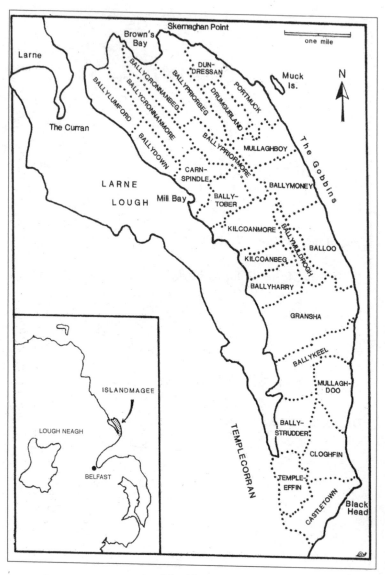

Islandmagee

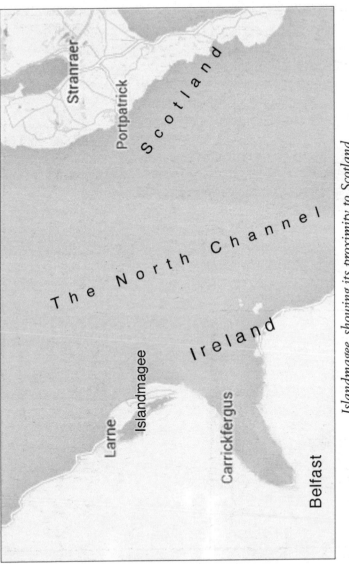

Islandmagee, showing its proximity to Scotland

HISTORICAL NOTE

The Plantation of Ulster in the early 1600s was a policy of colonization authorized by the British Crown. It proved to be a turning point in the history of the region. The majority of the land held by Irish chieftains was confiscated and used to settle planters, who were required to be English-speaking and Protestant. Most of these settlers were Lowland Scots, generally Presbyterians, who came because land was promised.

The colonization system was designed to stamp out rebellion and to 'civilize' the Irish – in the preceding century Ulster had proved to be the most stubbornly Gaelic part of Ireland. The Plantation's primary aim was to build a loyal British community on Irish soil. Although the Irish were intended to be displaced by this land redistribution, many remained on poorer land close to their ancestral holdings. The Plantation is regarded as one of the most significant historical events leading to the present-day partition of Ireland.

"The Devil came to me and bid me serve him." Tituba, a slave accused of witchcraft at Salem in 1692.

". . . these detestable slaves of the Devill, the Witches or enchanters . . . merits most severely to be punished . . ." From *Daemonologie* by James VI of Scotland, later James I of England, published 1597

Prologue

Islandmagee, County Antrim, Ireland.
Tuesday, January 13th, 1641
From Maud Bell to Frazer Bell, Pall Mall, London.

My dearest husband,

I pray God you have not already heard of the violence which took place on Islandmagee two nights ago, for I know you would be consumed with worry about all of us here. I write to set your mind at rest that neither I nor our beloved children were caught up in the Fever which swept through the island. Indeed, Fever is the only way to describe the madness which has taken hold of the place, turning neighbour against neighbour and causing many to follow where Peter led – renouncing those they once knew well.

My nerves are all of a-twitch, my ears strained from listening for sounds (in relation to what, I scarcely dare to imagine), and I have not slept more than brief snatches these past three days. Rumours abound: it is difficult to separate the truth from wild fancies. Yet the truth is already Dreadfull enough without embroidery stitched over its face. However, there will always be those who seek to exaggerate what is gruesome enough in its own right. Anyhow, my dearest, I cling to the hope that the storm has now passed.

The first inkling we had about something afoot came on Saturday, when our good friend inside Carrickfergus Castle sent word advising the household to stay indoors during the coming days. He was quite _exact_, and more than a little Alarming. On no account were we to stir abroad if we valued our lives. He urged that the livestock be brought into the barn, all doors and casements bolted, and no callers admitted, under any circumstances, even if they were friends and neighbours we knew and relied on. TRUST NONE, he said, underlining those two words so heavily that the page was ripped. Unsettled though I was by his counsel, I was swift to follow it. For as you are only too well aware, we have been quaking over reports of the most shocking atrocities carried out by the Irish against our people in other parts of Ulster. Their abominable rebellion proves them to be the Savages we always suspected they were.

As soon as I read the communication from the Castle, I made sure to keep close by me at all times, primed and loaded, the musket you left for our protection when you were forced to travel far from home during these Unruly Times. (A journey that went sorely against your inclination, Frazer, as I know right well.) Do not be alarmed, for we are all safe – despite the madness that has gripped Islandmagee.

And now I must tell you what I witnessed, though I have to confess to doubting my memory when I go to set down these events. As you know, the entire region has been in a state of agitation for months but we convinced ourselves it might pass us by, here in our small patch of Heaven on Earth. It was not to be. Still, I must hold fast to the belief that what happened has acted as a fire does, cleansing and purifying.

But back to that Sunday (can it only be two short days ago?) when the GATES OF HELL opened before my eyes. All day long I felt considerable unease. In part, it was because of the message from the Castle, grateful though I was to be

4

forewarned. And in part it was because we were trapped inside our home, and Islandmagee, which had always seemed to embrace us, took on a more sinister hue. The children were restless, begging to go outside to play. I hardened my heart and refused every plea, and for most of the day we sat quietly in the parlour, while I read aloud from the Bible. I made the three of them memorize a passage from Isaiah ("So do not fear, for I am with you; do not be dismayed, for I am your God. I will strengthen you and help you; I will uphold you with my righteous right hand") and, as I tested them on it, I confess my powers of concentration were woefully impaired.

When night fell, my disquiet did not diminish. I took the musket to bed with me, wishing you were by my side instead of this half-yard of cold metal, but determined to protect our home and our chicks as you would have done. Eventually I fell into a troubled sleep, strange shapes flitting through my slumbers, until a Fearfull Clamour woke me. Without stopping to light a candle, I raced to the window, where the moonlight spread its timid light over a scene of Utter Havoc.

A handful of yards from our door, a scramble of people were being swept along in a great jumble of panic and confusion. I watched, not quite comprehending what was before my eyes, until all at once I understood they were being chased. No sooner had this realization overtaken me than I saw it was all women and children in flight. Most of the women had babies in their arms, and some also carried a tiny passenger on their backs, while the bigger children clung to their mothers' skirts and tripped along at their heels.

Behind them was a band of foot soldiers with axes and broadswords in their hands. A few more were on horseback, officers I presume, who appeared to be holding back their mounts to stay with the body of men. Such whoops and filthy oaths issued from them that I wanted to stop my ears. They howled at the women, telling them to get ready to meet their master the Devil. There must have been at least twenty women, possibly more, and each of them appeared to have at least one or more small children. Burdened though they were, the women were outrunning the soldiers. Strange to say, no noise came from the Hunted that I could hear, though they must have been panting from their exertions. I wonder if the mothers were too intent on escape, the children too terrifyed even to cry?

I lifted your spyglass to continue observing their progress, and as I put it to my eye I saw a small boy trip and lose his grip on his mother's skirt. His was the first child's voice I heard raised. "Mammy! Mammy!" he called. The wind snatched up the Pitifull Bleat and blew it back to me. She twisted her head, searching for her offspring as she was propelled forward, and shouted out a name – I think it may have been Owen. But the poor woman was caught fast in the charge and could not turn back. The boy, who can have been no more than three or four years, was knocked to the ground in the stampede, and as he lay there a pair of mounted soldiers came upon him. To my horror, they made no effort to avoid the child. Frazer, he was trampled underfoot. His soft little body must have been ripped into ribbons beneath their horses' hooves.

Now the Gobbins Cliffs were reached. There was nowhere left for the runners to go. Sea stretched before them, soldiers behind. The pursued pulled up short, huddling at the brink. A sound came at last from the women. You could not call it a wail because this noise was not human. It was the moan an animal makes when it is caught in a trap, and can find no way out short of gnawing off its own leg. If I live to be a hundred, I hope never to hear such a cry again.

I continued watching: afraid to keep looking, and just as afraid to turn away. Moonlight glinted off the unsheathed blades of the soldiers, and bounced off the faces of the women and children as they turned to face their hunters. A few, not many, fell to their knees. I saw one supplicant hauled back to her feet by a companion. Hands cradling small heads, they gathered their children closer to them. And waited.

Even as I go to write what happened next, I can hardly bring myself to frame the words. I shudder to think such a scene could be played out in our beloved Islandmagee, this Bed of Roses transformed before my disbelieving eyes into a Crown of Thorns. I know the soldiers were our own troops, charged with defending our lives and our holdings in the name of His Gracious Majesty King Charles, and these people they hunted down were our enemies. Yet what I saw will Haunt me for as long as I live.

The women and children stood at bay. A pause seemed to hang there, and I had enough time to notice the pursuers outnumbered their prey by more than two to one. Having cornered them, the soldiers were hesitant about their next step. "Remember, this is God's work! God and the King's!" shouted one of the men on horseback – I suppose he must have been their captain. "Time to finish what we started!" called another. And the soldiers advanced.

[Fragment of letter ends here. The Bell Letters are held in the Linen Hall Library in Belfast, Northern Ireland – part of a collection relating to the 1641-2 rebellion in Ulster.]

Chapter 1

It poured fit to need the Ark again when Mary Dunbar came among us.

The night before she arrived, I woke ahead of daybreak. I wasn't given to fancies, but something unsettled me, and I lit a candle stub to keep the shadows in their place, though the mistress would have scolded about waste if she caught me. It wasn't the rain or wind that alarmed me. I slept in the loft, and the elements were closer to you there – many's the night you heard a creaking through the beams, as if a giant saw was cutting through the roof. I was used to any racket the weather could make. When a maid-of-all-work finally gets to her bed, nothing stands between her and sleep. My ma said it was God's reward for honest labour, and told me I was lucky to have a room – when she was a servant she slept on the kitchen floor.

I daresay it was the night whimsies disturbing me, and no wonder after the upset we had all winter long. A death in the house can go hard on those left living in it, especially when it's a slow passing. Old Mistress Haltridge wasn't long in her grave and had made no easy end of it. We were all of us still on edge.

Peggy McGregor, the cook, snored in bed beside me.

Comforted by the candlelight, I lay listening to the storm, and to Peggy's whistles and groans. But then I fell to fretting about my monthly courses, and what would happen if they did not come. I counted. They were overdue by three weeks now, and I was trying not to dwell on it, because I heard it said that watching for the blood only served to hold it back. But it was hard not to worry.

The rooster clearing his throat in the yard below brought my duties to mind. There was a visitor expected that day, and a guest would mean extra work. I was no lady's maid, but I would have to lend a hand with Mary Dunbar, brushing her clothes and fetching her hot water and so forth. Not that I minded too much. It made a change from the everyday. Besides, it might cheer us up to have company. The house had been cloaked in gloom since the death of my master's mother, with the bairns scurrying from one corner to another like nervous wee mice, hoping nobody would notice them. We were too quiet here now: the stream of callers trotting in and out to see the old dame, as if every day was market day, had dried up. Some called us a household in mourning, but that's not the right of it.

We were a household on edge. Watchful for what might follow.

Christian woman though she was, old Mistress Haltridge's death proved a vexing business. It should have been a relief, finally, when she breathed her last. Everybody wanted to believe her passing would bring the troubles to a halt. But something crackled in the air of Knowehead House still. Something bent on mischief.

The rooster crowed again and I had to set aside my fears for myself, as well as for the goings-on at Knowehead. Downstairs to the kitchen I took myself. I always liked early morning, before my bones ached and folk pulled me this way and that, wanting the sun, moon and stars from me. Oftentimes I would dawdle over a sup of milk, yawning and stretching to my heart's content. Waiting for the day to reveal itself.

But I had no liking for what it revealed this day.

At first, I failed to spot it. I went to the larder for the milk, and then I opened the top of the kitchen half-door a splinter, rain or no rain, to let in a breath of air. It was only when I crossed to the fireplace to see if there was any life left in the embers that I found it. A big, blue-black crow lay in the ashes. Dead as last summer. It had come down the chimney in the night, and must have been done for before it landed, because it stayed where it fell. Its feathers were singed by its resting place, but it wasn't the burnt reek that bothered me. No, what gave me the dry heaves was them two eyes like beads. Wide open and full of wickedness. But I breathed deep, stretched out my hand and lifted the bird by its scaly feet. Then I ran outside to dump it on the midden heap before anyone else saw the trespasser and made a fuss about omens. We had enough to put up with at Knowehead, never mind dead crows setting tongues wagging.

Knowehead House is on Islandmagee, a wheen of miles – fifteen or thereabouts – from Carrickfergus. The island is tucked into the north-east coast of Ireland, in the county of Antrim, and a nicer, more fertile wee nook you'd be hard pushed to find. It has been a God-fearing place since the Scotch folk settled it, these hundred years and more. What was papist, and pagan before that, was put aside. Everything was made tidy, with ditches between fields so you knowed what was what and whose. Aye, the planters were bent on taming wildness.

Yet something dark stirred on Islandmagee towards the heel-end of 1710, like an animal nosing out of its winter sleep. And by these early weeks of 1711, evil was abroad. Happenings to make you shiver were gathering pace. An old sheepdog, soft as butter, turned savage for no reason and attacked the Orrs' baby, leaving its life hanging by a thread.

Another time, the sky turned dim and a black circle crawled across the sun, blocking its light. All that was left was a fiery ring round the outside. The darkness slid away after some minutes, but not before causing terror far and wide, with folk sinking to their knees and wailing about the end of the world. Even after it passed, all were certain it would bring down bad luck.

Worst of all were the whispers about Hamilton Lock being spotted again, walking about at night as though he was lord and master of the island – though by rights he should have been turned to dust some forty-five years ago. If ever a man ought to be keeping the demons busy, piling on the faggots, Hamilton Lock was him.

If the ghost of Hamilton Lock was abroad, folk agreed misfortune would surely follow, for there never was a man born of woman to match him in wickedness. From the stories you'd hear, he was a fellow could trick his way into the New Jerusalem and make merry mayhem among the saved. Anybody that clapped eyes on him always saw him near-hand to Knowehead House. One of the elders who called over to pray with the old mistress spied him by our barn, called out his name – and was thrown by his mount as soon as the words left his lips.

No two ways about it, it was ill-starred for Knowehead House that such a fiend should pitch up to mock and frighten us, just as the old dame turned feverish and took to screeching all manner of ungodly things. It left folk thinking he had some hold over her. Especially as strange things began taking place at Knowehead at the same time.

Belongings went missing, disappearing for days before turning up in the rarest places. I found wee Sarah's rag doll at the bottom of the turf basket, and the key for winding my master's tall clock in a pitcher of milk. When I cut into an apple tart, what should be inside but one of the mistress's shoe buckles? Before long, the hens stopped laying and we had to send out for eggs, while my master's greyhounds refused to come into the house – even with bones to tempt them.

Then there was the day Peggy McGregor found a hoof-mark outside the front door, sunk deep in the earth as if meant to act as a warning. Soon after, wee Sarah said she could hear feet on the roof at night, dancing a jig to fiddle music. Another time, her brother Jamesey insisted he saw a black dog with a long red tongue at the casement. The young master swore it spoke to him in a man's voice, asking him to slip out and follow him. The childer took to refusing to kiss their grandmother goodnight, as had been their habit – they said whispers came from a big wooden chest in her bedchamber.

Your head would be noddled trying to follow what was going on. The best you could do was say your prayers and mean them, and sleep two or more to a bed. And, during it all, old Mistress Haltridge was raving away, saying evil had returned to Islandmagee.

But maybes the evil was there all along, biding its time. Looking for folk to use.

◖ ◖ ◖

I was twelve when I went to live at Knowehead House as maid to the Haltridges, with plenty to keep me going from sun-up to sunset. My master was James Haltridge, Gentleman, born on the island same as myself, and he loved it the way I do though both his parents were reared in Scotland. My life has been commonplace, but my master was well-travelled. He visited lands where he conversed with men whose faces were as black as boot leather and as red as roof-tiles. He saw bears baited by a pack of dogs, and oxen roasted whole on a river wider than the length of Islandmagee, turned entirely to ice. He was chased on the high seas by French privateers, aye, and outran them, too. But for all those sights, he said there was nowhere on earth to match Islandmagee with its braes and its

13

burns. "It burrows into your heart and spoils you for anywhere else," he said oftentimes. I don't seek to make a paradise of it, but I have to agree with him.

Mind you, every paradise has its serpent.

The mistress never cared for the place. Maybes Knowehead never took to her, nor her to the house. It can be hard on a woman to leave her people and live among strangers when she weds. What was happening inside her own four walls made her nervous, forbye. She stopped feeling safe in bed at night, especially when my master was away from home. That winter he was oftentimes in Scotland, trying to smooth over a legal dispute in the family involving an inheritance. It meant the mistress had most of the burden of the old dame's illness, and she became a tricky patient to manage as her fancies caught hold.

Old Mistress Haltridge took to screeching that Knowehead should be tumbled down, stone by stone – once, she even leaped out of bed and tore at the plaster on the walls till her fingers bled. That was odd, for a woman who used to say in the whole of her health, "Don't think me boastful, but Knowehead House is surely one of the finest properties on the island."

Nobody could argue with that. It was built for my master's father when he was minister here in the parish of Kilcoan More. I always loved how the road curved away just in front of Knowehead, pushing uphill, inviting you to catch your breath and notice how everything belonging to it was as neat as a new pin. Looking back, you saw a long, thatched house with lime-washed stone walls, rising two floors high, when only a few here were built to such a height. Trees planted near-hand gave shelter, and every year blackbirds nested in them – it did the heart a power of good to see them wee scaldies with their wide-open beaks. One of the trees always gave a fair crop of apples, and many's the tart we filled with them.

We had a dairy and a hen coop, as well as stabling for the horses, while at the far end of the yard stood a barn. The piggery and cow byre were on the downward slope, on account of the smell and mess. Dirt never bothered me, nor my master. The mistress was town-bred though, and never accepted the way the hens had the run of the yard. The notions she took would put a duchess to shame.

We ate well in Knowehead. The land looked after you if you looked after the land. The Scotch settlers believed in working it, and the new folk were busier than the Irish they replaced. They ploughed and dug. They pulled rocks out of the yellow soil and gathered seaweed to use as manure on the potato crop. They fattened and enriched the fields so there was no need to let them lie fallow. "God helps those who help themselves," said the planters. But the Irish called them cuckoos, and every now and again tried to shake them out of their nests. Except the Scotch weren't for being pushed out. They built sturdy nests, and defended them with arms – aye, and with soldiers from Carrickfergus Castle.

Some might say Knowehead could have been fancier, but I say it was a house built for living in rather than admiring. Rooms were added on as my master prospered. It was a solid, practical place, fit for purpose and serviceable, like a gown that gives years of wear and takes kindly to patching.

The mistress was right about Knowehead, all the same. There was something other about the house. I noticed it the first time ever I set foot in it. Once in a while, it could give you a feeling – as if something was there, just out of the corner of your eye. A movement, quick as a fish through water. And your heart would skip in your chest. It was a house made up not of doors and floors alone. That's the best way I can explain it. You'd have to stand inside Knowehead and breathe it in to understand what I'm trying to put across.

"I'd sooner go to the poorhouse than spend a night in Knowehead," my friend Mercy Hunter said every now and again. It never stopped her accepting gifts from old Mistress Haltridge, though, to pass on to her mother – like warm stockings the good dame knitted, though her fingers ached from holding the needles, and a blanket handed over with a blessing one bitter winter. Many's the one had the benefit of her kindness about these parts.

I stood up for Knowehead when anybody passed remarks about it. All the same, I knowed something was not quite right. The place was twisty somehow, like the horns you see on the odd cow.

But it was a manageable twisty. Till Mary Dunbar landed in on top of us. She was a beauty, and beauty causes a disturbance. It brings disorder, despite seeming orderly to the eye. There was something twisty about her, daisy-fresh though she was.

The reason Mary Dunbar came among us was because my master was obliged to make another trip, and felt guilty about leaving his lady yet again. Mary Dunbar was cousin to the mistress, and would keep her company. My master was a merchant, part-owner of a schooner that traded between Ireland and Barbados. Since he was a Presbyterian, he could not earn his living from the law, nor from any government position such as the courts or the excise office. And whether he attended it or not, he had to pay tithes to the established Church. As he said himself, you might just as well be a papist, except you'd be damned in the afterlife.

Word came that a shipment of sugar, delayed by ill winds, had docked at last, and he needed to go to the Custom House in Dublin to see about selling on the cargo. But my master could see his lady was having a time of it, between nursing his mother and trying to hold her head high against the gossip – not that he ever allowed there was anything in it. He was blind about what went on at Knowehead House but he could not fail to notice how jumpy the mistress had become. He insisted it was lack of sleep from nursing his mother that made his lady give way to imaginings. But that wasn't it at all. Her nerves were in ribbons from what she witnessed in the house.

I saw some of the same things myself and they couldn't easily be explained. It was near-impossible to keep candles lit by old Mistress Haltridge's bedside because something kept snuffing them out. And at times, when you sat with her, you'd hear footsteps in the yard below, circling the house. A man's footsteps, heavy and purposeful. But there was never anybody there. I never clapped eyes on ghost or demon – I could not have stayed in service with the Haltridges if I did. But there was definitely a shadow in her bedchamber that took the shape of a man, though if you looked hard it melted away.

Towards the end, the old dame kept up a caterwauling that would make a body's ears bleed. One night, from dusk till dawn, she called on the Devil by all his names: Satan, Beelzebub, Lucifer, Anti-Christ, Fallen Angel. When my master was told, he made out she was railing against the Devil, but Peggy McGregor and I were agreed it sounded more like she was calling on him.

My master could pretend all he liked – and he would never accept there was anything untoward at Knowehead – but the strain took its toll on the household. I daresay he was just as upset as his wife, but at least he was able to saddle up his horse and leave everything behind. The mistress was tied to the house. And the household's habits were turned throughother, between the doctor calling every second day, the neighbours in and out like Jack-in-the-boxes, and the minister and elders spending a good deal of time under our roof praying over the old dame – all of them needing to be fed.

His lady was at the end of her tether, so my master came up with the notion of inviting Mary Dunbar to leave her parents' home in Armagh and visit with us in Islandmagee.

"You can't ask someone to be a guest in a household where

death might knock on the door any day," said the mistress. "Your mother could take her last breath this very night."

"Who knows God's design, Isabel? And you need a companion. No harm in sending an invitation – you often speak of Mary."

Ten years lay between the cousins, but they were on friendly terms before the mistress married my master. Back then, before the Dunbars moved away, they lived near-hand to one another in Belfast. As a wee mite, Mary Dunbar used to follow the mistress about, and she made a pet of her. My master had only met her once, and scarcely knew the young lady.

It was on Candlemas Day that the mistress sat down at her writing desk to ask if Mary might pay a visit. I recall it clearly: the weather was sunny, and I thought I'd get a head-start on the cleaning.

"This is shapin' up to be the best day in months, mistress. I've a good mind to put the beddin' on a bush to air, and have a go at beatin' out the rugs."

"Mind you don't disturb your master's mother, Ellen. She's asleep now after another restless night. I could do nothing to pacify her."

"I'll work well away from her side of the house. But it would be a shame not to take advantage of the sunshine, even if there's no heat to it."

"Do as you like, I cannot direct you. I have my household accounts to tally, and a letter to send by Noah Spears to Port Davy if it's to make the post. Money goes nowhere these days. It's scandalous it will cost me thruppence to get word to Aunt Dunbar." She straightened her cap and wiped a mark from her skirts. Fierce particular about her appearance, was the mistress.

"Never you worry about me, mistress. I'll look about for what needs doin'. A day like this is a gift from the Almighty and it's a sin to waste it."

"I'd rather see it dull, today of all days. '*If Candlemas Day* be fair and bright, winter will have another flight.' That means it's bound to turn wintry again. The old sayings have the right of it."

The mistress was always looking for causes to be unhappy. She was never one to see the good in anything. She whinged about all the time my master spent away from home on business, without being grateful for the presents brought back for her – he never returned without a trinket in his knapsack. I remember a pair of buttercup-yellow stockings – silk, if you don't mind. Worsted ones weren't fancy enough for her. No wonder the minister spoke to her about the sin of vanity. She was the most prideful woman on Islandmagee.

It gave the mistress a lift when her aunt answered by return of post. She was excited enough to read it out to my master, not noticing I was there, polishing the furniture with beeswax, the smell making my head light.

"Listen, James, Aunt Dunbar writes she can spare my cousin right willingly: '*The change of scene is exactly what Mary needs after being cooped up all winter. Your uncle and I have been racking our brains for some place we could send her to take her out of herself. We worry about her being too much alone and prey to her thoughts. An only child can be somewhat isolated. It goes hardest on sensitive girls such as our Mary – their fancies seem to take shape more readily. However, I feel confident the fresh air and company on Islandmagee will do her a world of good. Your invitation is a godsend.*' Do you think we might be able to keep her till after Easter, James?"

"She might stay for good if we find her a husband, sweetheart. And that should be no trouble if she takes after your side of the family."

"I know you're anxious to attend to business. Will you still be here when she arrives?"

"It depends on Mother. What kind of son would I be, to go haring off to Dublin and risk missing her last words? I'll just have to be patient. It's only twice in our lives we're obliged to wait around: the first time for birth and the second for death. I can spare my mother a few more days. The poor soul is agitated enough without me taking off, and causing more distress. These visions of hers are the rarest thing – I never knew the like of them. I daresay if my father was alive he could find the words to put her mind at rest. But I can't seem to make her understand she's safe here in Knowehead. I'm afeared she's not in her right mind at all. You know, only the other day she begged me to take her away from here."

"I heard her. James, would you not think of humouring her? She must have her reasons."

"I'm surprised at you, Isabel. She's not well enough to travel. Besides, Knowehead House is where she belongs. It's where we all belong."

"But if it's causing her agitation. If she sees things that unsettle her . . ."

"It's all in her mind. I'll hear no more on the subject."

Aye, he could order his lady silent, but he couldn't force his mother to stay quiet. Only the night before, the old mistress had roused herself to cry, "The Haltridges are being punished! It willnae stop at me. There's a curse on this family. It will hang over us till there isnae a Haltridge left on Islandmagee!"

"What are we being punished for?" asked the young mistress, but my master stepped in and started spooning a potion into his mother, before answer could be made.

I thought the old dame would resist, and force him to listen to her, but by then she was spent. She fell back on the pillows, her strength used up.

Old Mistress Haltridge died on the 8th day of February, and as soon as ever she was in her grave my master started making arrangements to leave. Don't think him cold-blooded – he loved his mother, his eyes were red-rimmed at the funeral.

But time and tide wait for no man. "It's the living I need to consider now," he told his friend Frazer Bell.

My master's mother was taken four days before Mary Dunbar came among us. They never met. Would it have made a difference? It's possible. Dead, the old dame could be turned this way and that to suit others' needs. But if you met that decent woman for yourself, if you looked into her eyes and saw the charity in them, you might not be so quick to bandy her name about.

Knowing the young lady was on her way meant my master was easier in his mind, making preparations to leave. That didn't stop his lady from going at him, hammer and tongs, the day before he set off. I was preparing the bedchamber opposite theirs for the visitor, lending it a few of the mistress's dainties to make it more welcoming, and I couldn't help hearing their squabble.

"James, now your mother's gone, there's something I want to raise with you. Maybe you might think about it when you're in Dublin. My love, could we look about finding someplace else to live?"

"Surely you're not picking up where my mother left off, Isabel? She took a strange fancy, brought on by the fever. I see no earthly reason why we should leave our home."

"But I don't like it here. It's not as if I haven't tried. I'm nine years under this roof, after all."

"Aye, Isabel, I know it's nine years. Nine joyful years, I was foolish enough to believe. I brought you here as a bride, and you told me you never saw a house that pleased you as well."

"That was before –"

"Before what?"

"Before I lived here. Before I knew what it was like."

"You're talking as much moonshine as Mother did on her deathbed. But she wasn't herself then."

"Was she muddled, James? Was she truly? I thought her

21

lucid to the end. And with her dying breath, she tried to warn us. She saw Hamilton Lock – here in this house."

"She imagined she saw Hamilton Lock. There's a world of difference."

"She called out his name. She threw her Bible at him. She ordered him, in the name of the Lord Jesus, to stay away."

"My mother never knew Hamilton Lock. It was just a name she put to a nightmare she had. But it's a debauched name – best forgotten."

"Your mother saw his ghost. She was convinced of it. She told me he poisoned the air in Knowehead."

"Isabel, you try my patience. Forget about Hamilton Lock. The idea of his ghost disturbing Mother is flim-flam. Nobody else saw a thing. Admit it, you saw nothing when you were with her."

"Sometimes I felt as if somebody walked on my grave."

"You 'felt'. Never mind what you felt. What did you see? Nothing. A dying old woman conjured up the bogeyman, and you let yourself be taken in by it. I'm disappointed in you, latching on to her superstitions."

"It's only natural this is where Hamilton Lock would come – didn't he live here?"

"He did no such thing."

"Not in Knowehead House, but his family farmed our land. Our barn was built where their cabin used to stand. Noah Spears told me so."

"Noah Spears should hold his tongue if he wants to keep his job tending our stock."

"Don't be a crosspatch. Noah only spoke the truth. The Locks were moved off the land when your father became minister here. What's ours was theirs before."

"Sir Moses Hill owned the land, not the Locks. He had every right to move them. My father came here by invitation, to tend to the spiritual needs of the landlord's tenants."

"James, bring me and our children away from here. I'm

begging you. Something isn't right about this house."

"I'd sooner take leave of my senses than take leave of Knowehead. I'll be damned if I quit this house any way except feet first."

"How can you swear at me? You promised on our wedding day you'd always treat me with kindness."

"Forgive me, Isabel. I lost my head. But you're the only one who wants to leave. The children are happy here."

"Maybe before. But these past months have been hard on them. They had the night terrors when your mother lay dying. Sarah's scared of her shadow now. And Jamesey's all full of bluff and bluster, but I know he isn't himself."

"The children are fine. If they heard things that frightened them, they'll soon forget."

"Others won't. Once your mother started using that name, tongues clacked. I told the servants I'd turn them out if they repeated anything Mistress Haltridge said. But the neighbours were in and out of the house, visiting her bedside. Word spreads. Folk have been saying an illness like hers couldn't come from God. And that Hamilton Lock was a . . . was a . . ."

"Spit it out."

"A messenger sent to bring her to his master the Devil!"

"Damn them all to hell for their malice! I'd like to take the gossipmongers and shake them till their teeth fall out. Shame on you for listening to tittle-tattle. I thought you had more spirit. It makes me sick to the pit of my stomach to think anyone could spread vicious lies about a pious Christian who never did harm to anybody, her entire life!"

"James, don't upset yourself. Nobody thinks any of it was your mother's fault. But we can't pretend it didn't happen. It was a warning to us."

"Can't you see, we'd be giving them an excuse to spread even more rumours if we turned tail? We have to hold our heads high and weather this. The Haltridge name mustn't be tainted. Not just for my sake, or Mother's, but for Jamesey and Sarah. Isabel, sweetheart, I'm relying on you. You must support me in this."

"James, you were away a lot over the winter, while I was here. In the thick of it. Things happened in this house that made my blood run cold."

"What things?"

"You know as well as I do. I've told you often enough. Things that sound stupid in the light of day, but they can't be explained away. What about the time Sarah was pushed out of bed? Or the candle that was toppled, all but setting fire to the house. And once, when you were away, I felt an icy hand clamped to my mouth as I lay in bed, but when I struck a light there was no one."

"These things are accidents or imaginings. Every house has them, after dark."

"Why won't you listen? What mischief has to overtake us before you see sense? You make me out to be a silly goose when I know in my bones something's not right."

At that, she burst into tears, and my master was helpless against them.

"There, there. Nobody's calling you a silly goose. You're the bonniest woman on Islandmagee. And I haven't forgotten how you behaved like a daughter to my mother when she needed one. You were a blessing to her. Didn't she leave you her pearl ring, when she could have said it should be put aside until Sarah was old enough to wear it? Hush, Isabel. Hush. Mother's gone now, and all the upset is dead and buried along with her. Try to be brave for a day or two longer, and your cousin Mary will be here with you. The pair of you will be so delighted with each other's company you'll have no time for me when I get back from Dublin. Come here, sit on my knee and give me a kiss, and let's have no more quarrelling."

My master preferred surfaces to be smooth. No matter what lay beneath. He was always inclined to escape from unpleasantness, counting on all being well when he returned.

The funeral meats were not even finished before he saddled up and was gone. And our household of women and childer did what we do best. We waited.

Mind you, I had plenty to occupy me, keeping the house and everybody in it warm and fed. No job too messy for me. I scooped out the ashes from their fireplaces, emptied their chamber pots, and wrung the necks of their chickens. My hands were like lumps of raw meat at the end of the day.

It was no great odds – I was born to be a worker. From when I was no age, Ma told me I should thank the Good Lord for fashioning me hale and hearty, because a strong back would outlast a pretty visog. "It might outlast the face but not outshine it," laughed Da, who melted at a pair of bright eyes, like most men. Ma always said to pay him no heed. "Your face is the way the Man Above intended it to be," she used to say. "He drew it Himself, and He knew what He was about."

I can't deny the Lord God drew my face, but He didn't put His back into it the way He did when He tackled Mary Dunbar's. Now, she had a face to linger in the memory. We all thought she was a gift from above sent to lift our spirits.

Little did we know. She tested us sore, and no mistake. For a slender lass, she cast a long shadow.

Chapter 2

The mistress was worried Mary Dunbar's coach might have to turn back on account of flooding, with the day being so wet, but she had to send Noah Spears in to Carrickfergus with the ass and cart anyway. Coaches didn't venture out as far as Islandmagee. Noah was busy chopping wood, and grumbled about being taken from his work to ferry folk about, but I think secretly he liked an outing.

Noah was a bachelor, with less hair on his head than a wee scaldy – and no wonder, because he was old when Adam was a boy. But lately I found myself watching him, wondering if he might be tempted to take a wife. Would a young woman in his bed make up for another man's child in her belly? Best cross that bridge when I come to it, I told myself. I might escape the consequences of my sin yet. I tried not to think about whether he could be the answer to my problem as he carried in Mary Dunbar's trunk.

The young lady's spirits were high despite the lashing rain she travelled through to reach us. She smiled at me, a dimple popping into each cheek, as I took her woollen cloak, heavy with water, to dry in front of the kitchen fire. She had a lambskin rug as well, to cover her knees on the journey, and it was soaked through. Behind her smile, you could see the visitor was tired after her journey – and no wonder, for she had to rise in the wee small hours to catch the coach on its way through Armagh. Them coaches stop and start at every turn round, between passengers getting on and off and letters and packets being collected at inns.

The mistress was as excited as a bairn about having a guest. Islandmagee was lonesome for her taste – towns were Mistress Haltridge's preference. "I can't buy as much as a button without ordering the horse made ready," she complained many's the time. I suppose it was natural, for a glover's daughter who grew up above the shop, used to constant hustle-bustle. That's where she came by her taste for fine plumage. Not that the island was the place to indulge it. The meeting-house was not meant for parading in showy bonnets, though it never stopped her.

Islandmagee is no island, by the by. The master told me it was a – wait now till I think of the word – a peninsula, which means it is almost an island but not quite. A strip of land ties it to the mainland, the way a bonnet's ribbons hold it on the head. May as well be an island, because we're tucked out of the way here. And that's how we like it.

The mistress urged the visitor into my master's leather-and-mahogany chair next to the fire, in the parlour, leaning behind her to plump the cushions. Then she called for a hot toddy to warm her cousin, in case she might have caught a chill. She made a show of telling me not to add the honey till the hot water was mixed with the whiskey, as though I was a simpleton. I daresay she wanted her cousin to think she ran a tight ship. They were yarning away, nineteen to the dozen, as I carried the tray through to the good room. This was a chamber the mistress was proud of, with its flagstoned floor. The rest were floorboards or clay covered with rushes.

"I'm not so much tired as sore, Isabel, from being thrown round inside the coach. It almost overturned more than once. The roads were slippery from rain."

"James says the public thoroughfare has holes the size of a cartwheel. Only the other week, he spoke of going to our neighbours and taking up a subscription to have them repaired. Did you hear any news on the coach?"

"There was talk of the Earl of Antrim's marriage to an English lord's daughter. And of an apothecary from Lisburn, deceased a year since, whose house and shop are being sold to the highest bidder because the heir can't be tracked down."

The mistress fussed over her cousin, who was sitting there like a queen in her cap with lace lappets. If you ask me, only the promise of this visit kept her from taking to her bed after my master set off. I never knowed a woman so fond of her bed.

I set the toddy on a table fornenst Mistress Haltridge, before crossing to the fire to build up a blaze. I took my time, so as to steal a closer look at the young lady.

"I was sorry to hear about your mother-in-law passing over, Isabel."

"She'll be missed. She was a great help with the children – at least until a few months ago."

"Mama said you wrote and told her she took some odd fancies towards the end."

I dropped the block of turf I was holding, and Mistress Haltridge flashed a warning with her eyes. Mary Dunbar looked from one of us to the other, peeping out through a mass of curly hair.

"Never mind standing there swinging your arms, Ellen," said the mistress. "Go and see about the children. They'll want to come and bid their cousin welcome."

There was only a year between Master Jamesey and Missie Sarah. They were firm friends for the most part, though they could fight like cat and dog when the humour was on them. I was afraid this would be the very day they'd tear strips off each other, and them in their Sunday best, under strict instructions to keep their clothes clean. But they were good as gold, waiting in the nursery, the wee girl holding her babby-doll and her brother with a tin soldier in each hand. They ran at me in a rush of arms and legs when I opened the door.

"Can we go down now?"

"I'll show her my soldiers."

I checked their hands were free of dirt before leading them downstairs. Then I waited by the parlour door while the childer approached the guest, Missie dropping a curtsey the way her mother had taught her, the young master tilting his body into a stiff bow.

Mary Dunbar kissed them both. "I've made your acquaintance before, Jamesey, but you wouldn't remember. You were still crawling."

"And me? Did you meet me?" asked Sarah.

"No, this is our first time. But I can tell we're going to be the best of friends. I've brought you a yard of ribbons from my father's shop – I'm going to plait your hair in the latest fashion."

Sarah wriggled with delight. Mary Dunbar possessed the happy knack of being the centre of attention without doing anything to draw the eye.

Back I went to the kitchen to discuss the newcomer with Peggy McGregor. She styled herself housekeeper, but cook was nearer the mark, and she was ancient, so the heavy duties fell to me. The Haltridges kept her on because she came to Islandmagee from Scotland with my master's father when he was given the living in Kilcoan More. She was there long before the old minister brought his bride into the house. Peggy was a good cook, I'll grant her that, but no help with the labour of scrubbing floors, drawing water from the well or beating the laundry clean. Lately, I even had to help with the cooking, because she was a right slowcoach and the meals would never be ready otherwise. I didn't mind – cooking was a useful skill. In time, I hoped I might be taken on as the cook myself. I didn't want to be a maid-of-all-work all my days.

"Peggy, I could'n tear me eyes off her hand holdin' the hot toddy glass. I never saw such totie wee fingers. They would'n be out of place on a child of ten summers."

Just then Mercy Hunter burst through the back door, all of a tizzy. She must have run the whole way from Ballymuldrough. Her news tumbled out of her.

"This is on'y a flying visit. I cannae stop. The minister's been called out to wrestle with sinners. Sammy Orr an' Ruth Graham were discovered in a state of fornication." She waited to see we were suitably shocked that a tenant farmer and his maid were found sinning. "They were caught ruttin' in his stable like animals. Naked as a chicken ready for the pot, was Ruth Graham. At least he kep' his shirt on. His wife came upon them an' sent for my master."

I felt a giant fist take hold of my heart and wring it slowly.

"I'd a thought Fanny Orr would be pleased at a break from child-bearin'. Is it six or seven she has now?" said Peggy.

"Six wee Orrs. Three of each. Sammy never tried to deny it – how could he, with no britches to cover his arse? But he said he did'n know what come over him – he must a been tempted by God's Ape. The minister says 'tis proof the Devil's cloven hooves are clatterin' about Islandmagee." She widened her eyes, shuddering.

"Well then, Mercy Hunter, I wonder at you riskin' your immortal soul to step out to us." Peggy had little patience with Mercy – even if she was as interested in her news as the rest of us. Oftentimes, she said Mercy Hunter had a tongue too long for her gob.

"How so, Peggy McGregor?"

"If Aul' Nick is abroad an' temptin' folk, he might spot your apple cheeks as you go skitin' across the fields an' try his luck with you."

Those cheeks paled, but Mercy held her ground. She had more talking to do, and Peggy wasn't going to put her out of her stride. She edged over to the fire to warm her nether regions. "Sammy Orr and Ruth Graham will be shamed afore the congregation, their sin named from the pulpit. They'll be put on stools in front of everybody to make confession – it'll take a month of Sundays afore the minister reckons them repented. Fornicators are his pet hate."

The giant fist gave my heart another squeeze.

"Sammy'll weather the storm. His wife'll give him the could shoulder for a while, but that's as much as she can do. Ruth'll not get off so handy. She'll be turned out of their service. And then what's to become of her? If she goes home, she'll be beat by her da till there bain't an inch of flesh on her body. Still, maybe she's as well takin' the hidin'. After she losses her position, no mistress from these parts will touch her. She'll have to go as far as Carrickfergus, maybe even Belfast, to look for work." Mercy lifted the back of her skirts to let her legs have the benefit of the heat.

I spoke up, wanting to believe Ruth had a chance of a future, even when it was clear she had no easy time ahead. "I hear there's agencies that find you places. I saw one in a journal from Dublin my master give me, to practise reading." My master taught me to read, and some lettering as well, when most maids can just about make their mark. Many's the time I watched him take out a penknife, choose a feather from a goose wing and fashion it into a quill.

I produced the *Dublin Intelligence* from under the settle and read it aloud. "'*At the Blue Leg in Castle Street is kept the Intelligence Office, after the same manner as in London, where any Persons may be furnished with Men or Women Servants or Nurses. Likewise such Servants as can show Certificates of their Good Behaviour may be placed in Positions.*' You see? Thon place could maybes find Ruth a job."

"Hell will freeze over afore Fanny Orr gives Ruth a certificate of good behaviour after what she got up to with her Sammy," said Mercy. "An' Sammy Orr wud'n dare go agin her. Ruth's reputation is lost now. She can never get it back."

Masters are hard to turn down, I thought. Every maid knows that – every mistress, too, even if she chooses to blame the maid. And then I thought: Pray God he has'n planted a child in her.

The others stared at me, appalled. I hadn't just thought it – I had spoken my fear aloud.

Mercy and me, we knowed Ruth Graham all our lives – all three of us grew up together, tumbling in and out of each other's cottages, and it was a struggle to imagine her with Sammy Orr. He was father to a brood of childer as thick in the neck as him, including the wee one savaged by the sheepdog turned wild. For Ruth to give herself willingly to a man who dribbled over his tankard of ale, and slapped any backside he could get away with handling, was a right waste. You could see it with a gentleman like my master, who changed his linen regularly and had coaxing ways to turn a girl's head. Any maid could be forgiven for weakening under temptation from him. But Sammy Orr was another kettle of fish entirely. Satan's hand was at work here, sure enough.

Peggy read my thoughts. Well, some of them. "The Devil makes work for idle hands. Mistress Haltridge and her guest need their supper. Mercy Hunter, the minister could be back home already and wonderin' why you're out gaddin'."

"Not at all. He's on'y gettin' goin' with the prayin'. The master loves a good pray." Mercy was a sauce box, but she carried it off. The pretty ones always do. She turned to me. "What's the visitor like? Did she bring a big trunk with her?"

"Time enough tae chinwag about visitors when the work is done," said Peggy. "You run along now, Mercy Hunter, and see you step over me herbs if you take a shortcut through the vegetable patch."

I walked Mercy to the end of the yard, where we dallied by the barn.

"How are yiz managin' without your master, Ellen?"

33

"A guest in the house helps. It takes our mind off things. And she's a wee dote – she'll do us all a power of good. The mistress has'n looked so cheerful since afore the aul' mistress took ill. Master Haltridge was brave and relieved when he heared the visit was agreed."

"You're too fond of thon master of yours, Ellen. Your face shines when you mention him. A cruel word from him wud cut the heart out of you. Does he ever steal a kiss when nobody's lookin'?"

"Whist! Not every man is like Sammy Orr." I tried to sound unconcerned but I couldn't help blushing.

"Ach, would you listen to her, lettin' on to be shocked! He has a gleam in his eye, your Master Haltridge."

"Stop it now. My master is a gentleman – he'd never take liberties."

"He wud'n be the first gentleman to fun hisself with a maid. Look at you, Ellen Hill, you're as red as a rooster's comb. You've been cuddlin' with your master, have'n you? You can tell me, I'll never let on – not to a soul."

"Mercy, please, that's enough. You'll cost me my place if Mistress Haltridge hears you."

"It's the quiet ones need watchin'. You look like butter would'n melt in your mouth. But you've been sneakin' round with your master, same as Ruth with hers." She dug her elbow in my ribs, and let out a squawk.

By now, I was desperate to shut her up. "You mustn't say such things. I know you're only havin' a joke, but imagine if the minister or one of the elders overheared you. They would'n see it as a bit of fun. A-coorse I think my master is a braw-lookin' man, and maybes he does like me a wee bit, but it would be madness to give in to him. He's too far above me in station, and wed already forbye. If I sinned with him, and was punished with a swollen belly, I'd have to leave Islandmagee."

"You and your precious Islandmagee. Given half a chance,

I'd shake the dust from this place off my feet. Aye, well, I'm on'y teasin', Ellen – no need to get so het up. Stay out a few minutes longer – it's dull up at the minister's house. You'd miss a body to have a laugh with."

I let her gabble, lost in my own thoughts. Remembering how sweet my master's lips tasted. If it was only kisses, it might be no great harm, but kissing led to touching and touching led to forgetting. And forgetting was something I should never let myself do.

Except I had.

How did Mercy guess? It only happened the once. It was on a day when he was very low, between his mother's illness and her screams that Knowehead should be tumbled down. My master came to me for comfort, and I lost my virtue to him. That's the truth of it. I had fallen, God forgive me. I looked up, and my misdeed was in front of me. It happened in this very barn I was standing beside. Now I was in a right state, waiting for my monthlies. Praying for escape from the fruits of my sin. Pledging and promising it would never happen again.

My master flattered me into it. "I don't know how we'd manage without you, Ellen. You're like a candle, straight and tall," he told me, and it went to my head because nobody ever praised me like that before. Ach no, I was lying to myself. It wasn't only his sweet words that made me give in to him. There was also the longing way he looked at me, as if he saw something in me nobody else did – that's what made me stay for his kisses. Aye, and kiss him back, his breath tasting of apples. I lost my virtue that day.

What was done was done, but I knowed I must take care not to fall again. Even though his touch gave me pleasure, I can't deny it. How and ever, the risks were too great. Ruth Graham was a lesson to me. Even if I was lucky – Sweet Lord, have pity – and no child was sown inside me, I'd lose my place if we were caught.

35

It would be a relief to talk it over with somebody, but I could confide my sin in no one. Especially not Mercy Hunter. She wasn't bad-hearted, but as sure as night follows day she'd blab my secret to somebody.

By and by, I said, "I must go on back, the mistress might be askin' for me."

"Is it quiet now, about the place at night?"

"I'm not follyin' you, Mercy."

"Ach, don't give me that. Sure the whole of Islandmagee knows whose face the aul' dame saw at the foot of her bed."

"Catch yourself on. She had your master with her at the end. The minister was prayin' at the top of his voice over her when the Almighty took her to His mansion."

"Somebody come for her, all right. But not everybody thinks she was gathered to the Lord's side. Some say Hamilton Lock was sent for to bring her in the other direction."

"Mercy Hunter, Mistress Haltridge was a Christian soul. If she was'n saved, there's no hope for the rest of us."

"Aye, she was a godly woman. But my master says evil likes to pit itself agin godliness. 'An' sometimes Lucifer gets the best of the match. Mistress Haltridge was touched by an unclean thing, an' died howlin' like a dog. You better watch yourself, Ellen Hill. Because from what I hear, Hamilton Lock is far from finished with Knowehead House.'

ꞏ◖ꞏ ꞏ◖ꞏ ꞏ◖ꞏ

Next morning, Mistress Haltridge told me to help Mary Dunbar with her unpacking, and I was glad of the chance to look at her gee-gaws. I knocked on the door of the young lady's bedchamber, and was given leave to enter. She was standing at the casement. Not much of a view from there, if you ask me. Larne Lough is nice enough – it's saltwater, by the by, on account of being an arm of the sea – but you can't get a look at it from her chamber. All you can see are boggy fields with rushes growing in them. Her lambskin rug was over my arm, dried off in the kitchen overnight, and I laid it on the floor by the side of the bed. It would be cosy underfoot when she had to use her chamber pot at night.

"Which way are the cliffs?' asked Mary Dunbar.

I jerked my head to the right.

"I saw them yesterday. I begged your farm hand to drive up for a look, after he met me in Carrickfergus. He took some coaxing. Said it was nearly dark, which it was. But he gave way in the end. I only had an impression of steep, grey crags, though just being near them gave me goosebumps. I must walk as far as the cliffs and take in the sights properly."

"Them's the Gobbins. They lie about a mile from here, pointing east toward Scotland. Two hundred and forty feet high, in some places. Best not go wanderin' up thonder. Leastways not with the wind so high. There's more than one poor soul been blowed over them cliffs and met their end on the rocks below."

"I know about that."

I gave her a look that would smash china. "What do you know?"

"That women and children died there."

"Aye. So they did. But we don't talk about it in these parts."

"It's not the only thing you don't talk about, is it?"

"I don't get your meanin', mistress." I waited but she didn't respond. "I was sent to help you unpack, mistress. Will I put away your clothes?

"Do."

The whiles I worked, she watched me. Her clothes were scented with rose petals. We used lavender for the same purpose here, storing it in the chests where clothes were kept. I dried it myself every autumn, and scattered it through the rushes on the floor. The mistress was finicky about having plenty of dried lavender about the place.

I let my fingers stroke her gowns, feeling the quality. The waists on them were totie. There wasn't an ounce of spare flesh on my bones, but I could no more fit into one of those dresses than I could force my way into wee Sarah's frocks. One gown had fine lace at the collar, and she told me it was brought on a trading ship from a convent in France.

"I hope the rain did'n disturb you in the night," I said.

"Not the rain. But I did stir once. My head gave a bump against the mattress that shook me out of my sleep. It felt as if someone had pulled the pillow from under me."

"Maybes the pillow fell out."

"I could have sworn I heard laughter. Still, I found it on the floor – I expect I was tossing and turning. Anyhow, I lay awake for a while after that."

"My ma tells me to say prayers if I cannot drop off to sleep – prayers allus help you nod off if the night be's long."

"I'm afraid I forgot to say any prayers at all last night. I thought I'd do it in bed, but I went out like a candle. At least until that business with the pillow. Have I shocked you?"

Now, to tell you the truth, she had: I would sooner serve slops instead of goose for the family's Christmas dinner than go to bed without saying my prayers. But just because she made you feel you could talk to her like an equal didn't mean I was touched in the head enough to try it.

"Say twice as many the-night, mistress."

Her next question knocked the wind out of my sails. "Have you ever done something wicked? Something you were afraid to admit to a living soul?"

"I could'n rightly say," I managed to get out.

There was no power on earth would make me tell her about what I did with my master. I thought about palming her off with the trick Mercy Hunter and I got up to last Midsummer's Eve, with a looking-glass dipped in the white of an egg. We only wanted to see the faces of our future husbands – we meant no harm. Mercy said an Irish wise woman told her to do it. But a noise frightened us and we dropped the glass and broke it, before either of us saw so much as a shadow. Mercy and I swore one another to secrecy. The kirk took a dim view of such doings. And then I wondered if Mary Dunbar had done anything wrong herself, since she put the question, but I could not make so bold with the mistress's cousin as to ask.

It seemed as if she meant to speak some more on the matter, but a tap came on the door and Mistress Haltridge appeared.

"Still here, Ellen? You mustn't dawdle – there's plenty needs attending to about the house."

"Nearly done. I've been holding her back with my chatter." Mary Dunbar smiled at me. "I can finish off here. Thank you for your assistance."

I was out in the passageway when the mistress called me back.

"Have you seen my blue apron?" she said. "It's not with the others."

"I washed it three days ago, and put it away. You saw me do it, mistress. The best linen tablecloth and napkins were washed the same day. You locked the chest after me."

"It's not there now. Someone must have borrowed the key." She jangled a ring of them from the belt at her waist, giving me a sharp look. "Be sure and find it. Money doesn't grow on trees."

So much barging over a length of material. That was typical of the mistress. She was always yammering about farthings, and knowed how every coin was spent.

Her being so particular over the apron made me keep an eye out for it as I went about my duties. But there was no sign. Imagine the rumpus if it had been one of her coloured shawls from the West Indies that went astray. It was only an apron she hardly ever wore, except for making preserves, a skill she was vain about. Mistress Haltridge was not one for aprons – she was keener on giving orders than joining in the work it took to run a household.

⋐ ⋐ ⋐

It was a week after Mary Dunbar's arrival, and I was alone in the kitchen. Peggy was outside feeding leftovers to the greyhounds: she petted them for my master's sake, since he had a fondness for them. He wasn't only being sentimental – don't think that about him – they had their use for hunting. The Scotch are not a people with time for idle decoration. Everything earns its keep.

I was resting my feet on the hearthstone, brooding on how there was still no sign of my monthlies. Normally I was regular as rain, and by now I feared the worse. You'll have to do somethin' about this, Ellen Hill, I told myself. You can't let it slide. Making do and mending was something I had plenty of experience with, but this problem was maybes beyond mending.

I shook myself. No good could come of me sitting there with one hand as long as the other. I put my hand into the darning basket, and took out one of Sarah's wee stockings. But when I looked at it, my courage gave way – and afore I knowed it, my head was resting on my knees, my breast was heaving, and I found myself overcome.

Ach, master, you ought to have knowed what was likely to happen, I railed at him in my thoughts. I should have said something before he rode off, but I was still hoping for the best then. And with all the fuss about his mother's funeral, there never seemed to be the right time. Now, I wondered should I write to him. But commonsense told me I had to deal with this myself. What could he do, so far from home? He must care for me a little, though, I told myself. Didn't he take pains to share his learning with me? It gave me comfort to dwell on it. The mistress disapproved – I heard her argue with my master over it. "A maid has no business with an education, James. She'll get above her station and be spoiled for working. What a waste that would be, after me taking such pains to train her." That was a bare-faced lie, because it was the old mistress who troubled herself on my account, and showed me how things should be ordered.

"Isabel, you'll lose nothing by it. She's a clever lass, a hard worker. You should not begrudge her the chance to profit from reading the Good Book's wisdom. Hasn't she as much right to its healing as any of us?"

A clever lass. A hard worker. In my heart, I guarded those words. My master had no calling to follow in the footsteps of his father, the old minister, yet he had a winsome way with language that would have lifted any sermon. And dearly did he love the Bible. Once, he told me it was full of yarns that would make your hair curl, and he read it for enjoyment as much as for advice.

The mistress could not defy my master when he was set upon a course. All the same, I could see her dislike of the time he spent on me by the way she loaded me with tasks once our lessons were over for the day.

As if my daydream summoned her up, Mistress Haltridge appeared in the kitchen. Usually she rang for us, or sent one of the childer. Quickly, I wiped my sleeve across my face and jumped up, dropping wool and needle alike.

"I need you to keep an eye on my guest and the children. I have to lie down."

I bent for the ball of yarn. "Are you unwell, mistress? Shall I bring you some calves' foot jelly?"

"That will not be necessary – it's only my monthly courses. If I rest till the cramps pass, I should be fine."

She had her monthlies and mine were late. Not just late but unlikely to come now. A fierce envy flooded me. The mistress had everything and I had nothing – not even my usual pains.

"You look strange, Ellen. Is anything the matter?"

With an effort, I smoothed my face clear. "Nothing, mistress."

41

"It didn't look like nothing."

"I suppose I'm a bit tired. We've all had it rough this past while, with the master's mother and the strange things she came out with."

Mistress Haltridge flared up. "I forbid you to talk about that. I've told you before: if I hear you've been gossiping about this family's business to outsiders, you'll lose your place here."

"I meant no harm, mistress. Pardon me."

"Just mind what I say. Now, make yourself useful and bring me up a hot jar. My cousin will attend to the children – they're fast friends with her already. But you see to it they do as she bids. They might test her authority."

Peggy crept back in as soon as she left. I wouldn't be surprised if she had dallied outside to avoid her. The greyhounds must have fed quickly because their yipping started up again. They were always whiney when their master was away.

"Was that the mistress in my kitchen? I dinna like her comin' doon here."

"Tell her so, then."

"What did she want?"

"She's takin' to her bed."

"Coddlin' yourself is dangerous. She laces herself too tight, that's her trouble. It's a wonder the minister doesnae check her on it. Tight lacin' is a vanity."

"The mistress likes to keep herself trim. It's a compliment to her husband."

"Compliment me arse. He made a dry bargain in our mistress – the match was nowhere near good enough for him. She did'n even bring much of a portion, for all her high-steppin' ways. He'd a fared better fetchin' over a bonny wife from Scotland."

"He follyed his heart. Is that not to his credit, Peggy?"

"Hearts can be changeable."

"I know less about hearts than wee Sarah. But I cannae stand about gabbin' – the mistress is waitin' for her hot jar."

I found her in bed, the shutters closed against what grey light was offered on that February afternoon. She did look wretched, poor lady. Some women are more afflicted by their monthlies than others. I never suffered much: a dull throbbing in the pit of my stomach for a day, but nothing to hinder me going about my business. "Hard work takes your mind off aches and pains," my ma always said. I would have traded ten years of my life for that niggle in my belly now.

Remembering how nice Mary Dunbar's clothes smelled as I unpacked them, I had brought lavender water with me to sprinkle on the mistress's pillow. I thought it might put her in mind of brighter days ahead. Once in a while I took pains to please her, though it was always a fool's errand. Just as it was this time. She raised herself up on an elbow and complained the scent made her head pound.

"Leave me be and check on the children. I don't want them misbehaving, especially Jamesey. He can be boisterous when his father's away from home."

"Where are they, mistress?"

"My cousin brought them to her room to show them some baubles in her trunk."

As I was leaving, I saw the keys the mistress wore at her belt lying on a chair. Quick as a wink, my back to her, I lifted them and slid them into my pocket. Then I slipped downstairs to the cupboard where my master's wines were kept, and stole a bottle of brandy. I'd have need of it this night for what I knowed I had to do. Then I tucked the keys into the bottom of the mistress's sewing basket – this could be a silver lining to all the belongings going astray in Knowehead.

When I went to Mary Dunbar's chamber, she was on her lone, perched on the window seat, looking out at the countryside. The young lady turned her bright face to me.

"Jamesey says Scotland is only thirteen miles from

Islandmagee. That's closer than Carrickfergus. Can you see it from here?"

"Times you can, if the day is clear. Not from Knowehead, mind you. You'd want to be looking over from Gransha or Mullaghboy. Winter's better than summer for sightin' it."

"Have you ever been across?"

"Me, mistress? Sure how would I get a chance to travel? I have'n even been the length of Belfast. Peggy McGregor was born in Scotland, in a place called Portpatrick. She says there's not much in the differ between it and Islandmagee, exceptin' Scotland has fewer papish superstitions left over from before."

"I've heard about Islandmagee's superstitions." She gave me a sidelong look.

I didn't like the sound of that, so I took a few paces towards the door to show I had work to do. She carried on, as if nothing had been dangled. "James took Isabel to Edinburgh for their wedding trip. She says it has a castle even more magnificent than the one in Carrickfergus. How is my poor cousin? Is there anything I can do for her?"

"The mistress hopes to sleep. It's the best way for her to deal with these aches. She'll feel the better for it when she wakes up, and might be fit for a sup of broth. Where are the bairns, mistress?"

"They ran off to meet some playfellows. They said they had their mother's permission, and promised to return before dark."

I knowed they didn't have the mistress's say-so, but judged it wise not to stir up trouble. "If need be, we can tell her they were gatherin' firewood. I'll press on, then. There's cheese waitin' to be made in the dairy."

"Stay and talk a while. I'm lonesome today. You'd think I'd be used to being on my own, with no brothers or sisters. But it's never as quiet as this at home."

All the chores I had to see about before I could lay down

my head that night came to mind. Never mind what needed to be done that called for brandy, as soon as I had the house to myself – and as much courage as I could screw up. But I hadn't the heart to refuse her, and I suppose I was curious. We didn't get many outsiders on the island. Most folk were born and bred on it, and marrying in wasn't all that common. So I folded my hands in front of me, and waited to hear what was on the young lady's mind.

"Isabel says she hardly ever goes junketing. Are assemblies or musical evenings never held? Aren't the islanders bothered about news of the outside world?"

"Well, mistress, the outside world is'n half as interestin' to us as our own doin's. But a crowd gathers about my master when he returns from one of his trips. Folk do be curious to hear the latest news from the coffee houses in the city. He's a great man for reading the gazettes they keep there. Sometimes he brings back a couple, and they be passed roun' till the pages turn to rags. He even lets me read them, so he does."

"You can read?"

"Why, a-coorse, mistress. Presbyterians believe in learnin' for all. The Good Book was meant for everybody to take comfort from. I can write as well." I don't know what got into me then – it wasn't like me to draw attention to myself. "Look," I said, and breathed on the window pane, before tracing some letters.

"What do you read about in those gazettes?"

"Faith, they can be dull enough, full of battles with Prussian troops and Danish dragoons, and the treaty negotiations after their silly wars. And sure, what are they to us here on Islandmagee? Wine at three shillin's a gallon, or a horse for sale that paces well – such like is more to our taste."

She made room on the window seat. "Sit here, Ellen."

"Beggin' your pardon, mistress, I prefer to stand." Imagine if Mistress Haltridge caught me!

"Tell me what else you read about in your master's gazettes."

"I've a weakness for the advertisements. One time he give me a gazette to keep, and I brung it home when I had a half-day off and read it to my da. He thought it strange the way the advertisements ran sideways along the edge of the page, fillin' in space where there was no news. But Ma said it was thrifty. Da loved hearin' about rewards offered for lost dogs and stolen horses, or wigs and false teeth for sale. He said he could listen till the cows came home. Thon's real life, says he. Not the high jinks of generals and dukes."

"I like reading about highwaymen."

"My da does and all. There's some believe the Good Book is readin' enough for anyone, and have no tolerance for other books. But my master is a broad-minded man and gives me all sorts to read. He allus takes pains to help me better myself. Even though I be vastly content with my station in life, mistress."

"You miss your master, don't you?"

I started plumping the pillows on her bed, till I could speak without giving myself away. "We all miss him. The household is livelier when he's at home. It gets a bit stale without Master Haltridge – he's a breath of fresh air."

"You sound quite the pet."

"Ach, no, mistress, don't say such things. He's just the best of masters and the kindest of gentlemen." Nervous at the thought of my master's weakness for me being noticed, I started gabbling to cover it. Even though I might not be able to cover up for him, when push came to shove. "Peggy McGregor has knowed him all his life, and she maintains he has a heart bigger nar his body. Me master loves Peggy's cookin'. He allus comes back a greedy guts for a bowl of her beef stew. They send out dishwater from the kitchens in them inns where he puts up, and charge a king's ransom for it."

"Why does he travel so much?"

"I suppose he does what he must, to keep his business affairs in order."

"My cousin hates him journeying so far from home. She can't abide being left here, in a house with only women and children. She says it sets her teeth on edge to hear the wind howl, like lost souls calling from the other side."

"Aye, the wind can make your skin crawl."

When first she was wed to my master, the mistress and the old dame were company for one another – especially at night, sitting in the parlour, after the bairns went to bed. My master's comings and goings weren't so hard to bear then. It was only when his mother fell ill that the mistress started to mind his being away so often. She told me once she felt like a prisoner at Knowehead, instead of its mistress. Best not to share this with the young lady, I thought. Mistress Isabel Haltridge was well able to speak for herself.

Mary Dunbar looked me up and down. "How old are you?"

"I turned nineteen in November past."

"So there's a year between us. I had my eighteenth birthday in December. Do you have a truelove?"

I shook my head. I might be soft on my master, but I wasn't so soft as to claim him for a sweetheart.

She went on, "I've had a proposal of marriage already, but my father rejected him. Freddie – Ensign Montgomery – was with the infantry in Armagh. He had the shiniest boots I ever saw. I thought him exceedingly handsome in his regimentals. But he had the name of being a rake and a trifler, though he swore I reformed him. My father wouldn't hear tell of an engagement. He said it was only a notion of mine to wed him. He's always complaining that I take too many notions." She heaved a sigh. "I'd be glad to marry a soldier – there's nothing like a man in uniform, with all those gold buttons and braid. Do you truly have no sweetheart?"

"Sure who'd look sideways at me?" The bottle of brandy

danced before me, and the purpose I had for it. And my skin betrayed me with a change of colour. I daresay the young lady thought it was modesty, though in truth it was shame.

One man had looked sideways at me – and more, forbye – and now I was suffering for it, in the way sins of the flesh were usually punished. I towered over most folk on Islandmagee, men as well as women, and the Good Lord saw fit to fashion me from serviceable materials. The only man ever to notice me was my master. And, in gratitude, I was weak.

But it was hard to be strong round a gentleman such as my master. I recalled the first time I understood he liked me – as a woman, rather than as a maid who served his family faithfully. It was in October past, and my eyes were delighting in the red and gold of the leaves as I walked to Carnspindle on a half-day off. My master rode up behind me on his dappled grey stallion, and before I knowed it, he leaned down and pulled me up in front of him. Just for a minute or two. Should I live to be a hundred, I'll never forget how it felt inside the circle of his arms. Like queen of the castle, I was. But it was broad daylight, and anybody could have come round the bend in the road.

"Master," I said, "what if someone should see and tell the mistress?"

"Say my name and I'll set you down," he said.

"James," I whispered. It was the first time ever it passed my lips.

And he said my name back to me – "Ellen" – as if it had meaning, instead of a word to shout out when something was wanted. Then he eased me down to the ground, letting his hand slide over the swell of my hip.

Mary Dunbar drew me back to the present. "A gentleman called Frazer Bell bowed to my cousin and me at the meeting-house yesterday. My cousin says he has no wife."

"He's a neighbour of ours, mistress, and great friends with

my master." It was said of him he preferred reading poesy to the Good Book, but I didn't repeat the scandal.

"My cousin was disappointed he did not tarry to speak to us. He seemed in a hurry to be away. Still, there were several other gentlemen who asked to be presented to me."

Mary Dunbar had no shortage of admirers when she made an appearance in our meeting-house on the Sabbath. The meeting-house is a fine, T-shaped building put up by the old minister, Master Haltridge. Visitors always stop to look at the sundial scratched on one of the outside walls, with the date on it: 1664. I saw folk stop to look at Mary, too. Their eyes lit up the moment they clapped them on her dainty wee frame. She was as fragile as a dandelion clock. Heads were turned by that cloud of curls and her complexion as pale as Frazer Bell's prize doves. There was the novelty of a new face, of course, but even so, hers was not a face you would tire of quickly.

"Tell me a story," begged Mary Dunbar.

"Sure I know none fit for a young lady."

"The children say you have a gift for storytelling."

"I grew up round tales, my da's a great man for them. I tell the bairns the odd yarn, to while away an evening. But you would'n pay any heed to them."

"Still, I'd like to hear one. I heard stories about Islandmagee on the coach from Armagh." She darted the same look at me as before: the one that made me want to walk away from her.

I played stupid. "Stories about what a paradise it is here? We're left alone on the island, maybes on account of being surrounded by water on three sides."

"The land gobbled up by water . . . No, it was stories about Hamilton Lock."

"Better not blether about the like of him, mistress. No good comes from dwellin' on his wickedness."

"But stories about wicked people are always more interesting than stories about good people. A man who sat opposite me on the coach said his ghost was haunting Knowehead House. Is it true? Have you seen him? I wonder if I shall!" She trembled, and not entirely from fear.

"For the love of God, mistress, don't go repeatin' that."

"So it's true!"

I swallowed. I didn't want to say it was true, and I wasn't certain I could say it was untrue. "I've never laid eyes on him, and I trust I never shall. Them that see Hamilton Lock get no luck from the sight of him. How could they, and him bad to the backbone? He was the sort of man would steal the Cross from under the Lord Jesus."

"I heard he was a handsome, black-haired man, a full head taller than anybody else, with eyes that danced."

"He had honeyed ways with him. So they say." Suddenly I noticed a bloodstained handkerchief knotted round her thumb. "Why, mistress, have you hurt yourself?"

"I broke my nail just now, on the chest where my clothes are stored. It bled heavily for such a minor mishap."

"Shall I get you some salve?"

"It's stopped now. But I'm afraid there's blood on the floorboards. I suppose it'll scrub off."

"I'll fetch some rhubarb leaves from Peggy's vegetable patch. Nothin' to beat them for shiftin' bloodstains."

A clatter of footsteps on the stairs signalled the childer's return. They burst through the door. "Come and see the swans on the lough, Cousin Mary," said Sarah.

Mary's eyes shone. It was as if she was told we had sunken treasure in the lough. "I didn't know you had swans here."

"Hard winters, the wild ones come into the lough for shelter, mistress." I was never pushed about them. Too fancy for my taste, with their dazzling white plumage, set off by orange bills bordered in black. And people said such daft things about them. Nonsense about them being silent till they sang their swansong, for instance – that's just plain wrong: they whistle and snort, so they do. I've heard them with my own ears. In harsh weather, sentimental folk on Islandmagee feed the swans, but I never gave them so much as a breadcrumb. Let them root around for themselves. Beauty was always getting preference, whether it took the shape of a bird or a woman.

Mary stroked Sarah's hair. "Have you ever noticed how their necks are shaped like an S? For Sarah. That makes them your special birds." The child smiled fit to crack her face in two. Mary Dunbar looked thoughtful. "If I could choose to be any creature on God's earth, it would be a swan. Their beauty moves me. I can't bear ugliness – there's something sinful about it. I don't know why we talk about somebody being as ugly as sin. If you ask me, it should be as sinful as ugly."

With that, she threw her cloak over her shoulders and went off with the childer, hand in hand. I stood at the casement to watch them. The lettering I had set down with my finger stood out on it. I might only be a maid, but at least I could do script like a lady. I looked past the words, to Mary Dunbar beyond the glass. She had her skirts up in her hands, racing the bairns, forgetting herself. But my ma always warned me women should never forget themselves. It leads to trouble. Whether you be maid or lady.

I brooded on our visitor. Could it have been chance alone that brought the name Hamilton Lock into the conversation during that coach ride from Armagh? What if Mary Dunbar had raised it herself? She seemed to have some purpose in mind with her questions – she wasn't just passing the time. I felt a prickling on my skin, and it struck me some folk are born to whip things up, come what may. That's just how they're fashioned. Maybes they cannot help themselves.

Chapter 3

Nobody noticed me slip in to see to the candles in the dining room before supper. Master Jamesey was telling a story, with Mary Dunbar and Sarah as his audience.

"If you walk too close to the cliffs, the Magee ghosties will get you. They watch and they wait. And before you know it, their hands reach up to grab you by the ankles and wheek you onto the rocks. They can crush a skull like a head of cabbage."

"Less of that nonsense!" I snapped. Jamesey reddened. It was all Peggy McGregor's fault – she was forever turning the childer's heads with this jabber.

"It's not seagulls you hear crying at the Gobbins," piped up Sarah. "It's the ghosts of the Magee women and their babbies, begging the soldiers for mercy."

"Whisht now. No more of that. It's only one of them yarns we touched on, Mistress Mary. The wee'ans have no business repeatin' it."

"So there was no raid on the Magees of Islandmagee by soldiers who rode out from Carrickfergus Castle? They weren't all slaughtered, the whole clan of them?" asked Mary.

I busied myself hooking up the casement shutters. They helped to block out the roar of the wind, or maybes it was the sound of the sea crashing on the rocks, floating across the fields to our ears. Or, if you believed the tale, neither wind nor waves but the crack of hooves, carrying men with blood on their blades and more bloodshed in their hearts.

Mary Dunbar wouldn't take the hint. "Long before I came here, I heard about what happened on Islandmagee. My old nurse told me the story. She said every Magee on the island was put to the sword that night – or worse. Not a man, woman or child survived." She looked meaningfully at me. "And a soldier called Hamilton Lock was the ringleader."

I sighed. "Aye, there was a raid. But it was a long time ago. Getting' on for seventy years now. Only one toothless aul' dear minds it, and she was a wee cuddy at the time. She says no soldiers rode out from the castle, that's fancyin' up the truth. And God knows this truth needs nothin' added. The soldiers came from Ballycarry – they were quartered out that direction. Some were on horseback, most of them on foot. All of them were fired up after bein' in a shebeen."

"But is the rest true? Were the Magee men run through while they slept in their beds? And the women and children chased to the cliffs, and forced onto the rocks at sword-point?"

"There were bodies found caught on the rocks below the Gobbins, and fishermen saw more floatin' in the water. The corpses were all women and bairns. I doubt if they went willin' over the cliffs."

"The soldiers were avenging the Scotch people," said Jamesy. "It gave the Irish a lesson they never forgot."

"The Irish would have cut our throats," put in his sister.

"It chills my blood just thinking about it," said Mary. "If it's true, that is. You hear conflicting accounts."

"Things happen when men go to war, mistress. Things it's best not to dwell on. All's peaceful in these parts now."

"And Hamilton Lock? What did he do?"

"What didn't he do, more like. Some say 'twas him paid for

the drink to flow like water in thon shebeen. He fixed it with the landlord to keep it comin'. And all the time they were tipplin', he reminded the soldiers about the wrongs done to the Scotch settlers. Then when they were quare and worked up, he put forward a bloodthirsty scheme. He was the one stoked the fires of vengeance, and led the way. Without him, it might only have been men talkin' in their cups. Childer, you need to get a move on and tidy yourselves afore supper. By the way, mistress, I cleaned the blood off the floorboards in your room. Rhubarb leaves do the trick every time."

I took myself back to the kitchen because I'd had enough of Mary Dunbar for now. Questions, questions, and all of them about Hamilton Lock. I was starting to have doubts about the mistress's cousin.

◖◗ ◖◗ ◖◗

Mistress Haltridge was well enough to join the family for supper, though her appetite was slight. When the old mistress was alive, Peggy and me dined with the family, but now she was gone my master's wife made up her mind we should feed in the kitchen. Putting on airs and graces for her cousin's benefit. It was no odds to me. I could take more enjoyment from my meat without her passing remarks over the way I used my penknife to cut it, or yammering about how much I ate. Sure, where was the point in being maid in a gentleman's household if you couldn't eat your fill?

Poor Peggy was not able to taste her own food any more, with all her teeth lost. She had to soak bread in milk before she could manage it, and most nights she dined on a bowl of mashed turnip. While we ate, Peggy quizzed me about the visitor. I said she was quick to ask about what happened at the Gobbins – I couldn't bring myself to mention Hamilton Lock's name.

"Better about the Gobbins than about the aul' mistress," I

added. "At least what took place at the cliffs was ne'ther today nor yesterday. Thon business with Mistress Haltridge is too close for comfort."

"She'd be better still not gabbin' about anythin'. Nobody likes a chatterbox. Jus' you chew on that, Ellen Hill."

We finished our meal in silence. Peggy McGregor could let her tongue run away with her as well as the best of them, but nobody ever sees the mote in their own eye.

As I was clearing the table, Peggy spoke up.

"I'll wager Sammy Orr is the reason the mistress took to her bed. Not her monthlies. She'd have heard all about it after prayers at the meeting-house yesterday. Tongues were flapping like loose sails in the wind."

"Aye, it was all the gossip. But why would our mistress take that to heart?"

"No mistress likes to hear about a husband givin' the glad eye to one of the maids. It makes all mistresses feel at risk. They hate to think of lassies leadin' on their foolish men." Peggy shuffled to the fireplace, holding the furniture for support, to check on water boiling in a pot there for the dishes.

"Who's to say it was Ruth Graham leadin' on Sammy Orr?" I said. "He could a coaxed her."

"No odds if he did. It's her job to say no, as loud and often as need be. And to tell the minister if he keeps on at her. Whether he sweet-talks or forces her, her answer must be the same. A maid has no business actin' the wife to her master – in partic'lar when he has one already. No good can come of it. Never you forget that, me lass."

"I don't know why you're sayin' that to me. I've allus been a good girl."

"I was'n born yesterday. Ne'ther was the mistress. You've been making big cow eyes at the master for months now. You want to watch your step."

Horrified at being caught out, and afraid the mistress

might have her suspicions too, I went back to the dining room to clear away their platters. Mary Dunbar and the mistress were discussing a gown the mistress was making for wee Sarah, and Mary said she had buttons to match the flowers in the cloth.

"May I see them?" asked the child.

Mary turned to me. "Would you fetch my sewing box? The buttons are inside. The box is japanned, and about so long." She held her hands nearly a foot apart. "I'm nearly certain I left it on the window seat."

I saw the sewing box at once. Near-hand, the lid of the chest where her clothes were stored lay open. When I went to close it, something blue near the top caught my eye. What should it be but the missing apron, folded neatly with the strings wrapped round the cloth. At first I was pleased, because the mistress held me responsible for its disappearance, but when I lifted it I noticed knots in the apron strings. I counted eight on one side, one on the other. Nine in all. Too many to be an accident. And these were bulky, deliberate-looking knots. I grew up watching fishermen knot their nets: I know when a knot is purposeful.

I brought the apron downstairs to Mary Dunbar, thinking she might have an explanation. I must have spent longer in her room than I realized, staring at what I found, because the visitor was alone at the table, tracing circles with a finger on the cloth.

"Do you know anythin' about this, Mistress Mary?"

She reached out both hands for the apron, and took it from me. "What is it?"

"The missin' apron the mistress was vexed about."

"But why should I know anything about it?"

"I found it in your bedchamber. In the chest."

"Who'd leave an apron in my room? Surely my cousin isn't suggesting I scrub her floors!" Her laughter died away as she touched one of the knots. "How curious they are!"

"These are no ordinary knots. Knots stand for fastenin' magic – somebody has tied a charm into the apron. It's a way of castin' a spell on the owner."

"That's daft, Ellen."

"It's as true as I'm standin' here afore you."

"This is a God-fearing household – my cousin's husband is son to a minister of the Lord. Spells would have no sway here."

"But look, there are nine knots. Three times three – the number must have meanin'."

"You might just as well say there's meaning in eight knots on one side and a single knot on the other."

"Maybes there is."

"These knots are only significant because we cannot take our eyes off them. Very well, I'll put paid to that." She began to unpick one of the knots.

"No, Mistress Mary. You're releasin' the evil. Don't do it, mistress. Please! Stop! Listen to me! None but the witch who tied these knots can undo them. The only way round it is to burn the apron – it purges the sorcery."

She was working at a second knot. Shocked and scared, I forgot myself and put my fingers on hers to stop her. Her flesh was on fire, and I dropped my hand at once. Then I ran like the wind for Mistress Haltridge, who was hearing the childer's prayers.

"I found the missin' apron," I panted.

"Good, I hate carelessness. It's no way to run a household."

"But mistress, its . . ."

"Have you torn it?"

I shook my head. "Its strings are knotted."

"Well, knots can be unpicked. Stop making a mountain out of a molehill."

"These are no ordinary knots, mistress. They look like . . ." I didn't want to say it but I had no choice. I took a deep breath. "They look like witches' knots."

She made fists of her hands. "Show me."

By the time we reached the parlour, the apron ties were bare of knots. Mary Dunbar held the garment, staring at it. She looked as if she was waiting for something.

"Mary, I see you have my apron."

"Yes, it was found in my bedchamber."

"My maid says the strings were knotted."

For a long moment Mary did not speak. I thought she meant to deny the knots, but then she tossed her head. "They were in a state, but I managed to smooth them out."

"There was nothing odd about the knots?"

"There was a right dose of them. Here, Isabel, have your apron back."

The mistress shook out the apron to examine it. From between its folds, a white flannel cap with a frilled edge fell out.

"What's that?" A wobble was threaded through Mistress Haltridge's voice.

I said nothing, though I knowed as well as she did what it was. She waited for me to pick it up, but I could not bring myself to touch it.

Finally, she bent for the cap, holding it by the ribbons, her arm stuck out as far as it could go. "Do you recognize this, Ellen?"

"It belonged to the aul' mistress."

"One white cap looks much like another," said Mary.

The mistress pointed to the letters AH embroidered on the edge. "Anne Haltridge. James's mother."

"Throw it on the fire, mistress. Only place for it." I ran to the fireplace and used the poker, setting the flames dancing. She stared into the fire, frozen. I went back to her and plucked at her sleeve. "It must be burnt, mistress. Sooner the better." Still nothing. "Thon cap belongs to the dead mistress," I reminded her, and she came to life.

She darted forward and hurled it in. I nudged the scrap of

material with the poker, pushing it into the heart of the blaze.

"I don't understand," said Mary.

The mistress and I watched as the cap curled and blackened, shrinking to nothing, and we held our tongues. You see, Mistress Anne Haltridge was buried in that cap.

༄ ༄ ༄

Peggy chewed on the stem of her clay pipe the whiles I told her about finding the apron with witches' knots on its strings – and the bonnet hidden inside.

"The mistress should a burned thon apron, as well as the cap," she said.

"Once a thing's touched by witches it's no use to man nor beast. Mind you, the mistress would hate to see a perfectly good apron go to waste. Thon tight-fisted nature o' hers will be her downfall."

"I never thought to tell her to put it in the fire – it was the cap put the fear o' God in us. It must a been robbed from the aul' dame's grave. If there's witchin' afoot, young Mistress Haltridge must be the target. The apron belongs to her."

Peggy took the pipe out of her mouth and pointed it at me. "The mistress reads her Bible every night. Witchcraft cannae harm her."

"The aul' dame read her Bible night and day, and was wife to a minister forbye. Yet she was witched into her grave in this very house. The bonnet is a message from beyond the grave. I don't like it. I don't like it one wee bit."

"We have horseshoes nailed above all the doors to keep us safe. Trust in God and in horseshoes, lassie."

At that, I put words on the dread that was gathering in my mind. "Horseshoes cannot keep out evil that's inside a house already."

Peggy heaved herself to her feet, never letting on she heard me. "Me aul' bones need their rest. Be sure and say your prayers afore you go to sleep. Put your faith in the Lord and he'll never let you doon."

After she left, I finished redding up the house, and prepared to do what I knowed I must, in the hopes of bringing on my monthlies. I had a remedy from the Irish wise woman that Mercy and I paid, after she promised we'd see the faces of our future husbands in the looking-glass dipped in egg white. When I went to leave, the scraggy old woman had held me back, in a surprisingly strong grip, and whispered the makings of it to me. She said I'd need it one day. I didn't believe her – didn't want to believe her – but that need was come, less than a year later.

That night, I was bent on brewing up her mixture. Many's the lassie went to her grave trying to do what I intended – drinking a poisonous concoction that killed her, as well as the child she was seeking to miscarry. I didn't know if mine was any safer than theirs. I didn't want to die. My only hope was that the sooner I acted, the less the risk. The wise woman said it worked if a lassie took it early enough.

Mary Dunbar's bell rang just as I was about to give it a try. Vexed though I was, the bell could not be left unanswered, and so I lifted a candlestick and went to her. She was tucked up in bed, although the curtains round it were open so she could see out. She let on she needed me to trim the wick on her candle, which was guttering, but she was well able to do that herself. Really, she wanted to question me.

"While I was waiting in Carrickfergus for Noah Spears to collect me, I heard another story. It was about a Magee boy on the night of the massacre. He hid in a great chest when the soldiers came looking for him and his family."

"Aye, so 'tis said."

"It was a good place to hide. But they found him and killed him anyway.'

"That was Philip Magee. He was ten years old." I should have stayed silent, but I could not help myself. "They did'n

61

find him – they tricked him into givin' hisself away. When he did, they murthered him."

"He must have been terrified."

"I daresay he was'n the only one. It was a night ruled by terror."

"What made him show himself, I wonder?"

"They coaxed him out with promises about bein' helped to safety." I was about to say something further, but bit my tongue. There was nothing to be gained from telling her any more of the tale than she knowed already. No good could come of recalling how Hamilton Lock and Philip Magee groomed horses together, and the boy trusted the man. How Lock called out Philip's name, and he left the safety of the chest. How Lock put his hand on Philip's shoulder, looked into his eyes, and stuck a dagger into the side of his neck. Then the soldiers battered him to a jelly for nearly making fools of them.

Ten was young to die, and such a cruel death. But they were violent times. Thanks be to God, Ireland was well settled now. Nineteen was young to die too, said a voice in my head, but I paid it no heed. I could not afford to.

Mary went on, "Do you suppose it was a chest like that one?" She pointed to the domed wooden box, with a huge iron lock on front, where I found the apron. It had squatted in that chamber since first I came into Knowehead.

"Aye, it could be, mistress."

"I wonder if it's the same chest?"

"I har'ly think so."

"But it might be. It looks old enough. It's certainly big enough – I could fit in there myself. I have a fancy this is Philip Magee's hidey-hole. He'd have stayed alive if he kept inside. Papist or not, you have to pity him."

"What on earth sets you to thinkin' on such a thing?"

"I thought I saw blood on the chest."

"Maybes some got splashed on it when you cut your

finger." I brought the candle closer to the box. "I can see nothin' on it. I fear you're imaginin' things, Mistress Mary. You're in a strange place, when all's said and done."

"Look there – that dark patch on the lid."

"That could be anythin'. Butter, or a wine stain, or even just some weatherin'. Tell you what, I'll take rhubarb leaves to it in the mornin'. If there's blood, they'll shift it, never you fear. Let me pull the curtains round your bed now, mistress, and you can settle down for the night."

I was impatient to go back to the kitchen. There she was, hoaking for things to worry about, when some of us hadn't far to look. Still, the chest started nagging at me, as well. Old Mistress Haltridge told me it was in the house when she arrived into it as a bride. It was a gift to Minister Haltridge, she said, from a member of his kirk called Castle. She made a joke of it, saying such a chest belonged in a castle. I didn't pay much notice at the time. But thinking it over, I remembered my da telling me about a family by the name of Castle, gone now from Islandmagee. The reason he mentioned them was because we were out for a stroll, past Philip Magee's house, and he said the Castles moved in there after all the Magees were killed.

At that, my hand flew to my mouth. When I took it away, I made the sign against the evil eye.

Back in the kitchen, instead of getting on with what I needed to do, I dilly-dallied by the fire. I was like a dog sitting on a thistle – wanting to make a start, but loath to leave the fireside. Mary Dunbar had left me unsettled, with all her talk of blood and killing, and the turf rustling in the grate didn't comfort me like it usually did.

Time and tide, Ellen, I reminded myself, and stood up. I had no choice but to take my fate into my own hands. I put water on to boil above the fire, and lifted the knife out of the drawer in the kitchen table. Quickly, I chopped the herbs I had gathered earlier from Peggy's patch, muttering a prayer, though by rights I shouldn't be calling on God's help for what I was about. Next, I poured myself a beaker full of my master's stolen brandy. "It's not wrong to take the bottle from his store – he's the one got me into this mess," I said out loud. To stiffen my backbone, I took a long swig of the dark golden drink, waiting for the water to heat. When it was bubbling, I stirred in the herbs, adding more brandy to thin it down.

I drank the potion standing up. The heady sweetness of the brandy could not mask the sharp taste of the herbs laced through it, and I shuddered as I swallowed. Then I sat fornenst the chimney corner, waiting for the brew to take effect. As I did, I fretted. Maybes it would have fitted me better to worry about what I had just done. Instead, my mind fell to picking at what was going on under this roof – I daresay I couldn't bring myself to study too close on the ifs and ans of the drink I took, and why.

Whether Peggy admitted it or not, what was happening at Knowehead was a bad handling. I always knowed it was not like other houses. But I told myself if I didn't bother it, then it wouldn't bother me. People whispered about an impish presence there, before ever I went to work for the Haltridges. Why it should be, I can't tell, but Knowehead was no ordinary house. You might go to set down a bowl, and miss the table altogether. Or trip over a step if your mind was elsewhere. Chairs were cowped up, eggs broken, flour scattered on the floor. At times, you'd feel a cold draft where there was no cause for it. Or a door might swing open with nobody behind it. You grew accustomed to such things. If you didn't make a fuss, if you just waited it out, everything settled down again. I never paid much attention to these quirks – they were part of life at Knowehead House.

But they became more noticeable during the old dame's illness. The house acted up during those months. The young mistress thought it was the ghost of Hamilton Lock tormenting a dying woman, and she wasn't alone in holding that suspicion. If he was able to leave Hell when it suited him, where else would he come but here? This patch of land had been his home. Everything went quiet after Mistress Haltridge was taken to meet her Maker. Too quiet, maybes. Hamilton Lock might only be biding his time.

I counted the chimes on my master's tall clock in the hall: eleven o'clock, half past eleven, midnight. Shortly after the twelfth bong faded, a pain in my belly doubled me over. It was like the kick of a horse. Beads of sweat sprang up along my hairline, and more sweat trickled between my paps. My stomach rose to meet my throat. Gagging, I managed not to give way until I staggered outside to the midden pit, where I heaved everything up. What came out of me was lost amidst all the family's waste. When I was done, I lay on the ground, not caring about the filth.

By and by, I pulled myself to my feet, took off my cap and put my head under the pump, opening my mouth to the gush, letting the cold, clean water wash everything away. Dirt, doubts and all.

Back indoors, I threw a shawl round my damp shoulders, put a hot jar to my aching belly, and fell into the battered old rushbottomed chair by the fire. I knowed I should slide in beside Peggy to catch a few hours' rest, for whether well slept or not, screek of day would bring no let-up from work. How and ever, the thought of climbing that ladder was too much for me. I nodded off where I sat.

Until a cry came from upstairs. It wasn't a scream – not much more than a kitling's mewl, but I'm a light sleeper and the house was still as the grave that night. It sent me shuffling to the passageway, hunched over and nursing my tender front. Was one of the childer having a nightmare? Sarah had been disturbed by all the pother with her granny, bless her heart, and it had got to the stage where she wouldn't go near her for love nor money. But once my master's mother was bedded down in St John's graveyard, there hadn't been a peep out of the wee lassie.

I listened, but there was only the hoot of thon big owl that liked to rest himself on the tree outside Mary Dunbar's bedchamber. Maybes I dreamed it. Little wonder if my sleep was restless that night. Into the silence, the clock bonged three times, and the cry came again. This noise was made by no child: it was a woman, and she was in distress.

I was still a bit fuddled, between the brandy (and what was in it) and boking it all up afterwards. Along with whatever else was in my belly. But those cries weren't answered by the slap of feet upstairs, so it was up to me. Moving slowly, my insides tender and my throat raw, I went and held a candlewick to the embers of the fire. Then I lifted the brass nutcracker from the drawer in the kitchen table and slipped it into my apron pocket. Shielding the flame, I picked my way through the house.

At the top of the stairs, I took a moment to think. The call had to be down to one of three people: the mistress, Mary Dunbar or Peggy. Peggy was furthest away, under the roof. The mistress and Mary Dunbar were on the first floor, in rooms near-hand to each other. I tiptoed along the passageway, quiet as a mouse, and checked under both doorways for a line of light. Nothing. Now what? The mistress had taken a sleeping draught, and would be crotchety if I disturbed her. If I was making a mistake, I guessed Mary Dunbar would be less put out. I opened her door a crack.

"Isabel? Oh, it's you, Ellen. Come in."

She was sitting up in bed, without a candle lit, the casement shutters open to the moonlight. There was a full moon, and by its light I could see the bedchamber was in a shocking state of disorder. The young lady must have been searching through her clothes, because the lid of her chest was open, the contents spilling out and scattered willy-nilly.

"I thought I heared you call out, mistress. Was there something you wanted?"

"The moonlight's strong. It woke me."

66

"Pardon me, but it stands to reason you'll be disturbed if you leave your shutters unhooked."

"They were shut when I got into bed. Someone opened the curtains round my bed, too. You drew them closed yourself, when you fixed my candle."

"I must'n a fastened this latch right. There's a trick to it. You tuck it in here. It stops it flyin' open. Were you after somethin' in partic'lar from the chest?"

She gazed round at the jumble, and I was pleased to see she didn't take it lightly because her hand flew to her mouth. "It's worse than I thought."

I lifted her cloak, rumpled in a heap beside the wooden box, and shook it out. "We'll soon have everythin' shipshape. I hope you found what you were after."

"None of this is my doing."

I smiled. "Jamesey says the same when he gets things in a muddle."

"You don't understand. This has nothing to do with me."

"Whatever you say, mistress."

"It was like this when I woke up. At first I thought I was dreaming. Then I realized it was no dream. Someone went to the chest and took out all my clothes." Shocked, and scared too by the look of her, she leaned back against the iron headboard. "Don't you see? Somebody's rummaged through everything I own. There's my spare nightgown, inside-out on the chair. And look at my comb – some of the teeth have been broken off!"

Weakness from what I dosed myself with earlier made me sit down without asking her say-so. Never had I done such a thing in front of a lady or gentleman, but my legs refused to hold me up any longer. "Maybes you did that to the comb yourself, mistress? Tuggin' at a knot?"

"Why would I damage my own belongings? See my ribbons, dangling in the water jug, and my best gown tossed in a ball on the floor. I think the lace is torn." Tears sparkled in her eyes. "Are the children playing a trick on me?" "If they are, they'll be punished sore for it." Master Jamesey had become contrary, inclined to be disobedient, although Peggy said it was only the boy's attempt to draw his father's attention. As for Sarah, she did her brother's bidding. Still, I could not believe Jamesey and Sarah would tease their cousin in such a hateful way. Yet if Mary hadn't done this herself, I couldn't easily explain it away.

Mary Dunbar threw back the covers and got out of bed. She paced about in her bare feet. "Why does my cousin jump like a scalded cat when I mention her husband's mother? She changes the subject every time."

"She cud'n a been kinder to my master's mother during her illness. She used to sit with her of an evening, and read to her from her favourite book, *Sermons on the Covenant*. That was a book that belonged to the aul' minister. His lady was terrible taken with it."

"Well, of course Isabel looked after her well when she was ill, it was her Christian duty. But why should she mind talking about her now? Do you know what Mistress Haltridge died of?"

"It's not my place to make guesses."

"Her name was mentioned by some of the coach passengers."

"Take no heed of waggin' tongues."

Contrary though she sounded, I could tell she was looking to have her mind set at ease. There was only a year between us. But the more I saw of her, the more childlike she seemed to me. I had to give up being a bairn at the age of twelve, when I was packed off into the world to earn my keep on account of the clatter of wee'ans Ma had after me. But Mary Dunbar was left to grow at her own pace, a slow one in most ways. Apart from how she was with men. That came natural to her, as I saw when she dimpled at those who bowed to her at the meeting-house, and allowed our neighbour, Hugh

Donaldson, to pick up a glove she dropped. I had a half-notion she dropped it deliberately, to win the courtesy. Anyhow, I tried to give her some reassurance.

"The elders prayed in every room of the house durin' Mistress Haltridge's sickness," I said. "All was left peaceful after she passed."

"Why did they need to do that?"

"They judged it prudent."

"Why?"

"Prayer never goes to waste. There now, that's enough questions. Back to bed with you."

"Please, Ellen. Why did the elders say prayers in every room?"

"If I tell you, do you promise not to let on where you heared it from?"

"I promise."

I spoke in a whisper. "They thought there was somethin' let loose in Knowehead House. Somethin' hungry. And pitiless. They were afeared of what it might do."

Mary Dunbar stopped her racketing about the bedchamber and came right up to me, her face inches from mine. Her voice was a blade. "Hungry for what?"

I knowed I'd said too much. "Never you mind. Now, I'll redd up here in the morning. It's too late to clatter about doing it the-night, and I'm a wee bit the worse for wear, tell you no lie. Must be somethin' I ate. You hop back into bed. We'll leave this candle burnin' for you, Mistress Mary. It'll be a comfort in a strange house, so it will."

She let me hap her up, gentle as a lamb, and I managed to get myself off to the attic, though it's a mystery to me how I managed to mount that ladder. My head was spinning, between what I had just seen and what I had done earlier. What if the things we chose to brush away during the old dame's illness – candles blowing out for no reason, footsteps in the yard, shadows on the wall – turned out to be the build-up of something more than simply mischief? And what if trouble on a grander scale was unfolding now?

Spooning my poor sore belly into Peggy's warm back, I closed my eyes and tried to fight off wave upon wave of dread washing over me.

Chapter 4

I dropped off in the end. The next thing I knowed, Peggy was tugging me awake, saying everyone in the house had overslept. Yawning, I rubbed at the crick in my neck, from lying at a funny angle. Something warm and sticky itched between my legs, and I sat up. Hardly daring to believe, I put my hand down to feel what was flowing out of my body. Blood. A weight flew off my shoulders. Peggy was grumbling away about something and nothing – how I'd need to get the fire going so she could make a start on breakfast, and the hens were back in another flap and not laying again so there'd be none of the boiled eggs Master Jamesey liked – but nothing could spoil my relief. She could have told me there'd never be another egg laid anywhere in Islandmagee, and still I'd have wanted to kiss her. I scrubbed myself with water from the jug, and found one of the rags I used at this time of the month. Then I followed her downstairs with a light step, blood-stained nightdress balled up in my hand and needing a soak.

Peggy was outside hunting for eggs, just on the off-chance there might be the odd one hidden away, when the house boiled over into uproar. Mary Dunbar showed the mistress the state of her bedchamber, before I had a chance to set it to rights. The bairns were suspected right away. The poor wee pigeons were threatened with a cuff on the ear if they didn't own up, and were left feeling miserable – nobody likes being accused in the wrong.

"Go home. I don't want you here no more," said Jamesey to Mary Dunbar.

"Me neither," said missy, his sister. "Keep your ribbons."

"Make your apologies to your cousin at once," said the mistress. "If your father was here, you'd be thrashed with his belt."

"If Father was here, he wouldn't blame us for something we never did," said Jamesey.

"Wait till he hears how you cheek me behind his back. He made a point of asking if you were being good in that letter I had from him yesterday. Now I'll have to write and tell him how naughty you are, for a big boy and girl of eight and nearly seven. The worry it'll give him, and your father trying to do his best for us all, so far away in Dublin. You should be ashamed of yourselves."

The children hung their heads. They were sent to copy out the Ten Commandments in their best script, with special attention to the fifth, and forbidden to go outside for the rest of the day. I thought it hard on them, and was surprised at the young lady for not speaking up on their behalf. But the danger which had passed me by left me inclined to make allowances for everybody. Maybes she believes them to blame, I told myself. As for Jamesey and Sarah, I'd sneak them in a treat as soon as I could.

Mary Dunbar was as out of sorts as missy and the young master. To please her, the mistress suggested they take the ass and cart and pay a call on a neighbour above in Gransha. This was a great concession to the young lady. But Mary told her she was in no humour for small talk with strangers. So the pair of them sat with long faces, working on a new rug for the parlour. The mistress was determined to have it finished by Easter Sunday. I had my eye on the old rug for the loft. The wind whistled between the boards, up there at the top of the house. I was waiting to catch Mistress Haltridge in a good mood, but this wouldn't be the day, I could see that.

Moods are catching, and soon everybody was downhearted. Bar me, I have to confess. Tender though my body felt, my spirits were released. What I had done with my master – what I must never do again – would go unpunished. At least in the here and now. I'd have to answer for it in the hereafter.

Anyhow, a visit from Frazer Bell was welcome in our gloomy household, carrying the crisp air of outdoors into the parlour.

He tossed his slouchy grey hat onto a side table. "I've come to pay my respects to your guest, Mistress Isabel. I promised James to keep an eye on things while he's away. But I've been guilty of shameful neglect. It's all hands on deck during lambing season."

"I know how it is at this time of year, Frazer. Ask Noah for help if the lambing gets busy."

"We're over the thick of it, touch wood. Where are the bairns? Do they know about the ducklings on Donaldsons' pond?"

"They're in disgrace. The ducklings will have to manage without them."

"It's I who should be in disgrace. Worry about my ewes drove me away so fast after prayers on Sunday, I did no more than bow at a distance to you and your cousin."

"Allow me to introduce you now. Mistress Mary Dunbar of Armagh, meet Islandmagee's most eligible bachelor, Mister Frazer Bell, who has known my husband at least three times as long as I have."

"You sing my praises too kindly, mistress. But it's true – I have known James since the day he was born, practically. We learned how to skim stones and scale trees together. He was always better at climbing than me. It's a pleasure to make your acquaintance, Mistress Dunbar." Frazer bowed.

He was not known for paying particular attention to ladies, though they enjoyed his company as much as men did, for he was a tonic. He had a merry nature, and usually had everyone else in high spirits along with him, though if you thought about what he said afterwards it never seemed out of the ordinary. It was just his glad-hearted way of putting things over. Usually it was some jest about how a ship had been wrecked over Donegal way, meaning the cost of fancy wines would fall miraculously.

But only a pockle could fail to see he was immediately struck by our visitor. You can always tell when a gentleman notices a lady. It's no different when a lad notices a lassie. Mercy Hunter says it's a way they have of looking: taking everything in. Frazer Bell leaned on the mantelpiece, gazing down at Mary – just on the right side of polite – and ignored the glass of claret I knowed to fetch him straight away, without waiting to hear would he prefer punch. Usually he glugged it back in a swallow or two. This time, I doubt if he even saw the glass at his elbow.

His voice was gentle as he addressed the guest. How did she find Islandmagee? Was it her first trip? How long could they persuade her to stay? I wondered what sort of figure he cut for a young lady who had already turned down an officer. His coat was not an eye-catching scarlet, but a good grey cutaway, a match for his eyes. He wore no fancy wig, but his own thatch was a thick chestnut brown. And his face, with its scattering of moles on his left cheek above the side whiskers, was an honest and well-meaning one. They were of an age, but he was no match for my master: neither as tall as him, nor as even-featured. Still, I'll not deny he had his charm.

Mary Dunbar peeped through her halo of curls at Frazer Bell. Some women blossom in a gentleman's presence.

"Would you allow me to show you something of Islandmagee, Mistress Dunbar? There are some ancient remains of interest."

"Frazer knows the island like the back of his hand," said the mistress. "His family has lived here for generations."

"Only since the 1630s, Mistress Isabel, when my grandfather – for whom I was named – sailed across to stake a claim on some land. But I flatter myself I do know Islandmagee. Mistress Dunbar might like to explore the caves at the Gobbins. There is one called Moses Hill's cave, where Sir Moses Hill hid out when the Irish were on the rampage, back when the Scotch first planted Ulster."

"Do all the caves have names, Mister Bell?"

"Not all, Mistress Dunbar. A few do."

"What other names do they go by?"

"Stop!" the mistress burst out and we all looked at her, startled. "I mean – stay a moment. I've often wondered how come a servant such as Ellen has a name in common with Sir Moses." She turned to Mary Dunbar. "He was the landlord in these parts."

Everybody looked at me, and I stuttered at so much attention. "I can't tell how it is we share a name. But there are plenty of Hills about here. Ordinary folk, not gentry like Sir Moses and his people." I backed away.

"Often, tenants took a landlord's name," said Frazer.

"Anyhow, that's enough history," put in the mistress.

"Wouldn't it be fun to get up a party and pay the caves a visit?" said Mary. "What do you say, Mister Bell?"

"I say why not, mistress. Spring is in the air at last."

Which only goes to show how taken he was with our guest, because most days it would skin you.

  ⅎ ⅎ ⅎ

The following day, Peggy and I sat in the kitchen, taking our ease before it was time to prepare supper. Peggy produced a plug of tobacco and bit off a chunk with her gums, tapping it into her pipe. "Mister Bell slipped it to me yesterday," she said, with sly delight. He knowed her from boyhood, and often brought dulse for her as well. It grows down by the rock pools at the foot of the Gobbins, and folk gather it to dry and sell at the fair. But Frazer Bell liked to give it away.

We each had some claret, Peggy and me, which I managed to wheek away after Frazer's visit before the mistress saw there were leftovers. I preferred port wine, but it was a treat, all the same, and I smacked my lips over it. How could you not savour something when you knowed it cost thirteen pence a quart? The mistress was always listing the price of goods, like a big stick to beat you with. But sometimes it just served to sweeten stolen pleasures.

The peace of the late afternoon was broken by a violent tug of the parlour bell. It used to be that the mistress would come to the door and call if she wanted me, but I suppose she liked to look fancy in front of her cousin. I was expecting to be scolded for some transgression or other, but when I entered the room the mistress was trembling, her face drained of colour.

Silently, she showed me the book of sermons she used to read aloud to old Mistress Haltridge. Pages were ripped from it. She pointed towards the fireplace. Blackened remains of paper were strewn on the hearth, as though put there on purpose after they were part-burned, to show what was done.

"Tell me you did it for a jest and we'll say no more about it," she said.

"Mistress, I had no hand, act or part in this."

"My husband used that collection of sermons to give you reading lessons, did he not?"

"Aye, and other books. But I would no more put one of them in the fire than my own right hand."

"The children deny it, too. It was their grandmother's favourite book. Hearing me read aloud from it was the only thing that gave her peace, in her last days." She pushed it into my hands. "Get rid of this. I can't bear to look at it." She flopped down on a seat. "It's starting up again. Knowehead is cursed."

She was only saying what I thought myself. For a moment I felt overwhelmed, but then I brought the bairns to mind. The household would be undone entirely if both the mistress and me gave way to our fears. One of us had to stay strong.

I took a deep breath, bunched my hands into balls, and willed my voice not to betray my own doubts. "No, mistress, you must'n let yourself think that way. Please God the hauntin' is dead and buried along with the aul' mistress."

"It's too much to hope for. You know as well as I do that your master's mother saw a man in this house. A man who had no business to be here, but he came and went at will. And he'll go on coming and going as he pleases – why should he stop now?"

"We have to remember she was'n well."

"Her body was ill, not her mind." She looked me in the eye, not as mistress to maid but as woman to woman. "Towards the end, when I sat up with her at night, she used to say things. But she wasn't talking to me. She was talking to a butcher of women and children. She took that book out of my hands and held it against her heart, as if it could protect her from the Devil himself. You never saw such desperation in a person's face. She was pleading, Ellen. Pleading with Hamilton Lock. Telling him the Haltridges had never harmed him, and there was no reason to bear ill-will towards us. I was terrified when I heard that. I interrupted to ask why Hamilton Lock would want to hound us. She said it was because of where we lived. It was down to the house."

A tight feeling came over me at that, as if my skin was shrinking and didn't fit my body any more. The mistress shuddered, close to tears, and I wasn't far behind. I put the book down and made so bold as to put my arm round her, taking as much support from her as she did from me.

"Hush, mistress, try not to say his name out loud." My

mouth dried up, and the rest came out in a croak. "It could maybes conjure him up."

She rested against me for a minute before shrugging me off – too proud to lean on a maid. "My husband forbids me to speak his name too."

"Name a thing and you give it power. Especially a name steeped in evil like his. Did the aul' mistress say anything else?"

"She was bargaining with him to leave her grandchildren be. 'They're innocent,' she said. 'They don't deserve to be taken. Take me instead.' And he did. But she might not be enough for him. Maybe he wants more. Oh sweet Lord, he's still here! I can feel it! Can't you?"

I wrung my apron between my hands, and it's a wonder I didn't make a rag of it, so tight did I twist it. "Aye, mistress, I can feel something amiss in this house."

"I think he's trying to tell me something, Ellen. He's letting me know he heard me reading from this volume of sermons – and a holy book is just paper that can be burned, as far as he's concerned." We both looked at the book with its scorched and torn pages. She rubbed her forehead, where a vein popped out. "This act of mischief is just a tease. I fear there's worse to come. James had no right to go off and leave us so soon. I'll have to send for him – I'm not able for this on my own. But he won't thank me for disturbing him in Dublin. The news was far from good in that last letter I had from him. He says his affairs will occupy him for longer than he bargained. He expects to be away for weeks, unless I bid him come home."

Only a few days ago, I'd have jumped at the chance of seeing my master, and passing the burden of my secret on to him. Now, though I was as fearful as her, I thought we should call on help closer at hand. With the best will in the world, my master would take some days to reach us. "Speak to the minister, mistress. Him and the elders helped us in the past."

"Should I? But folk will talk about Knowehead House if the kirk has to come here again. James won't take kindly to it."

"Maybes the kirk will be fit to put a stop to the things goin' on in the house."

"I'll sleep on it. I know we need help but James really won't thank me for drawing attention to the family. I'm afraid he'll hold me to blame, rather than . . ." Unable to finish, she pressed her lips together, trying to control herself. "We have to hope for the best," she said finally.

"Hope for the best and prepare for the worst," said Peggy, after I repeated what passed between me and the mistress. She sucked her gums. "I had that Dunbar lassie doon with me whiles you were with the mistress. Questions, questions. She's a right Nosey Nellie, for all she's a lady."

Later, after Peggy went to bed, my mind started chasing its tail. Tell you no lie, I thought about clearing out from Knowehead House. Something told me to pack my bundle then and there and walk back home to Carnspindle, black night though it was. I could be there in no time if I went by the pads through the fields. A matter of minutes would leave me ready for the road. I had nothing much to take – no call for a trunk or a cart ride for the little I owned. Shanks's nag would do me.

From when I was no bigger than a blade of grass, Ma taught me the one lesson she said I needed in life. What can't be cured must be endured. But that night my mind was nipping at me, and I thought I wouldn't be able to manage much more of it. Not this time. Sure I was only a cuddy, when all's said and done.

I put my mind to thinking about a new place. There would be an opening for a servant at the Orrs' farm, with Ruth Graham in disgrace, but I hardly liked to benefit from her misfortune. Or put myself in the way of that goat Sammy Orr. I had a narrow escape with my master already. There had to be other places. Only the other week, Mercy Hunter told me about a family at the foot of Muldersleigh Hill looking for help. They had soldiers staying with them, and needed a hand with the cooking and cleaning. She was half-tempted, on account of her weakness for uniforms, but it looked like a heavy workload.

But I pulled myself together. A job in the hand was worth two in the bush. The money I earned was wanted at home to help fill the bellies of all the wee'ans Ma had popped out. Seven of us living, the youngest only four years old. Da was too fond of rum for his own good. Islandmagee was crawling with shebeens and you'd swear he made a pledge to keep each and every one of them going strong. He was a carpenter by trade, but a drinker by inclination. The carpentry took him to sea as a young fellow. Most of the menfolk in these parts either go to sea or farm the land, and ships need carpenters. That's where he came by his taste for rum. Ma says he drank because he missed the sea but I took that with a pinch of salt. Drinkers can always find an excuse.

No, I couldn't leave my livelihood and that was that. I forced myself to remember how much better off I was, in many ways, at Knowehead House. The helpings were plentiful, and I only had to share a bed with Peggy instead of four to a pallet at home.

But if I was staying at Knowehead House, I'd need to keep my wits about me. And my distance from my master.

≋   ≋   ≋

Mary Dunbar appeared in the yard the next morning, as I was coming back from rounding up the dun cow after it strayed on the road. By rights, Noah Spears should have seen about it, but he was nowhere to be found. The greyhounds let out a few yips when they spied her. But when I hushed them, they settled down quick enough – they were getting used to her.

"You're up with the lark, Mistress Mary. There's buttermilk in the larder. Come inside. Will I fetch you a beaker?"

"I had stomach cramps last night. I was in agony with them."

Now that I looked at her properly, I saw a shadow under each eye. "I'm sorry to hear it. Was it something you ate?"

"It was a warning. Some visitors came to my bedchamber."

"At that hour of night? How did they get in?"

"Through the window. Or they could have come in by the keyhole. Walls would never keep them out."

"I'm not follyin' you, mistress."

"Witches. They were plotting together. I didn't dare shut my eyes till cockcrow."

"Witches?"

"That time I unpicked their knots and thwarted their spell. They mean to harm me for it. You should have stopped me untying those knots in the apron strings."

"Pardon me, mistress, but you were thran, so you were. There was no stoppin' you. I did my best."

"I didn't understand. You should have made me see the danger."

I disliked the way she was loading all the blame on to me. "I'm sorry you could'n sleep. A nap after breakfast might help you catch up. Now, I have chores to see about."

I tried to get past her, but she blocked my way, slight though she was.

"This house scares me. Does it not scare you?"

At that, I relented – she was only a lassie, after all. "Look, the sky's clear this morning. Why not take a walk and clear your head of all them fancies?"

"They're not fancies – I heard the witches as clearly as I hear you now."

"Did you see them?"

"No, only their voices. But I know they were there. Three

81

of them. I couldn't move a muscle while they were in my bedchamber – I was paralysed."

"Three women, mistress? Or was one of them . . . a man?"

She hesitated. "They were all women."

That was a relief. But then I remembered Mistress Anne Haltridge's cap in the apron folds. "Was one of them an aul' dame, white-haired but with black eyebrows?"

"They all kept their backs to me."

Peggy hobbled out with some leftovers in a pan for the pig. "Good day, mistress. It's shapin' up to be a nice, soft day. I trust you slept well."

"How could I, tormented by witches half the night?" And back indoors she ran.

'Witches?' Peggy asked me.

"Aye, on account o' thon handlin' over the knots in the apron," I said. "I'm afraid I called them witches' knots. I should a held me tongue. It's put the notion o' witches in her head. It must a been nigglin' at her these past few days. She thinks the witches who tied the knots into the apron came back, and have been in her bedchamber – plottin' agin her."

"Why would witches be bothered with a lassie like her? Surely they'd have other fish to fry?"

"To punish her for spoilin' their spell. So she says."

"Witches have places where they meet an' cast their spells. I never heared tell of a young lassie's bedchamber bein' one of them. Besides, if there's badness about, who's to say witches are behind it?"

"Who else could it be? Somebody playin' tricks?"

"Could be. It might be the livin', all right. Or it might be . . ."

She said no more, but I knowed what she meant. It might be the living. Or it might be the dead.

※　※　※

During supper, the mistress rang for me. "She'll wear that bell out, if she does'n wear me out first," I complained to Peggy. "They'll be lookin' for more salted herrings, I daresay. I'll bring some in, to spare my feet." I had salted them myself, under Peggy's direction, and they were a tasty mouthful.

But nobody was thinking about food when I entered the room. Everyone was staring at Mary Dunbar. She had her chair cowped up and was standing by the table. Her body was arched like a hissing cat's, teeth bared and eyes fixed on something that clearly nobody else could see. I took her to be in a trance. I threw her one look, and told the bairns to go to Peggy in the kitchen. Missie Sarah was willing, poor frightened pigeon, but Master Jamesey's eyes were popping in his head and he seemed inclined to stay and gaze his fill.

I clapped my hands. "Run along now – tell Peggy I said yiz are to have a honeycake apiece."

The mistress was panicky. "She doesn't answer when I speak to her. Watch. What ails you, Mary? Mary, can you hear me?"

Silence. It was as if the young lady was no longer in Knowehead House. She was somewhere inside her head – and it was not an agreeable place to be, judging by her expression.

"She's having a fit. My aunt never said she fitted. I wouldn't have asked her to come and stay with us if I'd been told. I don't know what to do. Do we click our fingers and snap her out of it?"

She was asking me questions I had no answers for. I was only a maid, not a physician. But one of Ruth Graham's brothers used to go into a trance when he was younger, and I tried to mind how her ma was with him. She never startled him out of it. She always let him be, and he'd come to on his own.

"We must take care not to alarm her, mistress. She'll come round in her own good time."

"But we can't leave her like this."

I chewed my thumb, trying to think what to do for the best.

"Let's move her closer to the fire. Maybes the heat might bring her out of it." I took hold of an arm, but it was like trying to shift a tree because Mary Dunbar was rooted to the spot. I was no weakling, but I gave up the attempt. I passed my hand in front of her eyes, and she didn't blink. "What brought it on, mistress?"

"I have no idea. Jamesey was teasing Sarah that we were eating rabbit rather than mutton. You know how she feels about bunnies. It got her all het up. I scolded Jamesey, he started kicking his feet against the table leg, and Sarah was pulling at my gown and gabbling away. Then I heard what she was saying. 'Mama, something's the matter with Cousin Mary.' When I looked up, she was frozen solid. Buried under a sheet of ice. Just as she is now. She's not here at all."

I touched Mary Dunbar again. "Come to the fire." I kept my voice low, the way you'd handle a sick animal. "You'll feel better when you're all cosy." But her attention was fixed on whatever she was staring at. And it gave her no pleasure.

"I'm at my wits' end." The mistress tugged at the strings of her cap. "Run up and check her trunk – see if there may be some physick she has forgotten to take."

"Aye, I'll do that." I backed away slowly, unable to tear my eyes from that empty face. Its blankness filled me with foreboding. Less for the young lady than for what it meant for the household.

"On second thoughts, Ellen, don't leave me alone with her. Not while she's having a fit."

"What happened?" It was Mary Dunbar.

"Mary, my dear, you're back with us. How are you feeling?"

"Peculiar, Isabel. As if I nodded off in the middle of doing something. But I don't feel rested – in fact, I'm bone weary. Where have Jamesey and Sarah gone? Are they in bed?"

"Don't you remember what happened?"

She screwed up her eyes. The voice was reedy, and the

words came slow, at first, but speeded up as her memory returned to her. "I was cutting my meat . . . I looked up and couldn't see you any more . . . I just floated away . . . and found myself somewhere else. I think it must have been a cave – I could hear the sea outside, and smell the saltwater. There was a bonfire, and a group of women round it. It seemed to be a meeting place. One of the women had a skull – I think it was a human skull – there were tufts of black hair on top. She was holding it up in the air, chanting a name. '*Hamilton Lock! Hamilton Lock! We summon you up, Hamilton Lock!*'"

The mistress held her throat, eyes searching out mine. I shook my head, warning against cutting in.

"The women circled the fire, in a sort of procession, repeating that name. '*We call on you again, Hamilton Lock!*' Next, the one with the skull sang out '*She is waiting!*' and the flames leapt higher, and the others called '*Waiting for you!*' And then, all together, they shouted '*Mary Dunbar is waiting for you, Hamilton Lock!*' Their voices are ringing in my head still. They were gleeful cries. Triumphant cries." She began shaking. "It was vile to hear my name coupled with his. I was in terror, Isabel. Mortal terror."

The mistress wrapped her arms round her cousin, stroking her. "I'll take care of my cousin – you see about the children, Ellen."

"Aye, mistress, but then we need to get help. This has to be all mixed up with the aul' mistress. I know you don't want Knowehead talked about. But you can't hold off any longer. You need to ask the minister and the elders for help."

"I'll send for him the morning. It's too late now to drag him out."

"Mistress, if it was me, I would'n waste another minute."

"No, first thing in the morning is time enough. I don't want this to appear worse than it is."

I gaped. Mary Dunbar was saying witches used Hamilton

Lock's skull to call him back from the dead. How could it be any worse? "But Mistress Mary had a vision of what sounds like Lock's Cave. It has to be searched."

"I – I suppose so. But, Ellen, don't you see? Folk will say my cousin is possessed. She'll be shunned – her reputation will never recover from it. Let's leave it one more night. I'll give her one of my sleeping draughts, and hopefully she'll have a restful night. Perhaps in the morning she'll tell us it was all just a vivid dream. Now, do as you're told and see to the children."

I could push it no further for now, but decided to remind her about fetching the minister straight after breakfast. Even if she disliked the nudge.

Back I went to the kitchen, to find the bairns standing by the half-door, as though they'd just as soon be outside as in.

"I want my daddy," said Sarah.

I picked her up and cuddled her. "He'll be home soon, chicken, with stories to tell about Dublin." She pressed her face against my neck, crumbling the uneaten honeycake in her hot wee paw. I ran a hand through Jamesey's hair. We had tried to protect them from what happened in Knowehead House before their granny died, but they still caught sounds young ears ought not to hear.

While I have breath in my body, I'll never forget the look in them dead eyes of hers when I went to close her eyelids for the last time. The mistress couldn't bring herself to touch her, and it wasn't fitting to let someone outside the family do it. So I had to nerve myself to stand over the old mistress, and press the flaps of skin down over them eyes that stared like they were seeing a vision of hell.

And I'll tell you this much. Mary Dunbar had the self-same look in her eyes when she was tranced.

⟨⟨@ ⟨⟨@ ⟨⟨@

We got Mary Dunbar off to bed and the mistress sat with her a while, but the young lady nodded off almost at once. The mistress told me to look in on her on my way to bed, because I was always the last to go down for the night. But the visitor slept like a newborn.

Next morning she woke, sunny as June, and took the bairns out for a dander after breaking her fast. Missie wasn't keen, and the cub made a lip, but their mother made them go. The childer had turned against Mary Dunbar. Still, the fresh air would do her a power of good, and it was as well to have wee legs near-hand. They could run for help if she took another turn. But I had a word in the mistress's ear. The upshot was that Noah Spears went along with them. "You lassies are a holy terror, so you are," he said, but he was only too willing to juke out of working on the land for an hour. Looking at him, I thought how addled in the wits I must have been, worrying about my monthlies, to think of him for a husband.

When the coast was clear, I told the mistress I was ready now to step over to Ballymuldrough, to tell the minister about Mary Dunbar's vision in a cave.

"Don't you have butter to churn?"

"Aye, but butter can wait. The minister should be told about this cave with a skull in it. He'll want to order it searched."

"Yes, he will. And think of the fuss – all laid at Knowehead's door. My cousin seems much improved today. I really can't spare you to go gadding about on errands."

I scowled, but I couldn't disobey her.

Out in the dairy I was a long time at my task, and the mistress came by to inspect the work.

"The butter is slow to come. Do you have a horseshoe on the bottom of the churn?"

"A-coorse I do, mistress. Sure the world and his wife know you could never churn butter without it."

"It's taking its time."

"Sometimes it just does. There's ne'ther rhyme nor reason to it."

"Aye, well, that's true enough. I'll leave you to it. I might take a walk and see if there's any sign of Mary and the children."

"I could go and speak to the minister when I'm done here, mistress." I knowed I was pushing it, but the thought of Lock's Cave had filled my mind as I churned.

"Ellen, I've already told you to let it rest. 'Tis possible it could all pass over. It might – mightn't it?'

I dropped my eyes to the churn. If I gave her the answer she wanted, she'd make a liar out of me. So I said nothing.

She cleared her throat. "I was wondering if I should have my cousin to sleep with me in my bed. Perhaps she doesn't like retiring on her own. That could be why she's jittery."

"Does she not usually sleep on her lone, mistress? She told me she has no sisters."

"True enough – she's the only one of my aunt's children to survive infancy. You're right, we'll leave her be in the guest chamber. She's settled there. One more thing: if Mercy Hunter calls for a blether, I expect you to keep quiet about this. It would be a shame to see my cousin's name sullied in the mouths of tattle-tales."

◦◦◦ ◦◦◦ ◦◦◦

I made sure to sound as if I wasn't a bit un'asied when I asked the wee'ans how they fared with Mary Dunbar. Jamesey talked about the Brent geese flying low over the lough. Them lingering here was a sign of the hard winter we'd just come through – usually the geese would be gone by now. As for Sarah, she jawed away about all the rabbits they'd seen. There wasn't a word about Mary Dunbar having another attack. I hoped that was an end to it.

When I met Noah clattering about the yard, I brought him into the house and served up a tankard of ale. Playing nursemaid to visitors wasn't part of his job, after all.

He downed it quickly, wanting to be on his way home to his own parcel of land. But on the doorstep he mentioned something that sent me after him, tugging at his sleeve.

"What was that about a wooden chest, Noah?"

"The Dunbar lassie says there's a man hidin' in the chest in her bedchamber. I tould her I'd go up an' chase him, but she says none but her can see him for now. I daresay she was havin' a wee joke at my expense." He wiped his mouth on his sleeve. "I pity the man takes up wi' her. She looks soft as a feather bed. But she's thran as the day is long."

I let him go. Thran, he said. Stubborn, headstrong – someone not easily turned back from the path they were on. I was thoughtful as I closed the door after him.

Chapter 5

That evening I was worn out, and sat by the hearth with the mending basket on my lap, lacking the strength to do any work. The only light was by the glow of the fire and the moon shining through the casement. Peggy McGregor was nodding off beside me, grumbling in her sleep. Most days, you never got much use out of her company come nightfall. The fire was smoking because the chimneys needed sweeping. It was up to the mistress to send for the sweep, but it must have slipped her mind. The house was higgledy-piggledy and no mistake. A gust of wind came down the chimney and sent black smoke flapping round us, and Peggy woke with a start.

"You were sound there."

"I was dreamin' about the time I come across here first from Scotland with the minister."

"I daresay them were happy days, Peggy."

"We were young. That's always to the good. But . . ." she studied some old burns criss-crossing her arms ". . . the first year or two were far from 'asy.'

"I suppose everything was new to you, and you knowed nobody but your master?"

"Ach, it was more than that. There were things not right here. It took a long while afore I felt safe in my bed."

"Were you afraid of attack?"

"There's no denying the Irish didnae want us. But we had soldiers to protect us, and muskets of our own forbye. What the Irish liked or disliked was ne'ther here nor there, providin' they could be kep' down. And mos'ly they were. But there was somethin' else didnae want us. And that was harder to manage. We should'n be here, lass. That's the long and the short of it." Shivering, she held up her hands to the fire.

"But Islandmagee was a wilderness till the Scotch came. The land was goin' to waste. We only took what the Irish lacked the sense to look after, and see how we improved it."

"I bain't sayin' we've no right to be in Ireland. We've earned what we hold in Ulster." She gripped the arms of the chair with both hands, heaved herself to her feet, and leaned in towards me. "But Knowehead House went up where it had no business bein' put."

My eye was drawn to her shadow, climbing the chimney breast till it all but covered it. For the first time since I met her, Peggy McGregor was a large presence.

"When I came here as a young woman, the aul' folk said there was somethin' Other about this patch of land at Kilcoan More. Nothin' should ever a been built here. The Locks were warned agin puttin' up their house, over where our barn stands now, but they would'n listen – and look at the luck they had. Ne'ther father nor son died in their beds. Then along came my master the minister, an' he insisted on buildin' here too. Folk were even more agin it by then. It would'n do, they said. Not when a great Stone sat where Minister Haltridge meant the house to go: a lump of rock put there deliberately, maybe, for what purpose we could not guess, by a race of heathens long since vanished from the face of the earth. He was tould on no account should the Stone be disturbed. But the minister was'n for budgin'. He said he refused to be ruled by superstition. It was no easy task to move thon lump of rock. But down came the Stone and up went the house." She tottered to the door. "A pagan message, he called thon Stone. I've said enough – I'm for me bed."

"Wait, Peggy. What was the message?"

"Dinna play the innocent with me, lassie. You ken how it is as well as I do – you're livin' here long enough. Knowehead House is different because of where it stands. This patch of earth is Other. It's like nowhere else on Islandmagee. Or in Ireland, for that matter. We're trespassers in Kilcoan More. Our walls and fences have no business here."

Aye, as soon as she spoke the words, I understood how it was. Trespassers – that's exactly what we were. She knowed it, I knowed it and the mistress knowed it. So did the bairns, young as they were. My master was the only one who wouldn't or couldn't admit it, as stubborn as his father, the minister.

Peggy put an end to our yarning by saying her bed was calling to her, though it wasn't yet late by the moon. We kept early hours on Islandmagee. Most folk did. Even so, she was sleeping more and more these days – I suppose she wasn't getting any younger.

After she left, I was restless. For something to do, I went to the walk-in larder for an apple. They were wrinkled after a winter stored in dry sand inside a barrel, but still sweet and only a little faded. No sooner had I pulled one out than I began to hear a banging noise from somewhere in the house. Then, as I listened, wondering what it was, I heard the mistress calling me, her voice spiky from fright. I dropped the apple and tore out as fast as my feet would carry me.

Mary was in the master's heavy leather-and-wood seat in the parlour, arms folded round her body, rocking backwards and forwards. Each time a judder went through her, the front legs of the chair were lifted up and crashed back down. You'd never believe such a slight wee thing could make as much racket.

The mistress was beside herself. "She's having another fit."

"How long has she been like this?"

"A few minutes. The rocking is getting more violent – she'll bite her tongue in half if she carries on."

The young lady's teeth chattered in her jaw, but the flames were blazing up the chimney.

I bent towards her. "Mistress Mary? Are you cold?"

I half-expected her not to hear me, like before, but she answered. "Help, they're jiggling me up and down!"

The previous fit was nothing compared to this. Her eyes had stared at something then. Now they rolled about, the way an animal's do in pain.

"Nobody's jigglin' you," I said. "You're in Knowhead House, among friends."

"They say they'll keep it up till they shake the teeth out of my head."

"Who is doing this to you, Mary?" asked the mistress.

"The witches from the cave. They're intriguing against me. They've sent their shadows to torment me."

"But why do they intrigue against you, Mary?" she asked.

"Their master orders it." The chair stopped moving and she shrank back into it, a look of horror on her face. "She has a whip in her hand!"

The mistress and I exchanged glances, helpless.

"Keep her off me. Someone stop her, for the love of God!" She pulled off her cap and aimed it at something. It sailed through the air, landing with a plop on a chair back. A shriek fit to raise the dead burst from her. "She's ripped my skin off. Look at her laughing. Oh Christ above, I can't stand the pain!"

I brushed back her hair which was sticking to her face, trying to calm her. Dark pools of sweat gathered at her armpits. She trembled in my arms, clutching at her thigh. I lifted her skirt and petticoat, but there was nothing to see. Yet there was no doubting her pain.

"She has the whip still. The others are urging her on. They

say my flesh is going to be striped red and white by the time they're through with me."

"Do something, Ellen!" said the mistress.

My mouth fell open. What could I do?

"Make them go away. This is hell on earth!" Mary Dunbar was panting, her ribcage rising and falling like a bellows.

I sucked on a loose length of hair, and for once the mistress didn't pick me up on it. How could we save her from an invisible enemy? Her squeals were real enough.

"We can't manage on our own any longer," I said.

Mistress Haltridge nodded. There was no more talk of tongues flapping about Knowehead.

"I'll run out now," I said. "I'll not come back without help."

"Be careful. It's dark outside."

"I bain't afeared of the dark, mistress."

The mistress didn't like to let on she was nervous of the dark. "You could miss your footing and fall into a shuck. That's all I meant."

"I ken the pads through these fields like the back of my hand. I'll be back with the minister afore you know I'm gone. You need to stay with the young lady, mistress."

"But what if she attacks me?"

"I'd be more afeared of her harmin' herself. Never you leave her alone for a minute."

"Very well. But we need to give Mary something to pacify her. There's no telling what she might do in this state. Before you go, tell Peggy to mix up one of her cordials."

"Aye, but the best service we can do her now is to have her prayed over. It was the only thing gave the aul' mistress any peace. Somebody needs to get down on their knees and ask the Good Lord to send your cousin back to us – because she's bein' taken places no Christian soul should go."

Peggy was awake, the blanket clutched under her nose, when I went flying back to our sleeping place in the loft. I was in such a rush, I caught myself a clip on the head from the roof beams.

"A body would think she was bein' hit by the hammers of hell," said Peggy.

"Maybes she is. Best stir yourself. I've a message to run, and the mistress is wantin' cordial for the young lady."

Peggy wrapped a shawl round her shift and climbed down to the kitchen after me. Muttering away, she took out a wooden bowl and pestle from the cupboard, whiles I tugged on a pair of worsted stockings and kilted up my skirt. Jumping over shucks was muddy work, never mind the cow claps. At first I thought Peggy was mumbling a string of complaints as she mixed dried herbs. But as I went to pull the door shut behind me, I realized the sounds coming from her lips were something else entirely. They were prayers.

꿩   꿩   꿩

On the way to Robert Sinclair's house, the only creatures I saw were some whitricks, looking about their supper like as not. Mercy Hunter answered my tap on the kitchen door. She was dying to know why I was sent to fetch the minister, and pinched me for answers leading me in, but I was in no mood to satisfy her curiosity. This would get out soon enough.

Mister Sinclair was in his study preparing his sermon. He was a man of some fifty years, with a face marked by smallpox, and a wig that vexed his head, because he was forever scrabbing underneath and never put it back straight. The kirk in Scotland sent him to us in the back end of the 1690s, to take John Haltridge's place after he was carried off. His wife was reluctant to come, or so they said, and found no shortage of reasons to take the three-hour boat-trip home to her own people. She was there now, helping a sister who gave birth to twins late in life. The minister and his wife had neither chick nor child. His congregation laughed at him, behind his back, for tolerating an absent wife. It was the worst of both worlds, they said.

I gave a bob, minding my manners. "Sir, Mistress Haltridge begs you to come at once. She has a guest in trouble."

"I'll come gladly. I presume it's the young female relation she's been bringing to the meeting-house. But what kind of trouble does the visitor find herself in?"

"Sir, she says witches are meddlin' with her."

The intake of breath was sharp, though he tried to disguise it by clearing his throat.

"There's something else, sir. She says the witches cast their spells in a cave. It sounds as if it might be Lock's Cave. I'd say it needs to be searched."

"I'll go to Knowehead House at once."

He rang the bell, and Mercy Hunter came so quick she must have been on her knees by the keyhole. She had the run of the house, with no mistress to bring her to heel. "Mercy, tell Thomas to saddle Sobriety, and look sharp about it. Then bring me my cloak."

She rolled her eyes at me on her way past.

The minister fumbled among the papers on his desk. "Where did I set my Bible?"

"Please, sir, is that it sitting on the chair? It's lying open at one of Paul the Apostle's epistles."

"So it is. Paul has useful words to say about fornication which I intend drawing to my flock's attention. I hope you are a good girl and stay pure in mind in body. Remember, your body is shaped in God's image and likeness and not intended for idle amusement."

"Aye, sir." I had learned my lesson the hard way.

He placed the Bible, a braw book made of panelled calfskin, in a leather satchel. Something occurred to him, and he peered at me over the top of his reading spectacles. "You can read? You knew the page my Bible was open at?"

"Aye, I can write, an' all. My master taught me how."

"Good. In our faith we believe in reading the Word with our own eyes, rather than depending on someone else to deliver God's message. But you would do well to restrain your reading to the Holy Scriptures. They are meat and drink enough for any man or woman."

"I do read the Bible, sir. There's a copy of it in Knowehead. Master Haltridge was civil enough to say I could borrow it whenever I had a mind to practise reading."

The whiles Mister Sinclair gathered himself together, I thought about the lessons I had with my master. They were the happiest times of my life. The reading came first, before we moved on to lettering. At first, my master intended only to teach me to draw the symbols that set down my name. But he said I had such a knack, it would be a shame not to take it further. He put the first quill ever I held into my hand. His hands were soft, the nails clean. Cleaner than mine. Softer, forbye. He said what he was about to give me was worth more than rubies: "It raises you above the herd." Them were his exact words. I was only half-listening to Mister Sinclair as he droned on like a goodwife on market day. Instead I was remembering the touch of my master's hand against mine, as he showed me how to hold the quill. Such gentleness there was in him. I never knowed much gentleness in my life. It left me defenceless when I met it.

Mercy landed back in with a black woollen cloak over her arm, a hat and a pair of boots. The boots were clabber from tip to toe. I should have been ashamed not to take a scraper to them boots before handing them over. But Mercy was a clattery being, and Mister Sinclair pulled them on without noticing. She was always yammering about him being tight-fisted, insisting she could get higher wages elsewhere, but he was an easy master for those of a slothful disposition.

"The King James's Bible is the only chainmail a man needs against sin," he said. "It was that far-sighted monarch's gift to his subjects. A Scotchman, of course, like myself. The king, who is grandfather to our own Queen Anne – long may she reign – ordered the translation of the Bible into the common tongue, so that all his subjects could read it. The papists opposed it, Rome-ridden lackeys that they are. But it was the king's crowning achievement.'

I thought about our queen. She buried all her babbies, one by one, poor lady, and so her people were her children now. Even queens don't get everything their hearts desire.

As I followed the minister out, Mercy dragged me back. "Ellen, what's goin' on?"

"Mary Dunbar. She's taken a fit."

"What kind of fit?"

"I could'n say."

"Pull the other one. You're a finder-outer. You worry away at things, gettin' at the whys an' wherefores."

That stopped me short. It's always a surprise to have our natures laid bare. "You're a fine one to talk, Mercy Hunter. Any word of Ruth?"

"Back home, bein' bate black and blue by her da. Pleasures have to be paid for, as me master is never done remindin' us."

"No time for idle chit-chat!" called the minister. "You can ride behind me, Ellen Hill. My mare's a strong animal and will carry two."

Thomas Kane, his man, held the bridle of a roan horse with a white flash on her forehead. Mister Sinclair used a starting block to mount, and still managed to make a poor shape at it. I scrambled up behind, with a push from Thomas Kane, and no sooner was my backside on the mount than the minister clicked his tongue.

We could not help but touch each other, with me seated behind and holding tight to his belt through his cloak, as Sobriety jogged towards Knowehead. Maybes that's why he spoke of fornication.

"Carnal lust is no venial sin but a serious one which pollutes the body. God ordered man to abstain from fornication, speaking through Paul. Fornicators are lowering themselves to the ranks of dogs and swine, and by their –"

Some of his words were lost in the clop of hooves and the creak of saddle and reins, but I couldn't think of myself as a pig, let alone my master. Yet what my master did with me counted as fornication in the minister's eyes. In God's eyes, too. I knowed he'd want us to do it again. But he'd never push himself on me – he'd take no for an answer. Provided I was strong enough to say him nay. A wee voice in my head whispered I had fallen already, so what difference would a second time make? But another voice said only a pockle would take such a risk after the near-miss I had.

I closed my eyes and, from a pocket in my mind, lifted out the soft words my master spoke to me on the day before he rode off to Dublin. He came to me then, promising we'd take up where we left off when he returned. "It's not a sin to hold each other, Ellen. Don't think of it as sinning." He slipped his hand inside my clothes, stroking my secret place, and the pleasure of it left me weak – not shocked, the way I should have been. It drew a sound from me, louder than was seemly, and he put his other hand over my mouth. Its suddenness was a slap. Above the hand, his face was panicky, and it was like a splash of ice water. I saw he feared discovery, and it helped me to pull away. I would have spoken out then, giving shape to my fear that I was carrying his child, but wee Sarah ran up and the chance was lost.

The minister's voice drifted back to me. "There are some men who hold fornication to be no more than a pastime, like shooting or fishing. Their day of reckoning awaits them."

But was it truly fornication if a maid loved her master – and he loved her just a little?

༄ ༄ ༄

When I arrived back with the minister, both Peggy and the

mistress were sitting with Mary Dunbar, Mistress Haltridge
being reluctant to wait on her own. Mary was resting, her
head against the chair back, but her eyes opened at our
approach.

"I am one of God's chosen ministers." Mister Sinclair laid
his hand on her head. "I have come to pray over you, child."

He told us to kneel, and led everyone in the Lord's Prayer,
Mary joining in. When it came to the line "*And lead us not
into temptation*," she wheezed as she held her stomach.
"They're punching me!"

The minister gave us a sign to continue praying, but our
voices were drowned out by the din as Mary cried about
blows raining down on her. We tailed off, and the minister
alone was praying. Instead, we were watching.

"No, I won't do it. You can't make me!" yelped Mary. All
at once, she rolled up her sleeve. "See how they persecute
me?" A row of bruises covered her arm. "Stop nipping me. I
won't say it. You can pinch me all the colours of the rainbow,
but it won't change my mind." She showed us more bruises
on the other arm. "Sir, send them away, I beseech you.
They're peeved with me, because I try to stand up to them.
They tell me I must do as they command, or they'll torture me
twice as hard. *Ouch!* All right, I'll say it. Give me peace and
I'll say it. That chanting fool in the black cloak is nothing but
a long streak of misery. No wonder his wife put a sea betwixt
and between them."

Mistress Haltridge gasped.

"And Isabel Haltridge is a peacock who'd turn slut for
sixpence, while that maid of hers is a horse-face who'd never
get the chance."

"It's not the lass speaking, but some fiend using her tongue
for its own ends." The minister rose to his feet and stretched
out a hand, finger pointing. "Get thee hence, witch or devil,
whatever you be. You have no power in this God-fearing
house."

Tick-tock, went the tall clock in the hall. *Tick-tock*.

She burst into a cackle I never would have believed could come from her mouth, if I had not heard it with my own ears. Her body jerked, as though seized by the middle and thrown back with great violence, and spittle dribbled from both corners of her mouth.

The minister couldn't help himself – he jumped back. But then he gathered himself to do battle, lifting his Bible above his head with both hands. "You besoms using this poor maid can defy me, but you cannot defy the Good Book. '*Even though I walk through the valley of the shadow of death, I fear no evil, for You are with me.*' Jesus Christ has given His promise on it."

I noticed the mistress do something with her right hand. Something those governed by popery do. She made the sign with fingers they call blessing themselves. I was surprised, but let on to see nothing.

The minister went forward a pace to make up the ground lost. "In the name of our Redeemer, I order you to speak. Who are you?"

Mary Dunbar panted like a dog, tongue out.

"Who sent you?"

She thrashed about, giving him no answer.

"Why have you come here?"

At that, she looked him full in the face, sneering. "*Vengeance is mine, sayeth the Lord.*"

"How dare you quote Holy Scripture! By the power of this Precious Book, I command you to leave this girl in peace. Her soul belongs to the Lord. She has been washed by the blood of Christ. Let her loose – I cast you out into the place from whence you came. Go, you servant of Satan. Go, in our Saviour's name. Begone!"

Mary Dunbar's writhing halted. As sudden as a thunderclap, the casement shutters banged and the candles guttered. Peace floated over the room.

"Look at Mary's face," whispered the mistress.

Where before it had been twisted into ugly shapes, now it was gentle. Her eyes had been clouded, now they were clear. You never saw such innocence in a face. She stood up, wobbled, and sat back down.

"I'm thirsty."

I poured her a glass of water, and she drank it in a single swallow.

"How do you feel, Mary?"

"My throat hurts, Isabel, and – oh, who tore the seam of my gown? Here at the waist? It's coming apart."

The minister held out both hands to Mary and took hers between them. "I am Robert Sinclair, Presbyterian minister here on Islandmagee. You have been unwell, but I hope we have cured you of what ails you."

She freed one of her hands to smooth back her hair. Her voice was husky as she said how honoured she was to meet him, and how much her cousin admired his speaking voice. He preened, despite his scolding about vanity in others.

"Peggy, help Mistress Mary to prepare for bed and then slip off yourself," said the mistress. "Ellen, we should offer Mister Sinclair some refreshment after his efforts. Fetch food and wine."

"No wine, thank you, mistress. Sobriety is my horse and sobriety is my nature."

"Forgive me, how could I forget your sermons on the monstrosity of drunkenness? You are an abstemious man, Mister Sinclair, a credit to your calling. But you must have something to eat before you set out for home."

She led him into the dining room, while I trotted off to the kitchen for a fruit tart on the larder shelf. He was known to have a sweet tooth. I added some cheese and a brace of apples to the tray, along with a pitcher of milk, and carried his supper through to the dining room.

The mistress was shivering. I took one look, and poured

her a full glass of port wine, without adding water as I usually would. Then I busied myself at the fire, adding timber rather than turf to build it quickly. When I looked up, the minister was mouthing something at her.

"You may speak freely, Mister Sinclair," said the mistress. "Ellen Hill has my fullest confidence. She has been with this family for seven years, and has never disappointed."

My ears burned. She never spoke flatteringly about me in my hearing. Indeed, I was the cause of friction between her and the master, because of his insistence on tutoring me.

"Admirable. As I was saying, I see no reason to make a connection between these episodes involving your young relative and the unfortunate incidents surrounding the death of Mistress Haltridge Senior. Granted, she was laid to rest only recently. But I think the fact you are experiencing further, ahem, disturbances, is no more than coincidence."

"But, Mister Sinclair, you led the elders in prayer in every room in the house. I don't understand why our troubles are back."

"Aye, I did indeed. As the Good Book says, *'If any be sick among you, let him call for the elders of the Church, and let him pray.'* James 5:14."

"But why are we plagued again?"

"I cannot answer that, Mistress Haltridge. However, I fear there is a malevolent force afoot in Islandmagee. The Devil is rightly named the Spirit of Fornication, and I'm just now dealing with a pair of fornicators not three miles from this door. No doubt you have seen them chastised at the meeting-house – Samuel Orr and Ruth Graham. A minister must spare no effort to curb debauchery and excess. We have a commission from God to do it. Our vigilance against the Prince of Darkness and his snares can never be relaxed."

"Could that malevolent force you speak of be a restless spirit which has managed to get into this house, Mister Sinclair? The spirit of a man so depraved with vice that he can flit about on earth long after he should be roasting in hellfire?"

"Men and women have an infinite capacity for sin. But spirits, no matter how degenerate, cannot withstand the strength of prayer."

"But what if prayer only keeps such a wicked spirit quiet temporarily? What if its evil is rooted too deep to dig out?"

"Beware the temptation to surrender to despair, Mistress Haltridge – another sin. Prayer and faith conquer all. But I'll make allowances, in view of the circumstances."

"My cousin came to this house with a blameless character, but now she's behaving like one possessed. I fear she's being acted upon by something odious. Just as my late mother-in-law was."

"Calm yourself, dear lady, you are overwrought. Entirely natural, but you must be strong. Sit down – you'll tire yourself out pacing around." He tapped his chin with his fingers, the way he did when a windy elder was droning on too long at the meeting-house. "The situation of the house is a wee bit lonely, I'll grant that. But you have to control your imaginings. You must pray, aye and fast too, for the courage and strength to overcome the obstacles God chooses to set in your path. Remember, two children are in your care while your husband is away."

"But it's happening again – things that can't be explained. What if the shadow that used to cover the wall by Mistress Haltridge's bed comes back? And instead of staying a shadow, it takes shape as a man? What if someone else dies?"

"What if, what if? Dinna fash yourself, Mistress Haltridge. The-morrow, I'll bring the elders to pray here, and if there be malice in this house it will be forced to turn tail and retreat to the place from whence it came."

"If there is malice? You still say if, after what you witnessed tonight? Hamilton Lock's ghost is at work here, there's no other explanation. He's behind this!"

"That name should not be spoken in a God-fearing household."

"Don't you see? He's toying with us. I dread to think what he intends." As she spoke, she birled the stem of her glass until it snapped, and wine splashed over her gown.

I rushed forward to take away the broken pieces before she cut herself. As soon as he decently could, the minister lifted his hat and bag, eager to be away.

I followed him to the door.

"Has my mare had a handful of oats?"

"And a drink of water, forbye. Sir, you have'n forgot about Lock's Cave?"

"Aye, the cave needs to be searched. I'll organise a party of men to do it in the morning. If a coven of witches is meeting there, they will be dealt with severely. Have no fear on that score."

When I went back to the mistress, she asked me to make sure all the doors and casements were bolted before I retired – the master's last task at night, and hers in his absence. But this night, she hadn't it in her.

After locking up, I looked in on the bairns, and was glad to see the pair of them sound asleep. But I could not make myself check on Mary Dunbar. Enough was enough. I dragged myself up the ladder to my nest in the attic, where, unusually, Peggy lay awake.

"The mistress should send thon lassie straight back to Armagh on the next coach. She'll cause merry mayhem here afore she's much older."

I took off my cap and unpinned my hair, letting down the plait. "Maybes it's not the young lady behind the mayhem. You hinted as much yourself the other night in the kitchen."

"Aye, well, I daresay I should'n blame her. She's part of this, but not the cause. Still an' all, her bein' here is stirrin' things up. The Haltridges have aye been respectable folk: men of the cloth and men of business. They come from right, sound Presbyterian stock. I bain't sayin' it's the lassie's fault. But she's doin' harm to the Haltridges' good name."

"The Haltridges' good name is already muddied. We might not like it, but that's the truth." She turned her face to the wall. "We'll need to start bakin' early the-morrow if we have the elders ploughterin' through the house again. All that prayin' gives a man an appetite. Say your prayers and blow out the candle, lassie."

"Peggy, what's goin' on here bain't Christian. First the aul' mistress sees things, now the young lady does. It's e'ther witchin' or hauntin'. An' maybes it's both."

Chapter 6

Next morning, I brought the young lady breakfast in bed. Her face was like a lump of bleached driftwood. I knowed before I put the question to her, but I asked it anyway. "What sort of a night did you have, Mistress Mary?"

"The witches came again. They took my candle, and burned me with it, laughing at the stench of scorching flesh. They said it reminded them of their master."

"Their master the Devil?"

"Aye, he's a devil, but he has a name. Their master is Hamilton Lock."

That name again. There was no escaping it. "How many witches came?"

"A nest of them. At least six – maybe more."

She pushed away the food, and as she did so something caught my eye. I pulled back the sleeves of her lawn nightgown. Burns like giant, angry skitter-jabs stood out on the backs of Mary Dunbar's totie wee hands. It was impossible to look on them without flinching. "My Lord above, you need salve for that. I'll fetch some, and tell the mistress to come and see about you. Them burns look desperate sore."

She swung her legs out of bed and walked barefoot to the

casement. Something in her manner made me reluctant to leave her, even though the burns needed attention.

"What are you lookin' at, mistress?"

"I'm trying to see the Gobbins."

I wondered if the search of Lock's Cave was under way yet, and what it might throw up. Mercy Hunter would have the news on that before I did.

"You know you can't see the Gobbins from here – the direction's wrong. But stay away from them cliffs, for the love of God. Imagine if you took a fit by them. Besides, those are rain clouds in the sky. This is a day for the ducks and nothing else."

"Tell me a story, Ellen."

"Later, mistress, after we see to your burns."

"Where do you find all your stories?"

"From my da. The yarns he can spin – there's nobody to match him."

"I asked Noah about the slaughter at the Gobbins, the day he picked me up from Carrickfergus. You want to have seen the look on his face – I thought he was going to make me get out and walk."

"You must'n go broodin' on the like of that, mistress. It's no good for you."

"Why does nobody ever want to talk about it? Noah denied any such bloodbath took place. He said it was a tale put about by the Irish to stir ill-will. And when I asked Isabel, she told me it was just a story used to frighten children, and probably all exaggerated."

"We don't go in for idle talk here on the island. Nobody could call us blabbermouths. We believe in silence. Least said, soonest mended."

"But why deny what happened?"

"Some folk prefer to forget."

"You can feel it in your bones, Ellen: things happened there. You can smell it in the air."

"Aye, well, I'll give you no argument as to that."

110

She pressed her poor burned wee hands against the cool glass on the casement. "What did the Scotch people on Islandmagee do while the Magees were being killed?"

"They closed their ears and their doors."

"Hadn't they neighbours and friends among the Magees? Couldn't they have warned them, at least?"

"The Irish were – what's the word my master told me? – presumptuous. They thought this land belonged to them. What happened at the Gobbins taught them different."

"Are there any Magees left here?"

"Never a one."

"Weren't even the children spared?"

"The soldiers could'n risk it. Childer grow into men. Men able to carry a grudge. And a sword. Now, I'm away to get salve. Eat your oatcakes and butter. You need to get your strength back – you look frail."

"Mistress Anne has forbidden me to eat so much as a crumb. She says it's my punishment. She's angry with me because the preacher came to the house."

My heart gave a judder at the mention of that name. "Who's Mistress Anne?"

"She's chief among my persecutors."

"I thought their leader was a man." I lowered my voice. "Hamilton Lock?"

"He's there in the background, giving the orders, but he has a woman who passes them on to the others. Her name is Mistress Anne."

"Who told you she goes by that name?"

"You sound vexed with me. I heard the others call her it."

"Was that all? Did they call her anythin' else?"

"No, just Mistress Anne."

"And you're certain-sure Mistress Anne was the name they put on her?"

"Positive. How could I forget anything about my tormenters?"

"Did you get a look at her?"

111

"I'm never able to see her face – I see the others but not her. I don't understand why you're sharp with me, Ellen. It's not my fault I'm terrorized. A dog wouldn't lead this life."

I busied myself making her bed, to give me a chance to think. Some believed if you were witched into your grave, your spirit would be unquiet. Folk would be only too willing to believe the worst of Mistress Anne Haltridge. She was a decent soul – much good it did her, when push came to shove. Folk were slow to blether about the old dame while she lived. But dead and gone, her name could be blackened.

Did Mary Dunbar know what a wasps' nest this would stir up? Maybes she hadn't added up two and two. Or maybes she had.

"Should I not tell anyone about Mistress Anne? Will it make everyone as cross as you?"

I forced a smile. "I'm not cross, mistress – worried is all. Every man Jack of us is in a pother about this. If you know the names of any witches tormentin' you, then it would be wrong to hold them back. But these matters are beyond me – sure what do I know about witchcraft? Best talk to the minister when he comes again with the elders. He'll keep you straight." I went to the casement. "Let me take a look at them clouds. Aye, it'll pour from the heavens the-day, so it will." I breathed on a pane and traced some letters on it with my finger. I never could resist showing off my writing skills. "Now, Mistress Mary, if you cannot eat, at least you can wash. You rest here, whiles I fetch hot water and clean linen. You'll feel the better for it."

I almost said cleanliness was next to godliness. But I stopped myself in time.

❦   ❦   ❦

The household was on edge, waiting for Mister Sinclair and the elders. I brought the childer into the kitchen to give Peggy and me a hand with the cooking, and to take their puzzled wee minds off the goings-on. But they hadn't the heart for helping with Peggy's broth, although usually they begged to be allowed to toss the chicken feet into the pot. Instead they asked questions we let on not to hear.

It was a sin to see their worried faces looking up at us, wanting reassurance. Their father was what they needed, not a helpless maid and an ancient cook. I wished my master's work did not take him so far from home, but it was like wishing day was night, because it was either business or the Church for him – and his nature lacked that certainty you see in men of the cloth, where they feel able to tell others how they should live. He was not a man to judge others by too strict a code. Nor to live by too strict a one either, as I knowed only too well.

"My babby has run away," said the wee missie.

"Has she indeed? Why would she do that?"

"She doesn't like it here."

"That ugly bunch of rags is a silly moo, just like you," said Jamesey.

Sarah burst into tears.

"We'll find your babby-doll, never fear," I told her, before rounding on Jamesey. "Now look what you've done. You're her big brother, your job is to mind her, not set the poor lassie weepin'."

"This handlin' is goin' to get worse afore it gets better," said Peggy. "It's bad for the bairns, so it is. The master ought to be sent for."

"Aye. But till he is, we'll have to do our best to look out for the wee'ans. Same as the last time."

Jamesey's eyes darted between our faces. "Little jugs have big ears," I said to Peggy, walking past her to the back door, where I threw a handful of grain to the hens. They came flocking and clucking, but the rooster did not stoop to mingle with them, even for food. He remained on his perch on an overturned wheelbarrow.

"Isn't that just like menfolk?" Peggy indicated the fowl. "Leave the women to root in the dirt, and let the men stay above it all. Even a man like our master. I ken how it'll be. We'll see ne'ther hide nor hair of him till this sorry business comes to a head."

I did not like her attacking Master Haltridge, but I recognized the truth in her words. Still, I was determined to do my best for his two wee pigeons. For their own sake. But for his, too. Above the rooster's coxcomb, the clouds were melting away, blue showing through in gaps. Maybes the rain was going to pass over, after all. I turned to the bairns, who were watching me as if I could turn black to white, dear love them. "The rain might on'y be a bit of a mizzle. The pair of yiz could go and play with the Baxters."

"They're not our friends any more," said Sarah.

"Quarrels can be mended. Run up to their farmhouse and see if they want to play."

"No."

"Do as you're bid, like a good lass."

"They won't play with us. They said our granny won't stay in her grave. She went in the ground but she won't lie in it."

Peggy's eyes latched on to mine.

"Never worry about them," I said. "The middle boy of the Baxters is a born troublemaker – you're as well away from him. How about if the two of you go callin' on the Widdy Patterson instead?"

"She smells," said Jamesey. "I'd rather go hunting for birds' nests."

"You leave their eggs alone. Besides, your sister is too wee to be climbin' trees. Goin' to see the widdy would be a Christian act. You know how she loves to hear all the news. She allus gives yiz peppermints."

"Would'n the widdy jus' love to hear the news from this house," warned Peggy.

"Say nothin' about your cousin's dizzy spells," I said.

"Can I tell her about the ribbons she brought?" asked Sarah.

"Yes, tell her all about the ribbons, chicken."

"I don't want to sit about with no Widow Patterson talking about no ribbons," said Jamesey.

"Now, Jamesey, you know right well she'll let you ride her donkey if you ask nicely."

He pulled his catapult out of a pocket and stretched the string, letting it snap. "Sarah has to do as I say. You have to tell her I'm in charge."

"You are not!" said Sarah.

"I am too."

"Not."

"Am."

"Not long now afore the elders pitch up an' start prayin'," said Peggy.

I took the hint, and bundled the pair into their cloaks and stout shoes, along with a pot of blackberry jam for their hostess, and instructions to mind their clothes on the brambles.

When Mistress Haltridge, my master's mother, was in the whole of her health, there used to be a dose of praying in Knowehead House. Hail, rain or shine, she called us all together for household prayers at eight o'clock every night. Half an hour, and sometimes longer, we were on our knees. We let that habit slip when she wasn't herself any more. The young mistress was never as anxious about her servants' immortal souls. I daresay she thought our wages and victuals were enough – and as regards eternity, we could fend for ourselves.

        ❦   ❦   ❦

"Let us, with a gladsome mind,
Praise the Lord, for He is kind.
For His mercies aye endure,
Ever faithful, ever sure.

Let us blaze His name abroad,
For of gods he is the God.
For His mercies aye endure,
Ever faithful, ever sure."

The hymn-singing lifted the cloud inside the house, and I hummed along as I went about my work, changing the rushes on the floors. They freshened up the place and kept the stoor down. I was making good progress, until a round of screams brought me up short. I raced to the parlour. It was a good job I always made sure we had plenty of rushes on the floors – with the amount of running I was doing lately, I was at risk of slip-sliding all over the place.

Mary Dunbar's face was cherry-red, her limbs jerking like a puppet's. "Stop! Stop! Stop!"

"Keep singing, friends," said Master Sinclair. "All together now: '*Let us, with a gladsome mind –*'"

The squawking broke out again. It was an appalling sound, and I had to put my hands over my ears to block it out. The elders were all ruddy men, from spending their days on the land, but that caterwauling stole some of their healthy colour.

I saw Randall Leaths there, along with Joseph Esler, Hugh Donaldson and Bob Holmes. They were sober men, married with families, except for Holmes, who was too set in his ways to tolerate a wife. Donaldson was a Samson who could do the work of three or four and, though he was an overfed, snorting bull, it was a comfort to have him in the house. As for Leaths and Esler, they had been good neighbours to us during old Mistress Haltridge's illness. All four of them looked at Mister Sinclair now, waiting for his lead.

The minister scratched under his wig. "Lord, keep us steadfast in your work." He was stuck for words after that, scrabbing away at himself. "We must pray for deliverance for this poor soul," he came out with at last. Everyone fell to their knees, while he remained standing. "Mistress Dunbar, you must renounce your sins, which give the Evil One authority over you."

Mary Dunbar neither moved nor answered, which must have lent him courage. He approached her and placed a hand on her head. "Bear witness before this congregation –"

At that, she was overcome by a monstrous coughing fit. Her eyes watered, her hand clawed at her throat, and it seemed as if she would hack up her insides. Finally, she had some respite and fell back, panting.

Mister Sinclair set off preachifying again. "Some say there be no witches at all but only aged and ignorant crones, deluded in their imagination. I say this is another of Lucifer's snares, to put us off guard. We must be ever vigilant against witchcraft, which is a sin against God."

"Amen!" said the company.

"By nature, a woman is more likely to enlist in the Devil's service than a man, for women are more lustful and easier led."

Mary leaned forward and boked up a flow of egg-yolk-yellow pus on his coat. Everyone jumped off their knees and leaped back, although one or two could not avoid being splashed. The minister stood where he was, his gob hanging open like a fish on a slab. If it wasn't so serious, I'd have laughed at the visog on him. A clink sounded as some objects, caught up in the stream of vomit, bounced off his coat and onto the floor. The lumpy liquid splashed across Mary's clothes, and still she retched on. When she was finished spewing, the mistress propped her head on her lap and fanned her, whiles I took off my apron and mopped at Mister Sinclair.

"Sir, if you gi'e me the coat I can take it to the kitchen and work at it," I offered, and he pulled it off right willing.

Hugh Donaldson took up the poker and separated out the bits and bobs brought up by Mary: a large ball of hair with chicken feathers through it, two waistcoat buttons and a candle stub.

"Did my poor cousin bring up those buttons?" asked Mistress Haltridge.

Donaldson nodded.

I would not have believed it, if I had not seen it with my own eyes.

The candle looked like an ordinary wax stump to me. But Randall Leaths said, "Thon's left over from a Black Sabbath ritual, so it is."

There was silence.

"We wrestle not against flesh and blood but against demons," announced the minister. "Mister Donaldson, give me those objects for safekeeping. I will pray over them later, for fear they may be tainted. We will need them for evidence of witchcraft."

Mary Dunbar opened her eyes. They swam with appeal. "Help me, sir. I throw myself upon your mercy. My tormentors plague me beyond endurance."

He kept a safe distance, but answered with civility. "Rest assured I will do everything in my power to return you to the grace of our Redeemer. You will not be left to fight them alone. Can you tell me, are they here now? Do you see them in this room?"

All of us cast nervous looks left and right.

"No, sir, but two of them were here a short time ago."

"Can you identify them?"

"One had a face that was whole on one side, but puckered red flesh on the other. The eyebrow and eyelashes were singed off."

"I know an aul' biddy has a face like that," said Randall Leaths. "She lives hard-by the burn at the bottom of Charlie Lennon's field. One look from her would frighten a horse without blinkers."

"Fetch her here," ordered Mister Sinclair. "Let's see what she has to say for herself."

Randall Leaths rubbed his chin. "I'm not sure I like to go

next nor near her if she be a witch. She might put a hex on me."

"Take Joseph Esler with you, and remember you are both godly men. Your faith will protect you."

"I know the one you're talkin' about," said Esler. "Becky Carson, she's called. There's no harm in her. She was married to a shepherd, but he's a long time dead. None of their childer made it past birthin'. She's none too steady on her feet. I mind she got thon injury to her face from noddin' off into the fire one night. Granted, it har'ly looks pretty. But we cannae hould that agin her."

"If she is blameless, she has nothing to fear. But she must be brought in to stand before Mistress Dunbar. The guilty cannot look upon those they have wronged without giving themselves away. Fetch her here. We'll see how she conducts herself, and judge her on it."

The two elders lifted their hats and went out to where Randall Leaths' skinny old horse was standing, still in the cart shafts. It would have been Christian to unhook the mare, but Leaths was never one for applying Christianity to beasts. I followed them to draw water from the well, for steeping Mister Sinclair's coat, and it was clear from the way they dragged their feet that neither man had much liking for the errand.

"I daresay there's no harm in hearin' what she has to say for herself," said Joseph Esler. "We may as well bring her in."

"May as well," agreed Leaths. "Like the minister says, if she be innocent she has nothin' to fear."

Just then, Frazer Bell clattered into the yard on his high-stepping bay. He had a weakness for a thoroughbred horse, and his stallion was his pride and joy. He called it Lordship, and liked to say it was better bred than half the folk on the island. I thought the elders would have tarried to speak with him, but they were anxious to get their errand over and done with. Leaths flicked the reins and grunted "Hup now!" at his mare, both men nodding at Frazer in passing.

He called after them, "I hear a search party was got up for one of the caves at the Gobbins!"

Leath pulled the mare to a halt, and twisted round in his seat. "Aye, a boatful of men went round at first light."

"Did they find what they were looking for?"

"They found the remains of a bonfire and some candle stubs in Lock's Cave."

"That's all?"

"So far. But a watch is bein' kept on the cave now."

Frazer Bell dismounted and threw his reins at a post. "I should never have offered to take her to those caves," he muttered to himself. "Why did I ever mention them?" He made haste indoors without giving me the time of day, a lack of civility which was unlike him. The stallion rolled his eyes, and I kept clear of them hooves as I skited round for a bucket by the turf stack. I pumped water into it, and threw the jacket in to soak, without taking time to pound at the stain. Then I shot back indoors to see what was happening.

Frazer Bell and Mister Sinclair were having a difference of opinion. Frazer wanted Mary Dunbar taken to her bedchamber to rest, whiles the minister preferred her to stay in the parlour where he could watch her. As for our guest, her trials had exhausted her, and she sat like one of the painted statues in a papish chapel.

"In the name of humanity, Mister Sinclair, she must be allowed to rest. The young lady can barely keep her eyes open. Making a peepshow of her in this fashion is unseemly, and taxes her strength."

"How is she a peepshow? The only folk here are elders or members of the Haltridge household."

"She's about to keel over. Let her go to her bedchamber and close her eyes in peace for an hour, before you start parading every woman in Islandmagee who's suspected of brewing up a few potions."

"You're taking this uncommon lightly, Frazer Bell. Witches

are tools of the Devil, and witchcraft is a heinous transgression against God's holy laws. Besides, you forget the evidence found at Lock's Cave."

"You call that evidence? Anybody can build a fire and light a candle. It signifies nothing."

"I cannot agree with you, Bell. My primary concern is –"

Frazer cut in, "My primary concern is Mistress Dunbar. She's on the brink of nervous exhaustion – the strain is too much for her health." He spoke quietly, but his words carried force.

The minister reddened, his pockmarks standing out against the skin. "I have to consider the welfare of more than just one person – I have my parishioners to think about. Mistress Dunbar has named Hamilton Lock among her tormenters. That means something supernatural is afoot. And it's my duty to do battle with it. But I daresay there's no harm in her resting herself for a wee space of time. Mistress Haltridge, maybe you'd be good enough to assist your young relative to her bedchamber."

I went forward to help: Mary Dunbar was weak, and needed one of us either side to arm her along. But as we came near the parlour threshold, she started clawing for air, thrappling and choking. I hammered on her back, and still she wheezed, the tears streaming. Finally we sat her back down, and she caught her breath, managing to spit out that she could not pass through the door. The witches forbade it. Why, she could not tell. Out of spite, like as not.

"When I try to get by, I feel a thumb pressed here, pushing the life out of me."

"That's your windpipe," said Mister Sinclair. "Your air supply is being tampered with." He raised his eyebrows at Frazer Bell, as much as to ask how he could doubt this was anything but witchcraft. "Friends, let us pass the time while we wait with another prayer."

"No better way to spend an hour," said Hugh Donaldson.

"On the other hand, it might be no harm to take up the threshold. There could be a witch's charm under it."

Waiting goes hard on menfolk, who always like to be doing things. Even the minister brightened. Off went a couple of them to an outhouse to hoak round for some tools. The greyhounds were upset by them walking about the yard, making free with the place, and barked up a storm. But the men aimed a few kicks at the animals, fetched in what was needed, and set to work. After heaving and wrestling, with the minister giving orders and the other three men ignoring them (because he knowed nothing of hard work, though they'd never tell him so to his face) up came the threshold. And with it a smell of rotten eggs that would make your stomach heave. But there was no witch's charm.

"It's brimstone we're smelling," said Donaldson.

"Hell reeks like this," said the minister. "Only a thousand times worse."

I must have made a sound, because he fastened his eyes on me.

"Oh aye, not just brimstone," he went on, "but the stench of singeing flesh fills the air in the Devil's lair. The pain is excruciating, because miscreants know there can never, ever be any release from their torments."

The thought of eternal damnation left me feeling queasy, so it did. Messy though it was, I had to hop out over the ripped-up threshold, to have a sup of water from the pump in the yard. I'd heard similar talk before. But the smell of brimstone in the parlour brought home the consequences of sin – and the fate in store for sinners – in a way no finger-pointing in a meeting-house could match.

As I was collecting myself, Jamesey and Sarah came striddling back from the Widow Patterson's. I brought them into the parlour to their mama, where they grew big-eyed at the mess round the doorway.

"It must be nearly bedtime," said the mistress.

"Mama, we haven't had our supper yet," protested Jamesey.

She sighed, and sent him and his sister to Peggy in the kitchen, with instructions to eat there. Frazer Bell went down, too, for a time – and from what I saw, running in and out, he managed to tease them out of their fears.

Still, the rattle of Joseph Esler's cart in the yard perked everybody up, as a relief from the waiting. In came the elders with a scrawny, dark woman, well past middle years, mucky as a ploughed field after a week of downpours. Her greasy grey-brown hair was hanging loose, under a cap. After one panicky look at the assembled company, she dropped her eyes to the floor and folded her hands in under her armpits.

Mister Sinclair spoke slowly, in a loud voice. "Look up, woman. Let us see your face." She did as she was bid, but her hair covered her cheeks. "Move your hair out of the way. It should be pinned up, not left to flap, inveigling men into sinful thoughts."

Reluctantly, she pushed her hair aside with her left hand. A gasp went up from the onlookers. She was exactly as Mary Dunbar had said: one side of her face was melted by the fire from forehead to neck.

Mister Sinclair turned towards the young lady, who was shrinking back into her seat. "Is this one of your oppressors?"

"Yes, she's a witch. One of the women who meet in the cave. Keep her away from me. Hold her back, I implore you!"

"What have you to say for yourself, woman?"

The accused peered at him, confused. "Please, your honour, I dinna ken why I be here. The gentlemen on'y said you wanted for to see me."

"It's this young lady wants to see you. And she has seen all she needs. You have been found out, you devil's handmaiden. You have been dabbling in witchcraft, which is an outrage against God and makes spittle of the dew of His Grace." He nodded at the elders standing either side of her. "The kirk has exposed her wickedness. She must be punished."

The woman stretched out her hands towards Mister Sinclair, clawing at the air in front of his chest. "I ken nothin' of witchcraft, your honour. As true as God I dinna. Becky Carson is me name. I come from a decent family. We was never in no trouble."

The minister narrowed his eyes. "Enough of these false protests. You must confess your misdeeds publicly or divine punishment will be fearful. 'Tis your only hope."

"Your honour, I says me prayers mornin' and night. I bain't a witch. God knows I bain't."

"Mary Dunbar has denounced you for your abomination. Now it's up to the civil authorities to deal with you. You'll be handed over to the Constable."

She fell to her knees at this. "Dinna turn me over to the Constable, I beg you. He'll put me in gaol and I'll never set foot in me own wee cottage again. Please, your honour, I done nothin' wrong."

It was a pitiful sight.

Bob Holmes cleared his throat. "She's on'y a poor aul' woman."

"Slothfulness begets poverty," said the minister.

"So does old age, an' bein' left on your own."

"She was the cruellest of them all," whimpered Mary Dunbar. "She has a dirk – she sharpens the blade every day. She stuck it in my leg up to the hilt, and laughed at my screams. Don't let her hurt me again. She looks like butter wouldn't melt in her mouth. But she's vicious."

"Go through her pockets," said Mister Sinclair.

Randall Leaths dived into a pocket in her skirts, and held up a penknife with a bone handle. Most folk had one for cutting their meat.

The minister took it from him. "Is this the weapon?"

Mary Dunbar quaked. "It is. I could never forget it."

"I've heard enough. We have a monster in our midst. She should be locked up," said Mister Sinclair.

"Do you not want to pray over her first, in the hopes of reclaiming her soul from the Devil?" asked Frazer Bell.

"Public prayers are needed, to guard against the spread of this baleful visitation. As for this creature – witches are Beelzebub's messengers, and must be shown no mercy."

"Does Christ Jesus not preach mercy?" said Frazer.

"Witchcraft is the last desperate assault on mankind by the Lord of Villainy – it has been foretold. We must fight back, using every weapon at our disposal. Do not let pity blind you to its iniquities. '*Regard not them that have familiar spirits, neither seek after wizards, to be defiled by them.*' Leviticus 19:31. I'll visit this besom in gaol, and give her an opportunity to throw herself on God's mercy. But first, she must confess her wrongs. Otherwise her sins will lead her to the scorching flames placed in hell by divine justice. Do you hear that, witch? Hellfire is waiting for you – an eternity of agony."

"You are quick to condemn her, Mister Sinclair." Frazer Bell locked eyes with the minister. "She denies the accusation. Where is your proof?"

Silence fell. Doubt showed on some of the elders' faces, until Mary Dunbar spoke up in a timid voice. "I saw her make water on the Bible, while her sisters in Satan hooted and cheered."

The minister's head whipped round. "When did you see her do this?"

"Last night. I had another vision of their witches' Sabbath, in their cave beneath the Gobbins. They defiled the Good Book to show their contempt for its teachings."

Her words caused alarm among the company.

"We did'n search Lock's Cave till this morning," said Joseph Esler. "We must a just missed them vixens."

"At least there's men watchin' it now," said Randall Leaths. "If they come back they'll be caught red-handed."

"You see what you're shielding, Bell?" said the minister. "Witches committing acts of desecration. The Lord sends these imps among us to punish our negligence, and to remind us of the true way we must live: in humility, industry and faith. Do you deny that?"

"I'd never deny the need for humility, industry and faith."

"I'm heartily glad to hear it. But have a care whose part you take. Some might judge you for it. Beware the swelling of false pride, which makes you imagine you can rescue the damned from the Devil's clutches. Leaths and Esler, remove this contemptible creature from my sight. She shall not sully a God-fearing household one minute longer."

"Where should we bring her?"

"Directly to the Constable. He has the authority to hold her until the Mayor swears out a warrant for her arrest. After you hand her over, you must go to Carrickfergus to the Mayor, and lay the complaint before him. She will have to face charges of disturbing the peace by witchcraft. Tell him I said she was too dangerous to be left at large. Gaol is the place for this despicable sinner. Inform the Constable that I will write out a full account of her transgressions this night for Mayor Davies, and send it directly to him by my man, Thomas Kane."

At that, Becky Carson fell to yammering about not having a soul in the world to speak for her, although Frazer Bell had gone to considerable trouble to stand up to the minister on her account, and Bob Holmes had defended her, forbye. It was risky for Frazer Bell to press Mister Sinclair so closely, but he was a gentleman always inclined to champion the underdog.

All at once, Becky Carson tried to throw herself at Mary Dunbar's feet – to plead with her, I daresay. But the men thought she was making a run for it, and caught and held her, none too gently, because her cap was knocked off her head. Leaths tied her hands behind her back with some rope from his pocket, before helping Esler to drag her outside to his cart. I picked up Becky Carson's cap, bogging though it was, and ran after them to put it on her head myself. She thanked me as if I had given her a fistful of guineas.

Back indoors, Mister Sinclair was full of business. "How many guards are posted at Lock's Cave?"

"Four men," said Hugh Donaldson.

"We must double the numbers. I'll put out a call for volunteers. Another night of devilry on Islandmagee cannot be tolerated."

"Mister Sinclair, if they cannot meet at Lock's Cave, is their power at an end? Or can they cast their spells elsewhere?"

The minister wiped his forehead with a grubby handkerchief, and mopped under his wig. He seemed at a loss for an answer.

Mary Dunbar stood up. "I believe I might be able to pass through the door now."

She arched an eyebrow at Frazer Bell, expectant – shades of her unwitched old self – and he offered his arm. She cut a dainty figure alongside his broad-shouldered frame. At the door, she lifted her skirts above the ankle with her free hand, tilted her chin, and stepped across the shambles of the ripped-up threshold.

"Praise be to God," said everyone, relief raising our voices high.

All except Frazer Bell. He said nothing. He looked sorry when she let go of him, mind you me.

As soon as Mary Dunbar left the room, the mistress remembered the children.

"High time they were in bed. Peggy should have thought to send them," she tutted. "Tell the pair of them I'll be in to hear their prayers in five minutes. Unless you'd prefer to hear them, Mister Sinclair?"

He agreed that he would, and I felt sorry for the poor wee mites, who'd be landed with some sermonizing on top of their prayers.

Now the mistress recalled her obligations as a hostess and offered the party a bite to eat. Meal times were at sixes and sevens with all the to-ing and fro-ing, and stomachs could be heard rumbling. Without waiting for her say-so, I carried in extra candles to cheer the place up, and set about blowing life into the collapsed remains of the turf blocks. I fancy the minister was pleased with himself for laying the problem to rest: I could hear his voice booming downstairs, from the nursery, as I went between kitchen and dining room. Peggy was told to sit with Mary Dunbar, so I had it all to do myself.

I was lifting down the big tray when Fanny Orr came in the back door. She fairly gave me a start, creeping in like that. I couldn't understand why she didn't go to the front, since it was the mistress she'd be wanting. We saw little of Fanny, with her brood of bairns to look about. Ruth Graham used to deliver her messages, but she was without a maid since refusing to have Ruth back in the house. Sammy was being slow about a replacement, to spite her.

"Is your mistress at home?"

"She is, Mistress Orr. Mister Sinclair and some of the elders are here. I'll bring you up to the parlour."

"No, I'll wait here. You run on up and tell her I'd like a word in her ear. But keep it quiet."

It was plain she didn't want to go next nor near the holy fellows. I suppose she'd had her fill of them, after Sammy was caught with Ruth. Even when they take your side, they can be hard to stomach.

I put some beakers of milk and a decanter of burgundy wine on the tray and carried them up. I knowed the kirk fellows wouldn't be wanting spirits, leastways not with Sober Sides hard-by. But the mistress might be glad of a glass of wine-and-water, and Frazer Bell certainly deserved something after his set-to with Mister Sinclair. Forbye that, if no wine was poured, how could I drink the dregs?

The minister was back downstairs, after putting the fear of God in the childer, and trying to do likewise with Frazer Bell over his wine-drinking. This gave me a chance to whisper to the mistress. Off she went to investigate. When I followed her a wheen of minutes later, the kitchen was empty. Fanny Orr was gone. In and out like a jack-in-the-box. No sign of the mistress either. I bit my lip, curious about what private business Fanny Orr had with Mistress Haltridge. Aye, well, time would tell – these things usually came out in the wash.

I popped a couple of apples in my apron pocket, to bring up to Jamesey and Sarah. After the minister's tender mercies, they might be glad of a bedtime treat. The mistress passed me on the stairs, as she came from the nursery.

"Surely you're not retiring for the night, Ellen? We have guests."

"No, mistress, I just wanted to find Peggy."

"Peggy's sitting with my cousin. Follow me, our guests need attending to."

I passed round pewter plates of food. Frazer Bell had no appetite to speak of, but he took another bumper of burgundy right willingly. Mister Sinclair made a hearty meal of the pigeon pie, while the two elders left behind, Donaldson and Holmes, got tore in to the haggery duff as if they hadn't clapped eyes on food since New Year's Day. They were the sort you'd rather keep for a week than a fortnight. I smiled to see them eye the wine, but make do with milk on account of the minister.

The mistress was talking to Hugh Donaldson about the news from Dublin in the master's last letter. "The oaf who carried it stored it so badly it was sopping wet, and I was hard-pressed to read it. He can't have kept it in a pouch. The ink had run all over the pages. Still, I was able to make out the most of it. I'm hopeful another week or so will bring my husband's business to a finish, and he can come home to us."

"I take it you've written to him about what's been happening in Knowehead in his absence?" asked Bob Holmes.

"Not yet. I'm trying to spare him worry. And, thanks to you gentlemen, all the unpleasantness has been taken care of, now."

"Best keep him informed, all the same, Mistress Haltridge."

Teeth gritted, she answered, "Yes, I must. Thank you for the reminder, Mister Holmes."

Bob Holmes was right – my master did need to know. I hoped she would act on his advice. The mistress was mistaken in thinking we could manage. And over-hopeful in thinking we were out of the woods, maybes.

"Dublin's not the far side of the world. Imagine if James Haltridge's affairs took him over and back to the New World, you would'n clap eyes on him for months on end," said Hugh Donaldson. "A cousin of mine trades with the colonials in New England, and he's never done puttin' to sea."

The mistress shuddered. Whatever her faults, I'll not deny she loved my master.

"A member of the congregation in my old parish, across the water, left a most devout legacy," said the minister. "He paid for the Bible to be read aloud to the savages of Massachusetts."

"Why Massachusetts? Were there no savages closer to home?" asked Frazer Bell.

"Your levity is excusable after the warfare waged this day, Mister Bell. Though I have observed your attendance at the meeting-house can be slack. The road to hell is paved with backsliders."

Frazer's eyes flashed. "I honour the Lord's Day as God's holy time."

"Tell us about this Bible-reading in the colonies," the mistress put in.

The minister was slow to answer, horns locked with Frazer Bell. But when she repeated herself, he turned to her. "The good wife who made the bequest greatly admired the writing of a certain Mistress Mary Rowlandson, a colonial woman who was wife to a minister."

"I've never heard tell of her," said Mistress Haltridge, gabbling in her anxiety to keep the peace. "Is it fitting for a woman to put pen to paper? Other than letters, I mean?"

"Not as a rule, but in this instance it was justified. She died recently, and I trust she has gone to her eternal reward. Her story has all the hallmarks of a parable, full of faith and forbearance. A true Christian, and not one in name only." He let his glance rest on Frazer Bell.

"You were telling us her story, Mister Sinclair?" said Hugh Donaldson.

"Indeed. Mistress Rowlandson lived in a frontier village in Massachusetts, and was kidnapped by savages during a raid, along with several of her children. She underwent an abominable ordeal at the hands of those painted heathens, but her faith in God helped her survive it. Eventually, she managed to escape. Or was she ransomed? Come to think of it, I believe the ladies of Boston raised a public subscription for her."

"How shocking – a white woman, dragged into the wilderness by whooping savages." The mistress fanned herself with her hands. "What happened to the children?"

"We must presume they turned savage, if they survived. But the Lord never sends us heavier burdens than we can carry. Mistress Rowlandson's unswerving faith enabled her to survive that trial. She accepted her suffering in a spirit of humility, and saw her Redeemer's hand in her release. Just as we must see His hand in this affliction which has befallen your household. Now, happily, lifted."

"My cousin says those Red Indians are instruments in the hands of Satan," said Donaldson. "He says the land is fertile but the savages cannae be trusted – even them so-called praying Indians who repent their pagan ways. It would put you in mind of some of the Irish."

"Satan has many instruments, as we witnessed here today. He is an old adversary of mankind's, and a beaten one. He was cast down into hell and furnished with chains of darkness. In his envy of man, for fully six thousand years he has tried to ambush us. If they could, he and his fiends would overthrow heaven itself." He shovelled a forkful of food into his mouth and kept talking. "God is mightier than a fallen angel, however. Any who keep His commandments have nothing to fear. So long as we trust to –"

Feet pounded on the stairs. Peggy, who could barely struggle between the kettle and the deal table, was fairly flying. "The lass is still witched. She says the other witches are vexed with her over Becky Carson. They're takin' their revenge: forcing her to dance, if you dinna mind. On'y I never seen dancin' like it. And Lord help me, I'd rather not see it again. Whatever it be, it bain't Christian."

Chapter 7

Frazer Bell bolted for the stairs, me following close behind. Such a sight to behold in a house that used to be home to a minister of the Lord's! Mary was dancing in her shift, with her cap off and her hair hanging loose – golden-fair curls streaming down to her waist. Even amid the commotion, I couldn't help but notice them, and wish the Lord had been a bit more generous to me. My hair was straight as a plank, and putting rags in it made hardly a haet of difference.

The minister, the elders and Mistress Haltridge crowded into her bedchamber after us. Over by the casement, Mary swayed, barefoot, to music only she could hear. She rolled her head on its long neck, paying not a whit of attention to us. A sighing sound came from all sides: the men's breath, quickened from watching her. A breeze from the open window lifted a strand of her hair, draping it over her eyes, and she pushed it aside. As she did, she noticed Frazer Bell. A change crossed her face. She put her hands on her waist and swivelled her hips, and a strap of her petticoat fell down, exposing the curve of a shoulder. Closer she rippled towards him, closer again, until cloth rubbed against cloth. Round in a circle she jiggled, hands high in the air now, and the pink tip of her tongue flicked across her lips.

A thought came to me then. Was it possible Mary Dunbar was the witch, and not the witched?

The men's eyes were bulging. Salome must have performed such a dance to earn John the Baptist's head. Even Mister Sinclair could not tear his gaze away – and I saw he was a man like any other.

It was Frazer Bell who broke the spell at last. "She's feverish. She doesn't know what she's doing. See to her, Mistress Isabel. Cover her up."

"Come to bed, Mary," coaxed the mistress. She put her hand on her cousin's arm, and whatever music the young lady was hearing came to a sudden halt.

Startled, she took in all the staring faces. "Why is everyone staring at me?"

Nobody spoke. A tree branch cracked against the casement, making us all jump.

"Sweet Jesus!" exclaimed the mistress.

"It's only a tree," said Bob Holmes, opening the window to show everybody.

Mary shook back her hair. "There's a wind tonight, you can hear it sing through the house. I like to feel the wind on my face." She turned to the casement and leaned out into the night air, closing her eyes and tilting her face to the darkness.

The barn owl that lived in the tree outside let rip with a bone-chilling screech, flapped his wings and flew straight towards the open window. Or rather, straight towards Mary Dunbar's face at it. His call had barely died away before he was pecking at her in a furious attack. Mary screamed, brushing at him with her arms, but still his hooked beak bobbed in and out. Frazer Bell snatched up Mary's wooden hairbrush and rushed forward. Feathers flew, the bird continuing to peck, dark eyes blazing, even as he was beaten, until Frazer caught him a thump on the head which drove him back. By now, Mary was in a craze, face and arms streaming blood. Frazer dropped the hairbrush and caught her in his arms, carrying her to the bed.

"Somebody shut that damned window!" he called, and Holmes fastened it up.

Mister Sinclair blethered about how the serpent could take many shapes, and we all needed to kneel and pray again.

"What we need is to assess the damage to this young lady's face," snapped Frazer.

I ran to the kitchen to fetch hot water and a rag, hoping her eyes hadn't been injured. What had come over the owl? He was like part of the family. My master was always commending him as a better mouser than any cat, and said he kept the bats down. I used to leave out bits of meat for him.

When I returned, the mistress had managed to soothe Mary Dunbar, but the blood was already drying on her face and her hair was sticking to it.

"You'd best send out for some special salve, mistress. Nothin' of mine can treat scars," said Peggy McGregor.

She spoke quietly, but the young lady overheard the words and let out a bleat. "Is my face ruined?"

"A woman's fortune is her virtue, not her face," said the minister.

"For the love of God, let it rest," Frazer Bell fairly snarled at him.

"Hush, Mistress Mary, hush," I said. "There bain't a mark on you. You're as bonny as the day you come among us."

I was no physician – I couldn't tell how well the tears in her skin would heal. But she caught me by the hand, spilling water over the counterpane.

"Do you promise?"

"Aye, mistress. I promise you'll be as good as new in a day or two."

"I'm taking a musket to that owl." Hugh Donaldson clattered downstairs. But he was back almost at once, reporting that the bird was lying at the foot of the tree, stone-dead. "You must have hit him a mighty crack with the hairbrush, Bell," he said.

135

"I had no choice."

"Aye, you did rightly."

Bob Holmes scratched his head. "It's not like an owl to go on the attack for no reason."

I took away the dirty water, jerking my head at Peggy to follow me. "Have you none of that oil you make from the leaves of white lilies?"

"Thon's for scalds."

"Would it not start the healin' on her face? Just till we look about somethin' better?"

"If it doesnae help her it willnae harm her. I'll see about some. She needs to rest, mind you. 'Tis the best cure of all."

"How can she do that with half of Islandmagee in her bedchamber, Peggy?"

"Aye, but she cannae be left on her lone."

When I returned, Mary Dunbar had her eyes closed. She was a gory sight, poor lady, with all the bloody marks on her face. I should have liked to pull the curtains round her bed, to give her some privacy, but I daresay it was better for her own sake to stay in plain sight.

Robert Sinclair and the mistress were in a huddle, and whatever she was saying left the minister dumbfounded. The mistress could tell he wasn't best pleased, and whispered some more, trying to persuade him round to her way of thinking. She might just as well have tried to move the Gobbins.

"I forbid it," he said then loudly. "As your minister I absolutely, categorically forbid it. Prayer is what's needed here. Not charms. I want to hear no more about it. It's the sort of folly that leads folk to forsake the Creator of Life and follow the Author of Destruction. Now, Donaldson and Holmes, come you with me. I need to consult with you."

The three of them left the room, and as soon as they were gone the mistress darted forward. She leaned over Mary Dunbar and wound a long piece of tape three times round her neck, dropping the ends inside her shift, out of sight.

"What are you doing, Mistress Isabel?" asked Frazer Bell.

"Hush, don't give me away. A well-wisher paid me a visit. She tells me this has never been known to fail."

The minister and elders came back and tried to get some praying under way, but it put the young lady in a lather.

"I've seen saner wretches in the lunatic asylum," Hugh Donaldson whispered to Frazer, whose forehead creased at the words. Donaldson seemed to relish the scene. Easy for him, with a quiet household to go home to – doubtless, he was thinking how his family would hang on his every word, with such a tale to relate.

When she recovered her wits, the young lady complained of a pain in her side. The mistress moved her shimmy to investigate. The tape she had put round her cousin's neck was tied at the waist now, knotted nine times. Eight double knots and a single one. Where each knot pressed against her, a blister was raised on Mary Dunbar's skin.

"What have I done to you, Mary?"

Mister Sinclair pushed in for a look, and his face flared purple. "I forbade you to use this charm. '*None can serve two masters.*' Matthew 6:24. Magic arts can heal no infirmity – this is merely the snare used by Baal to entangle mankind."

"I meant no harm." The mistress wrung her hands together.

"Charms and amulets are idle trifles without the power to heal. They have their origin in Satan." Spittle landed on her sleeve. "Where did you come by this Romish superstition?"

"It's just something I heard about."

"Someone must have told you about it, mistress. I insist on you identifying the wolf in sheep's clothing leading you astray."

"I can't remember. Just that it was a counter-charm – a papish priest passed it on."

"Show me this atrocious object."

The mistress unknotted the tape. "These are some words

from the first chapter of St John's Gospel on it. It dissolves away witchcraft."

"I order this piece of deception burnt. As I told you before, your young relative will be healed by the twin powers of faith and prayer."

"Prayers are no help to her, Mister Sinclair. She writhes in agony when she hears them."

"It is not Mistress Dunbar in torment, but the demons inside her. Any kind of magic, even self-styled white magic, is sinful. You cannot go to the Devil for help against the Devil. 'Tis a grievous mistake. Your defiance disappoints me. This tape is going straight in the fire. By rights, I should make you do it, Mistress Haltridge, but I can see you're not to be trusted. Don't think you've heard the last of this, mistress."

A wail from Mary Dunbar saved the mistress from shaping an answer.

"They're coming at me, seven of them, all at once! They say I'm for it now, after landing Becky Carson in gaol. Can you see them? They're flying past the casement, riding on the back of a big grey goose apiece. They're on their way in to me."

"Mary, the casement is shut tight. No one can get in," said Mistress Haltridge.

"They can creep through a mousehole, they can slide in by a crack. Shutters can't keep them out. Any minute now and they'll be on top of me." She tore at her injured face with her nails, breaking the skin again, and I reached for her hands to try and stop her, but was batted away.

Hugh Donaldson and Frazer Bell managed to take a hand each and hold it out from her body, whiles she twisted and gnawed at her lips.

"I thought the problem was solved by having that Carson woman gaoled," said Mister Sinclair, "but I see I was over-hopeful. A malevolent force has put down roots on Islandmagee. Hacking at them is insufficient – we must dig them up." He had a hoak round under his wig, scratching at his scalp. "This is proof of a witches' coven on the island. Such power over another soul can only be the result of a foul brood conspiring together – group witchcraft."

"But I thought Lock's Cave was being watched," said Hugh Donaldson. "How are the witches able to meet?"

"They must have a second lair. We'll have to mount a search for it. The Constable must send some deputies to help us. But whether there's one witch or an army of them, I'm ready to buckle on the Breastplate of Righteousness in the Lord's cause. I'll start by disposing of this trumpery."

He held out the tape, his face like thunder, and it made me think of how he was with Ruth Graham. Merciless. Heaping the lion's share of the blame on her. I couldn't see him going to Ruth's da and telling him to stop taking lumps out of her, either. He'd probably reach him a bigger stick. And Fanny Orr was putting all the guilt on Ruth as well, when she knowed what a goat her Sammy was. Something got into me then.

When Mister Sinclair went downstairs to burn the Romish tape, I made an excuse about needing to dry off his coat that got vomit on it earlier, and chased after him.

"I know who gi'e the mistress thon charm."

"Well? Speak up. 'Tis your Christian duty."

"It was Mistress Orr, sir."

"Was it indeed? After all I've done for her. I'll be having words with Mistress Orr the next time I see her. I'm not one bit pleased to see she has not shaken off her old influences."

Fanny Orr used to be a papist, afore Sammy Orr put his eye on her. She turned for the marriage, and for the sake of his few acres. Dirt poor, her people were. The mistress showed signs of being interested in the old religion as well.

When the minister returned, Mistress Haltridge was eager to make amends. "Mister Sinclair, my cousin tells us the Carson creature has no more power over her since the elders took her to the Constable. We should see about bringing her other persecutors to justice."

"Aye," said Donaldson. "A witch left at large can molest as she chooses. But it's a known fact a witch in captivity can do no harm."

"The perpetrators should certainly be taken into custody," said the minister. "Mistress Dunbar, do you recognize the women afflicting you?"

She quivered. "I could pick out each and every one of them in a fair-day crowd."

"Will you help us find them? Can you name them?"

"They threatened to kill me if I revealed their names."

"You must be brave. You have a Christian obligation to point out these witches. Can you describe them, at least?"

"I'll try." She counted on her fingers. "Their ringleader goes by the name of Mistress Anne."

"Imagine such a vile creature sharin' a name with our queen," said Donaldson.

"What does she look like? Where does she live?" asked the minister.

Near-hand, I could feel Peggy moving uneasily. Bad enough to hear the old mistress's name bandied about. But what if her face was put to the name? The family would never recover from the shame.

"Mistress Anne prevents me from giving her away," said Mary. "She doesn't take kindly to your intervention, Mister Sinclair. She threatens to have your likeness made, and roast it like a lark, and says you'll roast likewise. She boasts she can never be caught, no matter how hard we chase her, because she'll turn herself into a hare and run away."

The minister held his Bible close. "This Mistress Anne cannot elude God's justice."

Bob Holmes cleared his throat. "Is it not strange these so-called witches should allow the lassie the liberty of her tongue to denounce them?"

Mary Dunbar shrank away, but the minister flashed into

140

anger. "Do you question this young person's suffering? You saw for yourself how she's afflicted."

"Aye, I saw plenty. But do we drag every goodwife on Islandmagee before a cuddy just now landed in among us, on her say-so alone?"

"Godly women have nothing to fear by coming here."

"Still and all, the lassie may be mistaken."

"Mistress Dunbar is a stranger to this parish. How could she supply us with names unless she heard them used during one of their profane meetings?"

"Not wantin' to cast any doubt on her, but there's more than one way to skin a cat. And more than one way to latch onto a name. It's not fittin' for dacent folk to be tainted with such things. '*Do not plot harm against your neighbour, who lives trustfully near you. Do not accuse a man for no reason, when he has done you no harm.*' Proverbs 3:29."

The minister arranged and rearranged his wig as Holmes went on.

"Forbye, Mister Sinclair, why are you so quick to hand over these women to the civil authorities? Becky Carson's in Carrickfergus already, and she might rot there afore anythin' comes of it. Mister Bell riz the same point, but got short shrift from you. However, I've been studyin' on it, and to my mind he talked sense. Surely, as a man of God, you'd want to wrangle with sinners yourself and rescue them from the Devil's clutches? If he's usin' them, they deserve help as much as any strayin' childer of God. We must instruct them on the path to salvation, and regain them for the Lord. But we cannae do it so handy if we shove them in a dungeon."

Bob Holmes was a man with a wee bush of a beard – odd as two left feet, some said, because he would never eat flesh, though he loved his pipe. But he was held to be a sound judge of cattle, and people oftentimes went to him for advice when they were buying stock. His words swayed the minister.

"I need to seek guidance from some brother clergymen in

this matter," said Mister Sinclair.

Mary Dunbar's eyes rolled back in her head, showing only the whites. "They're here now!" she screeched. "They've brought a wild dog with them. Sweet Jesus, it looks like a wolf."

"I thought all the wolves were hunted out of Ireland," said Hugh Donaldson, from behind his hand. "There has'n been a pelt presented for the trophy fee this past lock of years."

"It's slabbering over me, I can feel its fangs on my flesh. Oh God, oh God, it means to make a meal of me!"

It was too much for the mistress, who ran from the chamber. Frazer Bell nudged me to go after her. Peggy came too, mumbling about something that couldn't be put off any longer, and squeezed past me, making for the stairs. I knocked on the mistress's bedchamber and was sent packing. I hadn't gone half a dozen paces when she opened the door and beckoned me back.

"It was unChristian to snap at you the way I did," she said. "You're a good girl, Ellen Hill. My nerves are in shreds from this. Bank down the fires to keep them going overnight, and see to it there are plenty of candles in all the rooms. No need to go back into my cousin's bedchamber." She patted my arm. Maybes she thought she was saving me from a spectacle she had no taste for herself. "I'll join the minister and elders as soon as I bathe my temples. It's not seemly to leave her there with only men."

I went along the passageway, pausing for a listen outside Mary Dunbar's door. In case I was needed – not to eavesdrop. The wild dog, or the wolf, or whatever she thought was attacking her, seemed to have gone. Smoke drifted out from under the door, and I guessed it was Bob Holmes sucking on his pipe.

The minister must have been smarting over Holmes' challenge. "Time can be better employed than by messing about with a stinking tobacco pipe," he said. "I used tobacco in my youth, and was bewitched by it. But I left it off because I saw it was another snare of Lucifer's to persuade men to waste time."

"Each to their own. Everybody has their own way of puttin' in time," said Bob Holmes.

The mistress's door opened, and I hurried down to the kitchen, to find Peggy standing on a chair, hanging a flint stone with a hole in it from a nail above the back lintel. She was none too secure, but I knowed better than to offer to trade places. Instead, I took hold of the chair back to steady her. The stone was one you'd find down by the lough shore, or maybes over by Brown's Bay. They were called elf stones – folk used them to keep witches away.

"The bairns should be sent to their grandparents in Belfast, Peggy. This house is no place for them. I'm worried about them, so I am."

She footered with the stone, making sure it would hold. "The mistress would never part with them."

"She needs to be tould."

"What are you lookin' at me for?"

"She'll listen to you afore she listens to me."

"She'll heed ne'ther one of us. If them chicks was'n sent away when their granny was ill, they'll not be sent away now."

"Their da was mos'ly here to watch over them when their granny lay dyin', but he's a long way from home this time. The bairns need to be taken somewhere they'll be safe."

"It's a mortal pity the master has to be away. He has a way of keepin' a cork in things."

"He could'n keep a cork in this, Peggy. It was bad enough when the aul' mistress lay dyin'. But it's different this time. It's stronger. And it's happenin' quicker. It's like a horse without a rider. There's no tellin' which way it'll go."

She came down off the chair, ignoring my outstretched hand. "You're a fly one, so you are. I see you suggestin' things

143

to the mistress. Makin' her lean on you. Mind you dinna bite off more'n you can chew."

I was taken aback. Me and Peggy, we always rubbed along well together. I tried to ease her workload in the house, out of respect for her years, though I never expected anything by way of thanks. But I thought she was grateful, in her own way. Why was she suddenly turning on me? I stuck my hands into my apron pocket, rooting for a fancy hairpin of my ma's I kept there. Whenever I felt far from home and on unsure ground, it comforted me. I could understand it if Peggy was jealous of the favour my master showed me, but her jibe about making up to his lady was a puzzle.

After all our years yoked together, I was saddened to see her take against me. But careless words at such a touchy time could be dangerous – I needed to remind her we were all at risk here, and had to stand together.

"Peggy, I wud'n be surprised if it was you filled Mary Dunbar's head with yarns about Hamilton Lock. You're the one fanned the flames."

Her guilty face gave her away. "The young lady pestered me about him."

"What did you say?"

"Just about his name bein' used as a bogeyman, to put manners on the wee'ans. I never went into the whys and wherefores. I should a knowed better. Dinna tell on me, lass. I'm a foolish aul' woman."

"So you didn't tell Mary Dunbar everythin', Peggy?"

"I tould her enough. She's a lassie can set you talking. I hope I bain't the cause of trouble."

"Aye, well, we'll see about that. I'm waitin' to hear what you said."

"Nothin' about witches gatherin' at Lock's Cave. I on'y said it was a spot dacent folk avoided. I never mentioned the skull."

"What about the skull?"

"You don't know? You're Islandmagee born and bred, I'd a thought you'd a heard." She felt her way over to the fireside, and put her back to me. "Maybe it was hushed up deliberate. I daresay folk were ashamed at what they felt had to be done to him. But you have to know how Hamilton Lock died, surely?"

"Aye. My da says the men of this parish went after him one night. Staked him to the ground, arms and legs outstretched. Drove a horse and cart over him, again and again, till every bone was broken and he had'n a breath left in his body."

"Did he say what was done to his remains?"

"Buried at Lock's Cave."

"After he died, Hamilton Lock's corpse was cut into pieces an' spread out, so he would'n be whole come Judgment Day and could'n enter the Kingdom of Heaven. They made six of him, and buried each part at a different spot. On'y the head went into Lock's Cave."

My mind went back to Mary Dunbar's fit, where she described a tribe of women round a bonfire, holding a skull and chanting: *"Hamilton Lock, Hamilton Lock! We summon you up, Hamilton Lock!"* I shivered.

Peggy's voice was cracked when she spoke again. "I've been studying on it, Ellen Hill. Ever since the aul' mistress was taken ill over the winter, things have been goin' from bad to worse in this house. Mistress Haltridge saw things. Things nobody else saw. But what if they were real enough? And what if Mary Dunbar is seein' the same things?"

"Do you mean the same things – or the same ghost?"

"Aye, you folly me rightly. Hamilton Lock's who I mean. It has to be him behind this. How his ghost made its way into Knowehead House, I could'n say. If prayers and bible-readin' could keep evil out, he never should a got in. But mark my words – he's under this roof, and any misfortune that happens here comes from him."

A chill ran from my neck to my heels, and I joined her

145

beside the fire, holding my hands out to it.

"And here's somethin' else to think on. Hamilton Lock has reason to hate the Haltridges."

The bell rang for service, interrupting her tale.

"Why, Peggy? Quick, tell me."

"No, on second thoughts, best say no more."

"Peggy! You would'n leave me high and dry, surely?"

But she laid her knobbly finger against her shruken mouth, and there was no budging her.

⧫ ⧫ ⧫

The minister's coat wasn't right dry, but he wanted it brought up to him so he could go home and work on his report for the Mayor, who was also the Magistrate. This would put the warrant for Becky Carson's arrest on a proper footing. He was also keen to ask for men to be sent out, to help lead searches for places where the witches might meet. He believed if they could be kept from gathering, their powers would be watered down. Hugh Donaldson and Bob Holmes looked as if they'd just as soon head off home as well. But Mister Sinclair advised the elders to stay.

"Lucifer is a subtle tempter. We cannot leave a houseful of womenfolk at his mercy. Mister Bell, you may go home if you have affairs requiring your attention."

Frazer Bell bristled. When Sobriety's hooves could no longer be heard, he proposed keeping a vigil over Mary Dunbar. This arrangement put us in a fix, because the young lady could not be left overnight in the charge of men. A female had to be present for the sake of her reputation. So the mistress volunteered me, Peggy and herself to take it in turns – even though the only thing you could count on Peggy to keep open was her gob as she snored.

It was agreed that me, Bob Holmes and Hugh Donaldson would take the first watch. Frazer Bell would wrap himself in a blanket and get his head down for a lock of hours in front of the parlour fire. Then himself, Peggy and the mistress would relieve us.

To my surprise, Mary Dunbar was sound asleep by the time I had the house redd up and joined the men in her bedchamber. I could no more close my eyes with two strange men gazing at me than I could sail a square-rigger. But I daresay so much had happened to her since she came to the island, she could hardly tell day from night. She was fully clothed, for decency's sake, with only her stays unlaced.

Her bed curtains were closed at the sides but left open at the front, so we could see her. Everyone sat in chairs as far back from the young lady as possible, so as not to crowd her. Tell you no lie, it was hard to be at ease, with our candles throwing shapes on the wall and our ears straining. We jumped out of our skins at the slightest sound.

"I knowed an aul' hag turned herself into a bee and stung somebody on the tongue. It swelled up and turned black as pitch," whispered Donaldson.

Holmes gave him a look, as much as to say he should hold his own tongue. We were all of us jittery enough without adding grist to the mill.

Then Donaldson produced a pack of cards from his waistcoat pocket, proposing a game to pass the time.

"Mister Sinclair would have conniptions if he got wind of it," said Holmes.

"Where's the harm?" said Donaldson. "Playin' for buttons does'n count as gamblin'. We have to put in the night somehow."

I fetched my button box and we played for a time, until Donaldson mentioned the buttons heaved up by Mary Dunbar – "Supposin' they belonged to the Prince of Darkness hisself?"– after which we lost heart for handling buttons of any description.

"I heared tell of a man who used to sweat blood," said

147

Donaldson. "Out through his skin it would come, all of a sudden. He had a fallin' out with a neighbour's widow, who had the name of bein' a witch. He thumped her boy for cheekin' him, and called the lad a devil's get. She cursed him for it, so she did."

"Does he still sweat blood?" asked Holmes.

"No, he come by a charm for it. He had to stand under the moon at midnight on Hallowe'en, and turn about widdershins three times, chantin' some words he was given."

"Yarns are all very well, but I daresay Mister Sinclair would tell us silent prayer is a seemlier way to pass the hours of darkness," said Holmes.

Silent prayer made it too easy to nod off. Heads were drooping before long. I have to confess to falling asleep myself. I tried to stay awake, but it was a battle with my body the mind couldn't win. I don't know how much time passed – it might have been minutes and it might have been hours – when a scuffling disturbed me. At first I thought it was mice. One time, a mouse ran up my master's sleeve and down the other one, bold as brass. Unless you keep a cat, it's impossible to be mice-free indoors. An owl will only keep them down in the yard. Our last kitling died during the old mistress's illness and we hadn't got round to replacing her.

I heard the noise again, louder than before, and jerked awake. Mary Dunbar was tossing her head on the pillow. Her face was in shadow, but I could tell she was awake because the candlelight made two pin-pricks of light behind her eyelashes.

It struck me then to wonder what it must be like to be Mary Dunbar. Was she frightened? She said she was, oftentimes. But what if it was excitement rather than fear that made her quiver? Look at her, with all these men jumping to her bidding, staying out of their beds to protect her from something only she could see. Then I felt ashamed for failing in charity. It's not as if any of this was her fault. It could as easily be the mistress afflicted by witches, or Peggy, or wee Sarah. Or me.

Hugh Donaldson was snoring like the long-legged sow in our smallest outhouse, making the candle flames flutter. A violent gust of air crashed through his mouth, and two of the candles were blown out. That left only one flame burning. Dim though it was in the chamber, I was too weary to stand up and light them again.

All of a sudden, I squinted at Mary Dunbar, hardly able to believe my eyes. The simplest way to put it is that she left the bed. But she didn't sit up and get out the way a normal person would – she seemed to slide out and land gently on the floor, as if supported by invisible hands. The young lady didn't fall, I know that much. It was too smooth, and there was no crash. It happened as easy as one of them wild swans gliding over Larne Lough.

"In God's name, leave me be," Mary gasped, gathering herself into a ball.

"Help her, one of you!" It was Frazer Bell, ready to take his turn, and getting an eyeful. The others leaped out of their chairs, rubbing their eyes and letting on they were watchful the whole time.

Frazer and Hugh Donaldson put her back to bed, and when she was recovered she said the witches were teasing her again. "They lifted me up, meaning to throw me out the window. But I brought to mind our Lord Jesus on the cross, and asked Him to pity my suffering for the sake of His own. At that, they let go of me."

Well, Hugh Donaldson and Bob Holmes were fierce impressed by this, and Donaldson said the Lord never let anybody down in their hour of need. He insisted on leading us in a prayer of thanksgiving. But whiles I prayed, I was thinking to myself how she was nowhere near the window. And I never heard her call out to the Lord Jesus, nor nobody else for that matter, although maybes she did in her own mind.

The next morning, Peggy fried collops for the household, and I served them up. Master Jamesey and the wee missie sat rubbing their eyes, making a lip at all the extra folk at their table, because Frazer Bell was still with us, and the elders.

"That's my father's chair," the young master said to Hugh Donaldson, at the head of the table.

"I'm only keeping it warm for your daddy."

"My father doesn't need you to do that."

"Mind your manners, Jamesey," said his mother.

At that, Sarah slid off her chair and hid under the table, and there was a whole hoo-hah about getting her back out.

I took myself out to the yard to work at the pots with a heather scrubber, trying to shift some of the baked-in dirt. Frazer Bell must have bolted his food because I made no headway before he was out after me.

"Ellen, did you get a clear view of what happened with Mistress Dunbar last night?"

I dried my hands on my apron and stood up. "I think so, sir, though it was gloomy in her bedchamber. 'Twas a pity only the one candle was left burnin'."

"Tell me what you saw."

"Well, sir, one minute she was in the bed and the next she was on the floor, and how she got there I could'n rightly say."

"Could she have fallen out?"

"She could and she could'n. There was no sound till you spoke up. There'd have been noise if she fell. It was more like she floated out. Did you not see, sir?"

"I'm not sure what I saw. I didn't see her float. But I didn't see her walk, either." He ran his hand over the bristles on his chin. "It's vital that we believe her. Otherwise she'll be sent to an asylum for the mad. It's either supernatural or lunacy – no other explanation is possible. And she'd never survive an asylum. Mary would be better dead than penned up with lunatics. I was in London a few years back, and did a foolish thing. You could pay a penny to go and view the inmates in Bedlam. As long as I live, I'll never forget the spectacle. Some of them were hardly human any more. The bestial side of their natures had overtaken them."

I noticed how he forgot himself, and called the young lady Mary instead of Mistress Dunbar or even Mistress Mary. He was affected by her, and that's the long and short of it.

Peggy was sitting at the kitchen door watching the hens the whiles he was talking, or thinking, or whatever Frazer Bell was at. She must have been listening. When he went back indoors, she spat on the ground. "Mad or bad, it makes not a haet of difference. Thon wench is bringin' down trouble on our heads."

"How can the young lady be held to blame for what's happenin' to her, Peggy? She's in agony, so she is."

"She's sufferin' – I'll grant you that. But she'll be the cause of a dose of it afore she's through. If you ask me, Mary Dunbar is being used like a funnel, to deliver trouble to our doorstep. Maybe if she was'n here, then n'ether would the trouble be."

Peggy had been at Knowehead for years before I was even born. She must know things about the house. But she had a habit of keeping her tongue stubbornly in her mouth if you showed too much interest in something. Still, I thought it worth trying her – she might let something slip.

"You know the other day when you tould me about your first year or two on the island, Peggy? You were none too happy about the aul' minister buildin' Knowehead House here. On account of him movin' thon big block of a Stone that stood where he wanted his house put."

"He never should a interfered wi' it. Bigger'n than a kirk, it was. Must a weighed a good ten tons. The master was warned agin interferin' with it, so he was. Folks were agin it.

Then an Irish wise woman tould him to leave it be if he knowed what was good for him. She said it stood there since time before time was counted. An' the aul' gods – gods that belonged to these parts, the way his never would – they'd be offended if it was moved. He had her whipped out of the parish."

"The Stone was broke up, was'n it?"

"Aye, took long enough, too. Weeks they were at it. The cattle they used to pull away the Stone from the earth caught some sort of sickness. Then one apprentice lost an arm. He was crushed beneath a chunk of rock that broke off and landed on him. Another lad threw hisself in Larne Lough. 'Twas said he had nightmares and kep' wakin' up in a sweat about the job they were at. The master had to do somethin' to put heart in the men or there'd be no workers left in the finish up. So he stripped to the waist and hammered away at the job along with them, singin' hymns and tellin' Bible stories."

"An' the Stone was dragged away, and Knowehead House built in its place?"

"Knowehead House went up where the Stone used to stand, all right. But the Stone might not a been ready or willin' to be replaced." A chicken pecked near the kitchen door, and she pushed it away with the toe of her boot. "I heared Hamilton Lock was never done hangin' round thon Stone. He was drawn to it, you might say."

"Was he there when the Stone came down?"

"No, that happened when he was on his travels – up to no good elsewhere, I daresay."

"Maybes it was when he was hidin' out in Scotland? When the law was lookin' for him? So my da says."

"Aye, so it was. He was gone for years, and when he came back he was quare and put out to find the Stone gone. Had words with Minister Haltridge about it. Thon Lock was a man with no respect. He tould my master he'd live to regret it. A-coorse, what might really a niggled him was the loss of his own wee cabin, knocked, too, to make way for our barn. Minister Haltridge found Lock's da another cabin, up Balloo way, and no harm done. But Hamilton Lock did'n see it that way. Nor about the Stone goin'. Fierce taken with it, he was. God alone knows what he got up to there."

"Maybes Hamilton Lock dabbled in witchcaft or some class o' sorcery, Peggy. Maybes that's why he had a thing about the Stone."

"I'd put nothin' past him. Come to think of it, some of the stones his wee cabin was built from were used in the makin' of Knowehead House. 'Waste not, want not,' said Minister Haltridge."

That gave me a jolt. It was almost as though Lock had lived under the same roof as us – an appalling notion. 'No wonder the aul' mistress got worked into a frenzy and tore at the walls in her chamber, thon time afore she died. Was that the reason Hamilton Lock had a grudge agin the Haltridges, Peggy?"

"Ask me no questions, I'll tell thee no lies."

And I could get no more out of her.

Chapter 8

The elders jogged off after breakfast, Hugh Donaldson holding on behind Bob Holmes, and it was plain as the snout on your face they weren't one bit sorry to leave Knowehead House.

Frazer Bell saddled up Lordship and left too, promising to return. He leaned down from his stallion and took the mistress by the hand. "You will not have to deal with this on your own, Mistress Isabel. I am a poor substitute, but until James returns – and I trust that day will be soon – you can count on me."

"I plan to write to James today, Frazer. But he thinks I exaggerate everything. I'm not sure he'll believe me when I tell him what's been going on."

"Then bid him come home and see for himself."

After he rode off, the mistress turned to me as I scrubbed the doorstep. "Your master won't thank me for taking him away from the affairs of business."

I sat up on my hunkers. "You could always tell him the lie of the land, and let him make up his own mind."

"I hope to shield him for as long as I am able. He must have no distractions from business. His mother's illness took his mind off affairs for longer than was desirable."

"I'd be inclined to let him know all the same, mistress."

"You mind your place, Ellen."

She went indoors to pen her letter, but came back almost at once to say Mary Dunbar fancied a dander, and I was ordered to go with her because the mistress was too worn out to tramp the countryside.

I wasn't too pushed about it myself. Just me and Mary Dunbar? You'd never know what might happen. The mistress read my face. She was holding my master's latest letter, in the process of answering it, and waved it at me. She knowed full well I liked to hear news of him. "Your master says he's ruined from paying for coaches. Listen, I'll read you a passage. '*I am unable to walk anywhere in Dublin for the state of the roads and the dirty condition of the streets. Coach hire is crucifying me – I was eighteen pence out of pocket today because I had so many calls to make. I took on a servant called Barney Goggin, recommended to me by Richard Pue of Dick's Coffee House, who makes the best coffee in the city.*'"

Oh ho, I thought, he's passing time in coffee-houses, hearing about the world's doings. Little suspecting the doings here.

"'*This fellow Goggin is full of bluff and blarney. He started off well, but as soon as I paid him he took to the drink and I saw no more of him until every penny was spent. Then he turned up looking sheepish and smelling like a tavern. I spoke to Dick Pue about him, because I cannot have an unreliable servant. Pue said my mistake was to give him an advance, and I should pay the fellow nothing more until I am ready to leave the city. He passed some amusing remark about what happens when Barney Goggin gets grog in – he makes a rhyme out of everything, and is known for it far and wide. I suppose I should give this Goggin another chance. It is inconvenient to take on another servant at this late stage. I call into Dick's Coffee House every day, because there is no better spot to chew over the latest news. It is in the drawing room of*"

Carbery House, formerly the Earl of Kildare's home, and is close to my lodgings (they are tolerable, by the way) on Skinner Row. Lawyers, merchants and various squires, up from the country, sit round his fires discussing politics and other news. The London Gazette, the Paris Gazette, the Flying Post and other newspapers are to hand, so we have all the domestic and foreign news. Auctions of books are held at the back of Pue's premises. I have bought some already, which will be of use in the children's education.' There now, my husband is thinking of us all, though he is far from home." She folded up the letter. "I should really put the children over their ABCs but I haven't the heart for lessons today. Take them walking with you and my cousin instead. Tell them if they come back with roses in their cheeks, I'll give them a treat."

"Where are they, mistress?"

"They went out to play as soon as breakfast was finished. They race outside any chance they get."

I set off looking for Jamesey and Sarah. Usually you'd find them teasing the rooster or jumping about in the barn, but there was no sign of them. As I hunted, I turned over the idea of writing to my master myself, to tell him how things stood here at Knowehead. But sending a letter to her master is not something a maid does easily. Besides, he might complain to the mistress about being slow to tell him and, in turn, she could accuse me of getting above myself. It was hard to know what to do for the best.

The bairns were in the top field, hanging round Noah Spears at his digging and sowing. Their faces fell when I told them they were to walk out with me and Mary Dunbar.

"Do we have to?" asked the wee miss.

"Why, what would you rather do?"

Jamesey piped up, "We wanted to sail paper boats in a barrel of water. Noah said he'd help us make them as soon as he's done here."

"You must'n keep Noah back from his work."

"Ach, let them be," said Noah. "They're out of harm's way here. If you catch me drift."

"Aye, I hear what you're sayin'. All right. Jamesey, Sarah, you mind you're no trouble to Noah."

"Can we go to your cottage for stew afterwards, Noah? Like before?" asked Sarah.

"It was rabbit stew," Jamesey whispered to me, "caught in one of his traps – but we never let on to Sarah."

The mistress pulled a face when I told her the children preferred to stay with Noah Spears, and she said they missed their father. "It's male company they're after," she added, as though defying me to gainsay her.

I scooted up the ladder to the attic for my woollen shawl.

Mary Dunbar strolled on ahead, and I found her among Peggy's rhubarb rows. Juking down, touching the leaves coming up, so she was. "Best let them be," snaps I, sharper than a maid should speak to a lady. But I was on edge at being in charge of her, with nobody to send for help if she took a fit.

We went east as far as the Gobbins, though I had to take her arm because her strength failed her before we got the length. I expected the young lady to quiz me again about the pointy rocks at the foot of the cliffs, and the bodies that were ripped open on them, for her thoughts ran to the morbid. But she only looked at the fishing boats, bobbing in the distance. With Islandmagee being an island, near enough, all but the poorest family had some kind of boat – journeys made by water were always quicker than by road. Many of Islandmagee's men earned a living before the mast.

The gabbon hawks shrieked at us, for being too close to them, I daresay, and Mary Dunbar went to the cliff edge to see if they were nesting. They were held in high regard by the gentry, who used them for hunting. I had to pull her back because the ground was treacherous after weeks of heavy rain. She hummed to herself, enjoying the outdoors. I liked it there myself, despite the duty of minding her, because nothing beats fresh air for blowing away the cobwebs.

"Local lads climb down the cliffs on ropes to collect seabirds and their eggs," I told her.

"You'd want to be sure of your rope," she said.

We chatted about the different families living on Islandmagee, and I told her how they came across from Scotland in the early 1600s, defying native and nature to build homes and farms. Others followed when they saw a good life could be made here.

The young lady had a powerful curiosity about the early settlers. "Were Hamilton Lock's people planters?" she asked, and I gave a wee jump at the offhand way she throwed in his name.

"Don't go namin' him – you'd never know what power his ghost might take from folk repeatin' his name."

"His name rings in my head, Ellen. I hear it morning, noon and night." I let on not to hear her, but she went on, "I heard he liked horses better than folk."

I was surprised into letting down my guard. "They say he had a way with horses – he could gentle the wildest stallion."

"Who told you that?"

"My granda knowed him as a wee lad. Hamilton was some years ahead of him, but they were acquainted."

"Is that how he earned a living? Taming horses?"

"As far as I know he did a dose of things. Most of them bad. He was in the army for a time, but he was too unruly to take orders. He went to sea forbye, and I would'n be surprised if he was as rowdy on the high seas as he was on the land. But there's more to Islandmagee than Hamilton Lock."

"What else is there?"

"Why, there's the land, Mistress Mary. It's the land that matters. And it's generous to the folk that work it. So is the sea, come to that."

"But the islanders profit from the sea in more ways than one, don't they?"

"Oh aye?"

"Smuggling. A wee bird told me the caves at the foot of the Gobbins shelter smugglers. As well as witches, of course."

Shivering, I pulled tight the grey shawl my mother had knitted for me and, as my fingers touched it, I thought of her sitting by the fire with the needles clicking. This past while, I was tied to Knowehead, without much leave to visit the ones at home. I wondered whether Ma fretted for me, on the back of all the gossip lately.

"Time we turned back, mistress."

She put her hand on my arm. "I've been in one of those caves, you know. At night. I was carried over the cliffs on the back of a huge goose sent by Mistress Anne. She said witch magic has more force behind it in Lock's Cave. But the coven can't use the cave any more, now that it's watched. They move from place to place. This angers them, and they take it out on me. Nowhere else suits them half as well."

"Where do they meet now? You should tell the minister."

She didn't answer. Instead, she said, "Hamilton Lock met a grisly end, didn't he?"

"I could'n say."

"I'll ask Peggy. She'll tell me."

"Hamilton Lock got what was due to him. That's all you need to know. He committed one crime too many for folk to stomach. I daresay he thought he could get away with anythin', on account of gettin' away with so much in his time."

"You mean he wasn't just part of the massacre? Did he do something else?"

"Hush now. That's enough."

"I'll give you a present if you tell me everything you know about it: half a dozen jet buttons from my japanned box. You can sew them on a frock. They'll turn heads at the meeting-house."

I knowed the buttons she meant and was tempted. My

master might admire me wearing them, I thought, before shaking myself. I must not go courting my master's admiration – it was too dangerous.

"Do tell, Ellen. All right, I'll make it a dozen buttons."

Maybes the buttons swayed me. But it struck me how it was high time Mary Dunbar understood why Hamilton Lock's name was blackened beyond repair – and why it was better left unsaid. She seemed inclined to see him as a figure of interest, rather than the thoroughgoing rogue that he was. But there was something else made me decide to tell her, too. I think it was because I was on standing on the self-same spot where it happened.

"Very well. But first you must promise not to breathe a word of this to the mistress. She'll give me my marching orders if she hears I've been blabbin' about him."

She held up both wee hands, two fingers overlapping on each. "I promise."

"I had this story off my da, who had it off his. It was back in the time of the Magee massacre, when blood ran like rainwater on the island. Hamilton Lock was only twenty or thereabouts, but he was strong and well-growed, and he hacked and hewed like a man possessed. He tore the clothes off the backs of the dead to wipe away the blood drippin' from his face, and carried on with his rampage. I heared he seized a suckin' babe from a cradle and stamped on its head with his boot, crushin' it like a nut. They say he laughed at the sight of its poor wee flattened skull."

The weight of this story was more than I could bear to tell standing upright. There was a rock a few yards away, and I walked over to sit on it, Mary Dunbar following.

"Hamilton Lock hated the Irish. I daresay he had his reasons. Hate like that does'n come out of nowhere. His hate ran straight from his heart into his sword arm: it was a fever he had. He was named by a young woman called Bridget McGill who survived the killings. She was in her brother-in-law Eiver Magee's house, down Carnspindle way, when the attack came. It was one Sunday night shortly after Christmas. A crowd of soldiers tore into Eiver's house, all fired up on drink, wavin' pikes and muskets about. That was the start of it. They killed all round them, afore headin' to the next house for more of the same."

"Isn't Carnspindle where you're from?"

"It is, aye. Bridget McGill said Hamilton Lock was at the front of the band that come bustin' into Eiver Magee's. 'Death to all papist rebels!' he bellowed, and fired a musket shot at Eiver. Bridget was standin' behind Eiver, and the bullet passed through him and into her throat. She fell like a stone. The next thing she knowed, Lock had her by the hair and was pullin' her to the door, past the bodies of family and friends. What he had in mind to do to her, the Lord only knows. 'No time for that,' someone shouted. 'We've a long night's work ahead of us.' So he let her drop, contentin' hisself with cuttin' off her girdle to give to some lassie he had his eye on. Bridget McGill played dead, and after the soldiers left she hid out by the rocks at the shoreline. Next day, she managed to get away in a boat. She carried a scar on her neck for the rest of her life. Long gone, she is now. But my da knowed her when he was a wee lad."

I sat for a while, watching the gulls dive for fish, yellow feet pressed tight against their bellies as they rose back, squawking, into the air. Lucky birds, with wings to lift them up the cliff face. By and by, I felt able to pick up my story again.

"Some say it was thirty families done to death, others say thirty people. The truth falls in-between. Truth usually does. My da did a head count and reckoned it at about seventy deaths. That's how it was when times were troubled. Kill or be killed. It was done to teach the Irish the penalties of insurrection. The Scotch general they sent over to protect the settlers – Munro was his name – he had this to say about the Irish: the more you scourged them, the better they learned to respect you."

"Unless they learned to hate you," said Mary.

"Aye, hate. That can be a powerful force. Hamilton Lock is proof of that. Anyhows, there was an inquiry into the massacre a dozen years later. This would be the 1650s, long afore you or I were thought of, mistress. Some of the soldiers were dead, but others were still about. Cromwell was in charge by then, puttin' order on the Scotch as well as the Irish. From what I hear tell of Cromwell, he'd a lost no sleep over what went on here. He's dead more'n fifty years, but the Irish still spit on his name. 'The curse of Cromwell on you,' they say. Anyhow, for the look of the thing, maybes, he ordered an inquisition into what went on here. His men took depositions, an' cobbled together an account of what happened with the Magees. A sorry tale it was. Even leavin' out the worst part."

"What was the worst part?"

I was too choked to answer. Instead, I listened to the waves crashing against the rocks below: such violence there is, in an incoming tide. But something worked on me to speak. I have a half-notion it was the story itself, forcing its way out. Insisting on being said aloud. I struggled with it, and lost. Easier to command the rain to stop falling, or sheep to lay eggs, than to hold that tale in.

"You only have to stand on this cliff-top and hear the wind and sea to understand how it was. The Magee men were e'ther lyin' in their own blood or tryin' to flee. But the women would'n leave their bairns, and wee legs could'n run fast enough. The soldiers rounded them up and chased them to the Gobbins. The way I heared it, they deliberately gave them a head start. The better to enjoy the hunt. When they got them the length of the cliffs, they did a Godforsaken thing. They drove the Magee women over the top, babes and all. Killing the menfolk was one thing. But what they did to the women and childer –"

A long sigh came from Mary Dunbar, as if she'd listened to enough. As if she'd like to be let off the rest. But I wasn't able to stop now.

"What they did to the women an' childer was done for sport. Hamilton Lock's notion of sport."

The words were like stones vanishing slowly through mud.

"The depositions given in to the inquiry tried to make out the bloodshed at the Gobbins never took place. As if anyone could invent such a story. Maybes folk were ashamed to admit to it – even them that had no hand in the deed. The inquisition Cromwell ordered said no evidence was found. Hearsay was all. But it happened. Oh aye. It happened. There were eyes to see it. To remember. And to pass it on."

After a long pause, Mary Dunbar collected herself. "You know so much about the island."

"Islandmagee is my home."

"Were your family among the first settlers to come over from Scotland?"

"I could'n say, mistress. That's before my time."

"But you were born here?"

"Aye, like my father afore me, and his father afore him."

"So you're been here for several generations?"

I gazed at the greens and blues and purples of the land, and a fierce love for it swelled inside me. "Islandmagee is in our blood, and let nobody say different. We have a right to be here." Surprise bloomed on her face, and I saw I might have been too insistent. "There's no place like it for gettin' under your skin," I said.

"My father says we improved Ulster greatly, by planting a colony and civilizing the Irish," said Mary Dunbar.

"I've heared it remarked upon often enough, mistress."

It was agreed among the Scotch of Ireland that Ulster was a wilderness before it was planted. Yet if you ask me, Islandmagee held itself apart from the people who settled it – planter or Gael. It was hospitable enough. But there was a distance. You could never truly possess the land.

I took a last look about me. "Time to make our way back, mistress. We've been gone longer than we should. And spoken of more than we should, maybes."

We walked at a snail's pace, for she was slow and I matched my steps to hers. It was hard to believe she was the same lassie who had frolicked with the childer, running to see the ducklings on Donaldsons' pond. I noticed that the welts on her face from the barn owl's attack were starting to heal already. Mary Dunbar was blessed with good skin. She might get away with only a few small scars.

Just before we went indoors, she put another question to me. "You said there was an investigation twelve years after the massacre. What happened to Hamilton Lock and the other soldiers?"

"Aye, well, there were too many dead Magees not to admit somethin' got out o' hand. In the end, they left the officers alone, but some of the soldiers were transported to Barbados. Not Lock, though. He escaped from gaol afore the ship sailed, and hid out in Scotland for a while. Years later, he turned up again on Islandmagee like a bad penny. Did some farmin' up Balloo way, on land his father was given by Minister Haltridge. He always claimed he was'n Hamilton Lock, but his brother Nathaniel. Folk knowed him, though. Hamilton could get a look in his eyes you would'n easy forget, my granda used to say. A look fit to slice a body in two."

"Was he not afraid of some Magee or other getting even with him?"

"There were no Magees left. They were all wiped out or fled to other parts. But if you ask me, that made no differ. Hamilton Lock was afeared of nothin' and nobody. He had a mean streak that ran from the crown of his head to the soles of his boots."

◖◖ ◖◖ ◖◖

No sooner was I back indoors, and had the young lady resting in her bedchamber, than a racket came from outside. I took a look through the half-door. Men on horseback were pouring into the yard. Their mounts were whinnying and rearing up, while my master's greyhounds yowled and snapped, dancing round their hooves. Above it all squawked the rooster, furious at this invasion of his territory. Such a commotion you never heard in all your live-long days. Jamesey and Sarah pelted in through the back door, breathless.

"There's men coming with muskets," said Jamesey.

"Their horses are all covered in dust," put in Sarah.

"And sweat," added Jamesey.

A dundering came on the front door.

"You sit here and be quiet as mice, till I see what this is about," I told the childer. Another thump on the wood showed it was an impatient caller.

I opened the door to Brice Blan, riding crop at the ready to knock again. It was the Constable, landing in to question Mary Dunbar. He had caked dung underfoot as though reared in a barn, but at least he had the sense to leave that clatter of deputies riding with him to kick their heels in the yard. Not that the greyhounds appreciated it: they were running about in circles, snapping at the intruders, while the mounted men aimed their boots at them.

"Nice welcome you lay on here," said the Constable. "If this is how you treat your friends, I feel sorry for your enemies. And from what I hear, you've no shortage of them."

Wee Sarah let a squeak out of her, and his eyes snapped to the bairns, who had followed me out to the hall. He scowled, cracking his riding crop against his boot.

"Go back," I said, and they didn't need telling twice.

Constable Blan had the sour breath and pinched face of a man whose meat lay restless in his stomach. It was said he could never keep down more than oatmeal. I heared he took a bloody flux if he tried to eat as much as a slice of black pudding. Looking at him, I felt like squeaking myself.

"I haven't got all day, lass. Where's your mistress?"

I brought him through to the parlour, where the mistress was cutting down one of the master's shirts for Jamesey.

"Good day to you, Mistress Haltridge. I'm not in the habit of beating about the bush. A woman by the name of Becky Carson is in my custody, and I'm making further inquiries about another woman answering to the name of Mistress Anne. Not much to go on – her accuser will have to furnish us with a description. The plaintiff is one Mary Dunbar, spinster, of Armagh. Now, I understand this person is not a native of Islandmagee, but lodges here and you can vouch for her. Is that right?"

"She's my cousin," said the mistress, as cowed as we all were, I suspect.

"Good. My task is to ascertain whether there be any substance to the charges laid against this Becky Carson." He raised his eyebrows to show it was a question, and the mistress nodded again. "She claims she was molested by witches here in Knowehead House in the townland of Kilcoan More. Correct?"

Mistress Haltridge cleared her throat. "There's no doubt about her being molested by witches, Constable. Only this morning, helping her to dress, I saw her back was scraped red-raw – the skin all worn away in patches. What else could it be but witchcraft?"

"That's not for you nor me to judge, mistress. But if she's been injured, the law will avenge her. Kindly bring the afflicted party before me so I can take the measure of her."

"Should we not send for the minister?"

"This is a matter for the civil authorities now, not the Church. Well, don't delay, bring her in." He tapped his riding crop, impatient.

Still, the mistress hesitated. "Constable, I wish the minister was here. He can shed more light on these matters than I can. It's no bother to send my maid for him. You and your men could have some ale, or a glass of brandy if you prefer, while you wait."

He twisted his lips into what passed for a smile. "I hope it's not smuggled brandy you're offering an officer of the Crown, Mistress Haltridge. A French vessel was spotted hard-by the Gobbins less than a month ago. I have information that a rowboat went out to it."

"Sir, the brandy comes from my husband's cellar, ordered from his wine merchant in Belfast. But I will not press you again. I was merely trying to be hospitable."

"I am here on business, not a junket, mistress."

"Very well, I'll have my cousin brought to you now."

She flapped her hands at me, and I went for the young lady. The door to her bedchamber was ajar, and I could see Mary Dunbar sitting on the window seat. Peggy McGregor was keeping her company, smoking her pipe, the pair of them yarning away. I stood on the landing to listen.

"Do you ever wonder which you'd choose in their place, Peggy? The point of a sword or the point of a rock?"

"I'd jump."

"Me too. There's always a chance in the sea. You might miss the rocks and swim to safety. But there's no chance at all on the end of a sword."

"It must be a horrible feelin', mind you, mistress. Fallin' through the air."

"Unless you still thought you might be saved. You could hope for just a few seconds more."

At that, I went in. When I told her the Constable was below, Mary lifted the lid of her sewing box, to check her appearance in a looking-glass inside it. She tweaked a curl, pinched colour into her cheeks, and was ready.

Brice Blan invited her to sit and told her not to be afraid because all he wanted was the truth. I half-expected her to collapse into a fit the minute he started quizzing her, because his manner was stern, but she held herself together tolerably well.

"I understand you've been abused by witches since your arrival on Islandmagee. Correct?"

"Yes, sir. Since I untied the knots in the apron and released the spell."

His eyebrows shot up. "Knots?"

"In an apron belonging to Mistress Haltridge, sir. It was fastened with witches' knots and I was foolish enough to tamper with them. When I did, a cap fell out belonging to –"

"We kept the apron," the mistress put in. "In case you need it for evidence."

"But the knots are no longer in it. Is that so?"

"Yes."

"Then it looks like any commonplace apron. It cannot be used in evidence. You were saying something about a cap, Mistress Dunbar?"

"It fell out of the apron. It had the owner's initials sewn into it and belonged to–"

"We do have some objects vomited up by my cousin, Constable Blan," said the mistress. "These could be used in evidence. Witnesses saw them appear from Mary's mouth. They can only have reached her stomach by supernatural means."

"Not necessarily. She could have swallowed them herself."

"Waistcoat buttons? A candle stub?"

He pursed his lips. "Fetch those objects, if you please, Mistress Haltridge. I need to examine them."

"Mister Sinclair took everything away to pray over them. He was here when she brought them up, you see. You should know that my cousin has had a number of fits, observed by various people of good reputation. During some, she loses the power of speech and movement and goes into a trance, her body frozen like a corpse. During others, she is sorely tested and attacked by witches, but is able to tell us how they taunt her. We hear her answer them and call on the Lord to shield her."

"Kindly stop handing over the evidence to the minister. Now, Mistress Dunbar is the only person able to see and hear the witches. Correct?"

"Yes. You counted eight witches in all, did you not, Mary?" said the mistress.

"There was a ninth but she died lately."

The mistress gave a start, and I blinked for the same reason she did, but we both of us held our peace.

Mary went on, "I saw a nest of them casting spells in a cave. They delight in wounding me cruelly, sir. Especially if I defy them."

"Lock's Cave has been searched, by order of Mister Robert Sinclair, our minister," said the mistress. "Some suspicious objects were found, suggesting a coven might meet there."

"Where are those objects?"

"Mister Sinclair has them."

Crack! Constable Blan's whip whistled through the air. It touched nobody, but we jumped out of our skins. He glared at the mistress, before turning back to Mary Dunbar.

"Is Becky Carson among those who beset you?"

"She was, but she hasn't come near me since being gaoled. The others are in a rage because of it. They say I will not know a day's peace till their sister goes free."

"Who are the others?"

"There is a mother and daughter I find particularly troublesome. The mother is a scold, only a couple of black teeth left in her head. I heard her called Mistress Janet. The daughter's name is Lizzie. The mother held me down while her daughter bit me. Forgive me, sir, I don't mean to be indelicate, but there is something you should see." She pulled up her skirt almost to the knee, and rolled down her stocking. A crop of bites bloomed along the right calf – the teeth marks clearly visible. "They attacked my leg because one of them is lame."

"Beauty is often a target for jealousy," said the mistress.

"And because I refused to blaspheme when they told me I must. They wanted me to say the Devil rewarded his servants more generously than Christ Jesus, but I told them I'd sooner die. They threatened to chop me into pieces and feed my flesh to pigs if I didn't say it, but I resisted them."

"Devil's strumpets, the pair of them. Are they from Islandmagee?"

"Yes, sir."

He stroked his nose. "A crippled girl with a barge for a mother should be handy tracked down. One of my men might know these women. Now, we need more information on the one you call Mistress Anne – the ringleader. And what of the others, Mistress Dunbar? Can you supply us with names or descriptions?"

Lines appeared on her forehead, and she rubbed at them, her head sinking into her hand. "I'm so tired, Constable. So very tired. I counted eight, but their faces are hazy now . . ."

"Perhaps if my cousin has a chance to rest, she might be in a better position to continue," said the mistress.

He muttered an oath, but went outside to speak to his men.

The mistress said quickly, "Mary, my dear, pray don't refer to my mother-in-law's cap again, unless you feel you must."

She opened her hazel eyes wide. "Why ever not, Isabel?"

"It's confusing. It has nothing to do with these other events."

"There were no witch's knots in the bonnet strings – they were in the apron ties," I said.

"Exactly," agreed the mistress. "It only muddies the waters."

Blan's footsteps hushed the three of us. "There's a woman has a name for rising a row with her neighbours, over by McCrea's Brae. She's called Janet Liston. Her husband is William Cellar – he's been up before the Magistrate on public order offences. A fine pair. They have a daughter of seventeen or eighteen years. Elizabeth Cellar has a stiff leg. I'll have them brought in to you, Mistress Dunbar, to see if you recognize them as your tormentors."

I knowed Lizzie Cellar: as quiet as her ma was quarrelsome,

she was inclined to be shy because of her leg. There was a problem when she was born because she was such a long babby. During the birth, one of her feet got caught and twisted inside her ma. It made me realize there were worse things than being the tallest lassie on the island. I wouldn't go so far as to say Lizzie Cellar was a friend of mine, but I suppose there was kinship of sorts. I used to think that there but for the grace of God went I, with a limp to match hers.

Could she really be consorting with the devil? Lizzie Cellar, who played tag with me and Mercy and Ruth Graham when we were childer, and was always the first caught on account of her leg? I was prepared to believe her ma was a witch, with that tongue on her like a stinging nettle. But Lizzie was a gentle girl. Still, Mary Dunbar denouncing both of them was a fact that couldn't be set aside. It looked powerful bad. My da popped into my head. "Facts can be shaped this way and that, like lumps of wet clay," he was fond of saying. All the same, it was hard to see how there could be an innocent reason for Lizzie and Janet being named.

I was in swithers. Nobody wants to have any truck with witches. Or even women accused of being witches. But I'd known Lizzie since we were childer. If the Constable surprised them at their cabin, Janet Liston was liable to burst out with anything. She had a temper that was easy riz. It would go better for her and Lizzie if they came of their own accord to Knowehead to face Mary Dunbar. If Janet Liston was brought in by Brice Blan, she'd be fit to be tied, and could give the young lady a tongue-lashing.

"Sir, not wantin' to jump in ahead of you . . ." I began.

The Constable was taken aback. He hadn't so much as looked at me since I led him into the parlour.

"But would there be any advantage in me steppin' down to the Cellars' house, and askin' them for to come here of their own free will?"

Brice Blan's eyes hooked on to mine, waiting.

"It might clear things up handy, instead of makin' a spectacle out of it," I said.

"Don't meddle, Ellen," said the mistress.

Part of me thought she was right. I might be getting into deep waters. Maybes I was taking too big a risk, trying to have Lizzie seen in a good light. After all, she might be a witch – the Devil was persuasive. He was a master at finding folk's weak spots, as I knowed to my cost. And if Lizzie was a witch, then her ma might be one, as well. The pair of them could take it into their heads to put a spell on me: I could be turned into a toad, or lose my speech, or my wits. I should have kept my mouth shut.

Too late.

"No, your maid talks sense," said the Constable. "No good can come of deputies riding from cottage to cottage, making folk fear a witch hunt. It'll only panic decent citizens. I take it you know this mother and daughter well enough to coax them to come in of their own accord?"

"I know them, sir. But I can't pretend I have any great sway with them." Maybes I could still back out.

"Aye, but you can tell them they won't be the losers by coming."

"I can say that, sir. I can't say if they'll believe me."

"It's worth a try. Stretch your shanks, lass."

During this exchange, Mary Dunbar was watching me out of the corner of her eye. Here's an odd thing about her. There were times when all the prettiness was drawn from her face, and I was amazed a body gave her a second look. This was one of those times.

Chapter 9

The Cellar family lived in a wee row of lime-and-stone cottages, each with a porch, on the east side of the island. The houses were thatched with straw and netted down with hay ropes held fast with wooden pegs. One of the houses was a shebeen, and that might have been why Lizzie's ma had a gob on her the size of Larne Lough. Her man was another one like my da, always spending his shillings before they were earned. That shebeen was too handy by far. If it was anything like the ones where Da went, it had sit-ins – to give folk every chance to sup their last bawbee.

I was nervous going in to the Cellars, and striddled the last few yards to their cottage, trying to gather up the courage. When I took the bull by the horns, Lizzie put on a brave civil welcome, though I fancy she was surprised to see me. Herself and her ma were at their spinning wheels by the window, catching the light, when I put my head in over the half-door. Lizzie said they were just about to have something to eat, and asked if I would join them.

It was smoky inside the cottage, from the straw they were burning instead of wood or turf, and my eyes started watering. The hole in the roof they had for a chimney didn't do much of a job. I was reared in a two-room cabin with earth floors like theirs, but it's no hardship to grow accustomed to better. At least their table was scrubbed white, and they were mannerly enough, forcing me to take a mug of buttermilk and an oatmeal square. Though I sat looking at the food, wondering if the buttermilk could be a potion to make my hair fall out, or hives pop up on my skin.

"Eat, lassie," said Janet Liston, and it sounded like an order so I bit in.

By and by, I came to the point. "I daresay you've heared about our troubles at Knowehead."

"It's been a hard knock for yiz. Aul' Mistress Haltridge no sooner wrapped in her windin' sheet, and now this," said Janet.

"Whist, ma," said Lizzie. "Dinna speak of the dead."

"I'm on'y saying, is all. Is it true her ghost walks through the house every night, groanin' from the weight of her sins?"

"Aul' Mistress Haltridge never knowingly committed a sin in her life." Janet Liston wouldn't belittle her whiles I had breath in my body. I calmed myself, and went on, "The troubles concern a relative of the young mistress's, lately arrived on the island. Mary Dunbar is her name, and she's plagued by witches."

"So I hear," said Janet Liston. "Can the kirk do nothin' for her?"

"Mister Sinclair is tryin' his best, but she swears there's a parcel of witches forever at her. One of them's been handed in to the Constable. But the witchin' has'n eased off, and the young lady says there's a coven out for her blood."

The women let out a couple of squawks, though they were content enough to settle down for a blether, little suspecting what else I had to tell them. My knees were knocking: it was a dry bargain I made in agreeing to this errand. But there was no handy way to put it over – I better just spit it out. "Mary Dunbar says a mother and daughter are in the coven. The Constable is above in Knowehead now. He thinks it might be the pair of yiz."

Janet Liston's rage blew up at once. She lifted the pitcher of milk and hopped it off the hearthstone, where it broke into pieces and splashed milk everywhere. The oaths that came out of her gob would have shamed a sailor.

Her daughter did nothing showy, but I could see Lizzie Cellar was shaken. It was hard not to pity her. "What do you think we should do?" she asked, when Janet's fury eased.

"Come to Knowehead House and meet Mary Dunbar. If she's mistaken, tell her so."

"The skitter o' hell. Jus' wait till I get me hands on her, I'll gi'e her plenty to be afeared of!"

"Ach, settle your head, Ma – losin' your temper is no help to us." Lizzie appealed to me. "Would it be safe for us to do that?"

"It's like this, Lizzie. E'ther go see her willin', an' make the best of it, or Brice Blan will bring yiz in. The young lady's sore afflicted, and it's agreed witchcraft is the cause."

"Witchcraft's a bad business to be named along of – nobody ever comes out of it well," said Lizzie, voice shaky. She was sore afraid, and I didn't blame her. There was no answer I could make. She looked me in the eye. "Folk'll say there's no smoke without fire."

I nodded. I was scared myself – and sorry to see her dragged into this, but it couldn't be helped.

"There's no power on earth can make me go and stand in front of thon wee hoor. I'll have to be hauled there by me hair!" shouted Janet.

"Think it over," I told Lizzie. "You'll have to face her, one way or the other, now she's named you. Mary Dunbar's a nice enough person, our own age, give or take. Act humble with her. She might take pity, and say yiz bain't the ones a-witchin' her."

The door slammed open and William Cellar came thundering in, demanding to know what all the caterwauling was about. He was a gulpin, known to have a temper the

177

equal of his wife's, so I took to my heels, not wanting to get on the wrong side of it. I was no way up the road when Lizzie Cellar came hirpling after, calling for me to slow down. It wasn't her fault she had a scold for a ma. I liked her, so I did.

"Me da says you have the right of it. We should talk to Mary Dunbar and tell her we've done nothin' wrong. Me conscience is clear, and so is Ma's. I know she carries on, but her bark is worse'n her bite. Me and Da, we'll bring her to her senses. We'll be along to Knowehead House shortly. I'm keen for to get this cleared up. It's a mistake, is all. Innocence will act as our shield . . . won't it, Ellen?"

She reached out her hand to me, and I squeezed it. "I hope so, Lizzie. Sure I know you would'n hurt a soul. I mind right well when we were wee'ans, you would'n step on a flower for fear of harmin' it."

"This is a test of our Christian faith, so it is. The minister was on'y after saying, last Sabbath in the meetin'-house, that we must all be God's obedient subjects and place ourselves under the protection of His divine will. He'll never see us wronged."

I was relieved. I didn't like to fail in my mission. Not that I was getting above myself, and I certainly didn't expect any thanks. But Lizzie might not be the loser by facing her accuser. Maybes the minister and the Constable would see she didn't have it in her to try her hand at witchery. And if she kept her ma on a tight leash, it was possible she'd be let off too. You couldn't be sure of the outcome, mind you. No two ways about it, it was a risk.

◎   ◎   ◎

Back at Knowehead House, I had to elbow through the Constable's men, all of them beef to the heels. Our yard was like a market square. Their horse dung was steaming all over the place, making everything look clatty. "Gi'e us a kiss," and

"Any chance of a wee drap?" they called after me, but I never let on I heard them.

Mister Sinclair had pitched up, and was deep in conversation with Brice Blan. If you ask me, the preacher couldn't bear to keep away from our household. Sure wasn't he cock of the walk here, quoting the Bible and laying down the law? Mister Sinclair had a companion with him, another minister by the name of David Arnold. He was the Church of Ireland curate, come to lend his support. Mister Sinclair would have sent word to him: he had to keep in with the established Church. They took a dim view of us Dissenters doing things under our own say-so.

Smartly turned out, was Mister Arnold – or the Reverend Arnold, I daresay he'd prefer to be called. You have to laugh at the airs and graces in other Churches. Plain mister is good enough for our ministers. Be that as it may, the linen at this Mister Arnold's throat was snow-white, his shoe-buckles shone, and there was not a single speck of stoor on his black frock coat. Some woman was attentive to him, for here was a sleek man and no mistake. He put me in mind of a sea-pig. And there was Mister Sinclair, looking like he hadn't changed his linen in weeks.

The minute the mistress caught sight of me, she ordered me to fill the baskets beside each fireplace. We were going through a lot of turf these days – it was spring outdoors, but indoors the house never felt colder. No chance of resting my bones for a bit, after footing it all the way to McCrea's Brae and back.

Constable Blan was quick to ask how my errand went. I was pleased to be able to report that Lizzie Cellar and her mother Janet Liston were coming to the house by and by. I kept my eyes down and stayed modest, so nobody should think I was claiming any credit. Not much chance of that round Mister Sinclair.

In he jumps, with his clabbery boots. "What does 'by and

by' mean? In an hour? Two? Are we to wait round on their pleasure indefinitely?"

"I took it to mean as soon as they can, sir."

"I trust they ken it's not a social call."

"They understand that well enough. Nobody takes it lightly, bein' named a witch." I forgot myself and was tart, and he spotted it.

"I would'n go feeling sorry for witches, lassie. Save your pity – if that's what it be. I trust it's not something more sinister." He turned to Mister Arnold. "If you ask me, these women take us for dunderheads. For all we know, they could be communing with Lucifer while we await their convenience." The other minister looked grave.

"Are these women friends of yours?" Brice Blan asked me, picking up on the sly suggestion put out by the minister.

"I tould you I knowed them, sir, and indeed everybody knows everybody on Islandmagee, sir. I would'n condemn a body afore hearin' what they have to say in their defence."

"Well said," came from Mister Arnold.

I wasn't expecting support from that quarter, and Mister Sinclair looked quare and put out about it.

Brice Blan tapped at his teeth with a thumbnail. Those teeth were as crooked as a country lane – no wonder he rarely smiled. "An hour here or there is immaterial. The plaintiff is resting. We might as well leave her be for a while. I want her refreshed, so she can concentrate on bringing to mind the names of the other witches."

I was let go about my business and headed off to the turf stack by the piggery. Noah kept it piled high, and always made sure there were sticks for kindling. "Nobody said I was to put a ring through their noses, and lead them along behind me," I muttered, feeling hard done by. One of the Constable's men carried the blocks for me, which soothed my temper.

As I took the load at the kitchen door, he set his boot on

the doorstep. "We were sent to search Lock's Cave again while you were gone."

"Oh aye? Find anythin'?"

"Ach, them fellows that looked it over before tramped here, there and everywhere. You could tell folk were about the place lately, but it could just as well a been the searchers. Blan gave the minister a right touch about it."

I laughed at the thought of Mister Sinclair being put in his box. When I did, the deputy leaned forward to whisper in my ear.

"Is it true the witches brewed a soup with earth taken from the grave of Mistress Haltridge? And used it at a Black Sabbath to summon her up?"

I slammed the door in his face.

But it wasn't so easy to slam the door on rumours. The longer this went on, the more outlandish they were growing. And tell you no lie, they put the wind up me – because there's often some truth in a rumour, no matter how far-fetched.

                  🙼   🙼   🙼

I was in the yard with Jamesey and Sarah, letting them help me to fetch water from the well, when I spied Lizzie and Janet crossing through the fields, along with William Cellar. They were still a fair way off. I waved, before telling Jamesey to run into the parlour and tell the Constable.

"Are they friends of yours?" Sarah asked.

I thought about Saint Peter, denying Christ three times, but still I could not bring myself to own them as friends. It wouldn't be safe. "Never mind your questions. When your brother comes back, the two of you are to go and play in the barn. At least you'll be dry – rain's brewin' in that there sky, and I don't want you catchin' your death of cold."

"But there's nothing to do in the barn, Ellen."

"I know, chicken. But it's better for you to play there than in your chamber." Who could tell what they might hear, under the same roof as Mary Dunbar and the two she had denounced as witches? I searched my head for a game. "How about if you bring your babby-doll, and Jamesey brings some of his soldiers, and your babby can get wed to one of the soldiers?"

"Jamesey will never play that game."

"Tell him I said he must. Hurry up, there's a good girl."

The young master arrived back, white-faced.

"What's the matter, Jamesey?"

"Cousin Mary is . . ."

"Is what?"

"Nothing. I wish she'd go home!"

I dropped the water and made for the parlour, where the company was occupied with Mary Dunbar.

She was sweating and trembling. "They're coming, the devils are on their way." The closer the trio came to Knowehead, the more agitated she grew. How she knowed is beyond me, because they couldn't be spotted from the parlour.

I went back to get the water, only to find the family standing outside the back door. They hadn't crossed the threshold, although I left the door ajar in my hurry. I signalled them to come in, but still they hesitated. Lizzie was leaning on a blackthorn stick, while Cellar must have had a bucket of water poured over him before he set off, from the state of his hair plastered to his head. Mind you, he looked a fair sight more respectable than earlier. All three were barefoot. I never knowed shoon, myself, till I came to Kilcoan More, when I was told I had to wear them, working for a gentleman's family.

"Best get this over with," I encouraged them, seeing how the big house overawed them.

Lizzie stepped into the kitchen, followed by her da, and finally her ma. I took a quick peek into the yard, and was satisfied to see the young master and missie skipping towards the barn.

Peggy looked the threesome over from tip to toe. "Witchcraft is a dangerous invention of Satan's," she said.

"It is, aye," said William Cellar.

"See yiz steer clear of witches. They'll bring nothin' but harm on your heads."

Lizzie rubbed at her leg through her skirts. I daresay the walk took it out of her. I knowed the longer they delayed, the worse would be Mary Dunbar's convulsions, so I urged the women straight up to the parlour, and told William Cellar to take a seat beside Peggy. Lizzie leaned her stick in a corner, not wanting to look like a cripple in front of the fancy folk.

By the time they stood in front of her, Mary Dunbar was tossing her head fit to snap her neck, and tugging at her fingers as though to tear them off. So much for my hopes of Lizzie and her ma reaching her before the attack got out of hand. The sight of them set her shrieking like a banshee. "Keep them away from me! Hold the witches back!"

Mister Sinclair took charge. "We'll do this one at a time. Leave the lass here, and take her mother outside."

The Constable gurned at having his men ordered about, but he nodded, and two of them did as the minister bid. Lizzie bobbed an awkward curtsey to the room and waited. She had a waterfall of sleek hair, as smooth as a horse's hide, which her bonnet didn't manage to cover entirely, and she put you in mind of a fawn, with her timid, wide-eyed manner. This graceful picture fell apart as soon as she walked, leaning forward and swinging her leg in a half-circle. But she looked like the last woman on Islandmagee to be in league with Old Nick. Even Mary Dunbar was silenced.

"Is this one of your persecutors?" asked Mister Sinclair.

Mary put her head on one side, her mouth opening and closing. Nothing came out.

"She could be under a spell," said the minister. "Witches have been known to freeze the tongues of their victims."

"What have you to say for yourself, Elizabeth Cellar?"

asked the Constable. "Have you silenced this unfortunate lady?"

"No, sir. I would'n know how. Nor would I want to, even if I did. I never seen her before – the young lady's a stranger to me. I have no cause to ill-wish her."

Mister Sinclair turned back to Mary Dunbar. "Answer, in the name of Christ our Redeemer. Is she one of those you name as witches? Is her name written in that hideous book kept by Satan which contains the names of all his disciples?"

No response.

Mister Arnold spoke up, his manner less bossy. "Let us hear more from the accused. Can you recite the Ten Commandments?" he asked Lizzie.

"I never learned all of them sir, just to be obedient, an' do as my elders and betters said. I know there's on'y the one true God, who gave His life so we might be saved, an' we have to love one another for His sake. Forbye that, we have to keep holy the Sabbath day."

"It would be preferable if you knew them all, but 'tis a good answer. Still, there's a difference between theory and practice. Now, I'm going to put a question to you, and I want you to answer in all honesty. If the answer is yes, we will help to wrest you from your malign influences. Do not be afraid of telling the truth. Elizabeth Cellar, do you worship a false god?"

"No, sir. I pray on'y to the Lord Jesus. I ask Him now to stand beside me and let yiz see I've always tried to be a good girl, and with the help of His tender mercy I trust I always will."

Her simple faith struck home with Mister Arnold. But Mister Sinclair didn't impress too handy. "Women are unchaste and false by nature," he said.

"Well, sir, I dinna deny we're weak and inclined for to stumble. But the Bible tells us the seed of the woman shall bruise the head of the serpent," said Lizzie.

"Genesis 3:15." Mister Arnold's eyes gleamed.

This gave Lizzie the courage to address Mary Dunbar. "Mistress, I dinna ken what ails you, but I'll say a prayer for you when I kneel down the-night."

Mary Dunbar still said nothing, and even Mister Sinclair challenged Lizzie no further.

"I believe we should see the other woman now," said Brice Blan. He flicked his riding crop at me, and I went out for Janet Liston. I found her back in the kitchen.

Maybes it was the Constable's men guarding the door – or maybes it was the waiting. But she had worked herself into a state, scarlet in the face. It was a pity Lizzie hadn't been on hand to keep her calm.

Her husband was saying, "Go 'asy, Janet, you need to keep your temper bridled," but she wasn't listening.

"I'm fair scundered with this," she burst out. "Who's thon cuddy to point the finger at our Lizzie and me? She wants to watch herself, so she does."

When I led her into the parlour, Janet Liston didn't wait to be addressed. She went on the attack. "What's she been sayin' about me? She has no business spreadin' filthy lies."

"We're here to establish whether they be truth or lies, Mistress Liston, and if you would cooperate –"

Whatever else Constable Blan intended to say was lost, because Mary Dunbar's voice came back. Eyes bulging, she let out a series of piercing screams, her finger pointed at Janet Liston.

"She's touched in the head," said Janet. "I'm sorry for her troubles, but it bain't anythin' to do with me."

"Liar!" screamed Mary. "Last night you boasted you'd have me turned into a pony and shod by the Devil. Then you'd ride me the length and breadth of Islandmagee till I dropped dead of exhaustion."

"I did no such thing – you need your gob washed out, lassie."

"Steady on, Ma." Lizzie laid a hand on her arm.

"An' let her away with any aul' nonsense that comes into her head? She's on'y shamming, she would'n know the truth if it took a bite out of her."

Mary jumped up and spun like a top, faster and faster, squealing as she turned. "It's those two witches doing it to me. They're making me dizzy. I can't stop!"

I kept a close eye on Lizzie and her ma, whiles the mistress and others ran to Mary Dunbar's aid. Lizzie was distressed, wringing her hands, but Janet stood grim-faced. Two deputies held Mary to stop her from turning.

Mister Sinclair rounded on Lizzie and Janet. "Now what have you to say for yourselves? You're bursting with corruption. Mistress Dunbar could have fallen and cracked her head open."

"Thon birlin' roun' is nothin' to do with me nor our Lizzie. She was doin' it herself, for attention. Shame on you, lassie. You have everybody else fooled, but I bain't taken in be your coddin' about. If you were mine, I'd gi'e you a lock of skelps to knock the badness out of you."

"Ma, mind what you say. Please."

"An' let her away with her bare-faced lies? No, Lizzie. This Jezebel won't rob us of our good names wi'out a fight." Her dark wee eyes blazed.

"Do you deny you have signed the Demonic Pact in your own blood?" demanded Mister Sinclair.

She threw back her head and laughed. "Satan would have to be satisfied with an X, for I cannae write."

"Dinna make a mockery of it, Ma. Say no more."

"Ach, you fine gentlemen are terrible 'asy convinced be a titter of playactin'. But how's this for a thought? How about if she's the one in league with the Devil? Doin' his biddin' in houndin' honest, God-fearin' folk?"

Robert Sinclair looked at David Arnold. Both of them looked at Brice Blan. Mister Arnold and Constable Blan let go of Mary Dunbar, taking a step back. You could have heard a feather fall.

Mary Dunbar flung herself on the floor and banged her head against the flagstones with a clatter to make your stomach churn.

"All the other witches are here now – they've got me by the hair. They say they won't stop till they shake the brains out of me." She thumped her head on the floor again, and the blood ran bright. The Constable caught her and pulled her to her feet, but her screeching continued.

Above the din, Mister Sinclair called to a couple of deputies, "Take those women outside."

"Feel free to tell my men what to do, Mister Sinclair," said the Constable.

The deputies hesitated, until the Constable made an impatient gesture. His men pushed Janet and Lizzie ahead of them out of the room.

"Take them away from this house," moaned Mary. "They want me to join their coven. I told them I'd never submit to Satan's wiles."

"Do we need to examine the man, William Cellar?" asked Brice Blan. "Does Mistress Dunbar complain of male witches?"

"Are you tormented by warlocks, Mary Dunbar?" asked Mister Sinclair. "Do evil men appear to you?"

"There is a man in their circle of vice. The witches called him up, but now he directs them. He is choked with malice."

"Who is this devil's spawn? Identify him."

"Hamilton Lock."

The name cut the air like a curse.

When Blan recovered, he turned to Mister Sinclair. "This is worse than I thought. Is this the first time Lock's name has been mentioned in connection with these disturbances?"

"Well, Constable, I must admit I feared Lock's involvement, because of the coven using his cave."

"I was under the impression the cave was chosen simply because it's out of the way."

"It's that, all right, but Mistress Dunbar believes these vixens met there to call him up. There are reports of his shade being sighted in these parts."

"I see." The Constable wheeled round suddenly. "Have you seen Hamilton Lock yourself, Mistress Dunbar?"

If he hoped to startle her, he was disappointed. She was the calmest person in the room. "He came to me last night. He seeks to make a witch of me. He said the Devil wants me to make a cake using my own water – from my body, if you catch my meaning – instead of milk. Once I eat it, I'll have the power to ill-wish whoever I choose. Prince or pauper."

"Depraved monster! How did you answer him?" asked Mister Arnold.

"I told him I'd rather die. He said that could be arranged."

"This hell's firebrand must be hunted down," said Mister Sinclair.

"I cannot give chase to a man who's dead," said the Constable. "That's your responsibility, gentlemen."

An almighty crash came from the kitchen. Blan charged along the passageway, me at his heels. William Cellar was in a lather to match his wife's. He had Lizzie's stick and was banging it about the place, rattling the pot hanging above the fire and splashing boiling water about. The Constable's men were trying to get that swinging stick off him, and not making much of a fist of it.

"Put a stop to this ruckus!" Blan bellowed at his men, but it was Lizzie who ducked in under the weapon and wrapped her arms round her father.

"Put it down, Da, you're on'y makin' things worse."

At first, he shaped to shake her off, but his fingers loosened on the blackthorn. She eased him onto a three-legged stool, at which point the Constable's men rushed in and grabbed him.

"We're done for, so we are," said Janet Liston.

"Ma, houl' your whist. That's the kind of talk started Da off."

"It's the Gospel truth. Thon lassie is too wedded to her own conceits to be turned aside now."

William Cellar struggled, hands pinned behind his back. "Did she denounce just you, or the both of yiz, Janet?"

"The two of us. She throwed a turn would put the fear of God into the Angel Gabriel hisself."

"That's enough. I will not tolerate a breach of the peace," said the Constable. "You women are for Carrickfergus. My men are bringing you straight to the Mayor, to have a warrant sworn out."

"You cannae lock up my wife and daughter on a daft lassie's say-so. She's the one ought to be locked up."

"Enough, Da. Whist." Lizzie laid both hands on his chest, calming him.

As for Janet Liston, all the fight suddenly went out of her and she fell to the floor, moaning. It was said she'd seen the inside of a gaol before, and I thought maybes she knowed what she was letting herself in for. Lizzie was too busy with her father to pick her up, and in charity I should have helped her to a stool. But to tell you the truth, I didn't move a step – I couldn't but ask myself if her collapse was a sign of guilt at being caught for a witch.

"Mary Dunbar is witched and somebody's responsible," said Brice Blan. "Your wife did herself no favours in there. She'd do better to keep a civil tongue in her head. It's a wonder you never taught her that, William Cellar. A man not fit to control his wife is scarcely much of a man." A couple of deputies snorted their appreciation.

Cellar groaned. "Janet has a habit of lettin' fly. I'll not deny it. Have the Mayor order her whipped. Or put her in the duckin' stool for a scold, if he sees fit. But for God's sake dinna bring witchcraft charges. If every woman with a temper on her was put away as a witch, the gaols would be full to bustin'. Me wife is no more a witch than she's the Lady Mayoress. But it's a slur there's no washin' off." His eyes welled up. "As for our Lizzie, she's good as gold – not one soul on Islandmagee has a cross word to say about her. I swear it afore God and man. She doesnae have a bad bone in her body."

"Well, somebody's tormenting Mistress Dunbar – she's covered in cuts and bruises. And you wouldn't be the first man to believe a woman's lies, Cellar. You har'ly expect your wife to tell you when she's off to hear a Black Mass, do you?" His laugh was a cruel sound, and his deputies grunted along with him.

At that, Cellar made a barrel of his chest, ready to take on Blan and all his men, but two of them held him by the arms.

Blan tapped his front with the handle of his riding crop. "I've no time to argue the toss with you, man. Your wife and daughter are bound for gaol, whether you like it or not. And you'll join them, William Cellar, unless you settle the head. You're like a bullock that smells blood."

"We need you on the outside, Da, sendin' word to anyone fit to help us. I'll look out for Ma and she'll look out for me. We'll say our prayers and trust to God. He'll never desert us."

The whiles Lizzie was talking, I wrapped some bread and meat in a cloth because prisoners were fed neither well nor regularly. Whether or not she'd been fooling with things she shouldn't, I didn't want Lizzie Cellar to starve. Forbye that, it was me coaxed the two of them to come and face Mary Dunbar, and look where it landed them.

When I pushed the food into Lizzie's hands, Janet Liston said, "You want to watch yourself, Ellen Hill."

"Why?"

"Thon one might take it into her head to point the finger at you."

"I've done nothin' wrong."

"Nor have we. It makes no odds when push comes to

shove. She's a holy terror. She can see the power she has – there's no stoppin' her now."

The Constable ordered mother and daughter taken away by four of his deputies, and said he was going back to question Mary Dunbar for more names.

When the kitchen was empty, Peggy came stumbling out of the larder where she had hidden away. She looked shaken, and I led her to the fireside nook to rest herself.

"The master is neglectin' us," she complained.

"Sure, Peggy, he doesn't know how things stand. The mistress seems loath to tell him, more fool her."

"He ought to be with his family. Ach, I'd give him a piece of my mind if I had him in front of me. Gaddin' about like that."

"Never mind our master. Have you spoken to Mistress Haltridge about sendin' the wee'ans away? I don't like them bein' in this house."

She shook her head, feeling in her pocket for her clay pipe. I picked it up off the floor, where she must have dropped it fleeing from William Cellar.

She managed a toothless grin. "We need to see about the rooster. He's naw been the same since this witch handlin' started up – he's gone off his food. Imagine if Mister Haltridge came back to find the rooster dead. The master bought the bird hisself, in Carrickfergus. He'd take it sore if he was gone. We need to tempt our laddie with a few morsels. Pet him and make a fuss of him. Roosters are no different to men, when all's said and done."

"You know a lot about men, Peggy, for one that was never wed."

"I see no ring on your finger e'ther, lassie. Men bain't hard to ken. It's women you can never get the right of – they be the ones hidin' secrets."

I blushed to remember the honeyed words my master spoke to me, as he slid his arm round my waist and coaxed me to surrender to him. But I held my nerve and answered Peggy. "Everybody has secrets."

"Do they?"

"Aye, Peggy. I daresay you have your fair share." I was only chancing my arm but she backed off. "Anyhow," I went on, "it's not just folk that hold on to secrets. Houses keep them too."

Peggy blew out a sigh that ended in a whistle. "Aye, you have the right of it. Some houses are inclined that way. They have a hidden side to them." She pursed her lips, searching for words. "But houses are on'y built on land, when all's said and done. They rise up on the land, and they can sink back into it. Men come and go. So do houses. But the land is still there. Land is there before and there after."

"Peggy, you were there when it happened. When the master's father pulled down the Stone to build this house. Was anythin' found under it?"

"There was nothin' found."

"I've been turnin' it over in me mind. I thought it must been a pagan grave."

"No, there was no bones."

I dropped my voice. "Could it a been somethin' belongin' to their priests, that they used in heathen rituals?"

"No, nothin' like that. But that doesnae mean it was empty under the Stone."

"What, then?"

"There was clay under it. The earth of Islandmagee."

"The earth of Islandmagee lies under every blessed house on this island, Peggy."

"But this corner of land is special. Why else would the Stone be raised over it? Why else would it be a place where heathen fellows gathered? Why else would a man like Hamilton Lock feel the way he did about it? He was bad, but he wasnae stupid. He knowed there was power to this place. If it took weeks to tumble the Stone and smash it to pieces, you can be sure it took twice as long to stand it there in the first place. No two ways about it, the Stone had a purpose. It was set up for a reason."

"How do you know? There's rocks and cairns all over Islandmagee."

"I saw the Stone, that's how I ken. It rocked, so it did."

"What do you mean it rocked? Would it not fall over?"

"No, it was cunningly done. Whatever way it was set down, it used to wobble back and forth, the way a cradle rocks. Not all the time. But if you looked at it for a while, it would. I saw it with me own eyes. 'Twas no accident – there was no wind doin' it. The rockin' happened as a warnin' to folk. It put the fear of God in me, watchin'." She took her pipe out of her mouth and pointed it at me. "It was to let folk know this part of Islandmagee is different to the rest."

"Different, how?"

"A thin place, folk whispered. Back when I come here first as a lassie."

"I never heared tell of a thin place."

"Them's spots where we be closer to the other world – an' the other world is closer to us. It's my belief the Stone was set up for to show that. As a signpost, you might say. An' that's why Hamilton Lock was drawn to the Stone."

I couldn't help myself. I gawked at her, and it put her on the back foot.

She coloured. "I'm sayin' no more. I dinna want them ministers accusin' me of truck with things no Christian soul should have dealin's with. And you'll keep your trap shut too, if you have the sense you were born with."

Chapter 10

A bell rang, and I wasn't a bit sorry. I wanted her to tell me what she knowed, but Peggy's talk of thin places made the hairs stand up on the back of my neck.

In the parlour, I was told to show Brice Blan out. He was standing over Mary Dunbar, looking none too pleased.

"It's disappointing you can only furnish descriptions or half a name here and there, as regards these other witches, but I'll waste no time in following up on them."

As I held the front door open for the Constable, he spoke to me. "Has Hamilton Lock shown himself to you?"

"Heaven forbid! I could'n stay in this house if he did."

"Your mistress says the same." He scratched his neck. "I can gaol highwaymen, murderers, even witches. I cannot gaol dead men."

Rather than take their leave with him, the two ministers decided prayer was called for, with everyone in the household ordered to join in. There was no choice except to submit, and the ministers raised their voices to heaven over Mary Dunbar.

While they prayed themselves hoarse, I turned over Peggy's words. If the Stone had been the doorway to a thin place, then Knowehead House must be that doorway now. But something had to unlock it. I remembered Mary Dunbar's story about

Lock's skull being used to call him up. Was his skull the key? I had no peace to think, with each man of God bent on outdoing the other, self-important voices filling the air.

"Eve's curse threatened us with the torments of hell, but our release from eternal destruction was bought by Christ Jesus, who endured a bitter death for our sakes," chanted Mister Sinclair.

Up piped Mister-calls-himself-Reverend Arnold. "As the Lord has His mysteries to bring us to eternal glory, so Satan has his mysteries to bring us to eternal ruin. These mysteries are not easily understood, for Lucifer's depths are hidden. But this sorrowful time can be one of learning for us."

Back came Mister Sinclair with, "We must reflect on why God let loose witchcraft among us. His wrath has a reason. Do not forsake us, oh Lord. Inspire us to renew our battle against sin."

On and on they harped till my head was fit to burst. The childer's fidgets got so noticeable that Mister Sinclair stopped preachifying to scold them. While they were chided, I let on I had chores that could wait no longer, and slid out to the cattle byre. Noah had milked the Galloway cow earlier, before going home to his own four walls, but I could always say I was checking she had enough fodder.

I sucked on a length of straw, trying to find a way through the maze of things I heard and saw, but didn't always understand. Earlier, Peggy said Hamilton Lock had a particular reason to hate the Haltridges. But she never would tell me what it was. Hate was a powerful reason for somebody to leave their grave, if a way could be found to do it.

Parsley, who was in calf, let out a moo and rubbed herself against me, as if she knew I was in a state and wanted to cheer me up. I fell to wondering whether she might miss my master's horse. Sometimes they were put together to graze in the same field, and always seemed perfectly companionable. Different animals can be right together, just as different people can. My master and I were always at ease in each other's company, no matter the gap in our station. Or was I fooling myself? Maybes his eye had been caught by a serving girl at his inn in Dublin, and she was helping him to pass the time agreeably. That was a thought gave me no pleasure, and I buried my face in Parsley's warm flank.

Hooves clattered up whiles my thoughts dallied. It was Frazer Bell and I was about to go out to him, but the mistress appeared at the door, and instead of holding it open to admit him, she pulled it shut behind her. They talked in the yard, Frazer's mount sniffing the ground. I strained to hear them, but their voices were low, until she moved him closer to the cattle stall, where I could follow their conversation.

"It's the house to blame, Frazer. I'm convinced of it."

"There's one way to test your theory. Move her to another house."

"But where?"

"She could come to mine."

"That wouldn't be proper. You're a bachelor – you don't even have a sister to keep up appearances."

"I have a housekeeper."

"Nevertheless, tongues would wag. We must preserve Mary's reputation. It's more important than ever, under the circumstances."

"Why not come too, Mistress Isabel? You could be her custodian."

"I can't leave my own household with James gone from home. The Lord knows, I'd give anything to get away from this place. But it wouldn't be right – James would take it amiss. I've given up trying to spare him worry, and written to ask him to come back to us."

"That was wise of you – he's needed here."

"I see I should have summoned him back before now. I'm sorry I ever invited my cousin here, Frazer. But would Mister Sinclair even permit us to move her? I don't like to speak ill of the minister, but you'd nearly think he relishes what's happening."

I must have made a sound, because they sprang apart as though caught canoodling. This witchery business had everyone looking over their shoulder. Your right hand hardly knowed what the left was doing – and was better off not knowing, forbye. I had no choice but to show myself, trying to look as if I wasn't eavesdropping.

The mistress spoke sharply to me, when I had a perfect right to walk along the yard after seeing to Parsley. "I wish you wouldn't sneak about like that – my nerves are rattled enough."

"Sorry, mistress. I was just headin' back to the prayers. Unless there's anythin' you'd prefer me to do?"

"No, you may rejoin the prayer meeting."

Frazer held the door open for both of us to go indoors, though the mistress was gurney at him giving consideration to a maid. The sound of voices reciting together sailed out. It sounded like Psalm 142. Frazer gave me a wee wink when her back was turned. But all I cared about was the snippet about the mistress bidding my master home. It wouldn't have hurt her to mention it to me. Even though it would take him some days to return to us, just the thought of him pointing his stallion northwards filled me with pleasure. I knowed it was foolish of me, but I couldn't help myself.

☙   ☙   ☙

"The longer this goes on, the more puffed up some folk get," said Peggy, as we toasted our toes at the fire that evening. "Mister Sinclair is cock of the walk these days."

"Aye, he has a strut to match the rooster. Except the rooster keeps hisself a sight cleaner." I allowed myself a wee laugh, but Peggy didn't join in.

"I dinna understand where thon lass comes be the names,"

she said. "She might be fit to say what the witches look like, but to my mind it's strange she can name them."

"She says she hears them call out to each other," I said. Peggy grumbled under her breath, and I asked her straight out, "Do you not believe she's witched?"

"Oh aye, she's witched sure enough." Troubled, she leaned in towards the fire, which showed up the hairs on her chin. "By rights, Hamilton Lock should never be able to quit his grave. The folk that paid him back for his wicked life took steps to pin him to the earth. But it looks as if he did find a way back, and this would be the first place he'd come."

"Does he walk here because his family used to live right here?"

"That'd be reason enough. But there's another, forbye. He died here, too. Out there, in the yard, hard-by the turf stack."

My eyes popped. All these years I'd been filling baskets with turf, never guessing.

"They say the shades of folk who die a violent death are allus drawn back to the place where their blood was spilled," said Peggy.

"But what happened? Why did he die here in the Haltridges' yard?"

Peggy didn't answer and I tried to get her to tell me more, but she let on to be deaf. In the end, I had to leave her be – it was time to go and see about the bairns. These days, Jamesey and the wee missie were tiptoeing round the house like a pair of scared mice. I gave them some gingerbread, and told them a story whiles they ate it. It was a happy story, about a magic kingdom under the sea where nobody grew old.

"Nobody dies there, do they?" asked Sarah.

"Not a soul."

"Good, because then they can't come back to haunt you."

It wrung my heart to hear her. I did my best for them, but it wasn't enough. They couldn't stay in Knowehead House – who knowed what nightmares it was giving them? After that wee wink from Frazer Bell, I decided to approach him. Maybes he could get the childer sent away. I watched for a chance to speak to him, and saw him go out to the yard. I slipped out behind, quick as a hot knife through butter, and found him in the stable with Lordship, his hand on the stallion's neck. That brute of a beast was whinnying, and as true as God the pair of them looked like sweethearts.

"Mister Bell," I began.

He carried on fussing round that animal, but looked over his shoulder at me with a pleasant expression. Which is more than can be said for the stallion: he flared his nostrils and pawed at the straw.

"Sir, it's about the childer. They ought not to be here. Not till there's an end to this business."

"An end to this business." His eyes took on a faraway look, for such a sensible gentleman, and he wasn't seeing the bairns. Then words spilled out of his mouth as if he couldn't hold them in. "Do you know, I wonder if an end is possible? It just seems to grow and grow. First it was that poor creature with the scarred face. Now it's the mother and daughter. At a push, I'm willing to believe the mother might be a witch. But not that gentle girl. Yet Mistress Mary has identified both, and insists they are her tormentors."

"About the childer," I tried again. "Somebody needs to do right by them."

"I'll speak to Mistress Haltridge. Noah Spears can take them to Belfast, to her people. If you look lively, they can be gone by noon. Tell Peggy to get ready to go with them."

"Aye, she'd be as well with a change of air. Between you an' me, I think Peggy is startin' to dote."

"She's not leaving for a change of scene. She's leaving for her own safety. Mary Dunbar has denounced Peggy McGregor as a witch."

"What?" I could hardly believe my ears.

"She named her just now."

200

I gawped. "But the two of them were allus jawin'. They seemed right and friendly. What made her turn so sudden?"

"You're asking for reasons when reason doesn't come into this. It's unfathomable. I can't share the kirk's certainty this is a bewitching. Yet there's no doubt Mistress Dunbar is in considerable distress: mental as well as physical. What can she gain from accusing innocent people? But I'm worried –"

He came up short, covering his face with his hand for a moment. It was a mortal shame to see such a superior gentleman at a loss, though he recovered himself speedily and let on to be stroking those handsome side whiskers.

"Only your mistress and I were present when the accusation was made against Peggy. But if Mistress Dunbar repeats it in front of ministers or elders, they'll treat it seriously. Peggy McGregor needs to get well away from Knowehead – the sooner the better."

And what about me, I wanted to ask? How safe was I here? If names were being thrown about as witches, what was to stop mine being put out there? Mary Dunbar could denounce me as handy as Peggy. My step was leaden as I went back indoors.

⟐   ⟐   ⟐

Mary Dunbar did repeat her accusation. She said it the next day, in front of the mistress and me when I brought the young lady a bowl of beef hash.

She turned up her nose at it. "Did you make that?"

"Peggy does the most of the cookin'. All I done was scoop it out of the pot over the fire."

"She's trying to poison me. Peggy McGregor is one of them. She's a witch."

"Ach, no, Mistress Mary," I began, but the mistress spoke over me.

"You're mistaken, Mary," she said, tart, as if scolding

Jamesey and Sarah. "How come you've only started mentioning this? Surely you'd have recognised Peggy before now?"

"I never saw her in Lock's Cave. But I saw her last night, when the coven met somewhere else."

"Where?"

"In a humble sort of cabin, I don't know where. Peggy tried to hide her face from me, but I knew her at once. Not all the witches go to every meeting – three or four at a time are sufficient to work a spell. They only need the full coven if they intend to do mischief on a grand scale."

"Peggy's an old woman, barely able to get about."

"Oh, Isabel, why do you doubt me? She flew there on a goose she calls Vinegar. He answers her bidding when she whistles for him."

"Mary, please stop this. Peggy McGregor wouldn't hurt a fly."

"She slapped me on the face. When she saw that I knew her, she was filled with fury, and had two of her sisters hold me. Then she lifted her arm above her shoulder and let fly with the flat of her hand. She was trying to make me cry. When I wouldn't, she said I'd end up in a bawdy house where I'd truly have cause to weep."

"Peggy has a stiff arm – she can raise it no higher than her elbow. For the love of God, Mary, be careful who you accuse."

"Maybe her master has cured it."

"James is no physician."

"I mean her unearthly master – Hamilton Lock."

The mistress caught hold of her cousin by the wrist. "Listen to me carefully. Peggy McGregor has served this household faithfully these many long years, and I cannot tolerate accusations being made against her. Especially in connection with that vile name."

"I'll tell the minister you're trying to silence me. And the Constable."

The mistress let her go brave and smart.

While this was going on, I remembered all the potions and salves Peggy was forever brewing up. She said the receipts were passed down through her family. But was it possible some of them were not come by honestly? I had shared a bed with Peggy McGregor for seven years, but how well did I really know her? And then I shook myself. Doubt begets doubt.

"Eat your hash, Mistress Mary," I wheedled, the way you would with a child. "You've wasted away since you come among us." I signed to the mistress, and she copied me.

"Do, Mary, there's a good girl. We need to bring some roses back into your cheeks."

"Mister Bell is worried to see you so pale, Mistress Mary," I put in.

Mary picked up the spoon.

"Aunt Dunbar won't be a bit pleased with the care we've taken of you when she sees you again," said the mistress.

The spoon clattered on the table. "Are you sending me home, Isabel?"

"Well, of course you'll go home some time. This is only a visit."

"But I'm not ready to leave. Don't make me."

"I couldn't, even if I wanted to. I had a letter from your mother today. Scarlet fever has broken out in Armagh. It wouldn't be safe for you to go home. Though how safe it is for you here, I'm at a loss to say."

"I like Islandmagee. I've never liked anywhere half so well."

The mistress flashed a look of surprise at me, and I was thinking the same as her. How could anybody like a place where they were bewitched?

"I know I've been plagued by witches here, but I couldn't bear to leave the island. Not now."

It dawned on me she must feel important, with ministers and elders hanging on her every word.

Mary Dunbar said, "You know, Isabel, maybe it wasn't Peggy McGregor I saw, after all. Maybe it was somebody who looked like her."

"Yes, that could be it. Just remember we all love Peggy here, particularly my husband. James would be devastated if anything happened to her." She stroked her cousin's curls. They hung limp now, in need of a wash. "Mary, we think it best to move you from this house to another one on the island – to test whether it's only here in Knowehead you're bewitched. I've spoken to Mister Sinclair about it. He's willing to have you stay with him."

"Mistress, is that wise? At least we can watch over Mistress Mary here. Who knows what might happen, and none of the family there to see about her?" I was choosing my words carefully in front of the young lady. What I really meant was at least we could keep a check on what she said – and who she denounced. But the mistress didn't catch on.

"I have discussed it with both Mister Sinclair and the Reverend Mister Arnold. They will protect her."

"Aye, but –"

"It's not your place to say 'but' to me, Ellen. Now, Mary, Frazer Bell recommends this course of action. James values his advice, and so do I."

"I trust Mister Bell. But I don't want to leave Knowehead," said Mary.

"Only for a wee while. To help you get better."

"Why do I have to go to Mister Sinclair's house?"

"He'd be on hand to pray over you. The minister is better able to watch over you than anybody else."

The young lady wrinkled her forehead. It took no stretch of the imagination to see she preferred a bed under Frazer Bell's roof than the minister's.

The mistress spotted the gurn on her. "Your safekeeping is our chief concern, Mary. You must try settling into another house, just for a few days."

"Of course I'll be guided by you. I know I'm causing you trouble. Oh Isabel, it's so good to get away from my father's house in Armagh. I felt stifled there."

"But you're beset here. You're the target of witchcraft." The mistress swallowed, and when her voice came out again it trembled. "Mary, there's something I've been meaning to ask you. This Mistress Anne you mention from time to time among your tormenters. Is she – do you think she might be – James's mother?"

"I never met the other Mistress Haltridge."

"But is she young or old? Tall or short? Fat or lean?"

"I'm not certain, Isabel, I've never had a close look at her. All I can tell you is this: the others dance to her tune. She has mastery over the witches, and Hamilton Lock has mastery over her. They seek mastery over me, too. But I will not yield. To her – or to him."

"I see. Spoken like a true Christian. Now, I must make sure the children are packed for their trip to Belfast. We have the loan of a carriage from the Reverend Mister Arnold, and Noah Spears is charged with driving it. I do hope he takes proper care. Noah is better used to carts than carriages."

"Send the wee pets in to say farewell to me, Isabel."

"I'm sorry, I cannot allow that, my dear."

"Why ever not?"

"It's not a good idea." She brushed down her skirts, avoiding her guest's eye.

When we were alone, Mary Dunbar appealed to me. "Will you bring Sarah and Jamesey in to me before they go?"

I shook my head.

"Why not?"

"If you bain't goin' to eat this hash, I'll set it aside for the greyhounds."

"Don't change the subject. Why can't I see Sarah and Jamesey? Tell me why. Or are you too much under my cousin's thumb to answer?"

Her taunt needled. "Because the childer are scared stiff of you."

She shrivelled up at that. Grown men and women being frightened of you was one thing, but nobody wants bairns cringing away. "I'd never do anything to hurt them. Does Mister Bell think I'd harm the children?"

"I'm sure he knows you'd do no such thing, Mistress Mary. A wee bird tould me Mister Bell admires you."

"Does he?" She smiled. "It's not my fault the Devil is trying to wind his way into my heart. I do my best to defy him. Mister Sinclair says women have always been easier to lead astray, ever since the serpent tempted Eve and caused the Fall of Man. But I'm resisting him with all my strength. I doubt if you could hold out against him the way I do."

"I doubt I could."

That pleased her. Still, she was regretful about the childer. "I should have liked to kiss Sarah and Jamesey goodbye."

"I'll do it for you, mistress."

"I wish you would." She hesitated. "Does the Devil never use his snares on you?"

"Ach aye, I've been tempted to badness – I would'n be human if I was never tempted."

"What kind of badness?"

I flushed at the memory of my master's eyes, cloudy with desire. "That'll do, now, Mistress Mary. I've no more time to stand about chitterin'."

❧   ❧   ❧

Frazer Bell came into the kitchen to wish Peggy godspeed. She looked relieved to be leaving, though she always insisted she hated travelling because it rattled her bones and left her noddled. He reported – in a glum voice – how excited Mister Sinclair was to have Mary Dunbar staying with him.

"I'm inclined to think the minister has witchfever," he said.

"Some are calling him the witch-hunter. Not everybody means it as a compliment."

"You stay well out of it, lad," said Peggy.

"I have to watch out for your master's interests."

"Aye, but look to your own while you're at it. A pretty face can cozen a man."

He laughed. "Peggy, I'm not one and twenty any more – my head's not turned by looks."

"You're a man – your head'll be turned be looks till the day you go into the ground. You mind what I'm tellin' you. Keep your distance."

He went out ahead of us to the carriage, and I gave Peggy McGregor some nuts for the childer, to pass the journey. She went to put them in her apron pocket, before recalling it was packed.

"Will you be able for the cooking, Ellen?"

"I should be, you taught me well."

"You're a quick learner. Remember not to use too much salt, and taste as you go along. You'll have a lot on your plate now, takin' on my job as well."

"I'll do my best. The mistress said we can send out the washin' and mendin' while you're gone, and buy in our bread. I daresay we'll get by."

"I daresay." The greyhounds set up a-yipping and a-yapping in the yard. "That reminds me, keep them dogs out of the rhubarb patch, or there'll be no crop come May. The master's fond of a rhubarb tart. By the by – you watch out for that master of ours. I've knowed him all his life, and he's good-hearted, but he's a man when all's said and done. He may give you soft words, but think on. Soft words butter no parsnips. You cannae rely on them."

"I don't know what you mean," I said. But I couldn't meet her eye.

"Plain girls are more at risk than pretty ones. If a man pays them attention, it turns their heads. I'm tellin' you this for your own good, lassie."

Cheeks on fire, I ran outside.

The childer were already in the carriage. They looked peaky, bless their hearts. Wee Jamesey had it in his head he was meant to be the man of the house till my master came home, and he was sorely torn about leaving. As for Sarah, she sucked her thumb like a baby, a habit we thought her cured of at least twelve months since. Frazer Bell was sitting in beside them, trying to raise a smile with his parlour trick. It was a knack he had, of balancing an egg on its end, and I've yet to meet anyone else who can repeat the trick. But Sarah and Jamesey barely looked at it. It was poor timing for them to be leaving finally, just as Mary Dunbar was on the point of going away too. But it was too risky to keep the bairns. Who knowed if the badness in Knowehead House would stay with us or follow her?

Peggy shuffled out, and I hurried to help her. While the mistress hugged the children, Peggy crooked her finger and whispered some parting words to me.

"I'd best tell you why Hamilton Lock would do the Haltridges down if he got the chance. Knowin' might help you guard the family's interests, when I bain't here to do it. I didnae see Hamilton Lock die, but I seen him pinned to the ground, and the menfolk talkin' over what they meant to do to him. Not everybody wanted to kill him. Some said he should be given a good hidin' and others were for handin' him over to the Constable. And then the minister spoke up." Her voice tailed off.

"Quick, Peggy, afore the mistress calls you to get in the carriage. What did he say?"

"He said *'An eye for an eye and a tooth for a tooth'*. Hamilton Lock had killed his own da, and had to pay for it. It sealed his fate. A great shout went up, and there was no more arguin' about what to do wi' him. Minister Haltridge saw what was comin' next and tould me and the other women to go on home quick. I seen one thing before I left, though. I seen Hamilton Lock spit at the minister's feet, and rain a dyin' man's curses down on him. He knowed the minister could a saved him. I think the minister had a bad conscience about it. He wrote it all down, gettin' it off his chest. Took hisself to his study and scribbled there all the next day. He tould me it was as well to have a record of Hanilton Lock's death. Not that everybody would a thanked him for it."

Creaking and grunting, Peggy climbed into the carriage with my help.

At that, Noah hupped to the horse, and the mistress cried out, "Keep the children well wrapped up if they go out in the evening, Peggy! The night air is dangerous!"

ᚼ   ᚼ   ᚼ

The breakfast dishes wouldn't wash themselves and the next meal needed a start made on it. Still, I took a break from my labours to watch Frazer Bell lift Mary Dunbar onto Lordship's saddle as if she was made of porcelain, to bring her to the minister's house. You should have seen the way he fussed over her. I thought he might have jumped on behind, and folded his arms round her to hold the reins. But he was not a gentleman to seek advantage. He set off on foot, leading Lordship by the bridle. I thought of my master, far away in Dublin. Did he think of me, at all, as he went about his business? As he ate, and drank, and lay down to sleep? I swallowed. Dwelling on the ifs and ans of my master in his bed at night would only give me unclean thoughts, and who knowed where that might lead. There was danger in dallying with my master, as I knew to my cost.

For the first time, there was just the mistress and me in Knowehead. She took to her bed – didn't even bother claiming she had the ague. I suspect she was just plain wore out, and wanted to rest herself. Bairns aren't the only ones like to put their heads under the covers from time to time. Still, it's an ill wind blows nobody any good, because it gave me a chance to hunt for the old minister's version of how Hamilton Lock died.

Maybes it was luck, or maybes it was somebody directing me where to look, but I found what I wanted quickly in my master's study. The old minister's Bible, tattered from a lifetime of use, lived in a glass-covered bookcase there. It wasn't often taken out – the family had their own Bible – but I knowed about it from doing the dusting. I hopped up on a chair and lifted it down.

John Haltridge was written in a dead man's hand. On the next page I saw my master's name, and the date he was born. Above and below it was a list of other babies, stillborn or living but a day or two. Mistress Anne Haltridge had it hard. I held the book by its spine and shook it. A dried-out leaf floated onto the desk, which somebody must have been using as a marker. It was followed by some loose sheets of paper, folded up and blackened at the edges as if rescued from a fire. Minister Haltridge's was a pinched script, not easy to read, but I ran my eyes over it again and again until the words took shape. It was an account of not one but two deaths. The first page was missing but I was able to follow the story.

. . . went immediately to see that his remains were accorded a Christian burial. His skull had been put in by a rock – the murder weapon left lying beside the victim of this Monstrous Crime, his blood barely dry on it. Such was the violence of the attack that splinters of bone and matter were protruding from his head. The parishioner who heard the altercation between father and son, and discovered the dead man in a pool of blood, informed me a lump of rock from the Stone was used to cave in his skull. There are pieces of it scattered about the earth still, though we tumbled it some years ago. The Stone had a distinctive yellowish hue, like no other stone on the island. I confess, the sight of it as a murder weapon reassured

me that I was right to have that Pagan Symbol pulled down, filled with misgivings though I was at seeing the use to which some of its leftovers were put.

However, I went ahead and performed my duty by reading from my Bible over George Lock's murdered corpse. He was more wedded to alcohol than was either proper or seemly, and less than regular in his attendance at the meeting-house, but it was a deplorable death. My wrath knew no bounds. Finally, Hamilton Lock had tried our patience too far. Since his return from Scotland, I had occasion to warn him about his behaviour frequently. He crossed my path more often than not, always loitering about my barn on account of his cabin having stood there once. The man sneered at my attempts to set him on the road to righteousness, and claimed I was an interloper on his land. Me, here by invitation from the good folk of Islandmagee, labouring day and night in the Lord's service. It was insolent, although typical of Lock. But never could I have imagined that he would stray so far from the path of the just.

After seeing the evidence of his Brutality in the form of his father's pitiful remains, I understood Lock was a diseased limb which needed to be hacked off before it corrupted the community. I called a prayer meeting, and preached a sermon reminding my flock how patricide is the most Heinous crime known to man – contrary to God's laws and man's. It goes against the rules of nature to steal life from him whose seed gave life to a man. My denunciations were passionate, I admit it freely, and my listeners were all attention. I told them a bolt of lightning from the heavens would wither the hand that turns against its father. I dwelled on his Barbarity – nay, his BESTIALITY. Scarcely had I concluded before the men rose of one accord, shouting that they would make Hamilton Lock pay for his crime. They were fired by outrage, and all impatience at the thought of waiting for the law to stretch his neck. I ought to have stopped them. There was still time to prevent their retribution. But I did not raise my voice against this Tide of Vengeance. I did not urge them to turn the other cheek. Alas, I must recognize my fault: I revelled in their passion – it matched my own. I, too, was incensed by this ultimate act of dishonour from son to father, a perversion of the most important kinship known to man. I regarded it as evidence of Satan's presence among us.

The kirk emptied of all the men. I tarried to reassure the women, and to order them to wait together there – though not all of them heeded me. When I caught up with my flock, they had tracked Hamilton Lock to my barn, and dragged him out. He was pinned to the ground with stakes and ropes a few yards from my front door. Even so, the miscreant remained defiant. From a bloody mouth, he laughed at them, taunting the men. Now that they had him, they were unsure what course of action to take, and debated it back and forth. Not everybody wanted to kill him. Some said he should be beaten soundly, others wanted to brand him on the forehead, the way the Lord God marked Cain.

And then they saw me. "Tell us what to do, Mister Haltridge," they said. "Give us guidance."

I looked at Hamilton Lock, and I did not see a man. I saw a beast crawling on its belly. I quoted from Matthew 5: 38. "An eye for an eye and a tooth for a tooth," I said. A roar went up, and Hamilton Lock's fate was sealed. Jeremiah Baxter had a rope, and made a noose for Lock's neck. Davy Holmes said hanging was too handy for such a fiend. "Press him to death," he shouted. Everybody looked at me, to see if I objected. I held my tongue. "Aye, press him to death!" they roared. Holmes spied my cart in the barn, and yoked my horse to it. Even now, there was still time to call for calm. But I stood by. Let him take his just desserts. Lock broke his father's skull – let him suffer broken bones in every part of his body.

Lock showed no fear as the talk went on round him – rather, he writhed, working at his bonds, struggling like a demon hot *from hell to set himself free. However, he was bound too tightly. Just before the horse and cart were driven over him, I gave Hamilton Lock the opportunity to own his sins, and ask the Merciful Lord's forgiveness. I told him he would fare better in the afterlife if he went to the Redeemer with the Abominable Stain on his conscience acknowledged. He spat at my feet, and rained curses down on me and mine. Even unto the seventh generation. At that, I nodded to Holmes at the reins. The cart trundled forward. The horse picked its way across the man, but the wheels were not so dainty. They passed over Lock's chest and legs, again and again, crushing the breath out of him. I heard his bones snap. I heard him labour to suck in air. But I did not hear him beg for mercy. Finally,* ~~troubled~~ *nauseated by what I had authorized, I turned my eyes away – unable to see it through to the end, and stay to inspect his battered carcass. Already, I knew it was no day's work to be proud of, and I . . .*

There was no more. Dazed, I pushed the pages back into the Bible, pictures of Hamilton Lock's last minutes tumbling round my head. Then and there, I had no doubt but that his ghost was hounding the Haltridges. I feared for the family. Aye, and I feared for myself, living in their house.

  ✺ ✺ ✺

I thought the mistress might have given me a half-day off to walk over to Carnspindle to see my ma and da, with only the two of us in Knowehead, but no such luck. The long and short of it was that Mistress Haltridge didn't want to be left on her lone in the house.

"With the help of God, our difficulties are at an end, now that my cousin is safe in the care of Mister Sinclair. You do think our difficulties are over, don't you?"

"It all depends, mistress."

"On what?"

"On the cause."

She chewed the end of her plait. "Perhaps you should call to the minister's house to inquire about how my cousin is settling in. But you wouldn't be gone long, would you? You could be back in an hour or so?"

"I can skip over and back in next to no time, mistress."

"No, leave it, you might get delayed, and then how would I manage? If there was anything amiss, we'd hear about it – bad news travels faster than forked lightning. Perhaps that maid of his will come to see you. She's always gadding about."

"Mercy Hunter might come a-callin'. She's dyin' about company."

"Very well. Leave it for today. If we hear nothing by the-morrow, you may run over to Mister Sinclair with a note from me."

"As you wish, mistress."

"But you'd promise not to stay away long? And you'd make sure to be back before dark?"

"Walkin' through fields at night does'n bother me. I'm not un'asied by the dark."

Her brow puckered, and I saw it wasn't my safety she was concerned about. Right then, I was all Mistress Haltridge had, and she needed me near-hand. The long and the short of it was she didn't want to be alone in her own house.

Alone, with whatever else was inside it.

Chapter 11

Mercy Hunter couldn't tear herself away from the minister's house, with the excitement of a witched lass in their midst, so I walked over to Ballymuldrough to deliver the mistress's message the following morning. Heavens above, but the place was in a flap: it was like walking into a henhouse after a visit from Master Fox. Mary Dunbar was missing.

I never saw Mister Sinclair so through-other. He wrung his hands like a big lump of a cuddy, maithering on about how he was responsible for her safety, and he didn't know how she could have vanished from under his eyes. Luckily David Arnold, the Church of Ireland curate, had the sense to organize a search party, with the help of Bob Holmes. The elder was giving out hand-bells so that if anyone found Mary Dunbar they could let the others know.

"How come yiz lost her?" I asked Mercy.

"Was it our job to lock her in? We thought she was here of her own free will."

"But did she leave of her own free will?"

"Aye, that's the question."

We looked at the men gathered in the yard, waiting for their orders.

"The house has been overrun with clergy since she landed

in here. Look at them, they're like crows." She nodded towards a group in black. "Mind you, even men of God have a vain streak. The smaller the man, the bigger the buckles on his shoon."

"Did anythin' happen the whiles she was here, Mercy? Was she troubled by witches?"

"It was quiet as the grave. Apart from all the ministers prayifyin' over her. Mister Sinclair was full of conceit, thinkin' no witchin' was possible inside his four walls. But he fairly guldered me name the-day, afore the dew was lifted off the grass. Such a state he was in, jiggin' from foot to foot, yellin' at me to search the house because the young lady was gone from her bedchamber. I looked high and low, and Thomas Kane went through the outhouses, but n'ether hide nor hair of her we found."

"The Constable will have to be tould," I said.

"Thomas has gone for him. The minister's hopin' the young lady will turn up afore he gets here. Between you, me and the wall, he's none too pleased about lookin' foolish in front of Brice Blan."

Mister Arnold was splitting the men into pairs, directing them to where they should search, when I went up and bobbed a curtsey. "Pardon me, sir. I'm the Haltridges' maid."

"State your business."

"Well, sir, Mistress Dunbar was allus talkin' about Lock's Cave. She said the witches took her to it, to work their magic. She might be there now."

"I see." He signalled to Bob Holmes. "I understood Lock's Cave was watched. But this young person believes Mistress Dunbar may be there."

"There was a pair of men livin' nearby kept an eye on it for a time, but I could'n rightly say if they're still watchin' it. They never saw nothin' suspicious. They might a give up."

"The caves must be seached, starting with Lock's Cave. Who can you send?"

"Edward Baxter, Billy Nelson and his brother Adam. Three sound men."

"Double the numbers. We must act on all information."

After the minister bustled off, Bob Holmes said, "Thonder cave's no place for a Christian soul to set foot."

"Aye. But Mary Dunbar said the witches gathered there because Lock's power was strong, on account of what was throwed in a hole in the cave."

"What do you know about that?"

"I ken it's where his skull was buried."

"And the rest of him?"

I met his eye fair and square. "You should know, Bob Holmes. Peggy McGregor says your people helped do what was done to his body."

"Aye, she has the right of it. My father joined in with what had to be done. Lock was the very offal of a man. As vicious as he was avaricious. He cud'n go into sacred soil on account of the monstrous sins he committed. And he did'n deserve to be put complete into the ground e'ther. The men from about here, we cut him up – it was the right thing to do."

"Maybes, but killin' him didn't put paid to him. His shade was left free to wander Islandagee."

"Impossible. We dug holes and pinned each part of him into the ground with a hazel stake. It was done so he cud'n walk again."

"The head, too?"

"Not the head. Nobody could bring themselves to touch it any more than they could help. My father said the sight of the leer on his face would unman you. Besides, a hazel stake wud'n pierce a skull. No, it was hidden away separate to the rest of the body."

"The job was on'y half-done, then."

Bob Holmes took his pipe out of his mouth and studied me, the way he'd look a cow over. "Ellen Hill, there's more to you than meets the eye."

"Better that than less to me than meets the eye."

"Are you sayin' we need to find the skull, and pin it to the earth – with a metal spike, maybes?"

"It might put an end to our troubles."

"Mister Sinclair would call it a heathen act."

"He would, sir."

He nodded. "I'll tell the men searching Lock's Cave to dig for the skull."

               ◖◖◖   ◖◖◖   ◖◖◖

"Dear Lord, is she wandering Islandmagee in her nightgown?" asked the mistress.

"Mercy Hunter said Mistress Dunbar's cloak and gown were gone."

"We must thank the Almighty for small mercies." She walked to the casement and looked out. "Was any mention made of Mistress Anne Haltridge?"

"Not that I heared."

"My cousin didn't talk about her at the minister's house, before she went missing?"

"Mercy Hunter never mentioned it, mistress."

"Good." She ran her finger over the shutter, checking it was dust-free, but her mind was elsewhere. "I can't help worrying –"

"Aye, mistress?"

"I shouldn't even say it. But it's been preying on my mind. I feel her presence in this house. It's as if she never left it."

"Mistress Mary?"

"No, Ellen, my husband's mother. I fear she might be part of these disturbances. Even though I helped wash her body, and prepare her for the grave with my own hands. The minister says she's dead and gone, and I mustn't keep trying to bring her back to life. To do that is to question God's design. But I feel she has unfinished business here, and wasn't

218

ready to be taken." She bowed her head into her chest, voice muffled. "I know what folk say."

"Folk get bees in their bonnets. They say more'n they should."

"They say Mistress Anne Haltridge lies restless in her grave."

"You must put such thoughts out of your mind, mistress. They'll only serve to fash you."

"I cannot help it. They overwhelm me. Oh sweet Lord, I wish I had never agreed to Mary coming to this house. Or leaving it either, unless it was to go home to her parents. Aunt Dunbar entrusted her to my care, and I have failed her. I should have listened to you, Ellen. You didn't want her going to Mister Sinclair's house. Oh Mary, Mary, what's to become of you?"

            ᠻᢁ   ᠻᢁ   ᠻᢁ

That afternoon, while I scoured the chamber pots at the back of the house, Mercy Hunter appeared at my side.

"My master thinks I'm fetching a jug of buttermilk from you. His corns have him crippled."

"He'll need to steep his feet for at least two hours in hot buttermilk to draw them out. A wee dabble is no good," I said.

"Ach, he can do as he likes. I bain't his skivvy."

I was glad to leave my task, and lead her into the kitchen. "Any news of Mary Dunbar?"

"None. Frazer Bell is headin' one of the search parties. He says she could be lyin' in a shuck with a broken leg. My master says if that's all's the matter with her, he'll be content."

"He fears the coven has her?"

"Aye. If thon's the case, she's better off dead an' buried."

"But, Mercy, the searchers might still be in time to save her."

"My master says the witches must a gathered for one of their unholy Sabbaths last night, to spirit her away. They must a cast a spell over our household, because none heared the young lady leave. Elders were sittin' up in the kitchen, whilin' away the hours of darkness, but they seen nothin'. By the by, Constable Blan has another witch. Mary Dunbar described her in detail yesterday, and was able to give part of her name. They brought in three women, just to be on the safe side, and she picked one out."

"Who is it?"

"Kate McAlmond – she lives up Balloo direction. She says she spent the night with a neighbour. But the minister says that makes no odds. It's well known witches can send their shapes to do their biddin' when their bodies are somewhere else. The Constable's men have Kate McAlmond in the stable, tryin' to get her to give up her partners in sin."

"Have you seen her? Does she look guilty?"

"I cud'n resist a wee keek. Even though me granny says a witch'll curse you, quick as look at you. She was jukin' down in the straw, shiverin' on account of the Constable havin' her ducked in the cattle trough to put manners on her. But she tould him nothin'."

Lightning was striking here, there and everywhere on Islandmagee. It could be any one of us next, I thought.

"Cat got your tongue, Ellen? Shove over there, you have the cosiest spot in the house." She jammed her shanks against mine on the wee seat I favoured.

"Mercy, if I was locked up, would you come and see me?"

"Why would you be locked up?"

"Innocent people go to gaol. Mistakes get made."

"The master says witches have deserted God, and anybody does that, they deserve to be punished. Bad enough if you're a heathen and never knowed God, says he, but to be given His grace and turn your back on it is beyond the pale. You'll burn in hell for all eternity, and the demons will laugh at your screams as they feed the fire." She stared into the flames.

By and by, I asked her did she want a drop of something. My master never noticed if we slipped the odd glass out of his bottles, and Mercy liked a sup when the chance came her way. There was never any drink in the minister's house.

"Naw, I have no stomach for it. I hear the searchers are goin' over Lock's Cave with a fine-tooth comb. Bob Holmes is mighty exercised about it."

"Aye, Mary Dunbar has a thing about Hamilton Lock."

"Why should she care about him?"

"Maybes on account of all the badness he got up to. She seems to find him . . . well, I har'ly like to say."

"What?"

"Excitin'. She's allus askin' after him."

"He was a wrong 'un, by all accounts. But sure all that was years ago."

"Some wrongs need to be righted," I said. "No matter how long it takes."

"What's that got to do with Mary Dunbar being witched, Ellen?"

"Nothin'. Just thinkin' out loud."

"Right and wrong. Wrong and right. Your head'd be noddled tryin' to tell them apart. I'm fed up of Islandmagee, so I am. Ellen, why don't you and me shake the dust of it off our feet? I've heared about assisted passages to the New World. We could ship out and be somethin' called an indentured servant, in Philadelphia or some such place, and work off the debt over time."

"Ach no, I couldn't bear to stand on the deck of a ship, watchin' Islandmagee disappear. I belong here."

"Well, I don't. I'll just have to go on me own then." Mercy cracked her knuckles, and tried to give her cheeky grin. "Anyhow, time I was on me way back to Ballymuldrough. No rest for the wicked." But it was only a ghost of a smile.

﹡﹡﹡﹡﹡﹡

Frazer Bell found Mary Dunbar, round about the time Mercy Hunter and I were yarning. She was soaked to the skin, lying hidden by rushes in the boggy field hard-by Larne Lough. There was a deep cut on her scalp, where she must have tripped and hit herself on something sharp, before passing out.

Frazer carried her in to us.

"Thank God," said the mistress, followed by, "What came over you, Mary?"

"I had to get back to Knowehead. The house was calling me."

"Why?"

"I answer its need."

"Best leave the questions till she's had a chance to rest," said Frazer Bell. "She wouldn't have lasted too many more hours out there in the fields."

I mixed Mary Dunbar one of Peggy McGregor's tonics, while she was put to bed with a hot jar and happed up warm as toast. The mistress dressed her cut and said she would sit with her through the night. I offered to share the watch, but she was afraid to let Mary out of her sight.

"It's on my conscience I nearly lost her, Ellen," she said.

Frazer Bell and Noah Spears were still in the house when I went downstairs. Their voices carried along the passage.

"Bob Holmes had us crawlin' over every inch of Lock's Cave," said Noah. "He was'n just lookin' for the lassie, whatever he was after. He would'n tell us, though – just that we'd know it when we found it."

"And did you?"

"Hard to say. We come upon something had the minister hoppin' about, mind you. 'Twas a wee poppet, of wood and wool, with a lock of Mary Dunbar's hair on its head, an' one of her ribbons wrapped round its body. Mister Sinclair says witches use them dolls for their charms."

֍ ֍ ֍

A letter came from my master, saying he was making arrangements to return to us, and it put a spring in the mistress's step – aye, and in mine, too, for all my need to tread carefully. I was never done running as more clergymen rolled up from far and wide for a gawp at Mary Dunbar. Islandmagee had never been so popular. Bob Holmes dropped by, and whispered to me there was no skull found in Lock's Cave. "Maybes the witches took it with them, to use wherever else the coven meets," says he.

Just as I was thinking there was nobody left to come a-calling, doesn't the Lord Mayor of Carrickfergus himself pay us a visit. And no wonder, with his gaol being filled by this one lass. Constable Blan brought him in, looking like the cat that got the cream as he presented him. The mistress was equally impressed, rustling about in a flame-coloured silk petticoat in honour of all her important visitors. She ordered milk punch to warm them up. It was well into March, but spring was backward that year, the few leaves barely taking the bare look off the trees. I heated some of Parsley's creamy milk, and added whiskey, sugar and nutmeg. It smelled so tasty, I couldn't resist a sip from each goblet before I carried through the tray.

The Mayor was a full-bellied gentleman by the name of Henry Davies. He dressed like an earl with rings the size of pigeon's eggs, and a coat with shoulder knots and a fur collar to keep chills at arm's length, as befitted the first citizen of Carrickfergus. His people were Welsh, and had done well for themselves. They pranced round as though born to lord it over us. None of them made old bones, mind you. All wealth and no health.

The Mayor took a pinch of snuff from a silver box in his waistcoat pocket, brought it to his nose and sneezed. He looked delighted with himself, once his eyes stopped watering.

"Nothing like it for clearing the head," said the Constable, though a good sneeze would have snapped him in two.

The Mayor let fly again, and Blan moved sideways.

The Mayor was full of his beehive, which produced the best honey in the land, according to him. Constable Blan nodded away at every blessed thing the Mayor said, but the mistress wasn't cut out for discussing husbandry. As soon as there was a pause, she volunteered me to fetch Mary Dunbar, who was resting. In fairness to the young lady, it must have been tiring having ministers constantly watching you to see if you were possessed, and quoting Hosiah and Exodus and what not.

"Before she arrives," said the Mayor, "I should warn you that I need to study this young person. We cannot rule out madness instead of witchcraft."

"Madness? Impossible." The mistress was put out at the slur, but she couldn't give the Mayor a piece of her mind. She looked to the Constable to back her up, but he knowed which side his piece was buttered.

The Mayor sipped his milk punch, and touched a handkerchief to his lips. "Unfortunately, it is possible. It is an explanation we have to consider. We must not presume witchcraft."

"I can assure your lordship, my cousin was perfectly sane till she came to Islandmagee. But naturally you must judge for yourself."

The interview started off civilly, with Constable Blan keeping in the background as the Mayor told Mary Dunbar he trusted she was on the mend, now that the women accused of scourging her were behind bars.

"Rest assured, we are moving swiftly to ascertain who – and what – lies behind these noxious acts committed against your person. Four women, all from Islandmagee, have been interrogated, and their examinations noted down. I am here to decide whether there is a prima facie case against them, and if they should be committed for trial."

"Mister Sinclair says it's the worst case of witchcraft he's ever encountered, your lordship," said Mary.

"Mister Sinclair is not the judge of this. A court of law needs evidence. None of the women you named have been in trouble before. There is nothing recorded against their reputations."

"Mister Sinclair says that's because witches are possessed of low cunning."

The Mayor raised an eyebrow. "Mister Sinclair is quite the expert. Now, is the bewitching at an end with four prisoners in my custody?"

"Oh no, your lordship. I'm still crucified by witches." She screwed up her dimpled face. "They torment me all the harder because I've given up the others."

"What are the names of your attackers? Where do they live? Where do they meet to cast their spells? It's your duty to denounce then."

"I want to do my duty, your lordship. They meet in different places now, to escape capture. Sometimes it's in a cattleshed, sometimes out in the open."

"And their names?"

"They come to me piecemeal: I can't bring them to mind all at once. At times, I only hear part of a name."

"But you must lead us to those who torment you. We will examine them, and see what they have to say for themselves."

"There is one witch I can easily describe. She has a hand like a claw, all twisted up into a fist and turned in on her body, and –" Mary Dunbar let out a howl, bending her head back as if her hair was given a sharp yank. She shook her head free and ran under the table, crouching there.

Mayor Davies nodded at some of the deputies, who helped her to crawl back out.

225

"I can say nothing more at present, sir. If I speak, my tongue will burst into flames and consume me."

The Mayor rounded on the Constable, his voice cold. "One of the women you brought in on this person's say-so is known to attend her kirk regularly. A witch couldn't kneel in God's house and pray. It's common knowledge."

The Constable's men grinned behind their hands at their master's discomfort, and I wasn't sorry to have him put back in his box.

"Somebody fetch my hat, I've seen enough," said the Mayor.

I followed him outside to where his coach was waiting. It was pulled by a pair of matched greys, their tails docked short so they wouldn't tangle in the harness or reins. A footman was mounted behind the coach, to open and shut the doors and carry a torch when it was dark. Before the Mayor climbed in, he stopped to give instructions to another footman trotting at his heels.

All at once a rumble came from the roof. It happened so fast, nobody saw it coming. A heavy chimney pot slid off the chimney stack, sailed down the roof as if gliding on ice, and crashed to the ground a matter of inches from the Mayor's head. The Constable barked an order, while the mistress rushed up and fussed over the Mayor.

He looked shaken. "There's no wind today. It's as still as the grave," he kept repeating.

"Is your roof in disrepair, Mistress Haltridge?" asked the Constable.

"No, James would never permit it. He's most particular about such things." The mistress stared at the broken remains of the chimney pot, while Mary Dunbar came to the door, looking equally dumbfounded.

"Step inside, Mayor Davies, while my men investigate this," said the Constable.

"Wild horses wouldn't drag me back inside that house." The Mayor rubbed at his chest.

Meanwhile, two deputies appeared with our ladder. They must have been poking round the outhouses earlier, because they knowed where to find it. They laid it against the side of the house and climbed up to check the roof. All eyes followed the pair as they prodded the remaining pots on the stack.

The Mayor stopped petting himself long enough to cup a hand round his mouth. "Have you found anything?" he called.

They shook their heads, scrambled down the ladder and approached Brice Blan.

"Steady as a rock up there, Constable. No reason for what happened."

"I can find a reason," said the Mayor. "Witches must be given no quarter. It's a mistake to show mercy, Constable Blan. Witchcraft breeds more witchcraft and infects the entire community."

The Constable stood to attention. "There'll be no slackness on my part, your lordship. I'll round up every last one of these women."

The Mayor whipped off his hat and bowed over Mary Dunbar's hand. "Mistress, you have been chosen for an important task. We rely on you for a complete list of every person you suspect to be members of the coven here on Islandmagee. Don't hold back. Describe them if you cannot name them. Constable, stay with the young lady, make a note of everything she tells you, and act on it at once. I'll send to the Castle for extra militia to assist your work. This must take precedence over everything." He drove away, still craning from his carriage window towards the roof.

The Mayor was easy swayed the minute he found himself in danger. When you get right down to it, fine folk and common folk aren't much to the differ.

As soon as his party was lost to sight, the mistress turned to me. "What shall I do about the chimney? It must be fixed, and Noah is too old to go climbing about on a roof."

227

"The minister's man, Thomas Kane, is said to be handy at that kind of work."

"I'll send at once and beg the loan of him."

"I'll fetch my shawl, mistress."

"No, not you. I need you here, Ellen. I'm sure the Mayor's servant will run the errand for me, if I slip him a coin."

She waved to the footman who had been ordered to stay behind, to gather up the remains of the chimney pot and bring them with him for evidence. He agreed to take the message, and while he tarried for her to write it, we passed the time of day.

"Your master looked quare and put out," I said.

"He's got it into his head witches are after him now. He wants some of the plasterwork taken down from an outside wall of his house, and a knife built in. It's to be seen to before sunset the-night."

We had a knife built into the house I grew up in. My ma mentioned it often, drawing comfort from its power to ward off witches. But I thought it was only the common folk took such steps. Imagine a gentleman as well got as the first citizen of Carrickfergus needing the same consolation!

And then I understood. I saw it with the minister and again with the Mayor. Witches put fear in men's hearts, no matter how powerful they be.

◆◆◆   ◆◆◆   ◆◆◆

Events skited along brave and fast after that, thanks to the Mayor getting involved. Soldiers from Carrickfergus Castle marched into Islandmagee, putting households into turmoil as they searched for places where a coven might meet, and for proof of folk dabbling in the black arts. These soldiers wore the English redcoat, rather than grey homespun like the militia who lodged in houses round about us. They threw aside mattresses and poked among the ashes of fireplaces.

Cattle stalls, hen huts, even pig pens were rummaged through. Later, I heard my parents' cottage was among those torn apart.

A dose of smuggled goods were found and seized – French wines and brandies, swapped for warm woollens to avoid excise duty. This was not what the soldiers were after, though their officer had the liquors loaded onto a cart, because gift horses should never be looked in the mouth. It was not regarded as a serious transgression – after all, the gentry were up to the same tricks, and any landowner on whose land a transaction took place could expect his cellars stocked for his trouble.

Certain books on palmistry were found in the home of one man, who sailed the high seas on the crew of a square-rigger in his youth, but he swore he had forgotten about them. Still, he was thrown into the cart, hands roped together. Some suspicious jars of ointment were discovered in the possession of a widow-woman, living in a mean sort of cabin hard-by my family. Ma said you could see from her skirts she wet herself, as she joined the sailor in the cart.

Knowehead House was excused from the soldiers' poking and prodding. The officer in charge, a popinjay called Captain Young, came by and told us so. He allowed his soot-black mount to rear up as he sat atop the beast, its hooves pawing the air – knowing right well we were watching. The mistress came to the door to see what all the commotion was about, and he introduced himself to her. What could she do but invite him in? Into the parlour he strutted, in his shiny thigh-high boots and spurs, accepting a glass of claret with the air of a man doing her a favour. I never saw a man wear his breeches so tight to the skin. It was downright indecent.

For all his self-importance, he couldn't help stealing peeks at Mary Dunbar. Not in the way a man looks at a pretty girl, mind you. I wondered if he was come to see Mary perform, since there could be no reason for him to call in person to

Knowehead. We were able to see and hear for ourselves what was happening round and about us. Besides, it was what he didn't say that mattered: we were let off because the soldiers were looking for hidden evidence of dabbling with the Devil. Whereas devilry was on public show at Knowehead – trumpeted far and wide.

Captain Young knocked back a bumper of claret and was eyeing the decanter when a knock came to the door. It was a lieutenant with dandelion-puff hair, informing him the search was completed and the prisoners were ready to be taken away and questioned.

"Duty calls," said Captain Young, and back he clanked to his troops.

Master Jamesey would have loved to see such a soldier up close. Later, I heard the captain released the sailor with a lecture, and the threat of worse, for holding on to such dangerous papers. The books on palmistry were burned. The old woman was let go, too, when the ointment turned out to be made of softened beeswax and herbs, a cure for stiff joints.

After the soldiers did their work, it seemed as if half the women in the county were marched in and out of Knowehead House to answer to Mary Dunbar. The search was extended beyond Islandmagee, as far as Carrickfergus. The young lady told the Constable one of her tormentors had pockmarks on her face, while another squinted horribly, and then there was the one with a claw hand she mentioned before, so dozens of woman fitting those descriptions were rounded up. Most of them were let go, but not before they were quaking in their boots at what might happen to them. As for those who weren't set free, it wasn't hard to imagine the panic they were in.

Meanwhile, men were posted at the caves, but there was no sign of anybody going about the Devil's work. Folk were staying indoors, and no wonder, for by now the island was in a state of bedlam. Word was out about Mary Dunbar. About what she could do to you, if she took the notion. Nobody knowed who'd be denounced next. Even the menfolk were nervous, though Mister Sinclair said women were more likely to be witches by a hundred to one, on account of a natural tendency to be false-hearted.

Sometimes Mary Dunbar looked a face over, debating with herself. Other times she had no hesitation, and Constable Blan would pull out his warrant from the inside pocket of his coat, and add another name to it. He liked to read it aloud, rolling the words: "*Complaint being made to me this day by Mary Dunbar of Armagh, and lately of Kilcoan More, against Bessie Mean of Ballycarry, wife to Andrew Ferguson, a tanner by trade. Whereas the above Bessie Mean, being accused and suspected of perpetrating divers acts of witchcraft contrary to the form of the statute made and provided against witchcraft by the first King James, should be taken up and committed for the same unto Her Majesty's gaol in Carrickfergus.*"

Bessie Mean gave the Constable a wee fright. "What's wrong with your head, man?" she said, after he read the warrant. "How can you not see this has more to do with Knowehead House than with thon Dunbar lassie?"

"Explain yourself."

Her round eyes, bright as a squirrel's, fastened on his. "Nothin' good ever came out of this patch of land. It twists the folk that live on it. It twisted aul' Mistress Haltridge, the minister's wife."

"Shame on you! You're vilifying somebody who can't defend herself," cried the mistress.

"I'm questioning this prisoner. Pray, don't interrupt," said Constable Blan.

"Is it nonsense, mistress?" said Bessie Mean. "Look me in the eye and tell me you've never felt something amiss in Knowehead. Look me in the eye an' say it. You, too, Constable."

"Hold your blether. It's not your place to quiz me."

"Are you sure there's nothin' in what I say, Constable? In

your heart, are you sure? I'm tellin' you here an' now, this house is crookedy. How could it be any other, when it stands on land where it has no right to be? Knowehead House is named wrong. By rights, it should be called Repentance House. Because them that live here have reason to repent it."

I'd seen enough and slipped back to the kitchen. A shape on the table caught my eye, and I stood stock still, looking. Time slowed right down. The flour jar was lying on its side, contents spilling out. I didn't leave the jar on the table – there had been no baking since Peggy went off with the bairns – but that wasn't what made me stare. It was the letters drawn in the flour. An *A* and a *H* were written there, clear as the skies above.

"I've been watching you."

My knee banged on the edge of the table as I jumped. It was the Constable. Quickly, I swiped the palm of my hand over the flour to wipe out the letters, acting on instinct to protect the Haltridges.

"You take everything in, don't you?" he went on. "That mind of yours is tickin' away under your neat linen cap. Tell me, do you know what Bessie Mean was on about?"

"Folk said daft things about my master's mistress when she was dyin'. Maybes that's what she's on about."

"What sort of daft things?"

My eyes fell on the patch of flour, with the track of my hand through it. I shivered. "They thought she was," my voice dropped to a whisper, "witched."

"Speak up, lass."

"Witched. 'Twas said she was witched into her grave."

His face turned red, the pockmarks standing out white against the skin. "Why was I never told about this? Answer me. Did nobody think it worth their while to let me know Mary Dunbar is not the first victim of witchcraft in this house? If this house was troubled before, it shows there may be a history of possession here."

"I thought you knowed, sir."

"I didn't. You folk up here on Kilcoan More keep your cards close to your chest. But how am I supposed to investigate something when I am not given all the facts? Well?"

"Sir, the mistress doesn't like us mentioning the aul' dame's death. She takes it to heart."

"Mister Sinclair could have said something. Or one of the elders." He was getting worked up, parading up and down the kitchen, muttering to himself.

I racked my brains for a way to calm him. "Maybes they judged it as well to let it lie. We all hoped that would be an end to it, when the aul' mistress went to her eternal reward."

"I'm the one to judge what information is important and what's not. And clearly it didnae end there, or Mistress Dunbar wouldnae have been plagued. Tell me, was your master's mistress bothered by the same witches putting Mistress Dunbar through her ordeal?"

"I would'n know, sir. I know nothin' about witches."

"Hmm. It stands to reason it would be one and the same coven. Islandmagee could hardly accommodate several. These witches must be exterminated – they cannot have licence to persecute decent folk. By the by, when is your master due home? It strikes me as downright peculiar for him to be away at such a time."

"We expect him any day now, Constable."

"I should hope so. I have questions I need to put to him. Such as why thon Bessie Mean thinks the land here at Knowehead House is – what was the word she used – 'crookedy'? Do you know why she should make such a claim?"

"She's upset, sir, she's just been outed as a witch. I doubt if she knows what she's ravin' about herself."

He flicked his riding crop against the elf stone Peggy had hung above the door. "I have no power to put crookedy plots of land in gaol, any more than I can imprison dead men. But I can throw the Devil's gets into a dungeon. Tell me, do you ken any more witches on Islandmagee?'

"No, sir. Maybes they've all been caught now, and we can go back to how it was before."

"It's never that simple. How about any that try their hand at doctoring, like Bessie Mean? Or whose babbies never live to see the light of day?"

"No, sir, never a one."

He frowned. "What about any meddlesome or quarrelsome women?"

I was scared at the way his questions were going. Any of us could be named a witch, if that was all it took. I breathed in, trying to stay calm. Don't lose the head, Ellen, I told myself. All you have to rely on are your wits.

"Sir, I be kept busy here – I dinna get much chance to pay attention to what goes on outside Knowehead."

"And how about what goes on inside Knowehead?"

"I can make no sense of it, Constable. I do as I'm told and get on with my work. I mind my place."

He rocked back on his heels, and changed tack. When he spoke again, his voice was wheedling. "You're a bright lassie, Ellen Hill. If you hear anythin', come straight to me. There's a guinea in it for you, if you name the right names, and give us something by way of proof."

A guinea was more money than I'd seen in my life. To whet my appetite, he produced a half crown with the Queen's face on it. He spun it in the air a lock of times, before reaching it to me.

"*Anna*," it read, and then some foreign words.

I handed back the coin right and quick, for fear I'd be tempted to keep it. It wouldn't be right to profit by others' misfortune. But when I saw the surprise on his face, I passed some remark about there being no need to pay me until after I did him a service.

"I hear there's lascivious women on the island who like

nothin' better than to flaunt themselves and tempt men to sin," he said. "Witches are known to provoke crude and unnatural desires. The Devil likes to set folk to fornication."

I was thoroughly alarmed now, but had no choice except to brazen it out. "I know nothin' about fornicatin', sir. I was brought up to prize chastity above all virtues in a woman." I pushed aside all thoughts of my master, and what I had given away to him so readily.

"And right glad I am to hear it. But word has reached me of a saucy lass by the name of Ruth Graham, who tempted a decent man to sin. I've a mind to see whether Satan was behind thon prank." He watched me the way a kitling sizes up a wee mouse. "What I want from you are the names of any other lassies up to the same rutting. Excessive passions and uncontrolled mating are the hallmarks of a witch."

"Ruth's run away. Nobody knows where she is, sir."

Constable Blan came closer. He was maybes an inch or two shorter than me, but it felt as if he was looming over me. "Appearances are deceptive. Witches come in all shapes and sizes, and some of them are a toothsome package. The Devil looks after his own. Them women need to be stopped in their tracks, before they go corrupting other men. Do you deny it?" I shook my head. "Good. The Mayor has issued a general warrant for the arrest of all suspect persons, and I'm intent on fulfilling my duties, should it take the last drop of my sweat. Oh aye. He'll not find Brice Blan wanting." His eyes glittered. "Now, think about this, Ellen Hill, afore you answer. Witches are damned. Anybody harbouring a witch is damned, too. There can be no forgiveness. No mercy. And no escape. So, are you for us or agin us? And if you be for us – you need to prove it. Well? Which is it to be?"

My armpits were drenched with sweat, and I knowed my face had to be shiny with it. Rattled though I was, I managed to buy a little time. "Could you give me a moment to collect my thoughts, sir? Maybes if I can just sit down, and bring to mind all the women I know, I might be fit to think whether they've ever done anything to raise doubts in my mind."

"Very well. Make sure you think hard. I'll return in a few minutes."

As soon as he left, I dashed into the pantry and poured myself a measure from the bottle of my master's brandy I had stolen, back when my monthlies were late. I kept the remains in a drawer there, hidden among a jumble of fishing twine and oddments. I swallowed back a long gulp, and considered a second helping, but held off to keep a clear head.

For all I knowed, I could be named as a witch myself. I thought of the potion I took when my monthlies were late, and tears started in my eyes. Was brewing that up enough to condemn me? I was guilty of plenty, even if it wasn't witchcraft. Sniffing, I rubbed a sleeve against the dampness on my face, but my fears were not so easily wiped away.

Maybes I was fuddled from the drink, or maybes I was more shaken than I realized. When I went to set the beaker down, I missed the shelf and it smashed into pieces at my feet. As I bent over, I saw it was the dead mistress's favourite beaker, the one she used to drink her bedtime milk from every night.

Hunkered down, the pieces in my hand, I asked myself what this beaker was even doing in the larder. It was kept in the dining room with the good china. I must have dawdled there looking at it, thinking all sorts of dark thoughts about messages from beyond the grave, because the next thing I knowed, Constable Blan was back in the kitchen.

"Now then, enough shilly-shallying: I want names."

Chapter 12

I was in a panic, and as sure as eggs is eggs the Constable would have tricked names out of me – innocent or guilty – if a brace of my master's greyhounds hadn't come yelping and pawing at the door.

Frazer Bell followed after, whistling. "Any chance of a bone for these boys?"

He caught sight of the Constable and the two of them looked each other over – not in a friendly fashion, either.

"Is there some service you require of the Haltridges' maid?" asked Frazer.

"I was just having a few words with her, before going about the Mayor's business."

"Important business, indeed. We mustn't detain you." And he stood aside from the door and extended his arm, as if to be gentlemanly, when it was plain he was telling Constable Blan to clear off. Not that he had any authority to do it. I doubt if even my master could have kicked him out.

The Constable threw me a crabbit look and threw Frazer Bell an even crosser one, but out he tramped.

"What did he want of you?"

"To name any I thought might be witches."

"And did you?"

"No, sir. I'm a good girl, I have no truck with witches."

"Of course not." He looked thoughtful. "A lie can be more powerful than the truth. Especially where people are ready to believe the worst of each other."

"I swear on the life of every member of my family, sir, I tould him nothin' but the truth. I have'n been within an ass's roar of a coven."

"Hush now, don't get upset. How about that bone for the dogs?"

൫ ൫ ൫

By now, there were seven women under lock and key in Carrickfergus gaol, four from Islandmagee and three from Carrickfergus, and a trial date was set. Once the seven were rounded up, Mary Dunbar experienced no more attacks, apart from one morning, shortly after breakfast, when she moaned about pains in her eyes. Metal spikes were being pressed into them, she said. Her eyes watered sore, and I bathed them to ease the stinging. When inquiries were made, it was discovered her complaints coincided with the hour the prisoners walked in the exercise yard.

I noticed something new about the young lady at this time: an odour came off her. It was unusual in a young lady so dainty. The pong came through her skin, as if something was curdled inside her and seeping out.

Frazer Bell still rode over to Knowehead House most days, and for the first time I spied some grey in that thick brown hair of his. I doubted if he had much heart for the poesy reading he used to delight in. Sometimes he looked bone weary. Yet duty or maybes just neighbourliness had him saddling up Lordship. He no longer seemed glad to be paying the visit, though he was always a welcome sight to us.

He was no sooner in the parlour on this particular day, when I heard him correct the mistress, from where I sat darning in a corner, quiet as a mouse.

"Did you not find Mister Sinclair's sermon yesterday rousing, Frazer? I confess, I shivered when he said there was an invisible agent at work on Islandmagee."

"There's an invisible agent at work here, all right, but it isn't the Devil. Whatever the kirk says. They've bent the law round to their way of thinking, but that still doesn't make it right."

"Hush, Frazer. You mustn't say such things about the kirk. It's dangerous."

While Frazer Bell was speaking to the mistress, he kept glancing at Mary Dunbar. You might almost have thought him a lover, unable to tear his eyes from his beloved. Except he had the anxiety of a lover, without the joy. She sat there, self-centred as a newborn, studying her lap and taking no part in their conversation.

"Not a single one of the accused has confessed to being a witch," said Frazer. "Mister Sinclair is visiting them daily, along with four or five other clergymen, trying to make them acknowledge their crimes. He exhorts them to throw off their infernal master and abase themselves at God's feet. But none follow his advice. Mister Sinclair says it shows how hardened the prisoners are in sin. But it could also be that they have committed none."

Just then, I saw the young lady lift a pomander from a pocket and hold it to her nose. So she was conscious of a smell. Whether she recognized it as coming from her, I cannot say.

"Are they being treated unkindly?" asked the mistress.

"Do you mean tortured? I know they've been kept awake."

"That doesn't sound so terrible."

"No? It's called 'waking the witch'. The prisoners are forced to walk about at night, and kept from resting the following day in the hopes lack of sleep will melt their obstinacy. Mister Sinclair says it's for their own good."

"He's worried about their souls, Frazer. He explained it to us: without confession, there can be no true repentance. They need to admit their covenant with Satan if they are to be saved. Only then can he be driven from their bodies."

"But what if they struck no deal with the Devil? What if these women are innocent?"

"Frazer, how do you explain the chimney pot that nearly flattened the Mayor? Or the injuries to my cousin? If these women are innocent, God will protect them."

"It's not that simple." Finally, he spoke directly to Mary Dunbar. "Mistress Mary, are there more witches? Or are we finished at seven?"

She raised her face to his. "Mistress Anne is always at me. She's the ringleader. She says we can lock up as many as we like, but she'll recruit more witches to take their place. The coven can never be crushed. She told me the Mayor has a new horse, and if he doesn't watch his step it'll throw him. New horses are skittish."

"This can't go on, Mistress Mary."

Her eyes strayed towards the window. "The swans are still on Larne Lough. I heard some of the elders talk about it – they don't usually stay so long. I'd like to go outside and see them again, but Mistress Anne forbids me to leave this house. Swans are said to mate for life. Do you suppose that's true, Mister Bell?"

"What will it take to stop this?"

"I should like to think it's true. But it's so hard to know what to believe. Once, I saw a pair courting. They kissed bills, and their necks made a heart shape."

"Perhaps the witches only have power over you because you believe they do. Why don't you test it? Why not step outside and see the swans on the lough? Mistress Isabel and I will go with you."

"I'd give anything to watch them glide along – they look so stately. My father tasted swan flesh once at a banquet. He said it was tough, though it looked delicate. I cried when he told me. It's a sin to eat them."

"Will I fetch your cloak, Mary?" Frazer's voice was a caress. "Will you come to the lough? So many women are locked up now there can be nothing to stop you."

"Oh, if you knew how I long to see the swans. If I stand at the casement and listen, I fancy I can hear the throb of their wings in flight. There are four pairs, aren't there? But I daren't risk it. Mistress Anne will punish me. She says she'll flay me till the flesh peels away from my body like apple skin, the way Pontius Pilate had Christ Jesus scourged."

"If this Mistress Anne is found, will she be the last? Will it stop there?"

She spread her hands wide in a helpless gesture. "I'd like Mistress Anne to be put in gaol. Then perhaps I can see the swans again. But she's crafty."

"Mary, listen carefully to me. Does Mistress Anne exist? Or is she only someone you see in dreams?"

She dropped the pomander, and it rolled off her lap, disappearing under her chair. Two red patches appeared on her cheeks. "It's not my fault witches persecute me. Day in, day out, people come to gape at me. The Constable is always badgering me. And when it's not him, it's Mister Sinclair, or one of the other ministers. I just want to be left in peace. I've stood up to the witches. If you only knew the half of what they wanted me to do. But I said no. I'm always saying no to them."

"What have they wanted you to do, my dear?" asked the mistress.

"I can't repeat it. It's lewd. They're always at me, making coarse suggestions." She speeded up, words tumbling out. "They'd have us all like beasts in the field, if they could. Sins of the flesh aren't sins at all, they whisper – it's only natural. You see how they pervert things? I cover my ears, but I can still hear them."

Frazer turned to the mistress. "Mistress Isabel, is there any reason for James's delay? High time he was home. The trial is fast approaching – your husband should be by your side. I can't imagine what might be keeping him."

"I thought he'd be with us by now. He promised to leave directly he appointed an agent to take care of business for him, but it's taken longer than he expected – he says it was a struggle to find anybody reliable. But he has written to say a man has been hired at last. I watch for him daily."

A bleat from Mary Dunbar drew the mistress to her.

"Mary, dear, would you like a rest? Why not lie down for an hour before supper?"

"I am a wee bit tired. My eyes are smarting again."

"Let me take you upstairs."

"Don't leave your guest, Isabel. I can make my own way."

Frazer Bell sprang to open the door for Mary Dunbar. I expected to be sent to keep an eye on her, but I stayed as still as a statue, and the mistress didn't order it.

"Mistress Dunbar's parents should also be made aware of the situation," Frazer said, after he sat back down again. "I take it you've been in touch with them about your cousin's delicate state of health?"

"Oh Frazer, I haven't mentioned anything about the bewitching. I couldn't bring myself to say it. I simply told Aunt Dunbar that Mary has been feverish and imagining things. My aunt said she would like to come and see her, but there is scarlet fever in Armagh and she cannot risk infecting us."

Shock was carved on his face. "Mistress, you must write and tell them everything as a matter of urgency. They'll hear about it soon enough – it's the talk of the county. And what if your cousin has seen witches before? What if she's made accusations in the past?"

"Surely we'd have heard."

"Not necessarily. Not unless your aunt chose to tell you. She may have wished to keep it quiet for reasons of discretion. We must assume nothing."

"Witchcraft is the only explanation. You can't think Mary is making this up, Frazer. You witnessed her convulsions. You know how she's suffering."

"Seven women lie in Carrickfergus and an eighth will surely join them. I don't know if any of the prisoners are witches. But I do know Mistress Mary Dunbar has sown suspicion, distrust and alarm in Islandmagee. It's tearing us apart." He gave a laugh that was closer to a bark. "Scarlet fever in Armagh and witchfever in Knowehead. Which has the better bargain, I wonder? And there's no looking to Mister Sinclair and his breed to bring healing. It suits them to have us going about in fear of witches. Their meeting-houses and chapels have never been fuller."

"Frazer, what you say is cynical, if not downright ungodly."

"I'm only telling you what James would, if he was here. I can't say if there's a coven. I can't say if women have pledged their souls to the Devil. But I have eyes to see other things. Dread has been drummed up among folk of every rank on the island: it's all anybody talks about. We need to make an end of this. If a witch trial is the way, so be it. But in God's name, let it stop at eight women." He lowered his voice. "The girl is dangerous. She points her finger, and a woman is brought in and falls to her knees. She points it again, and she's locked up. This is a young person of eighteen years, remember. It's bound to go to her head."

"Frazer, I can't believe Mary would do this deliberately. What possible reason could she have?"

"For attention. To feel important. Because she's deluded. I don't know. But I do know I have lived all my life on Islandmagee, and I can't believe evil walks here."

"Evil walks where it wills."

"Not evil on the scale Mary Dunbar suggests. Not on my island."

"Mister Sinclair seems convinced of it."

"What does he know about the folk who live here? Those who go looking for wickedness generally find it."

"Come now, Frazer, you're being unfair on the minister. He didn't seek out these disturbances at Knowehead. We sent for him, don't forget. The poor man is worn to a shadow trying to help us.'

"Maybe I do him a disservice. But I wish to God your husband was home. We need someone sensible near-hand."

"You're a true friend, Frazer. To be honest, I once thought we might have you for a relative, as well."

"How so, mistress?"

"You seemed beguiled of my cousin when you first met her."

"She had a glow."

"And now?"

He looked away. "I'm a crusty old bachelor. I don't know how to behave with women."

"You behave impeccably with me."

"Ah, but you –"

"Don't count?"

"On the contrary. Most assuredly, you count. You are a pearl among women, Mistress Haltridge. The truth is, I've grown too accustomed to living alone. Well, I've said my piece and I'll say no more. I trust the next time I see you, it will be with your husband by your side."

He rose, lifted his hat from a side table and was gone.

The mistress went to the casement to wave him off with her handkerchief. "Still here, Ellen? Run along and check my green woollen gown in the panelled chest for moth damage. This trial will be a spectacle for the common people, but I need to look my best."

I made my way to her bedchamber, thinking about how my master's arrival would brighten up the house. He was always laughing, teasing the childer, calling for food or wine, and planning fishing trips with Frazer Bell. He used to tease me, too, as if I was a bairn, but lately he was not so inclined to treat me like a wee lassie. And I had liked the change in him, though it had made me nervous as well. With just cause.

I found the gown: it had a grease stain on the bodice, but a dab with chalk should lift it. I held it to me, admiring myself. A generous mistress would give me her cast-offs, but Mistress Haltridge cut them down for Sarah. It was on the short side, but forest green was a colour that suited my red hair. Any gown I ever owned was grey or blue, on account of being dyed here on the island. Only shop-bought clothes came in such rainbow shades.

What would James Haltridge think of me, in such a gown? I asked my reflection. His eyes would linger on you, my heart replied – and I shivered at the thought. From pleasure. From a sense of risk, forbye. And maybes, wrong though it was, the risk lent colour to the pleasure.

         ⁙   ⁙   ⁙

That same day I fell into crabbit humour, trying to keep up with my own and Peggy's work. Out to the yard I ploughtered, with a bucket in my hand and my skirt kilted up to the knees, to bring slops to the 'greyhound sow'. She was called that for a reason – thon pig could clear fences, with her long legs. If I hadn't stayed to scratch her back with a stick, which set the old dame snuffling and squealing like a piglet, I'd have been back indoors and looking less trollopy without my much-darned blue woollen stockings on show. As it was, I heard hooves behind me and thought it was Frazer Bell.

"Am I forgotten already?" called a familiar voice.

I knowed it was him before ever I turned my head, but still I wanted the proof of my own eyes. When I was in swithers about my monthlies, and trusting to a potion that might be kill instead of cure, I thought maybes I'd feel differently about him when I saw him again. Not a chance. I let go of the bucket and went running up to him, as he swung his leg over the saddle and dismounted.

"Oh master, you're a sight for sore eyes! Welcome back, sir. Thank God you're home." I had to keep hold of my two hands so I didn't forget myself and reach out to him. How I longed to do it!

"Was I not expected? I sent a line by post to tell your mistress I was coming." He rested his hand on my shoulder, and my legs nearly gave way beneath me. His fingers kneaded the flesh at the side of my neck, just for a moment, before he dropped his hand. Two of my master's fingers were broken and set crooked, from trying to tame a gelding which ended up taming him. But no hand could have been dearer to me. His face was creased with tiredness, stubble on his cheeks and chin. There was dirt from the roads all over his coat, and a smell of horse off him. But my master had never looked so beautiful to me. My eyes never left his face – they were saying what my tongue could not.

He understood, and smiled at me. He had his own white teeth, my master – not rotting or crooked, like some. When he was in Dublin, he always went to a Spanish barber in a place called Temple Bar, and had them cleaned and polished. That smile of his melted away the hard ride, and I caught sight of what he must have been like as a boy, looking for birds' nests or collecting conkers.

"Have I been missed?" he asked.

"You're always missed from this house."

"Aye, but did you miss me?"

"I missed you, master."

For the space of a heartbeat, our eyes spoke to each other. And then the past weeks undid me, and I blew out a sigh.

"What is it?"

I longed to let it all pour out. 'Ach, master,' I wanted to say, 'my monthlies were late and I was afraid I might be carrying your child. A half-brother or sister to Jamesey and Sarah. But I took a cure for it, and all's well that ends well. Except I had it all to deal with on my own, and you far away from me. I was scared and lonely, and it was the hardest thing I've ever had to do in my life.' Instead, I said, "Ach, master, such a time we've had of it since you left."

"I came as quick as I could." He waited for me to say more, but I couldn't trust myself to speak, and so he began talking about the journey. I hoped he did it because he wanted to tarry with me a shade longer. "I stopped at Ardee for a meal, but the coaching house was a kennel, so I rode through the night rather than stay over – and here I am. Ready for one of Peggy's good, solid dinners."

"Peggy's gone with the childer to Belfast."

"So she has – it went out of my head. Your mistress told me about it in a letter. But you wouldn't see me go hungry, would you?"

"Indeed I would'n, sir." All at once, I realized my stockings were on show, all covered in darns, and I let down my skirt.

He rooted through his pockets. "I brought lemons, off a merchant ship that arrived in Dublin only the day before yesterday. You might be able to use some in a syllabub." He put one under my nose. "Breathe in," he invited.

You could smell the sunshine off it. Even better was the heat from his hand so close to my face. I was filled with the desire to bend my cheek into that hand, in the hopes he'd hold it the way he cradled the lemon.

Maybes my feelings showed in my face, because he said softly, "Did you ever think of me, Ellen?"

"Every day, master."

He went to speak, but the mistress came running out then – she must have seen us from the casement. "James! You're home!" And he caught her up in his arms and spun her round, his hat falling off. She buried her face in his shoulder, saying his name over and over. And I looked away.

"I'll see about some dinner," I said, and I might as well have been talking to myself.

೬ ೬ ೬

I fried up a feast of salmon for my master, and the whiles he ate I lit a fire in their bedchamber. The mistress tied on an apron and fussed over him, watching every spoonful that went into his mouth, while I toiled up and down stairs with buckets of hot water for him to bathe in front of the fire. He was anxious to wash off the muck from his journey, and his limbs were stiff from sitting on horseback. The mistress came up after me, to check I remembered to put towels warming on the fire screen, as if I'd forget anything bearing on his comfort, and when he followed her to their chamber she sent me off to unpack his bags.

As I sorted through his linen, it struck me how my master would prefer a bar of plain soap to the scented sort the mistress used, and I went to the storeroom and got one. But my mistress took it from me at their door. "Keep an eye on Mistress Dunbar. And don't disturb us again unless you're sent for – your master and I have much to discuss." I caught a flash of his wet back before she shut the door in my face. He was humming as he soaked, and the firelight danced on his smooth, light-brown skin.

I stood rooted to the spot outside their bedchamber. We had joined our bodies together in the closest act a man and woman can do together, but I had never seen his naked back.

I should have turned away, but no power on earth could move me from where he was. I heard splashing, and the mistress's laughter. "Here, let me wash you before you soak the place entirely." She begged for news of the city, and he launched into an account of the marriage between two dwarves in Dublin – a spectacle which attracted a crowd, including members of the gentry. The mistress was merry, calling for more details, and never once mentioned witchcraft or the goings-on at Knowehead House.

By and by, I realized I would be in trouble if I was caught there, and managed to pull myself away. Downstairs I crept, stopping to peep in at Mary Dunbar, alone in the parlour. Her head was close to the embroidery frame, working on her stitching. Once, she was never without a minister or a brace of elders at her elbow. But since so many witches had been uncovered, and her fits had stopped, the ministers were occupied with trying to wring confessions from the witches. As concerned for the black sheep as the white, they'd say. I wasn't so sure. As for the elders, they were avoiding Knowehead House. Mercy Hunter told me some folk went by the Low Road to save them passing the house.

I looked at the cause of it all. "Can I do anythin' for you, mistress?"

Mary Dunbar stuck her needle in the embroidery frame and came towards me, skirts rustling. "Do you like living here?"

"Islandmagee is in my blood. I can imagine livin' no place else."

"I mean in Knowehead House. How do you feel about the house, Ellen?"

"It's a fine house. But provided it has a roof that does'n leak, one house is much the same as another, mistress." My words were intended to keep her calm – I didn't want to have to cope with another fit – but in my bones I felt Knowehead was a house like no other.

"Is it?" She shivered, her eyes roaming from ceiling to floor to fireplace. "This house isn't like any I've ever set foot in. It holds itself apart from the folk that eat and sleep and go about their business in it. This house has a mind of its own. I sometimes think it could stand up and walk, if it took the notion. If walking fitted in with its plans." Her eyes fastened on mine, needy. "Surely you've noticed?"

"Houses don't have minds. Houses don't make plans." I was trying to convince myself, as much as Mary Dunbar, but I faltered.

"This house does." She brought her mouth close to my ear. "You must have heard it at night. Muttering away to itself. Creaking with laughter."

"That's just the timbers settlin'."

"I used to think it was the witches whispering to me. Trying to frighten me into doing what they wanted. Now I'm starting to wonder." She laid her knuckles against her eyes and pressed down. From behind them, her voice was bone-weary. "Maybe it's the house to blame. Maybe the witchcraft wasn't brought into the house by outsiders. What if it's part of the house already? Built into it, the way you'd build in chimneys and casements . . ." She took her hands away from her eyes. They were red-rimmed and blinking. "There's witchcraft here, all right. But have you ever thought the house might be the cause of it?"

My mouth went dry, my heart crowding my throat so that I couldn't manage a swallow. Mary Dunbar had read my fear. "Aye, mistress, there is something about Knowehead. You have the right of it."

"But why was I chosen? That's what I can't figure out. Why me?"

"Chosen for what?"

"To do the bidding of Knowehead House."

I should have gone back to the kitchen, leaving her to whatever thoughts were preying on her mind. I wasn't paid to be Mary Dunbar's nursemaid, and I didn't want her unsettling me with that kind of talk. For the first time in my life, I was sleeping on my own, but now I'd have welcomed Peggy's cold feet on mine. These nights, when I heard the house creaking, I lay there worrying about what was making the noise.

Or who.

I was afraid of what she might say coming back to trouble me that night, when I lay on my own in the dark. Aye, I should have gone away, but I couldn't help myself. Maybes I was jittery at having my own doubts about the house brought out into the open. But all at once I remembered them women penned together on the say-so of a lassie, the same age as myself, and I spoke my mind. "Are there no witches after all, mistress? Are you takin' it all back?"

A flash of panic crossed Mary Dunbar's face and she caught me by both arms, fingers digging into my flesh. "I cannot go back on it. The house wouldn't like it. It would find a way to make me suffer."

"You're sufferin' already, mistress. Maybes it's time for you to go on home. Back to your own folk. The house might a wanted you before, but it's finished with you now. You've served its purpose."

"Hush, can you hear it?"

"Hear what?"

"The house. It's listening to us." She cocked her head to the side.

I found myself listening too, though I couldn't tell you for what. I laid my hand, which was shaking, against my breast, and my heartbeat raced beneath it.

All at once, she shook herself, and returned to her embroidery. We might just as well have been chatting about the weather. She picked up her needle and said over her shoulder, "I want to be here. The house wants me too. I'd stay forever if I could. Perhaps I will. Just like Mistress Anne."

My knees were knocking together now. I edged towards the door, longing for the safety of my kitchen. "Mistress Anne is here?"

"Aye, she's always here."

"And what about Hamilton Lock?"

"It's different with him. Prayers used to drive him away. But he's stronger now. He comes and goes when he wants, and not on anyone else's say-so. But the house is using him too. The house is using all of us." She smiled, sweet as honeycake. "You too, Ellen Hill. Everything you do, it's because the house persuades you to it."

I left her to her sewing. Such talk was more than flesh and blood could bear.

I made sure to wedge the kitchen door open in case my master called for me – his merry face would cure this gloom. Then I fetched the broom to use the time profitably, hoaking out clocks from the corners. But Mary Dunbar had unsettled me, and in the end I brought the rush-bottomed chair to the door, and sat looking out at the hens.

When I went across the yard to use the privy, I saw the shutters on my master and his lady's chamber were closed. Back into the kitchen I clumped, torturing myself with pictures in my head. Finally, my master's footsteps sounded on the passageway overhead. He came down the stairs, opened the parlour door and greeted Mary Dunbar. A clatter followed, and an oath from him.

I rushed in. Mary Dunbar was on the floor, spittle shining on her chin, having a violent attack of the hiccups. It sounds little enough, but these were no ordinary hiccups. They ripped through her body with a violence that made your insides sore just watching. It was a wonder they didn't split her asunder. Her embroidery frame was cowped over, the skeins of thread tumbled every which way. My master had her propped up, thumping her on the back.

"Master, best leave her be, she'll likely take a few minutes to come out of it."

"Isabel told me she's been taking fits. I had no idea they were so brutal."

"Thon's nothin'."

Mary's hands, which had been hidden by her skirts, moved and settled on her belly. My eye was drawn to one of them. A thick darning needle pierced the hand, running for three or four stitches alongside a vein. The needle had been left stuck in, thread dangling, the way you'd pin it to a piece of material. Beads of blood oozed out.

My master saw what I did, swallowed, and looked away.

"I'll see to this," I said. "What happened your hand, Mistress Mary?"

The hiccups were dying down, and between gulps she was able to answer. "It's Mistress Anne. She said I told you too much. To punish me, she said she'd make a pincushion of my eyes. She tried to stick needles in, to blind me, but I held my hands over them."

I gritted my teeth, seized the needle and thread, and pulled it free from the skin. She let out a yelp at the pain, but it was done before she could struggle. Blood flowed out after it, and I pressed my apron to the wound.

"Why are you being punished?" asked my master.

"Mistress Anne is put out about me filling the gaol with so many of her kind."

"Who is this Mistress Anne?" Even as he said the name, he scowled. "Surely you can't mean my mother?"

The mistress rustled in, without her cap on, her fair hair loose on her shoulders instead of plaited round her head.

"Isabel, your cousin's talking about someone by the name of Mistress Anne. She seems scared to death of her. Have you any idea who she means?"

The mistress caught my eye, giving a slight shake of the head. "James, she throws out all sorts of names. The other day it was nothing but Mistress Latimore."

Mary began writhing. "Mistress Anne, oh Mistress Anne, for pity's sake, let me alone!"

"Should we not bring her to the couch, Isabel? She can't be comfortable on the floor. Ellen, take her legs."

I reached for her ankles, and she kicked out when I touched her. "You're hurting me!" I dropped her feet.

"Does she mean us or this Mistress Anne?" asked my master. Ignoring her protests, he caught her under the oxters and set her on her feet, still holding on to her. He pressed Mary Dunbar into a chair, and turned back to us. "Is this the first time she's used the name Mistress Anne? I fear it's no more than an unhappy coincidence. But I wish she wouldn't."

Mary Dunbar leaped out of her seat and sank to her knees, hands knit together. "She has the soldier's sword. Take it off her, I pray you!"

"Which soldier, Mary?" asked the mistress. "Do you mean Captain Young?"

"She's swinging it about. Forgive me, I never meant to tell on you, Mistress Anne. I'll say no more, I swear it on my life." The bones on her hands shone through onion-thin skin. "Sweet Jesus! She says she means to chop off my . . ." Mary Dunbar nodded her eyes towards her breasts, which she covered with her arms to protect them. "Have mercy! I haven't told them where to find you, or what you look like. They only have half your name."

"What's the rest of her name, Mary? Is it Mistress Anne Haltridge?" demanded my master.

Mary Dunbar paid him no heed. "Get the sword off her before she slices me up!"

"Where is she? I can't see her."

"She's made herself invisible. But she's in front of me. Surely you can see the sword, at least?" She fell backwards, banging her skull against a corner of the sideboard. She cried out and seemed stunned for a moment. "She nearly took my head off there! Mistress Anne, I told you I'd never denounce you. You must believe me. The Constable pesters me about you, but I haven't said a word." Tears poured down her cheeks, mingling with snatters and spittle.

My master turned to the mistress. "Has a physician seen her?"

"I never sent for one, James. When this started up, I didn't know what to do for the best. So I sent for the minister. I asked Mister Sinclair about having her bled. But he said cooling her blood would bring no benefit – she was gone beyond such cures."

"She should have been examined by a physician."

"What difference can it make now? The trial is going ahead at the Spring Assizes. Though God knows if Mary is able for the ordeal. Look at her now."

Mary had crawled under a chair, maybes because she thought Mistress Anne could not swing the sword in such a tight spot.

"It can't be my mother she sees – or imagines she sees. Mother couldn't lift a dragoon's sword, let alone swing it. This Mistress Anne must be somebody else, Isabel."

"Of course it's not her. The idea is preposterous."

"Besides which, my mother is lying peacefully in St John's graveyard. I saw her go into the earth myself."

"Look, James, Mary's visitor seems to have left her."

Mary had come out from under the chair and was sitting on the floor, dazed but calm.

"I hope she took her sword with her," said my master. "I don't like weapons being waved about in my parlour." He bent down and lifted her to her feet, setting her on the seat. Studying her face, which was blank, he asked, "What do we do with the girl after one of these fits? Put her to bed?"

"I'd leave her be – it's a mercy to have her peaceable after that racket. Dear heart, you look exhausted – you're the one should be in bed."

A secret look snaked between them, such as married couples give one another. I'd be better off working for Sammy and Fanny Orr, I thought. At least I wouldn't have to watch this. Kneeling down, I started picking up the sewing box contents spilled by Mary Dunbar.

"Isabel, we must think about bringing the children home from Belfast."

"Can't we leave them where they are until after the trial, James? Naturally I miss them, but I hate exposing them to this. We tried to protect them, but you can see how it is."

"No, they must come home. They belong here."

I couldn't bear to think of our wee pigeons brought back

so soon, even with my master to protect them from harm. "Master," I put in, hoping to sidetrack him, "maybes you'd care for a glass of Madeira. There's a bottle warmin' on the dinin' room hearth – I set it there the whiles you were bathin'."

"Ellen, you read my mind and know what I want before I know it myself. I'll have it in my study – there are some papers I need to look over. You're a treasure. I knew as long as you were here, there'd be common sense applied to any problem. Was I right, Isabel?"

The mistress waited a wee touch longer than I liked before replying. "She's a willing girl. But don't go giving her a swollen head – maids are ten a penny."

I banged the door on my way out.

꧁   ꧁   ꧁

The mistress followed my master into his study, instead of seeing about her cousin. I suppose she could not bear to part with him so soon after his return – and that I could understand. When I fetched in a second glass for her, she was perched on a footstool by his desk, leaning her arms on his lap and discussing what to do about Mary Dunbar.

"I need a day's rest," he said. "But the day after tomorrow, I'm delivering her home to Armagh. From there, I'll go to Belfast and collect Jamesey and Sarah. And Peggy, of course."

"We can't turn Mary out. There's scarlet fever in Armagh. A servant in my aunt's household has died of it."

"I see. Still, I'm inclined to think she should be sent away. There must be somewhere else she can go. Why should we have all the worry of her? She's her parents' responsibility, not ours. Did your aunt ever mention a tendency towards hysterics?"

"Not that I ever heard tell. But she was certainly eager for the visit to take place. Don't you remember? I showed you the letter. I'll look it out and see how she put it again. I recall thinking Mary must have been feeling poorly over the winter. Aunt Dunbar was more than willing to part with her, and I'm sure she mentioned something about her health. I presumed she meant her bodily health, but . . ."

"You must let your aunt know about the trial before she hears it from another quarter. It's a wonder you left it so long to tell me what's been going on. I know you mentioned there were difficulties with your cousin in earlier letters, but I had no idea how serious her condition was."

"Oh James, I didn't like to worry you. Besides, I scarcely knew what to say. It all sounds so scandalous when you try to put it into words. And I was a little ashamed, too, that it should happen while Mary was in my care. I'll write to Aunt Dunbar at once, now that you're back."

She grew moist-eyed, and my master dropped a kiss on top of her head. "Sweetheart, you've been a tower of strength."

The mistress noticed me at the fireplace, sweeping up some soot on the hearth, and her voice turned spiky. "Don't hang about like a useless head of cabbage – see to my cousin."

"Whether Mary Dunbar stays or goes – and my preference is for her to leave – I'm determined to collect the children," said my master.

"James, I wish you'd reconsider. For their sake, I mean. The atmosphere here has been far from healthy. There's been too much clamour and upset."

"Now you know right well you're a worrier by nature, sweetheart. I'm sure it wasn't as bad as all that. Things pass over a child's head."

"It's been perfectly dreadful, James, and the children weren't in ignorance of it." She caught sight of me, taking my time about quitting the room. "Are you still here?"

"Isabel, let the girl be. The children are coming home – my mind is made up. I'll brook no further argument."

The young lady wasn't in the parlour, or the dining room.

Her bedchamber was empty, too. Just as I was becoming alarmed, the greyhounds began barking. I looked out, and saw some of the Constable's men watering their horses. But there was no sign of their master. I made for the kitchen but, as I went to the door, I heard voices fornenst it. Brice Blan was conversing with Mary Dunbar. Strain though I might, I could not make out what they said to one another, so I hastened to throw open the door – at which they stopped talking. I flicked my eyes from her to him. Thick as thieves, they were.

"I gather Mister Haltridge is back from Dublin, Ellen."

"Just this day, sir."

"I hope he doesn't go getting any ideas about sending Mistress Dunbar away, now that he's home." He pointed his riding crop at the young lady. "She's needed here for the court case. She must stay till the law takes its course."

Mary Dunbar refused to meet my eye. Ach, she came across all sugar and spice, but she wasn't as soft as she let on.

"I'll take you to the master, Constable," I said.

He marched ahead of me, caking in mud as usual.

I lagged behind and hissed a few words in Mary Dunbar's ear. Just to let her know I was wise to her. "Eavesdroppers rarely hear anythin' good about themselves."

She opened her eyes wide. "I have no need to eavesdrop. The house tells me what it wants me to know."

Chapter 13

I did something that night I shouldn't have done: something I would have had to confess if I was of the Romish persuasion, which thankfully I'm not, being among the elect thanks to the Good Lord's mercy. I found the letter from Mary Dunbar's mother to the mistress lying on my master's desk, when I went to bank down the fire before turning in. She must have carried it in to show him. Curiosity overcame me. I remembered the gist of it, from hearing the mistress read it out to my master, but there was one part I wanted to check. My eyes skipped over the page. *Prey to her thoughts . . . sensitive . . . fancies seem apt to take shape more readily,* I read. And then a word I paused at. Aunt Dunbar called the mistress's invitation a *godsend*, underlining the word. Was there relief behind it? Or something more powerful again?

   ᘒ ᘒ ᘒ

The following day, the sun wasn't yet high in the sky when Mister Sinclair clattered up on Sobriety. He looked as if he could use a week's worth of sleep, and his poor mare wasn't faring much better. He had been riding the country on her, and no mistake. The roan was stiff in her legs and in sore need of a rubdown. He heaved himself out of the saddle, and hobbled towards where I was mixing pigswill. My master had given orders to fatten up the old saddleback sow for the butcher's knife.

"Is Mister Haltridge at home?"

"He's walking the land with Noah Spears, sir. I'll fetch him for you."

At each field I passed, the animals came to the gate to stare. It was odd to think how dull life must be for them on the island, when it was too lively for comfort among the men and women here. Especially the women. I found my master in the top field, talking to Noah about the hen house. He was woken by a fox barking in the night, and wanted to be sure the coop was secure when the birds were shut in after dark. It was the rooster he was particularly anxious about. My master was loath to lose his prized bird.

"Master, Mister Sinclair is in the house and anxious for to pay his respects."

"He might have left it till the afternoon." My master was irritable at having the inspection of his fields interrupted. He liked to check everything was shipshape following an absence.

"I daresay he has matters to discuss with you."

"Aye, well, I daresay he does."

We were in no hurry as we walked back to the house together. He matched his pace to mine, his shoulder bumping alongside, so closely did he stay by my side. I wondered what it would be like to have the right to put my hand in the crook of his arm, the way the mistress did. Maybes he was wondering things about me, because I saw him go to speak once or twice, but think better of it. Just before we rounded the corner where the house would come into sight, he stretched out his hand and pushed a loose strand of hair under my cap. It was always escaping its bounds.

"There was a lass in Dublin with hair your colour. She worked at the coffee house I favoured."

"I hope she attended to your needs, master."

"Not so sweetly as you.'

And then we were in the yard, and that was that. Before making for the door, he gave me a look that was just for me, a look such as I called up over and over again that night in bed, aye, and nights afterwards. Over his shoulder, he called out loud, for anyone watching to hear, "Don't forget my orders. I'm sure the minister would welcome a beaker of Parsley's milk after his ride, and I'll have some ale." He stopped and turned, pushing his old tricorn hat off his forehead. "Is Parsley still giving plenty of milk?"

"The creamiest on the island. There's nothing to match milk from a Galloway cow."

"But wouldn't all this witchcraft affect the milk? They say cows refuse to give a drop round them."

"We've had trouble churning the butter, master. But it comes through in the end. There's been no trouble with the milk. The hens bain't layin' well, mind you."

He let out a whistle. "I don't like the sound of that."

We parted again, my master to go through the front door and me to use the kitchen door.

Bringing in the drinks, I was just in time to hear Mister Sinclair let fly with his thunderbolt.

"The reason for my visit is not just to welcome you home, Haltridge, glad though I am to see you back on Islandmagee. I'd best tell you straight out – there's no way to sweeten this pill. The Constable means to dig up your mother's body."

Colour flooded my master's face. "But why would he do such a thing? It's uncivilized!"

"Believe me, I share your distaste. It gives me no pleasure to be the bearer of such tidings. But 'tis signed, sealed and settled: your mother's remains are to be brought out of the grave."

"What on earth are they expecting to find?"

"Anything abnormal. An empty coffin, say, or one in which the body is preserved unnaturally. If she's playing a part in this witching, the proof will be there in her coffin."

"Foolish blether! Of course she has nothing to do with what's going on here. She's sleeping the sleep of the just. It's sacrilege to disturb her grave – I refuse to permit it."

"The Mayor has ordered it, Haltridge."

"The Mayor must be bewitched himself, to stand over such a desecration."

"Hold your peace, man. Walls have ears."

"I don't care if they have tongues – aye, and eyes. This is unthinkable. The order must be revoked."

"Listen, Haltridge, we've had an atrocious time since you left. Surely your wife has told you? Mistress Dunbar has been sorely tested. She talks repeatedly about one Mistress Anne, the serpent's head directing this coven. We must track her down. Until she's caught, this vile sect will never be stamped out. I must confess, I'm full of fear for our community with witchcraft set loose among us."

"But even the Queen is called Anne. How can they dig up a Christian woman, a decent, upright soul who read the Bible every day of her life, simply because she shares a name with someone? Ach, man, it's barbarous!"

The minister took off his wig and held it against his chest, sighing heavily. "Haltridge, I'm not in favour of this. I said prayers over that godly soul's coffin as her remains were committed to the ground. I cannot believe she is anywhere except where we buried her: waiting to be gathered into rapture at the Lord's side. However, it's the Mayor's decision. The Church is in no position to go against the civil authorities on this. Distasteful though it is, it must be endured."

"I'm warning you. If my mother's body is dug up, there'll be repercussions."

"Haltridge, Haltridge, dinna fash yourself so. I mean to do my best by my predecessor's widow. I'll see to it there's as little disrespect as possible. I'll be on hand to pray over the remains again."

"Aye, and have a good gawp, too."

And in a whirl of fury, my master quit the house.

   ✿ ✿ ✿

My master's outrage, justified though it was, carried no weight against the Lord Mayor's command. The next day, Constable Blan and his men turned up at St John's graveyard with spades and ropes. They had a physician sent out from Carrickfergus with them: the Mayor's own sawbones, it was said. Word soon spread, and a crowd gathered. Frazer Bell rode over to Knowehead with the news. When he saw my master's face, he begged him not to do anything hasty, but he might just as well have put his hands in his pockets and whistled a tune. My master was gone before the words left Frazer's mouth. Hell for leather he rode out of the yard, scattering greyhounds and chickens in front of him.

Mercy Hunter told me what happened in the churchyard. She followed her master, who was part of the whole sorry business, however keen he was to wash his hands of it. Three ministers arrived to see the body dug up, each with a Bible tucked into his armpit. Some of the Constable's men looked queasy about the job in hand. Mercy said one of them had a jar he passed among his companions, before they made a start, and the Constable turned his back while they drank from it.

As the coffin was lifted out by rope, my master chased up. He let fly with a great oath when he saw them, and – may the good Lord forgive him – galloped over graves, setting clods of earth flying, to reach the Haltridge plot. He looked like a madman, according to Mercy: his handsome face was entirely transformed. It's a wonder they didn't drop the coffin back in when he bore down on them, hooves flying, howling like a banshee. "Grave robbers!" he shrieked. "Vultures!" He had his whip in his hand and lashed out at the gravediggers, right

263

and left, until a couple of the Constable's deputies managed to wrestle him off his mount. Amid the scuffle, he fell into the mound of soil dug up to reach his mother's coffin – earth got into his clothes, his hair, even his mouth. Two men knelt on him to restrain him, and a third held his head down. It's a wonder they didn't suffocate him. Brice Blan was jigging up and down in a passion at his orders being interfered with, and told his deputies to tie my master's hands with rope. He was on the point of having him muzzled, like a cur, until Mister Sinclair pleaded for him.

It was shameful that common men had the freedom to lay their hands on the master of Knowehead House. The world was gone topsy-turvy.

The deputies had another swig from their jar, doing it openly in front of the ministers, who complained to Brice Blan.

"Aye," says the Constable, mild enough once my master was trussed up, "that's sufficient for now, lads. Put it away, and let's finish what we started."

This didn't please the preachers, who wanted him to chastise instead of cajole.

All eyes returned to the coffin.

"They took a hammer to it, but they had trouble pullin' the nails out of the coffin lid," reported Mercy. "It looked as if they'd have to use a pickaxe to break it up. But the nails give way in the end, an' the lid slid off. Every man and woman in the graveyard stretched their necks for a closer look. A smell rose out of thon coffin that was enough to make you boke. Like rottin' meat, it was. The doctor steps up, a handkerchief pressed to his nose an' mouth, an' bends over the remains. I managed to squeeze in right an' close, and had a sight of what he was studyin'. Should I live to be a hundred, I'll never forget it." Shoulders hunched, she folded her arms.

"Would you a knowed her?" I asked.

"Not at all. It could a been anyone. Sure the body was

swollen up twice its size. She had her windin' sheet wrapped roun' her still. But you could see the face, hands and feet. And tell you no lie, you'd rather not see them. The skin had cracked and bust open, and the raw flesh underneath was on show. It was a kind of greeny blue instead of red. Any skin left on her was covered in big blisters. The doctor, he lifted one of her hands with a stick – I cannae blame him not wantin' to touch her – an' when he did, a nail fell off. He looked at it, as if debatin' would he let it lie, but then he scooped it up with a piece of slate lyin' on the ground, an' set it back in place. But he must a pushed down too hard, because the flesh on the hand fell apart like a piece of fruit gone rotten."

"What about her face, Mercy? Would you a known Mistress Haltridge by her features?"

"Ach, you might and you might'n. The eyes was sunk in an' the teeth stickin' out, twice the size they looked to be when she was alive. The on'y lifelike thing about her was her hair. There was masses of it. Sawbones started maitherin' on, things nobody could make head nor tail of, and still with that blessed hankie over his mouth, mufflin' what he said. But I tried to mind the most of it. Somethin' about the pressure of gases burstin' through the skin. And how it was part of the natural process, which varied dependin' on the time of year the corpse went into the grave. If you ask me, doctorin's a funny callin'. Anyhow, the long an' the short of it was he says your master's mother – or what's left of her – looked to be normal. Normal! If that's what'll happen to me, I'd rather go in a bonfire and be turned to ashes."

"My poor master, havin' to see his own mother like that."

"Aye, he took it sore. I may as well tell you, he was unmanned be the sight. Blubbed like a babby."

"Who can blame him, when all's said and done? Bad enough to see someone you love buried – but to watch them unburied must be beyond tholin'."

"Frazer Bell come along while the doctor was spoutin'

away. He had Mister Haltridge's dappled grey tied to his saddle – it bolted after your master was pulled off it. When he saw how Mister Haltridge was bound hand and foot, he tried to get the Constable to unbind him. But Blan would'n budge. 'Haltridge was crazed,' says he. 'He was like a man possessed.' But Mister Haltridge was well quieted down by then. Except the tears were trippin' him. Great big silent tears. 'She's been reduced to a side of meat,' says he. 'My mother's a carcass.' 'No, James, don't say such a thing about your mother,' says Mister Bell. Well, they put the lid back on the coffin an' into the grave it went, an' Mister Sinclair got stuck in with his prayifyin'. Frazer Bell, he kept on at the Constable to release his friend, an' finally he consented to let him go, an' Mister Bell took him away."

He must have brought him to his own house, to tidy him up before the mistress clapped eyes on him, because it was some hours later before the two rode up to Knowehead. There was nothing Frazer Bell could do to mask the master's black eye from his tussle with the Constable's men, which left him looking like a hooligan. The mistress let out a wail and asked him if he'd been in the wars. He grunted as I helped him pull off his boots, and grumbled about her making a song and dance about a wee bruise.

To keep the peace, Frazer Bell told the mistress there was a happy outcome to the day's proceedings: her mother-in-law was cleared of witchery. "Her body would have been preserved if she was a witch," he said. "The putrefaction was unsavoury to behold – but it puts Mistress Haltridge beyond suspicion."

"I've a right mind to go to law with Mayor Davies over it," said my master. "He smeared my mother by his actions."

"No, James, he exonerated her," said the mistress. "Let bygones be bygones."

"So the hunt for Mistress Anne goes on," said Frazer Bell.

◈ ◈ ◈

The next morning, the master had Noah Spears harness his grey stallion to the trap lying idle in the stable all winter, after the other horse was sold. He was set on going to Belfast to collect the young master and missie. I watched him oversee Noah, and wrung my hands wondering should I speak to him. If he refused to listen to the mistress, why would he pay heed to me? But I couldn't help myself.

I ran out to the yard. "Master, I know it's not my place to tell you your business. But would you not think on? The childer are best off where they be. Just for now."

"You're right. It's not your place."

"Forgive me, sir. I'm just afeared for the bairns. They're on'y wee."

"Knowehead House is their home. Nothing can harm them here."

"Whatever you say, master."

His black eye was bloodshot, and he was in a foul humour. I knowed before I said a word that he wouldn't take kindly to me questioning his decision. But I had to try.

◈ ◈ ◈

Jamesey and Sarah were full of chatter and importance about their daddy arriving out of the blue for them. Their happy shouts and kehoes brought the house to life. Even Mary Dunbar brightened to see their flushed wee faces, though they backed away when she went to take their hands. But Peggy McGregor didn't come back to Islandmagee with them. She had taken a turn and could not be moved.

It was no time at all before a mockery was made of my master's decision to fetch them home. It was me heard their cries, as the light was fading, on their second day back at Knowehead. My master was outside with Noah Spears, talking livestock (I always knowed where my master was – it was just something came natural to me) and I was bleaching his linen. This was work that should have been sent out, by rights, but I wanted to do it for him. A commotion sounded upstairs and my first thought was Mary Dunbar, taking another turn. But then I minded seeing her with the mistress in the parlour. I picked up my skirts and took the stairs two at a time. The noise was coming from behind Mary Dunbar's door – but it was the bairns' voices calling out.

"What ails yiz?" I said, and their shouts redoubled. I clattered the handle, but the door wouldn't budge. "Open up. Let me in."

"We can't. We're locked in," cried Jamsey.

"The lock's on the inside," I said. "Come on now, unbolt it."

"We've tried. It won't move."

"The bolt must be stuck. Give it a right, hard tug."

"I am tugging. It makes no differ."

Sarah burst into sobs. "My guts are being squeezed. It hurts!"

I dundered on the door. "Jamsey! What's goin' on?"

"Make it stop!" Sarah bawled.

I put my shoulder against the door and pushed, hoping to force it, but the solid Irish oak held firm. "What's the matter, chicken? What's bein' done to you?"

"My belly's strangling me."

"Jamsey? Is there somebody in there with you?"

"No. Yes. I'm not sure. I can't see anybody. But I think something's here. Something bad. It's hurting Sarah."

"Have another go at the bolt, Jamsey. It's at the top of the door. Can you reach it?"

"Aye, I have my hand on it now."

"Pull it open, there's a brave lad."

"I can't. I'm trying my hardest."

"Try some more. Do it for your sister."

"I'm doing my best. Nothing's happening. Sarah, what's

268

wrong? She's lying on the floor, Ellen, she's rolled up in a wee ball."

Sarah was whimpering rather than wailing now. "Mama. I want my mama."

"Her eyes have gone funny. They're like glass. I don't think she can see me any more."

I was beside myself. For the first time in my life, I felt anger towards my master. He should have known better than to bring the children back into such a house as this. But he wouldn't be told. "Sarah, chicken, I'll get you out of there, I promise. You'll be with your mama shortly. Jamesey, try the casement, see if you can open it." His footsteps moved away from the door, and I could hear him rattle the window frame. A creak and a sliding sound told me he was successful. "Good man. Now see if you can get Sarah over as far as the casement. You're a big strong lad, so you are. Pull her if you're not able to lift her. But Jamesey, go easy on her, remember the poor mite's sore."

"Up you come, Sarah." Through her moans, I could hear him helping her to her feet. "That's right, lean on me."

I flew downstairs and round to the back of the house. Below their casement, I could see his anxious face peering down at me. "Jamesey, I'm away for the ladder. You be ready to help her up on the ledge as soon as I give you the word." I raced to the barn for the ladder, scattering hens, yelling for someone to give me a hand.

My master appeared from the stable. "What's the matter?"

"Help me with the ladder. We have to get the childer out through Mary Dunbar's casement."

"What's wrong with the door?"

"Locked. Quit your dawdlin'."

Without raising an eyebrow at the way I spoke to him, he took an end of the ladder to carry it to the back wall of the house.

"Daddy," cried Jamesey as soon as he saw us. "I've got

Sarah but she can't stand up on her own!"

The wee missie wasn't fit to make a sound by this stage, and seemed uncommonly floppy from what I could make out.

"Well done, son. Do you think you might be able to keep a hold of her till I get up the ladder?"

"I'll try. But she's getting heavy."

"Good man. I'm on my way."

The lassie was only half-awake and not able to work with her brother, and he struggled to keep her upright. But my master lost no time in springing up the ladder, with me holding tight to the bottom. He leaned in through the casement and managed to pull wee Sarah through. Then, holding her against his shoulder, he carried her down one-handed.

Once outside the room, Sarah roused, and was less poorly.

"What happened, sweetheart?" Her father stroked her hair.

"I was being squeezed, Daddy. Something mean was inside me, squeezing."

My master lifted her and brought her in to her mother, before going upstairs to inspect the locked door. I followed him. The door opened without any trouble. Standing inside the room, I felt a prickle steal across my skin. It was a room I was in and out often, emptying the chamber pot, making the bed, and seeing to other chores. Now, something felt wrong about it.

The air crackled with a presence. I groped for an understanding of what it might be, and it struck me like a hammer blow. Malice. The room was alive with it. Shivering, I backed away. Outside in the passageway, I rubbed my hands over my arms, but the chill had taken hold. My teeth chattered.

"Nothing wrong with this door," said Master Haltridge. He seemed insensible to the presence in the room, intent on opening and closing the door and testing it. He clicked shut the bolt, unlocked it, shot it again. I stared at him. Could he really be untroubled by what was in the room? He leaned against the door frame, hands in his pockets. "What was all that about?"

"Sir, the door would'n budge. I tried. Master Jamesey tried. It was locked tight."

"From inside?"

"Aye, from inside. Ask Jamesey if you don't believe me. Why would I go harin' off for the ladder if there was no need?"

"I'm not doubting you. It's odd, that's all. Jamesey!"

The lad mounted the stairs, but shrank from setting foot inside Mary Dunbar's bedchamber. He stayed beside me in the passageway, where I slipped my hand into his.

"Son, what happened to Sarah?"

"She got pains in her belly. I thought she was going to die."

"Did she get aches like that when you were with your grandparents in Belfast, Jamesey?"

"No, I never saw her like that before."

"Were you picking berries? Or eating something you shouldn't have been?"

"It's too early for berries. We only ate the same as everyone else. Porridge and milk. Mutton. A gingerbread square."

My master footered with the lock again, trying to find a reason for the door to stick. "What were the two of you doing in here anyway? This is Mistress Dunbar's private room while she's our guest."

"We heard a whispery voice calling us, Father. It said our names. The door was lying open. As soon as we went in, it slammed shut. And then the voice started laughing. It was coming from the trunk." His eyes flicked toward the wooden chest, sitting there like a giant spider, and slid away again. He shuddered. "That's when Sarah's bellyache started. I was scared, sir. There was something in the chest. Something cruel."

My master flung it open, revealing a pile of Mary Dunbar's belongings. "Is it still here?"

"I don't think so, Father." He took a few paces forward and peeped towards it. "No, there's nothing now. But I don't like it here. Can I go now, please?"

My master scratched his head. "We'll all go downstairs."

He led us to the parlour, to where the mistress and her cousin were making a wee pet of Sarah.

"Mary, have you any idea why the children should believe they heard a voice inviting them into your bedchamber?"

"It must be the witches, James."

"But all the witches are locked up."

"All save Mistress Anne, the wickedest one of all."

"I see. Perhaps you'd be kind enough to give Mistress Anne a message from me." His eyes flashed fire. "Tell her to leave my family alone if she knows what's good for her."

He strode out and I followed him into his study. I couldn't let it rest after what happened in the bedchamber – my mind was full of the danger faced by the bairns.

"Master, what if it be the house and not witches?"

He presented his back to me. "You have been too much in my wife's company. She surrenders herself to imaginings about Knowehead, too."

"'Tis a house like no other."

"It's made of stones, like any house."

I dared to press on, though I was shaking inside. "But it's where it's built that counts, master. Some say it never should a been built. Not here."

"Don't make an empty vessel of yourself, blethering about matters you don't understand."

His words put me in a temper, so they did. I wasn't daft, whatever else I was. I tilted my chin up and answered him back right and bold. "There's none so blind as them that will not see."

"You mind your manners, girl." He started to say something else, but thought better of it. Instead, he passed a hand over his forehead, and dropped down into an armchair.

"Bring me some brandy. These have been a trying few days."

When I returned and placed the decanter and glass on a table at his elbow, he attempted to make amends. My master never liked to be on ill terms with anyone – not even a servant. Which was all I'd ever be to him, though my conceit fooled me to the contrary at times.

"Just a minute, Ellen. Don't go yet." He filled his glass and drank deeply. "Peggy was asking after you when I collected the children."

"Oh aye? What did she say?"

"That there was nobody like you for watching and weighing things up. It's a compliment – don't look so cross. I expect she's fond of you, after all these years. We all are." He gave me a look he'd never have chanced if the mistress was near-hand. "I was sorry to leave Peggy behind, and the poor soul so unwell. But she couldn't be moved. Strangely enough, she was in no hurry to come back to Knowehead House – you'd think she'd be eager to return to us, rather than lie among strangers. You know, something's just occurred to me. I wonder if Sarah might have picked up her stomach ailment from Peggy? That could explain her attack in the bedchamber." He finished off the brandy in his big balloon of a glass, looking relieved to have solved the mystery. "Pour me another."

When I was standing beside him, he put his hand on my arm. His voice was low, honeyed. "You slept with Peggy, didn't you? Now she's gone away, don't you find it lonely in bed at night?"

I set down the decanter for fear my trembling hands would drop it. "No, master, I don't get lonely."

"Never?"

"I be kept too busy."

"I was lonely for you in Dublin."

"Were you, master?" I fixed my eyes on the golden-brown pool of liquor.

"Aye, I was. I kept thinking about how cool your skin looked, and yet how hot it turned out to be when you pressed it against mine."

"Master, you must'n say such things! We have to forget we ever did that. It was wrong. We can't ever let it happen again. We have to be strong."

"I don't want to be strong, Ellen. Not if it means I can't touch you. There's no shame in what we did."

"But there is, master. It's a sin."

"Don't be cruel, Ellen. It's only a small sin. It hardly counts."

He took my two hands in his and started stroking them with his thumbs, a feathery touch that made my willpower melt away. Then he bowed his head and kissed my fingertips, one by one. I knowed I should pull away, but I was helpless.

He looked up at me and smiled, white teeth flashing, looking a wee bit disrespectable with his black eye faded to browns and greens. "I'm an early riser, like you. Tomorrow, I'm planning to head out early with my fishing rod. I'll leave at dawn. Why not slip out for an hour and join me? Before the household stirs."

I wanted to tell him I would. Aye, I will, master. I'd like nothing better. It was on the tip of my tongue to say it. But my brush with disaster the last time couldn't be set aside easily, and I hardened my heart. "No, master, don't ask me. One thing will on'y lead to another. An' I might end up shamed. It nearly happened the last time. I was at my wits' end, so I was, and you far from home . . ."

But all he could think about was his own wants. "You must call me James when it's just the two of us. It sounds wrong to hear the word 'master' on your lips, when I long for you to call me sweeter names. Say you'll meet me, Ellen. Just to walk and talk. Or to fish, if you like." He laughed softly. "Nothing will happen that you don't want to happen, I give you my word."

"No, master, I darsent. No good can come of it."

"I mean you no harm. I only have your best interests at heart. You must believe me."

"Harm would come of it, all the same. It allus does. I know, to my cost."

But he still wasn't listening to what I was trying to tell him. He stood up, walked to the door, and turned the key in the lock. Then he caught me by the waist, stroking a finger down one cheek. "You mustn't be so hard on us. I know you want this as much as I do. Don't deny it. Say yes, my bonny lass. Promise you'll meet me. Let's steal an hour together. Say yes."

Fool that I was, my willpower began melting. Maybes just a kiss or two, I thought. Maybes we wouldn't do any more. The thought of being alone with him for an hour was like turning a corner and chancing on a rainbow: an unlooked-for joy. He knowed I was weakening because he laughed again, as though we were conspirators. He sat back down and pulled me with him, onto his lap. As he nuzzled my neck, I closed my eyes, feeling my bones turn to water. Or maybes it was wine, because a feeling of warmth swept over me from head to toe.

"Open your eyes," he said. "I want to see what you're thinking."

I looked at him. His apple breath tickled my face.

"Your eyes are shining. Wait a minute, are you crying? Have I made you weep?"

"No, I bain't cryin'. I'm happy."

"You wonderful, special girl. You make me happy too. But we can make each other happier. Trust me. I'll look after you. Whatever happens, I won't desert you."

I wanted to believe him. My eyes fell on our hands, twined together, like those of trueloves. But wait, my hand was closer to a fist: red and swollen from work, veins standing out on the back. It looked ugly compared with his. I stared at them as his other hand roamed up my leg. I didn't want this reminder. But there it was, plain as day. Our hands showed up the difference in our stations. He could set it aside for a time, but I never could. What came of forgetting was too dangerous.

Panicked, I pushed him away, jumping off his lap and onto firmer ground. "You have to stop this, master. It's not fair of you to woo me."

"Ssh, don't make so much noise, Ellen. I'd never force myself on you. I thought you cared for me."

"I do, master, you know right well I do. But you have to let me be. For the love of God, let me be."

Just after cock crow, I listened to my master saddle his horse. He didn't need a mount to go fishing – he must be headed further afield. I was tempted to climb down my ladder and run out to the yard to him. My heart and my head were not in agreement when it came to James Haltridge. It went against the grain to refuse him. But even a pockle could see my story would end the self-same way as Ruth Graham's if I didn't take warning by her.

It was close on dinner time before my master came home, and he was in a foul mood. When he dismounted, he kicked away the greyhounds and tramped into the house, looking like he had supped with the Devil.

The mistress pattered up to him. "Where were you, James? I looked for you hours ago."

"Carrickfergus. On business."

"Frazer was here, asking for you."

"Frazer can go to hell. I'll be in my study. Send in a bottle of claret and some cheese, and on no account let anyone disturb me."

When Constable Blan and a dose of deputies rode in later, my master had no choice but to make an appearance. With them, they brought a woman in a cart. She was left in the yard with the deputies, where she stood, arms folded, looking round her: a big woman, with a fearless way about her, along with beefy arms and skitter-jabs the size of ha'pennies on her face.

"Jumped-up wee strap. He takes too much pleasure in his duty," grumbled my master, when I knocked to say the Constable was there. He held it against Brice Blan for digging up old Mistress Haltridge. But out he came, and into the parlour, where Isabel and Mary sat, and the Constable had made himself at home.

"Allegations of witchcraft have been made against a woman by the name of Margaret Mitchell – an unwed person, from Kilroot. We have reason to believe she may be the chief mischief-maker. If so, the coven's power is broken." The Constable had a strut to match our rooster's.

"It must be a relief to have the ringleader," said my master.

"Aye, but it has to be Mistress Dunbar who denounces her. And she has said on a number of occasions that the instigator is called Mistress Anne."

"Perhaps she used the name as an alias, to avoid detection."

"That's what I'm here to discuss with Mistress Dunbar." He turned to her. "You must face this Mitchell woman. Are you ready to do your duty?"

"Yes, Constable."

He knocked at the casement, and made a signal to his deputies to bring in the woman. "She's said to be a targe – all her neighbours complain about her picking quarrels with them. Information was laid before the Mayor, and we were sent directly to search her house. I personally discovered a wooden poppet, a close match to the one resembling Mistress Dunbar found in Lock's Cave. The woman claimed it was only a plaything, from when she was a bairn, fashioned by her da. But he's long gone to God, or the Devil, and in no position to say aye or nay."

A clatter outside the parlour door, and Margaret Mitchell was led in to stand before Mary Dunbar, as a tribe of others were before her. The young lady speedily agreed she was Mistress Anne, without any of the antics of previous denunciations. The big woman didn't take it as seriously as she should, and laughed at her, saying Mary must be touched in the head. It made no odds. The Constable was ready to believe her guilty because of the poppet, and Mary seemed unwilling to disappoint him. I couldn't help thinking this was hardly reason enough to name a woman a witch, and had no stomach to listen any longer, so I took myself off to boil water. Time I caught up on the cleaning.

I was lifting the pot off the fire when Mercy Hunter burst in, breathless at being whipped by the wind, and from throwing shapes at the Constable's men kicking their heels in the yard. She had news of a witch pricker lately come from Scotland.

"What does a witch pricker do, Mercy? Here, come to the well with me, I'm behind with my work."

"Why, he strips the prisoners and hunts with his brass bodkins for the Devil's tits, where familiars suckle their blood. Aul' Nick sucks there too, 'tis said."

She followed me out, and we watched as Margaret Mitchell was taken away by three deputies. "It'll be your mother or sister next," she told one of the men, and he hit her a clatter on the head. She was ready to strike him back, but they roped her hands behind her. Three other deputies remained, looking Mercy up and down. Men always noticed her.

"Every one of them women is refusin' to plead guilty, so more evidence is needed," said Mercy. "That's why Mayor Davies sent for the witch pricker. All witches are branded by a witch's tit. It gives them away."

Mercy was starting to think she knowed all about witches, on account of being maid to a minister.

A deputy offered to carry the bucket of water for us.

"We can manage," I said. "Give us a hand, Mercy, instead of makin' sheep's eyes there."

When she caught up with me at the door, I had to satisfy my curiosity. "Tell me, what does the witch's tit look like?"

"It's on'y wee, and you have to know what you're lookin' for. They try to hide it. It's masked as a freckle or a mole, or it might be put in some secret place – on their nether parts, or the back of the neck, up high where the hair grows. Once it's found, it damns you. Honest women have no such marks."

"But I have moles. I know you do, too, Mercy Hunter, for I seen them when we swum the-gether as wee'ans."

"Aye, but we don't let familars suck on them, do we?"

"I never heared tell of such a trade as witch pricker."

"My master persuaded the Mayor it was needful. Aul' Sinclair's smartin' since Mary Dunbar went missin' from his care. He thinks evil was visited on the island as a sign of God's disfavour, because folk are grown slack here. Sure your head'd be noddled listenin' to him bang his drum about it."

The water was bubbling on the fire when the parlour bell rang. "Mind that water does'n boil over," I said to Mercy, before answering the call.

The mistress directed me to serve ale in the kitchen to the Constable's men, and Mercy went out to the yard to call them in. She was keen to stay on and help, but I told her I could manage.

"Want them all to yourself, do you?" she asked, and I had to bite my tongue before I said something I might repent. It was bad enough having those great useless sides of beef in my kitchen, without watching them lose their heads over her forbye.

"Stay awhile, Bright Eyes," they called, when she waved farewell.

The deputies were a talkative crew, even before the ale loosened their tongues, and inclined to laugh up their sleeves at Mister Sinclair and the other clergymen.

"Them preachers are never done pesterin' the witches," said a baldy boy. "You'd nearly feel sorry for them. The questions they fire at the women would make your head spin. 'How long have you been in the snare of the Prince of Darkness? What promises has he made you? Do you keep toads, snakes or lizards, and caress them indecently? Confess at once, or lose your immortal soul. You'll know no peace till you confess.' I dinna ken how the witches thole it."

"Witches can stand anything, they're tough nuts to crack," said another. "I would'n go wastin' me pity."

"I'm jus' sayin' I would'n like to be on the receivin' end of them Bible-eaters. And thon dissenter, Sinclair, he's the worst."

"Ach, it makes a change for the witches. The worst thing about gaol is the boredom," said the third man, the one who had offered to carry water from the well. "You dinna ken day from night once the key turns in the lock. Any chance of some meat to go with this ale?"

I fetched them a platter of black pudding and a stale loaf, and they tucked in.

"Has a witch pricker been sent in to them?" I asked.

"Aye, yesterday. A Scotchman." The second man tore the bread apart with his filthy hands. "We had fun and games. He had us strip them to find their Devil's tit. You want to hear the yelps out of them."

"It har'ly seems right, strippin' them," I said.

"Right does'n come into it with witches," said the baldy boy.

His companions slapped their legs as if enjoying a jest.

"Buck naked, they were," said another. "Not that we could do much more than look. I would'n a minded pocklin' about a bit. But the ministers stayed close while we pricked them. Gettin' a good eyeful themselves, if you ask me."

"What do you know about prickin' witches?" I was

disturbed at the thought of Lizzie Cellar's clothes pulled off, her flesh handled by these apes.

"The pricker showed us how. The way to do it, see, is to blindfold them an' stick pins in their flesh. The Devil allus marks them, an' they never have no feelin' there after. They dinna know when the pin touches, so there's never a peep out of them."

"And do they cry out if it's just a freckle?"

"Oh aye, they squeal like pigs, some of them, if the pin goes in deep," said the third man. "Sometimes it draws blood."

"Did you find witch's tits on the women?"

"Not all of them." He wiped the back of his hand against his mouth and belched. "Not for want of tryin' with the young wan. She's a sonsey morsel. Her ma, a mouthy aul' sack, she fought us till we give her a couple of right slaps. We found a tit on her belly. Like mother, like daughter, I say. Maybe the young one needs to be stripped and searched again." And he shoved his elbow into the side of the fellow nearest him, and was thumped back, whooping.

I fetched them no more ale after that, even though one made a dumb show out of turning his empty beaker upside down. Listening to their blether, my dinner was threatening to work its way up my throat and out over the three of them.

◖◗   ◖◗   ◖◗

Frazer Bell called to discuss the arrests with my master. In the past, they had smoked many's a pipe whiles they mulled over politics and trade. Now all Frazer wanted to discuss was the witches. And, for a change, he and my master were not in agreement. Frazer felt sorry for the prisoners, while my master said they were a matter for Church and State to handle together, and honest men should stand aside and let them deal with it.

"Islandmagee will never be the same again," said Frazer Bell.

"Islandmagee can weather any storm. But I've had enough of witch talk. Can you believe it, Frazer? Bullocks are selling for up to four pounds and six shillings each in Dublin. The most you'd get for one here is two pounds, five shillings."

"James, don't pretend everything is all right now that a band of women have been arrested. A witch trial is upon us."

"Aye, I'm to give evidence at it. Will you be in court tomorrow?"

"The whole county will be there, I suppose I may as well join the rabble." His words had an edge. "I thought to spend the day on the land and miss the spectacle. But a sense of duty and a sense, I suppose, of inclination have acted on me. I feel the need to see this through."

The mistress was troubled by the coldness between such old friends. She put her hand on our neighbour's sleeve. "Of course you must go, Frazer. Would you stay home reading poesy on such a day? Mister Sinclair has volunteered to accompany us, hasn't he, James? To lend spiritual guidance."

"Folk are calling it the Islandmagee witch trial," said Frazer. "It's an outrage that Islandmagee's name should be tarnished."

"Islandmagee's name *has* been tarnished," said my master. "That's why the sooner this business is laid to rest the better. I'm relieved they have that Mitchell creature. No point in rounding up the small fry and letting the ringleader go free. I hear she's a woman of unruly spirits – apparently the dogs in the street are less quarrelsome than her."

"Being a scold doesn't make a woman a witch," said Frazer. He looked troubled. "Still, I can't deny Mistress Dunbar seems more her old self since the last of these women was locked up."

"She's much better," the mistress put in. "Her appetite is returning, and last night is the first in weeks where she managed to sleep right through."

"Mary says she thinks the witching is over now, Frazer," said my master. "Everything can get back to normal as soon as the trial is done with." Frazer let out a snort at that, and my master asked heatedly, "You appear to be some doubt about what's been happening here. How can you explain it, except by witchcraft?"

"I can't explain it. It perplexes me, all the same."

Silence fell, and I went to slip out to scrub the front step, grimy from all the comings and goings. The movement caught my master's eye. "Have you settled with Noah to take you in the cart to the Assizes tomorrow, Ellen?"

"Aye, sir. He's bringin' Mercy Hunter as well."

"See? The trial is an exhibition. 'Tis entertainment," said Frazer Bell.

"I'm not going to mock or to crow, sir," I said.

"You're going to see justice done, like a sensible lass," said my master. "Frazer, Mister Sinclair tells me a Good Samaritan is paying for a hot meal to be sent in every day to those witches. His initials wouldn't be FT, would they?"

Frazer picked up his hat. "Surely their poverty is proof they aren't in cahoots with the Devil? But folk are too blind to see it."

"Still, if they can't pay their bills in gaol, their possessions should be seized. That's only fair. Folk accused of crimes mustn't become debtors to the county." My master smiled with those white teeth of his, to take the sting from his words. "Cheer up – you look like a man who's been eating underdone mutton all week. Stay and dine with us."

"Thank you, no, James, I must be on my way."

When he was gone, my master said, "Frazer's a sound man, but he broods on things. Hang the whole damn lot of them, I say, and dump their bodies in a cesspit. If they hadn't been tricking about where they had no business, my mother's grave would never have been defiled."

Chapter 14

It was screek of day when Noah and me left Islandmagee to go to the witch trial, picking up Mercy Hunter on the way. Early though it was, we weren't the only ones on the road. As it grew lighter, we found ourselves in a procession of carts and carriages heading into Carrickfergus. That morning, I knowed it would be wet, because smoke came down the chimney. A dog eating grass is another sign of rain. But the weather did nothing to dampen our spirits, and conversation was gay between pilgrims. Among the women, there was a sense of relief at danger lifted: the witch hunt was over, and we not among those denounced.

We rattled through Kilroot, passing scores of folks on foot. The world and his wife were making their way to the same place as us. Many's the woman had her shoon tied round her neck, to save on leather till she reached the town.

Soon, the castle was ahead of us, with the sea behind it. No matter how often you saw Carrickfergus Castle, you couldn't help but be awestruck. Dark grey and mighty it stood against the sky – letting folk know they were in the most important town in these parts. The castle had a long, low keep stretching out into the waves, and whoever built it was a canny man because he gave it curved walls. No blind spots, see? My da told me that as a wee cuddy, and I never forgot it.

Traffic slowed right down, but we were happy to watch the militia practising their drill. Three mastiffs were chained to a gatehouse, with jaws that could crunch through bones as if they were blackberries.

Noah Spears had left off his usual torn smock, intending to make a good impression in the town, despite saying it was nothing but a den of thieves. And the town was making a good impression on him, or at least the castle was. "Them walls are twelve foot thick," he said. "Let the Frenchies try their tricks here, and see how far they get."

Some say the castle has stood in Carrickfergus these five hundred years and more. But I don't know if there's any truth in that. It sounds a powerful long time.

The crush meant we moved at a snail's pace. Noah told us to go ahead while he found a place to leave the ass and cart, and he would catch up on us. So out we hopped and joined those on foot. The courthouse was less than a cannon shot from the castle, but it took us a brave while to make our way to it. The crowd pushed and pulled us this way and that, but we gave the odd dig when we needed, holding our own.

Mercy stopped for a loaf of bread, but when the baker said he was looking tuppence for it, she laughed at him. "A bawbee's as much as it's worth. You're a robber, so you are."

At the courthouse, a crowd lined up. The double doors of oak, thrice the height of a man and studded with metal, were shut tight. Still, folk were in a holiday mood, eating and laughing and chittering about this and that – mostly the witches. If you put your nose in the air you could smell springtime, and it made folk itchy.

A woman in striped linen in front of us was ready for a chat. "Never let a witch's shadow touch you – it brings bad luck."

Mercy's eyes turned roundy. "What would happen?'

"Your fingers might drop off. Or you could loss the child

you were carryin'. Ach, you'd never know how the evil would fall on you."

"I heared a witch has no shadow," said another woman. "The Devil keeps it for her."

"Why do you suppose them witches bothered tormentin' the Dunbar lassie? Had they not more important folk to pick on?" said a man, wiping crumbs from his mouth with his sleeve.

"Jealousy," sniffed a woman you could see was a right blab. "I heared she's a pretty piece, and them witches all have faces on them like turnips."

"Will they hang?" asked a half-grown lad. "I'd give anything for to see a hangin'."

"Whatever they do with thon pack of she-devils, they darsent transport them – that's for sure," offered a man with a runny nose.

"Why not? On'y the other day a fellow was transported to a plantation in the Americas for house breakin'. Witchin' folk is worse."

"Witches can raise storms at sea an' wreck ships. No ship's master wud risk takin' them on board."

"My uncle says you want to see 'em kick when they're strung up," said the boy. "He watched a horse thief hang. Danced for a good half-hour on the end of the rope, so he did."

A rattle came from inside the courthouse, followed by a creaking, and a pair of soldiers opened the doors. When the crowd pushed forward, Mercy and I held hands to stay together.

"No sign of Noah," I said.

"He'll have to shift for hisself," said Mercy.

By now we were through the great hallway and inside the courtroom. I never saw such a high ceiling, nor so many domed windows – yet in no time it felt stuffy, the air stale from too many folk breathing it. The horse dung on the boots of the man in front didn't help. It was a brave handsome room, wainscoted from floor to ceiling, with great slabs of stone on the floor. Half the chamber was taken up with benches, and we followed the folk squeezing onto them. However many they were intended for, twice as many again crammed in.

There were men of the cloth wherever the eye fell. I never knowed the County of Antrim could hold so many. Grim-faced soldiers were everywhere, forbye. They were at the door, inside and out, and more of them standing round the walls. The only one who looked as if he had any use for gaiety was a drummer boy. You could see him longing to give a right old rat-a-tat-tat on the goatskin. Three or four haughty officers in jackets with a double row of polished buttons walked here and there between the troops. Spurs clashing and swords clanking, they turned heads. Mercy Hunter was in heaven when one of them gave her the eye.

A woman a few rows away from us took out a pasty and bit in, but a soldier knocked it from her hand. "No eating in the courtroom." She dusted it off and put it back in her pocket, complaining under her breath. But who can gainsay a man with a musket?

A buzzing went round when Mary Dunbar came in with my master, the mistress and Mister Sinclair. Everyone craned for a look. After all, it wasn't every day you saw someone who was witched. She seemed overwhelmed by the attention, peeping out from behind her cap with the lace lappets.

"Isn't she a poppet," said a woman nursing a baby at her breast.

"I wonder how she stood up to them besoms at all?" said another.

A hidden door opened in the wainscoting, and through it stepped a fellow in livery, wearing a powdered grey wig and shoes with red heels. He was lugging a staff as big as himself. He looked us over closely, before nodding at one of the captains, who nodded at a lieutenant. Out went a couple of soldiers, returning with a line of men at their heels. Twelve, in all. Well-got, they were, merchants or landlords or some such by the cut of them. Somebody said they were the jury. Red Heels tapped his staff again, and this time half a dozen solders and the drummer boy trotted out. They were gone no time before we heard the drum, followed by a tramp of feet, and the prisoners were led in. The drum beat made a solemn procession of it, though the wee drummer boy couldn't keep his face straight and a grin kept breaking through. The crowd was worked up by their arrival. "The witches," they hissed, and the soldiers had to push folk back and warn them to stay in their seats.

The prisoners squinted against the daylight. Their bonnets had been taken off them, though there was no call to show such disrespect, and their heads were close-cropped like wee scaldies. The scissors had sliced too close in places: scabs clumped where the blood was dried in.

"It's too bad they've been sheared," I said.

"Don't talk daft. A witch's familiar can cling to her hair," said Mercy.

I spied Lizzie Cellar behind Margaret Mitchell. Gaol had thinned her down so there wasn't a pick on her. She can't have done justice to those hot meals sent in by Frazer Bell. As for her beautiful nut-brown hair that used to fall to her waist, it was a sin to see it hacked from her scalp.

They were herded to a stand opposite the jury. Mary Dunbar let out a whimper as they passed near-hand, and the mistress put an arm round her kinswoman's waist. Another gentleman and his lady made their way across the room to them, and from the way they greeted Mary Dunbar I guessed them to be her parents. I was on the look-out for them. The mistress had invited them to stay at Knowehead for the trial, on account of the scarlet fever having passed over in Armagh, but they preferred an inn in Carrickfergus. Uncle Dunbar was a merchant, like his brother the glover, and liked to visit other shops when the occasion arose. There'd be no such chance in Kilcoan More.

"Order, order, order!" Red Heels banged his staff on the ground. "Pray be upstanding for their honours, Lord Justice James Macartney and Lord Justice Anthony Upton!" The concealed door was opened again, this time from the outside by a court official in the same livery as Red Heels, and two coxcombs appeared in scarlet robes and shoulder-length white wigs.

"Did you ever see such grand fellows in all your live-long days?" whispered Mercy.

Up they sat on thrones on a dais, under a coat of arms, and their conceit knowed no bounds.

"The court is in session!" bellowed Red Heels. A fine pair of lungs he had on him.

The judges looked to be about fifty. One wore spectacles and the other didn't. One had a yellowish complexion and the other didn't. Except for that, I found it hard to tell them apart.

The judge with glasses, Macartney, nodded to another fellow with more ruffles at his throat than you'd find on any petticoat. He was Clerk of the Assizes.

"We will open proceedings with a prayer," announced the frilly fellow.

A minister came forward and cleared his throat, covering his mouth with a hand, dainty-like, and hadn't he a ruby ring on it. Some men of God are closer to fops – Presbyters would never put up with such nonsense. "Christ Jesus, we ask you to bless this court and guide its deliberations towards a just and righteous judgment. We will now recite the Lord's Prayer." He squeezed his eyes shut. "*Our Father, who art in heaven, hallowed be Thy name . . .*"

Everybody joined in, nobody wanting to be thought ungodly.

I stole a keek round while the praying was going on, and saw faces from Islandmagee dotted here and there. Mary Dunbar looked a picture of innocence in dove-coloured cloth. The mistress was wearing her new cloak of plum velvet lined with rabbit skins, brought by the master from Dublin. The weather was mild, if damp, but she had to wear it on account of her need to turn heads. Mind you, she was pink in the face already from the heat of her fine feathers, and fanning herself constantly.

After prayers, the jury was sworn in, whiles the judges shuffled papers.

"Do we have any confessions among these documents?" asked Judge Upton. My, but his speech was polished.

"None, my lord. We have depositions from witnesses, and the plaintiff is in court to give evidence."

The judge studied the prisoners, who shrank beneath his notice. All except the big one. She gave him back look for look. "How do you plead?" he asked.

None of them answered. They seemed not to know they could speak up.

"All the prisoners deny the charge," said the clerk. "They have each lodged a 'not guilty' plea with the court."

"Stubborn hoors!" shouted a voice from the courtroom, and Red Heels banged his staff and called for order.

"We must hear how they plead from their own lips," said Judge Upton. "Prisoners have been known to change their pleas. Read out the charge to them."

The clerk lifted a parchment, and gabbled his way through it. He could read fast, I'll grant him that. It would have taken me half the morning, with all them long words.

"'*There being complaint made before us by Mistress Mary Dunbar of Armagh in the County Armagh, that diverse women are under high suspicion of sundry acts of witchcraft done against the laws of our Sovereign Lady Anne, by the Grace of God Queen of Great Britain, France and Ireland,*

Defender of the Faith, in the tenth year of her majesty's reign. These detestable acts, contrary to the statute of the first King James, were wickedly, maliciously and feloniously committed upon the body of the aforesaid Mistress Dunbar in the house of James Haltridge esquire of Islandmagee in the County Antrim. Whereby great hurt and damage has been done to the said person above named, who therefore craves justice.'" Then he read out the names of the eight accused.

Judge Macartney peered over the top of his spectacles. "You have been denounced as witches. What say you? Guilty or not guilty?"

"Spare me!" burst out one.

"All in good time. First you must answer the charge. Be you guilty of witchcraft, of which you are suspected? Yes or no? You must answer, so it can be recorded in the court documents."

One by one, the women said "Not guilty". Each time, Mary Dunbar shook her head and winced. Most of the accused answered in a mumble, irritating the judges. They wanted everybody to sing out loud and clear. But Margaret Mitchell called out "Not guilty!" right and plain, and didn't leave it at that, neither. "She has wronged me an' what she says agin me is false."

"The prisoner will confine herself to answering the question," ordered Judge Macartney.

Up jumped a skittery fellow in a bob-wig, with a visog on him like a kicked cur. He turned out to be the lawyer for the prosecution. "These women did shameful violence to the afflicted, the particulars of which I have here before me."

"Mister Blair will also kindly confine himself to addressing the court when he is invited to do so," said the judge. "We have not yet heard the formal indictment read into the record. Then, and not before then, does he have our leave to proceed."

The lawyer was a wee crawley-boy, thanking the judge for

slapping him down. Up he popped again as soon as he was given the say-so, going on about all the torture done to Mary Dunbar, between "body-arching spasms" and "bodily humiliations". Then he called the first witness to take the stand. There was a dose of ministers giving evidence, and before ever they were allowed to speak their piece they had to take an oath: *"The truth to tell and no truth to conceal, as I should answer for it on the Great Day of Judgment."* Every chance they got, they slipped in sermons about the Devil being an arch-deceiver, until even the judges were yawning.

The most preachy one of all was Robert Sinclair. Expecting to be on show, he had made an effort with his appearance: his coat was brushed, his boots scraped and blackened, and his wig put on straight. This was his big day, and he made a right song and dance about the part he played in battling Beelzebub.

"How did you first come to recognize these women as witches, as alleged?" asked Judge Upton.

The pockmarks stood out white on Mister Sinclair's cheeks. "The very fact of the accusation against these creatures damns them. Witchcraft is such a grievous sin that God would never allow an innocent person to be accused of it. Ergo, they must be guilty. These degenerate gets of the Devil must be brought to remorse for denying God's sacred commands. And they must be punished, mortifying their flesh for the sake of their immortal souls."

"It is up to this court to decide whether and how they deserve punishment, Mister Sinclair," sniffed the judge.

"Mistress Dunbar told me the coven had the power to raise Satan. He delighted in taking sods of peat, and throwing them at meeting-house windows."

"Why would Satan let himself be summoned up, and then be content with schoolboy pranks?" asked Judge Upton. "Surely he'd prefer to provoke war, famine and pestilence?"

"The Devil delights in any kind of mischief."

After all the ministers were done, my master was called. I felt proud of him there, with all eyes upon him. He made a braw show in his new navy double-breasted coat with the braid on the cuffs. He had nothing of the popinjay about him, but there was no doubting he was a man of consequence. Luckily his black eye was scarcely noticeable, or he might have looked less respectable.

I could see by the set of him he was a wee shade nervous, but he covered it up well and gave his answers with none of the embroidery that went before, describing the fit he witnessed at Knowehead. Then the lawyer thanked him for his help in leading the authorities to Margaret Mitchell, which caused a stir. My jaw dropped.

Mercy Hunter gave me a dig in the ribs. "You kept thon quiet."

"I knowed nothin' about it."

"Pull the other one, Ellen Hill."

"Whisht! I want to hear what the lawyer's sayin'."

"Perhaps you could explain to the court, Mister Haltridge, how you came to have your suspicious about the accused."

"Mistress Dunbar never named the woman who was causing her so much distress, but just lately she described her closely to me. Naturally I did my duty and passed this information on. Mistress Dunbar said the woman was without a husband, black-haired, heavily freckled, large rather than tall, and had fists like a man. Also, that she did not live in Islandmagee, but was near to Carrickfergus."

I was surprised at that, for I never heard the young lady say any such thing about Mistress Anne. She always said she kept her face hidden from her. Everyone turned to stare at Margaret Mitchell. She was, indeed, big, freckled and black-haired, and with those hands of hers she could have earned her keep as a butcher.

"How do you account for the discrepancy in names, Mister Haltridge?" Judge Upton put in.

"Mistress Dunbar explained that the accused used a false name to elude discovery. Forgetting, of course, that her victim was able to paint an accurate picture of her."

The lawyer continued, "I understand you were present when a conversation took place between the afflicted person and this Mistress Anne. Can you tell the court what you observed on said occasion?"

"On the first night following my return from Dublin, where I was engaged in business for some weeks, I was woken by a noise from Mistress Dunbar's bedchamber. When I investigated, she appeared to have an invisible visitor, whom she addressed as Mistress Anne. During the course of their conversation, Mistress Dunbar became agitated, and begged her not to tell lies, but to speak the truth as though the Last Trumpet had sounded."

"And what answer was made?"

"I could not tell, for the intruder was not just invisible but inaudible to me. However, Mistress Dunbar let out a pitiful moan. When I pressed her for the reason, she said Mistress Anne claimed there would be no Judgment Day. The Devil, her master, told her it was an old wives' tale."

A shocked rumble went through the court room.

"Following this encounter, Mistress Dunbar managed to furnish me with a detailed description of Mistress Anne."

My master was given leave to stand down, and congratulated on all sides as he returned to his place. I thought it odd, though, that I wasn't disturbed by Mistress Mary on the night he mentioned. The truth is, I tossed and turned on my pallet in the attic, thinking of him on the floor below me.

The lawyer turned to the jury. "Gentlemen, several of the accused were identified by means of descriptions as opposed to names. These descriptions are so detailed as to be beyond doubt. One of the victim's most vicious bullies had a squint, for example."

"Which of the accused is he referring to?" Judge Upton asked the clerk.

"Jane Miller, your lordship."

"Bring Jane Miller forward."

A woman was pushed towards the front by the clerk's assistant, and a ripple went through the crowd. She had a pronounced squint which gave her face an unfortunate cast, as though she was leering like those carvings in papish Mass houses.

"How came you by this deformity?" asked Judge Macartney.

She mumbled something.

"Speak up. What did she say?"

"She says she was born with it," said the clerk.

"The Devil marked her at birth," said the lawyer.

At that, a hissing rose up from the viewing benches, and the judges waved away Jane Miller.

"Where is the afflicted party who claims to have been molested by witches?" asked Judge Upton.

"She is here in the court," said the clerk.

"Swear her in."

Mary Dunbar made no move to get up. The clerk beckoned to her, followed by the lawyer, while Mister Sinclair leaned across the mistress and made a flapping motion with his hand. Grey about the chops, as if ready for her coffin, the lass stood up at last. But no sooner was she on her feet than she sat down again with a bump. The clerk minced his way down to fetch her to the stand, muslin ruffles at his chin fluttering. He led her forward, and lifted the Bible for her to take the oath, at which she swayed and fainted against him. Although he caught her most nimbly, he dropped the Good Book, which set the ministers tutting.

The fainting caused a stir, and even their lordships looked concerned. They sent water to her from their own jug, while the mistress forgot herself entirely and ran forward to fan

Mary Dunbar, though she looked as if she could use some air herself in her rabbit-skin cloak. When the young lady came to, she waggled her wee white fingers towards her throat. A gurgle came out, and she rubbed her neck, eyes bulging.

"Her voice has been robbed off her," whispered Mercy Hunter.

Mister Sinclair stood and asked for permission to address the court. "The young lady was in a state of the most prodigious apprehension coming to this courtroom, and begged to be excused. She said menaces had been made against her if she spoke out. I appealed to her not to shirk her duty, and she agreed to attempt to defy these fiends. But their combined might is too much for this courageous young Christian. Surely it is yet more evidence of their base arts."

"Very well, the young lady is excused," said Judge Macartney. "We have her deposition, which can be read into the record. When you're ready, Mister Crawford."

The clerk leafed through a sheaf of papers, cleared his throat and read aloud in a sing-song voice. It was all about the hows and wherefores of Mary Dunbar being tormented by witches.

"Were any of the accused witnessed attacking the plaintiff, Mister Blair?" Judge Upton asked the lawyer.

"No, my lord. They sent their spectres to do their monstrous work, which meant they were invisible to all but the afflicted."

"Is it possible the Devil could use someone's spectre without their knowledge?"

"No, my lord. I have submissions from three learned clerics on the matter. A person must give the Devil permission for his or her shape to be used."

"I see. Do any of the prisoners have witnesses for where they were at the time of the alleged bewitching?"

"Some do, my lord. But the prosecution proposes to the court that these accounts are worthless, since their bodies can be in one place and their apparitions in another."

Just then, a child had water spilled on its head by accident, and let out a lusty bawl.

"An odd place to practise that scriptureless habit of infant-sprinkling," a voice called out. There was general laughter, which the judges allowed to continue unchecked. I fancy they were ready for some relief themselves.

But in the midst of the merriment, a young girl leaped to her feet, shrieking words I couldn't make out. Those closest to her stopped laughing and turned to stare, and soon everybody fell silent.

"The walls!" she wailed. "What's happenin' the walls?"

The man next to her asked a question. The girl, who was maybe thirteen or fourteen and looked half-starved, shouted, "The walls are covered in blood! It's pourin' off them!" She looked down at her feet, eyes wild. "I'm standin' in it. It's lappin' at me ankles. Oh sweet Saviour, we'll all be drownded in blood!"

The woman nursing her baby let out a squawk. "Aye, I see it! It's like raindrops. Bloody raindrops. It's comin' doon thick and fast. Look at it spillin' out. This is God's judgment on us for harbourin' witches!"

Everybody turned to one wall, then another. Alarm swept the crowd. "Witchcraft!" went up the cry. As the terror spread, even the prisoners started yammering.

"I see it too! I see the blood!" screeched an old man, and soon there were five or six folk clamouring about the courthouse running with blood. "The blood of innocents!" yelled one man. "Preyed on by witches!" shouted another. Panic turned to mayhem. Those nearest the doors made a rush to get out, only to find them bolted. They started dundering on the wood, "Open up! Let us out!" A man with a red beard took a run at the prisoners, shaking his fist, and except two of the soldiers stepped forward to oppose his charge, injury surely would have been done.

Red Heels was getting nowhere banging his staff, but Judge Macartney put an end to the uproar. He beckoned to the sergeant, and spoke to him. The sergeant saluted the judge and stepped over to the drummer boy. A drum roll rang out. The boy's jaw was stiff with concentration as his sticks rattled above the screams. Meanwhile, the sergeant led away the girl who started the commotion. She went like one in a trance. Four or five more soldiers picked out others in the crowd who were fuelling the panic, removing them too. They were taken away through the door in the panelling from which the judges had come, rather than risk a stampede by opening the main doors.

Still, the racket continued, as folk tried to climb over one another to escape from the chamber. Mercy and me were nearly parted, pushed this way and that, but we linked arms and held on to one another. One of the ministers climbed onto a table and waved his hands at the crowd, and although his first words were lost in the din, it started to die down as folk turned to listen to him. An officer saw what he was doing and nodded to the drummer boy, whose sticks fell silent.

Now, the minister could be heard urging folk to be calm. "Do not fear, good people," he said. "Witchcraft has no power here. You are perfectly safe, I assure you." He held a Bible above his head. "This Holiest of Books will protect us. Let us sing a hymn together. '*How glorious is our heavenly king* – all together now – *Who reigns above the sky!*'"

By and by, folk joined in, and the panic eased off, with those who had left their places returning to them. Even so, it took quite a while for seats to be taken and order fully restored. At last, after what seemed like an age of confusion and noise, all was peaceful again.

"Such behaviour will not be tolerated in this courtroom," said Judge Upton. "One more squeak, and I will order it cleared. This is the Queen's court of law, not a fair-day junket. Standards must be maintained." He glared round him.

"Proceed, Mister Blair."

The lawyer said he meant to examine some of the prisoners, and called Bessie Mean. "You are accused of witchcraft, that damnable invention of Satan's. Who recruited you to this abomination?"

"I was recruited by nobody."

He let out a sigh you could have heard back on Islandmagee. "I repeat, who enticed you into a coven?"

"I was never enticed. I'm no witch."

"Remember you are under oath. I put it to you that you are a practitioner of an accursed art, as ancient as sin."

"I belong to no coven. God preserved Daniel in the lion's den and I trust to his mercy to preserve me the-day. I am innocent, and I pray to Him to prove it before this court. '*Oh give thanks unto the Lord for he is good, for his mercy endureth for ever.*'"

The lawyer did a jig on the spot, his shoon going clackety-clack on the floor. "You dare to mention God? He is calling upon you to confess, and recant your wickedness."

"I confess my sins freely, and with a humble heart, for God has lain on my shoulders far less than I deserve. But I say again, before a higher judge than these two gentlemen: I be no witch."

The lawyer dismissed Bessie Mean with a huffy flick of the hand, and called on another of the women. He made scant headway with her, or the one after.

Margaret Mitchell was next up, and she refused to admit she was a witch either, mocking him to his face when he called her a limb of Satan. He invited her to explain why she was named as a witch. She said the only reason she could offer was because she had helped at the lying-in of a neighbour, but the woman had died, and the child inside her. "I did me best," she said. "I know I have a tongue like the clapper of a hand-bell, but I would'n hurt a fly."

"Would you pray for Mary Dunbar?" he asked, and she

couldn't help herself. She threw the young lady a filthy look and said she'd sooner pray for Old Nick. That went down badly, and the lawyer was cock-a-hoop. He said he was through with examining the prisoners, and ready to do his summing up.

The judges gave their permission, though Judge Upton noted, "Tensions are high in this courtroom. I urge you to proceed with all speed."

Lawyer Blair tucked his hands under his coat tails and paraded before the jury. "Gentlemen, by their enchantments, witches have been known to raise mists and cause crops to fail. It is no stretch of the imagination to see how they might torture an innocent maiden, their malevolence excited by her refusal to be perverted to their loathsome cause. That which is baleful seeks always to contaminate. I put it to you that this is exactly what happened in the case of the unfortunate Mistress Mary Dunbar – victim of this deformed brood.

"If you exonerate them, you set them free to continue their infernal lord's work. You must stand sentinel against the Devil. If he had his way, you, your children and your children's children would boil in never-ending agony in hell's cauldron. It is clear that demons have established themselves in these women's bodies. Some of their answers to this court may have sounded plausible. They have even twisted scripture to their own ends. Do not be duped by their cunning, however. The law must show no mercy towards witches. Gentlemen, I call on you, I rely on you, I beseech you: do your Christian duty and find them guilty."

He sat down to a chorus of "Hear hear!" and was fawned over by his assistant, who treated him like the sun, moon and stars rolled into one.

Judge Upton asked, "Do the prisoners have anything to say in their own defence?"

None did, after the lawyer's outpouring. It would have taken the wind out of anybody's sails. They had no lawyer of their own. I heard a minister tell his friend they didn't need one, because the judges were meant to watch out for the prisoners' interests.

"Nothing at all?" repeated Judge Upton.

One of the eight called out in God's name that she was wronged.

"Houl' your tongue, you hell-hag!" shouted a man in the crowd, and no effort was made to silence him.

"Do we have any testimonials regarding the prisoners' characters?" asked Judge Macartney.

The clerk consulted his papers. "Depositions have been received regarding five of the accused, attesting that nothing criminal is known against them, and they are industrious and honest people. There are also depositions to the court which state that all of the prisoners are members of the Presbyterian Church, and regular in their attendance." The clerk turned over a page. "I understand a number of them were able to recite the Lord's Prayer when they were in prison. The captain of the guard has testified to it.'

The judges put their heads together and exchanged a few words. Judge Upton drank from his glass, straightened his collar and addressed the jury.

"The question for this court to decide is whether the plaintiff is the victim of witchcraft, or whether the prisoners are falsely accused by her. This is a perplexing business. It is beyond question that the plaintiff has been sorely tormented. This is supported by testimony from witnesses – gentlemen of the highest reputation, including those of the cloth. We have no reason to doubt her convulsions, or her suffering during them, and the objects she regurgitated have been inspected by this court. Nor is there any reason to suppose the plaintiff denounced the accused for malicious reasons of her own: the prisoners are completely unknown to her. However, proof that acts of witchcraft, contrary to the laws of our land, were carried out by the prisoners standing before this court is –"

He stopped and drank from his glass of water, Adam's apple bobbing. I daresay he was enjoying keeping everybody waiting.

"Thin," he continued. "It is an omission I cannot overlook. The apparitions described by the plaintiff in her statement are damning, but they were seen only by the afflicted person and there is no corroboration. Therefore, I am unable to advise conviction on the basis of them. Furthermore, a number of the accused can account for their whereabouts on the occasions under consideration. Mistress Mary Dunbar's visionary images are the sole evidence – everything else is circumstantial, hearsay or her word against theirs.

"I do not dispute that the whole matter is preternatural. But if the accused were really witches, and in compact with the Devil, they would not be regular churchgoers. Furthermore, confession is of the first order, yet none of the accused has confessed. Taking all this into account, it is my opinion that the jury should not bring in a guilty verdict. I recommend a verdict of *ignoramus*: no case to answer."

A hubbub sounded at once. "Shame," cried several voices. "'*Thou shalt not suffer a witch to live*,'" came from another.

"Silence in court," thundered Red Heels.

When the noise died down, Judge Macartney spoke. "I disagree with my learned friend. Witchcraft is the gravest offence known to man. Some say there be no witches at all, but only creatures silly in the wits. I am not of that view. There is no doubt in my mind that Satan's slaves walk among us, spreading their contagion. I see no reason not to admit spectral evidence: the pretext that these women were elsewhere was a device, intended to cover their tracks while their shapes visited Mistress Mary Dunbar, reviling and persecuting her. God is not to be mocked, however. Such diabolical wickedness cannot and must not be tolerated. I recommend a verdict of *culpabilis*: guilty."

This caused a racket too, but the voices raised were

approving. Both judges looked equally indifferent. The jury retired to consider their verdict. Onlookers stretched, and some predicted the twelve would send for candles and food, arguing long into the night. I stepped out for some air, and ran into Frazer Bell.

"What will happen to Lizzie Cellar and the others, sir?" I asked. "Will they hang?"

He footered at some objects in his pocket. "Even supposing they are found guilty, neither beast nor property has been damaged by them, and Mary Dunbar is the only human being harmed. By rights, they ought not to hang. But by rights they ought not to be on trial." He sighed. "The judges are divided. That's a good sign. It comes down to Mary Dunbar's word against that of the accused."

"Aye, but she's a lady." He said nothing, and so I pushed on. "Do you believe them to be witches, sir?"

"Ellen, I believe they're as innocent of witchcraft as you are – but they can trust neither to God nor man to clear them. Folk are only too eager to believe the worst of each other. Did you not notice how all the accused were poor, or old, or ugly, or in some way deformed? Or maybe just quarrelsome? It's enough to condemn them here. Yet I cannot deny that the peace of our neighbourhood is entirely disturbed. Something must be causing it. If not witchcraft, then what?"

The slap of hurrying feet made him look round, and someone shouted the jury was returning already. The twelve were gone for less than the space of an hour. As I went back in, I passed close to the accused. There was Bessie Mean, who brewed up Eyebright tea for my father after he was laid low with pains and couldn't work. And beside her was Lizzie Cellar, who came to Knowehead on my urging. A rank smell hung round the eight. I nodded at them, hoping to convey some fellow feeling, but they had formed a tight circle.

I compared them with Mary Dunbar, sitting there prim and proper with her hands hooked into one another, the way we

were taught in Sunday school. So genteel and elegant, she was
– she might have been new-minted. Only her mouth looked
out of place: her lower lip was ridged from where her teeth
had bitten through.

Chapter 15

"Guilty!"

The chairman of the jury spat out the word, and the eight prisoners burst into lamentations. Relatives in the court room added their voices to the hubbub.

Margaret Mitchell reared up, ready to do violence towards any of the jurors she could lay those hefty hands of hers upon. "Guilty me arse. May you never get meat on a Sunday," she snarled at the chairman.

"Insolent drab! I'll have you whipped," he flung back, though he looked shaken.

The clerk called for silence. "Pray be upstanding for the sentence of this court."

Judge Macartney did not look at the women as he spoke to them. "Have you anything to say before the court passes sentence?"

Their mouths stayed closed – even Margaret Mitchell's.

"Very well. *Probatum est* – the case is proved against you. Nevertheless, the court is inclined to leniency. The witchcraft you practised, while pernicious, was of the non-lethal variety. Count yourselves fortunate your victim appears to be in reasonable health, despite your insidious conspiracy against her. You are hereby sentenced to imprisonment of twelve months and a day, and are further ordered to stand four times in the public pillory. This will give you ample time to reflect on your scandalous behaviour."

"Bain't they to hang?" piped up a child.

A man answered him. "Naw, the-day's their lucky day. Maybes they put a spell on the judges, as well as on the lassie thonder."

The judges rose and went off together, with no sign of unfriendliness over their disagreement. Death, a whipping, or loss of liberty to those they dealt with was all in a day's work to them.

The soldiers prodded the prisoners and they shuffled out. Lizzie Cellar supported her mother, despite hirpling badly herself. I daresay Lizzie's leg was hurting from lying in a dungeon. Becky Carson tripped over her feet and banged into the woman ahead of her. Margaret Mitchell turned, and I was sure she would say something cutting, but she caught Becky by the arm and half-carried her along.

The crowd followed, danders up. When folk feel let down, anything can happen. One big ox of a fellow, who had to be a blacksmith from the soot only half-washed off his face, took a rope from round his waist and shaped it into a noose. He dangled it at the women, taunting, as the eight were loaded into a cart. Somebody picked up a stone and threw it at them. It bounced harmlessly against the wood, but Lizzie put her mother behind her for protection. Another man, whose aim was truer, took up a missile and it struck Lizzie in the face. She fell to her knees. Up went a roar of glee, and those closest to the cart started pounding and then rocking it.

The captain of the guard let fly with a string of oaths, lashing out left and right with the hilt of his sword, while his soldiers used their musket butts to try and clear a space round the cart. But as fast as they beat people away, more rushed forward to take their places.

"Get back, damn you to hell!" yelled the captain.

"What are you protecting them for?" came the jeers.

I had a good look at his face then, and saw it was Captain Young.

The blacksmith let out a shout. "The bitch! She's givin' me the evil eye!" Quick as a wink, he flung the noose at Lizzie and managed to get the rope round her neck at the first throw. Before anybody could stop him, he jerked her overboard into the sea of bodies. As she sank, I thought I heard her moan like a cow in labour before she was lost to sight.

Captain Young signed a command to his sergeant, and a volley of shots rang out over the heads of the crowd. It acted like a dose of ice water. Folk froze. A second volley and they scattered. The captain snatched up Lizzie, face down on the cobblestones, and threw her back into the cart with as little gentleness as she was taken from it. Then he leaped onto that black stallion of his, nudged it alongside the cart, and grabbed the bridle of one of the horses hitched to it.

"Let's go! Use your whip!" he shouted to the soldier at the reins.

He clapped his spurs to his mount, and the cart rumbled off at speed. Meanwhile, his sergeant lined up the remaining soldiers, their muskets trained on the crowd.

"Who's addled enough to die for a witch?" called the sergeant. "This time we're not firing over your heads."

◠ ◠ ◠

I didn't oftentimes get a chance to spend a wheen of hours in Carrickfergus. When I did, I liked to admire the handsome buildings and fancies in the shops – though Mister Sinclair said sober dress was more pleasing in the sight of God. Still, usually I enjoyed a look. But after the court case I had no heart to take my pleasure. And pickpockets were bound to be at work, so I was nervous of my few shillings. My purse was tucked into a pocket in my shift, but those rascals had nimble fingers.

Forbye that, I had an uneasy feeling about Knowehead. Anything could be happening in the house, with not a soul left to keep an eye on the place. There was no certainty that finding eight women guilty of witchcraft would end the pother there. Like as not, some new class of disturbance was lined up.

At least Jamesey and Sarah were over at the Widow Patterson's farm, rather than in the house. They had begged to come to Carrickfergus, but my master felt they were too young for such a spectacle, and arranged with the widow to keep them for the day. He wanted her to sit with them in Knowehead, but she said no power on earth would persuade her to spend time in that house, with only two bairns for company. My master wasn't a bit pleased, but he could find nobody else to take them.

I would just as soon have gone straight back to Islandmagee after the sentencing, and fetched them home. How and ever, Mercy wasn't ready to leave, and we still hadn't met up with Noah Spears, so I had no way back. There would have been space in the carriage my master hired – I could have sat with the coachman – but the Haltridges had gone off with the Dunbars and Mister Sinclair to dine in an inn. Whether grand or humble, folk saw this as a holiday.

Mercy and I walked about the square, arm in arm. At first she wanted to talk about the reed hoops worn by fine ladies, to make their gowns stand out. But there was so much to see that she soon left off chattering and stared her fill. A circle gathered round a Punch and Judy show with a hangman puppet by the name of Jack Ketch. Every time he popped up he was greeted by howls of laughter. Nearby was a man with a set of reed pipes, and a black and white spaniel in a ruff. When he played his music, the wee dog hopped up on its hind legs and danced along. It hardly seemed Christian but it was certainly droll.

Our mouths were watering, between the meat-pie stalls

and the jam-tart sellers – there was even gingerbread for sale in the shape of cats, a witch's familiar. Mercy gorged herself on it. Only the previous Sabbath, her master preached a sermon against gluttony, but everything went in one ear and out the other with Mercy Hunter.

"What news?" folk greeted one another.

"Guilty as sin," came the answer.

"They got off light," was a common complaint.

"At least they're locked up where they can do no more mischief." The speaker pointed to the pillory. It was raised on a platform in the market square – a fearsome-looking wooden device. "We'll get our chance to show the hoors what we think of them on fair day."

Apart from me, nobody was in any humour to go home. There was a stretch to the days after the long winter. And the trial had folk all worked up. Such a carry-on hadn't happened in living memory in these parts, though the ones lately come across from Scotland said they were common as muck over there. Witches were everywhere, and they knowed how to deal with them.

"Half the time we dinna bother with the law. If the kirk tells us a woman's been consortin' with Satan, we take care of her ourselves. Saves time," said a sandy-haired fellow. "The Scotch in Ireland be too soft on witches. It gives them a chance to lay their traps. Why do you think yiz had eight of them hussies lined up in the dock? You let them spread like fleas. That's why." Down came his hand on his thigh, with a skelp that raised dust. "Flatten the hell-faggots. That's how you handle witches."

A preacher started guldering about weak vessels being all too easy for the serpent to seduce, as far back as the Garden of Eden. "Beware the treachery of Eve," he warned, and the crowd became even more fired up. Especially the women, who wanted to show they had no truck with Lucifer.

"Them Jezebels should be hung," said one woman.

"Aye. Stretch their necks till they snap," said another.

"Hangin's too 'asy on them," said a man holding his wee daughter in the crook of his arm.

Then I heard a fine gentleman, in a velvet coat the colour of a grassy meadow, turn to another just like him and say, "Nothing matches the cruelty of the rabble, turned ferocious by ignorance and superstition."

But was he not there for the sport, same as everybody?

The mood was in danger of turning ugly again, till a peddler lightened it. He leaped onto a barrel and piped a few bars on his whistle. "Be warned by their fate – gather roun' for a tale to make your hair stand on end. Come closer, friends, and let me tell you the story of The Witches of Islandmagee." The crowd turned to him, hungry for diversion. "It happened here, good folk, right under your noses. The Prince of Darkness walked among yiz, and took the shape of a woman."

"Eight women!" shouted a voice near the front.

"But they got what was comin' to them. Evil did not triumph, friends. Justice was done today." The peddler piped a few more notes, stamping his feet to the beat.

"Let's get closer, I want to hear this," said Mercy Hunter.

Folk were joining in by the time the chorus came round again. One fellow, old enough to know better, burst into a prancing wee jig of his own invention. The peddler blew Mercy a kiss when he spied her. She gave him a long look in return, till I dug her in the ribs to remind her of modesty.

"You'd think butter wud'n melt in your mouth," she said.

It struck me that for all her sauce, Mercy was probably purer than me: a thought to steal any peace of mind a body might have.

When he was finished, the peddler skipped off the barrel, nimble as a frog, and someone reached him a pitcher of ale. I daresay he intended hawking his song further afield when he was through with us. Stories of witchcraft find a willing audience. Men and women are not so different from childer. They like to be frightened, just so long as the wicked are paid out in the wages of sin at the end.

I hardly like to confess it, but I bought a ballad – I was one of those fools soon parted from their money. The peddler winked, handing it over, but as I paid my thruppence I saw a mark on his left thumb that looked as if he was branded for a thief. "A burn from the fire," says he. No sooner was the money gone than I was sorry, because he offered to trade Mercy one for a kiss. Mind you, giving a ballad to Mercy Hunter was a waste – she could scarcely read more than her name.

The pamphlet showed a drawing of a woman fondling a goat, with her skirts kilted up to her knees. *Be Warned by Their Fate: The Witches of Islandmagee*, it said.

> *There once was a nest of foul witches*
> *Who worshipped the Devil not God*
> *They danced naked at fiendish assemblies*
> *Cavorting with he-goats and dogs.*
> *O, if they don't swing for their sins*
> *Then they'll surely roast*
> *If the law it don't stretch them*
> *Devil snatch the hindmost.*
> *On dark nights when good folk lay sleeping*
> *Their vice they indulged, to their shame*
> *By tormenting an innocent virgin*
> *Who bravely resisted their games.*
> *O, if they don't swing for their sins*
> *Then they'll surely roast*
> *If the law it don't stretch them*
> *Devil snatch the hindmost.*
> *The maiden was pure, incorruptible*
> *To prayers and her faith she held tight*
> *And the witches were tracked down and punished*

Putting paid to their Satan-stirred spite.
O, if they don't swing for their sins
Then they'll surely roast
If the law it don't stretch them
Devil snatch the hindmost.
So bolt all your casements, lock every door
Stuff rat holes and chimneys with rags
And pray God and his angels preserve you
From Islandmagee's evil hags.
Yes, pray God and his angels preserve you
From Islandmagee's evil hags.

  ◖◗ ◖◗ ◖◗

The day was wearing thin by the time we spotted Noah watching a wrestling match fornenst the Castle, and got our lift home from him. Mercy Hunter gabbed in my ear every step of the way: she was all delighted with herself because a value in coin had been put on her kisses. But I paid her no heed. I was thinking about what the pedlar said about justice being done in Carrickfergus courthouse.

Justice didn't feel all that satisfactory.

As we neared Kilcoan More, smoke appeared on the horizon. Not a lazy curl from a chimney stack, but thick clouds of it rushing upwards and outwards. My heartbeat pounded in my ears, louder than anything the wee drummer boy could manage – a fire meant death and destruction. Mercy clutched my arm. "Whose house do you think it is, Ellen?"

I shook my head. It could be any one of a number of places.

Noah Spears slapped the reins to persuade the ass to pick up speed. When we rounded the corner, we saw the cause of those grey plumes. The meeting-house had gone on fire.

"The minister'll go off his bap when he sees this," gasped Mercy.

314

The fire was nearly out now – others had reached the blazing building before us. But you could smell it still in the air. The sizzle, the scorched wood, the ruin. This was a fire that had raged away to its heart's content for a time. It must have caught hold while everyone was at the witch trial. It was a wonder anything was left above ground. The roof had caved in, and the doorway was in bad shape, but the blackened walls were holding up. The meeting-house was in a sorry state, but it was still standing.

"What happened?" Noah called to a soot-covered group of men.

Bob Holmes broke away and walked across, coughing. "Turf ashes were throwed on a dunghill over thonder. Our best guess is a wind blowed up, an' tossed some of them onto the roof timbers. That let the fire get goin'. A-coorse, it never could a taken hould if the whole blessed island had'n been in Carrickfergus, hopin' for a mass hangin'. It's a mercy there's a wall left." A coughing fit took him and he bent over, holding his knees, while Noah leaned down to hammer his back.

"There's more to this than meets the eye," said Noah, and we all nodded. He turned the cart to drop Mercy and me home.

"I never thought I'd say this, but I feel sorry for aul' Sinclair," Mercy said. "He's bein' punished for takin' a stand agin witches, so he is."

"Ach, maybes he is and maybes he is'n. It could be an accident."

"Oh aye, Ellen Hill. An' I'm a currant bun."

"I'm just sayin', is all."

"This is no accident. Not in the kirk. Not the-day above all days."

When it was just the two of us in the cart, I asked Noah, "What do you make of the fire?"

"It's a warning, that's what it is. The Hunter cuddy is right. Thon's no accident. God suffers the Devil to do as he likes in Islandmangee."

⟪Ϙ   ⟪Ϙ   ⟪Ϙ

The following day the Vicar of Belfast, William Tisdall, came to Knowehead to meet Mary Dunbar, and was disappointed to miss her because she had stayed the night with her parents in an inn in Carrickfergus. There would have been space for all of them in the house, but the Dunbars seemed to prefer to keep their daughter to themselves, though they promised to call soon. So the vicar had a wasted journey. He had taken notes in court, and said he was going to write up her case in a journal.

My master was far from pleased, and asked him to do no such thing. "Islandmagee is being turned into a laughing stock, Doctor Tisdall. We want to forget this. How can that happen if Mistress Dunbar becomes a figure to be pointed at on the street?"

"Can she put it behind her? I spoke to her while the jury were out. She disclosed that she was afflicted the entire time she was in court by a man's voice whispering in her ear. She said he was suggesting vile, unrepeatable things of a lewd nature. Surely she told you?"

"Mistress Dunbar did say something about it, but we naturally put it down to the strain. She was dreading the ordeal of the trial."

"She said the man was the notorious Hamilton Lock. The ghost of him, that is. I believe he has a close connection with this area. In all conscience, I ought to bring it to the attention of the Mayor."

"You can leave me to do that, if you see fit, doctor. I have an appointment with Mayor Davies tomorrow."

"Very well. *Sufficient unto the day is the evil thereof.*"

The Belfast vicar accepted some sherry wine and biscuits. As I was serving him, he asked whether I attended the Assizes in Carrickfergus.

"I did, sir."

"Did the case serve as a lesson to you about what comes of meddling where it's forbidden?"

"I'd never meddle where I should'n, sir."

"So you took nothing from the spectacle of the witch trial?"

"I thought 'twas a pity to see so many auld women in the dock. I was taught to honour grey hairs. Though a-coorse if they did wrong, they have to be punished. Except – gaol could finish some of them off."

"The old make way for the new. 'Tis the cycle of life."

"Aye. What's auld is oftentimes swept away. But what if it bain't willing to go? Say it resists – what then?"

Maybes I spoke out of turn, or was more kindled than was seemly, because he set down his glass and studied me. He looked ready to quiz me further, but the mistress sent me off with a flea in my ear.

While I was redding up after the visitor, I observed the mistress give my master a tap on the arm. "You know my aunt and uncle are due to call tomorrow to collect Mary's trunk. Will you miss them, if you have an appointment with the Lord Mayor?"

"I'm not meeting Mayor Davies. It's just a story I told that interfering vicar. Enough is enough. Mary must go home, and we must put all this behind us."

๙ ๙ ๙

When another day passed, the Dunbars arrived by carriage with their daughter, to pay their respects to the Haltridges before carrying her back to Armagh. They had tarried in Carrickfergus till they judged her able for the journey. As soon as Mary Dunbar was back in the house, the childer trotted up to hang off my skirts and get under my feet, though I didn't mind – the young lady's company affected their spirits. Wee Sarah was keen to be useful, bless her, and helped me fold the laundry that was being sent out for washing and pressing. But when the mistress told me to go to Mary's chamber and help the young lady pack her trunk, both wee'ans made a lip and stayed put in the kitchen, keeping their heads down.

Everybody agreed it was high time Mary Dunbar quit Knowehead House. Everybody but Mary Dunbar, that is. While I gathered up her belongings, she spent her last hours with us wandering through rooms, stroking walls, her forehead lined.

Horse hooves clattered up to the door, and I skipped downstairs to open it, expecting Frazer Bell to pay his final compliments. Instead it was Mister Sinclair, complaining about his kirk nearly burning down. In the parlour, he looked for the young lady at once.

"But where is Mistress Dunbar? She must have some insights into this fire, and the imps who connived at it."

I was sent to find her, and discovered her in her bedchamber on the window seat. But Lord above, such a sight met me. The japanned sewing box was sitting there, wide open, though I packed it myself. She had taken the shears from it – they lay on her lap still – and had used them to cut off her hair. Hunks of it were streeling in balls at her feet. The little that remained spiked round her head. Patches of her baldy scalp showed through, like a half-plucked chicken.

"Mistress, what have you done to yourself? What possessed you?" She shrugged.

I took the scissors away in case she did more harm with them – though the damage was done already, as far as her lovely curls were concerned. I tried to smooth down the hair, but up it spiked again, so I dipped the corner of my apron in her pitcher of water and dampened it flat. "Let's get your cap on, to cover the worst." When I tied her bonnet under her chin, she didn't look so strange. She sat there like Sarah's rag doll, letting me do as I liked. But when I tried to pull her to her feet, she held tight.

"Your mother and father are waiting, mistress."

"Go away. I can hear nothing with your chatter."

"But what is it you're tryin' to hear?"

"The voice."

"Whose voice?"

She didn't answer.

"Do you mean a witch's voice?"

She chewed on her thumb. "It's just a voice. It whispers."

"Is it a man or a woman's?"

"Hush, let me listen, I tell you."

I had no choice but to go back and let the mistress know the young lady was not yet ready to leave. "I'll handle this, Isabel," said her mother, seizing her skirts and marching towards the stairs. A good space of time passed before she brought her daughter down, while Mister Sinclair pulled at his stockings, bagging at the ankles, and droned on about how the dark shadow hanging over Islandmagee was not yet dissolved. Still more repentance was needed.

"Those fiends need not think burning the meeting-house can silence our prayers. Whether we raise our voices to heaven in a barn or a kirk makes no differ. Ah, Mistress Dunbar, I presume you heard about the mischief done to our kirk?"

"I did, Mister Sinclair," said Mary. "It does not surprise me."

"But the coven has been broken up. The witches are behind bars."

"Hamilton Lock is still here."

The minister paled. "Lock! Does he trouble you yet?"

"I hear his voice. At times, it feels as if my head might burst asunder listening to it."

"Had he a hand in the fire?"

"Of course. He told me about it in court. He sniggered to think of the upset it would cause.'

"Why did you not say anything?"

"I was forbidden to tell of it. His voice cannot be disobeyed."

The Dunbars exchanged alarmed looks.

"Now, Mary, remember what we discussed," said her mother. "You need rest and quiet."

"Yes, Mama."

"No more talk of a voice inside your head."

"Yes, Mama."

"But if the young lady has information about the fire in my meeting-house, she must be questioned," said Mister Sinclair.

"I regret that's impossible, Mister Sinclair. My daughter is far from well – her health has been under attack."

"As has my meeting-house."

"Mister Sinclair, my daughter has come through a shocking ordeal. She needs to recuperate. I am sure you would not want to risk her health any further. Come, Mister Dunbar, we must bring our chick home. Mary, kiss your cousin."

Mary Dunbar went to the mistress.

"Where are your curls, Mary? Your bonnet's all loose on your head. What have you done to yourself? Or has someone else been interfering with you?"

"Never mind that now, Isabel," said her mother. "Say your farewells, Mary."

"My head hurts, Cousin Isabel."

"Poor sweetheart. You'll feel better when you're back in your own bed."

"But I can come again for a visit, can't I? When I'm feeling stronger?"

The mistress stroked her cheek. "Of course, Mary. Or I'll visit you in Armagh."

"No, I must come to Islandmagee. My work here isn't finished."

"What work is that?"

"I – I'm not sure. To do as I'm bid."

Her parents hustled her outside, to where the carriage was waiting. I recalled her sewing box on the window seat, and raced upstairs for it. When I carried it out to the carriage, Mary Dunbar was standing on the top step, shielding her eyes as she gazed back at the house.

"I'm not supposed to leave Knowehead House, you know. I promised to stay. I keep thinking the house must be angry with me. But I can't tell how it feels. It seems – empty. Maybe it's resting. Everyone needs a rest sometimes."

"Who did you make a promise to, about staying?" asked my master.

"Why, the house, of course. Surely you talk to it too, Cousin James?"

Her father spared my master the need to frame an answer. "Get into the carriage, Mary. It's high time we were on the road."

I cast an eye across the fields. Still no sign of Frazer Bell. We had neither sight nor sound of him since the trial. Mary Dunbar must have thought he would call too, because she raised herself up on tiptoe, gazing in the direction of his land. The young lady sighed, dipped her head and entered the carriage, settling her skirts. But when her father went to shut the carriage door, she cried, "Wait, I haven't said all my goodbyes." She beckoned to me and put something wrapped in paper into my hand, saying I was to pass it on to Mister Bell. "Tell him I embroidered it myself."

The door was slammed, the driver flicked the reins, and the last I saw of the young lady was her totie wee face at the window. It was papery compared with her morning freshness on the day she arrived among us.

     ✑   ✑   ✑

The day after Mary Dunbar left Knowehead, Frazer Bell came galloping over on Lordship. He burst into the house, unshaven, in as thran a mood as ever I saw him. The mistress was lying down, and my master was glad of the company at first. But not when he heard what was on Frazer Bell's mind.

"James, we have to go to the Mayor together and convince him Mary Dunbar ought to see a physician. It's scurrilous there was no medical evidence given at the trial."

"That ship has sailed, Frazer. You should have raised it in court if you felt so strongly about it."

"I've been wrestling with my conscience, and I cannot stay silent. I ran into Mister Dunbar in Carrickfergus, the day after the court case. The lass is prone to imagining things – her own father let it slip. This past winter, before she came to Islandmagee, she fell into fits whenever anything crossed her humour. She accused a maid of turning herself into a black cat and prowling the streets at night. The Dunbars paid the girl off, thinking there had been some falling out between the two."

"Are you saying she made everything up?"

"James, whether she is designing or deluded, I cannot judge. But she has caused untold damage. People point to witchcraft when they can find no other explanation."

"What other explanation is possible, Frazer?"

"Not everything has an easy answer. Some things are inexplicable." Frazer Bell put his hand on my master's shoulder. "Come with me to the Mayor, my friend. There is no evidence Mary Dunbar acted out of spite, though she has caused suffering and hardship. We could say she was confused."

"Confused by Satan?"

"Possibly."

"In which case she must be the witch. Come, come, my friend, you're not thinking straight. Do you want Mistress Dunbar to take the place of those eight wretches?"

"Of course not. But perhaps they could be pardoned if we explain that Mistress Dunbar has made accusations before."

"Let it go, Frazer."

"I can't stand by and see an injustice carried out. And yet . . ." He dragged his hand down one side of his face. "And yet something happened in this house, James. Something that defies rational explanation. I've turned it over and over, and I can't make head or tail of it."

"What's done is done, man. Let sleeping dogs lie." My master patted him on the back.

Frazer Bell's broad shoulders were hunched with worry as he took his leave. He had the weight of the world on them, like that fellow Atlas my master told me about once. I waited by the door to give him his parting gift from Mary Dunbar, and he opened it in front of me. It was a handkerchief with a legend stitched on: "*The bright day is done, and we are for the dark.*" He would not accept it: "Throw it in Larne Lough or keep it, as you see fit." But he couldn't help himself – he had to ask about Mary Dunbar. "How did Mistress Dunbar look the last time you saw her? Was she cured?"

"No, sir. I would'n say so." I thought of her cropped head, and the tufts of hair standing up on it. How did she look, he wanted to know. Very well, I'd tell him. "She looked like them eight women tried as witches in Carrickfergus. That's how she looked."

Frazer Bell groaned, jumped on his horse and set off like an army of demons was in pursuit.

My master passed me in the hall. "Even if Frazer goes to him, Mayor Davies won't pay him a blind bit of notice. This is a knot that cannot be unpicked."

That gave me a jolt. It was knots being unpicked that started the whole caper off. I was reminded of those nine knots in the apron strings: eight on one side and one on the other. And there were eight women condemned as witches on one side of the court room, on the word of one woman on the other. Truly, a pattern was at work here. And for all we knowed, it was being woven still.

A heavy cloud continued to hang over Knowehead, blocking the sunlight. Mary Dunbar was gone, but there was something here still.

I walked on eggshells going about my work.

Chapter 16

The peace we hoped for at Knowehead after Mary Dunbar went away did not come. The air in the house was all stirred up, just the same as during the witching – sometimes, it felt as if I was wading through porridge while I went about the day's jobs. When a calf with two heads was born to Parsley, it looked powerful bad for the Haltridges. The creature drew breath for a matter of minutes only, and I never saw it, but Noah Spears helped birth it and he told me how unnatural and hideous it was. My master tried to hush it up, but word got out and folk kept their distance from us.

I had another reason to fret, during the weeks after the trial. Try though I might, I could not forget all those women in gaol. In particular, I was bothered by Lizzie Cellar being hauled into the crowd and beaten, until the soldiers saved her. She took some sore blows, and I wondered if anybody would treat her injuries. The sight of her face streaming blood plagued me. In the morning, when I splashed water on my cheeks, she looked back at me from the basin. At night, when I lay sleepless under the roof, listening to the rain drumming down, I wondered was she hearing the same sound in her cell. In the end, I asked my master for a day's freedom.

"You had a day off for the witch trial, Ellen."

"I did, master."

"Your mistress won't like you gadding about again so soon. Why do you want a holiday?"

"To go to Carrickfergus to visit Lizzie Cellar. One of them named as witches."

He raised his eyebrows. "Is she a friend of yours?"

"I knowed her when we were childer. But I've been no friend to her. I can do her a good turn now, though. She caught a stone in the face the day of the court case. Some ointment Peggy left behind might mend the blow."

He tapped a thumbnail against his teeth, considering. "How would you get there?"

"I'll start walkin', master, and hope someone might pity me on the road."

He took his time answering, making me wonder if honesty was the best policy. Maybes I ought to have told him my mother was ill and calling for me. But I didn't like to tempt fate.

Finally he said, "I'll take you myself. No time like the present. I'll fix it up with your mistress. Fetch me a chop and some ale, and we'll leave directly after I've dined."

⁂ ⁂ ⁂

I half-expected Master Haltridge to seize the chance to pay court to me as we rode along, me holding on to his belt with both hands – not even a basket between us, since the few bits I had for Lizzie were in a pouch at my back. I didn't believe he was playing the Good Samaritan for Lizzie's sake. But he clapped his spurs to the grey stallion's flanks and rode like the wind, making no attempt to woo me. I leaned in and breathed his clean smell, but could take no real pleasure in our closeness because my thoughts were nipping at me. I was never inside a prison cell, and not looking forward to my first time.

When we reached Carrickfergus Castle, my master pulled up by a mounting block so I could climb off. He did not dismount, but held my arm to aid me. Then he reached me down a coin. "You'll need this for the guard." Seeing I did not understand, he added, "To grease his palm. I'll meet you back here in an hour – you'll be well finished by then. A dungeon is no place to loiter."

   ≪@ ≪@ ≪@

The door clanged shut behind me. It was dark in the cell. Cold, too. The kind of cold that makes you hump your back. The kind that settles on your joints and gives them no let-up. There was no window, not even a slit to let in a slice of light. But the thing I noticed above everything else was the smell of decay: it was overpowering. A dozen midden piles would hardly send out a reek to match it. My belly heaved when the stink reached my nose, and I nearly lost my footing. I shuddered, wishing my conscience wasn't prodding me into this visit. But there was no help for it, so I took hold of myself, breathing through my mouth.

"Good day," I said. It sounded feeble. I cleared my throat and tried again, louder. "Good day." I forced myself forward and splashed through a puddle. Whether it was piss or rainwater I couldn't tell, but the handful of straw thrown on the ground was no use against it.

I squinted into the darkness. All I could make out were huddled forms. "Lizzie? Lizzie Cellar? Are you there? It's Ellen Hill."

A jabber came from several mouths, but you could not call it words.

My hand was shielding the candle given to me by the guard, for I was in the horrors at the thought of no light in this pit. Now I took away my hand and raised the flame shoulder-high. I could see the shapes were people, four of them. I moved closer, and they shrank from the orange glow.

"I've brought food. Here, you must be hungry." I unhooked the pouch I was carrying, pushed aside a napkin, and lifted out a drumstick. No sooner was it in my hand than a gust of hot, rotting breath blew in my face, and the chicken was grabbed. A pair of fierce eyes in a filthy face glared at me, gnawing the leg, swallowing the meat without chewing.

But then Margaret Mitchell slowed, and glanced behind her. She took another bite, before holding out the drumstick to a prisoner hunkered with her back against the wall. A lump of pale-brown flesh clung to her lower lip, and her tongue scooped it up. The taste made her think twice, and she looked again at the remains of the chicken leg. But she offered it still. When the woman did not take it, she shuffled forward and pushed it into her hand. The prisoner's fingers closed round it, without making any attempt to eat. Margaret Mitchell guided the hand upwards, towards Kate McAlmond's mouth.

I squinted at the other forms, trying to make out Lizzie. She must be here if the guard said so. A slumped shape, longer than the others, had to be her. Her hair had grown back a bit, covering up the scabs I remembered from the trial, but I couldn't see her face because it was pressed into her lap.

"Lizzie, it's Ellen Hill. From Islandmagee. I'm your friend. I have some salve here for you. So your face can heal. Lizzie? Don't you know me?" I juked down beside her, moving aside a patch of straw to find a safe place for the candle. She shrank back, whimpering. "It's all right, Lizzie dear. I'm here to help."

Another shape made a rush at me across the cell. "Stay away from her." It was Lizzie's mother, Janet Liston.

"Have a sausage, Mistress Liston. It's from our own pig."

She wanted to say no, but she was too hungry. She grabbed it with one hand and squashed it against her, while the other hand rested on her daughter's head.

"Has anyone been in to see about Lizzie?" I asked.

She shook her head, snatters dripping from her nose.

"I'd like to help her. I brought something to make her face better."

"You'd want to be a miracle-worker." She threw me a look, spiteful as a cat, before putting a thumb under her daughter's chin, coaxing Lizzie's head up.

I wasn't sure if I was seeing right. I lifted the candle off the ground and held it near Lizzie's face. There was a rope burn on her neck. But that wasn't what bothered me. No, it was her eyes that made my heart clatter against my chest. One eye was shut tight, and a half-moon scar snaked over it from eyebrow to cheekbone. The eyelid of the other was swollen and red, half-lowered over an eye that didn't move. The eye itself was covered by a milky veil. When I brought the candle closer to check, there was no change to the eye. It did not follow the flame as I moved it from left to right. It did not flinch from the light. It stayed just the same as if it gazed into darkness. Grumbling, Janet put her arm over her eyes to shield them.

But Lizzie Cellar was silent. Lizzie Cellar was blind.

❦ ❦ ❦

I didn't go to Carrickfergus to see the women pilloried on fair day. I have no stomach for such a display. But Mercy Hunter went, and reported back that the mob was vicious. Folk even took against the oldest dames, a sorry sight with their necks and wrists locked into the stocks, and their backs creaking from being forced to stoop. Mercy's master brought her with him to watch the full penalty of the law carried out. Not that she cared a haet about right and wrong.

She said all eight of them were put two by two into the pillory, the way the animals went into the Ark. "Folk riled up agin the witches," Mercy said. "But they were twice as angry when a fellow gave out to us. 'Pillorying prisoners is a relic of barbarism,' says he. ''Tis the law of the land,' somebody shouts back. 'A medieval law,' says he. 'The year is 1711, not 1311.' He shut up quare an' quick when they said they'd pillory him if he did'n watch hisself."

A bonfire was lit afterwards, where a piper played, and some of the men were the worse for ale, singing shanty songs.

"I met a tinker with rings in her ears," Mercy admitted. "They looked wile well."

"Your master would have kitlings if you turned up in earrings."

"The woman offered to pierce mine for a wee consideration."

"Mister Sinclair would put you out on the street."

"He would, aye. Still an' all . . ."

"Never mind your gee-gaws – what about the women in the pillory?"

She stroked her ears, and told me how Margaret Mitchell, above all the prisoners, irked the crowd. "She vexed folk, on account of answering back when they called her names. 'I'm no witch,' she shouted. 'If I was, I'd ask the Devil to take a bite out of yiz.' After that, instead of rotten eggs and sods of earth, a great gulpin wrapped a cabbage leaf round a rock and took aim. He hit her fair and square on the mouth. You want to have heared the gulder Margaret Mitchell let out of her. An' the minute she opened her mouth, half her teeth fell out. Folk laughed themselves giddy. A second stone caught her on the side of the head, and I think she might a fainted from the blow. It was hard to tell, the way the stocks kep' her on her feet."

She stayed her full time in the pillory, despite the injury. The captain of the guard curled his lip at the antics of the common folk. Mercy stayed near-hand to him, because she never could resist a uniform. "These Irish are unruly devils," he said to his sergeant. But he wouldn't give the signal to release Margaret Mitchell. A preacher took the captain to task. "We aren't Irish. We're the Scotch race in Ulster, and we've given our life's strength, aye, and our lives as well, to uphold the British connection here." The captain executed an elaborate bow and begged his pardon, but Mercy said he might have been mocking the preacher. Master Sinclair was an easy target.

"What about Lizzie Cellar?" I asked. "Did they hurt her?"

"Aye, she was pelted sore. No allowances were made for her bein' blind. Her ma asked to go in the stocks at the same time as Lizzie, so she wud'n have to watch her lassie suffer."

"Was she let?" I held my breath.

"She was." Mercy chewed her lip. "Lizzie looks like death warmed up."

She spoke some more about the witches' punishment, but my mind skittered away. Aye, I had a bad conscience about Lizzie Cellar. The visit I paid her did nothing to ease it.

"Ellen Hill, you bain't listenin' to a word I say. What's eatin' you, at all? The gurn on you would fright a babby. If you ask me, you need to find a new position. Knowehead is turnin' you crabbit."

"Sorry, Mercy. It's just that I'm doin' the work of two here, and it does'n look as if there'll be any let-up because there's still no word of Peggy McGregor comin' back to us. Thon distemper she took in her stomach has'n shifted. I've a broad back, but there's too much work here for one. If I could manage a decent night's sleep, it might help, but when I do get to bed I lie tossin' and turnin' and listenin' for noises."

I couldn't bring myself to admit it to Mercy Hunter but what really kept me awake was Hamilton Lock: having left his grave, he wouldn't go back to it so handy. He started with old Mistress Haltridge and moved on to Mary Dunbar – who would he turn his attentions to next? It could be me. And that was a possibility to keep even the hardiest soul awake at night.

"Do you hear noises after dark, Ellen?"

"I hear – I don't know what I hear. It might just be mice.

Or birds on the roof. It's not quiet in the house, that's as much as I know. I'm worn out, so I am."

"Aye, it's not what you'd call a cheerful place. I'm no sooner in this house than I'm lookin' over my shoulder. I only call because of you – and even then, wild horses would'n drag me in come nightfall. All the neighbours are givin' Knowehead a wide berth – I daresay you've noticed. I don't know how you put up with it here. Something's not right about this house. It'll never be right."

"Ach well, you get used to it. An' I have a terrible good master. They're not so easy to come by."

"You an' that master of yours. Mind he doesnae make a fool out of you. Or worse. Well, Ellen, if you willnae find a new position, then you must do something about the one you have. Talk to your mistress. Tell her you need Peggy back or another pair of hands. One or t'other. But you cannae go on as things stand."

❧   ❧   ❧

I told the mistress I was run off my feet, and she spoke to my master, who went to Belfast to see about Peggy. He could have sent a letter. But the way things stood in the house, I think he welcomed the junket. Lately, not a day passed but something went wrong. If it wasn't the casement clock stopping, it was the roof leaking – on a dry day – and if it wasn't the roof leaking, it was cracks appearing in the walls. As for Jamesey and Sarah, they ran about Kilcoan More from morning till night. Come suppertime, they had to be chased down and hauled back to the house – it was rare for them to come of their own accord. I never knowed a pair so unwilling to set foot in their own house. My master would never admit there was anything odd about Knowehead, but he leapt at the chance to ride to Belfast to arrange Peggy's return, even though he said he was only going because he could pay a visit to his wine merchant at the same time. The mistress wanted to go with him, but he said it wasn't fair to land me with the bairns on top of all my other chores.

But Peggy McGregor breathed her last on the day he went to see her – not long before he landed in, as luck would have it – and instead of arranging her return he wound up taking charge of her burial. She was laid in the ground in Belfast, instead of in St John's graveyard where she wanted to rest.

The mistress was agitated by that. How and ever, my master told her Peggy's life had run its course, and she was lucky to have a virtuous death. "It was more convenient to bury her in Belfast, sweetheart. I couldn't go dragging her remains back to Islandmagee."

"I hope at least you had the decency to see she was buried looking east."

"Of course I did. I was fond of Peggy. I've known her all my life."

"Aye, but not fond enough to honour her dying wish. And I know why. You're afraid of another funeral setting tongues wagging about Knowehead."

When he didn't reply, she took to her chamber for the rest of the day. It showed she wanted to do right by her old servant. If Peggy looked east in her grave, she'd be facing Jesus on His return to gather the godly with Him to walk the golden streets of the New Jerusalem. My master would have done anything for Peggy McGregor. Except give those who liked to blab more grist for their rumour mills.

꧁ ꧁ ꧁

The next time Mercy called for a chat, she told me Margaret Mitchell was left without a tooth in her head after her turn in the stocks. She had it from the minister. The following day, I said it to the mistress when she was helping with the dusting – even she could see it took more than one pair of hands to get through all the housework, and she didn't mind the light jobs. No chance of her taking on anything heavy or dirty, mind you. She wouldn't even climb on a chair and brush away cobwebs, though the spiders were making free with the house. Still, every little helped, and I was glad of what she was willing to do.

She must have repeated the story about Margaret Mitchell to my master, because he paid for a barber to attend her in gaol. He was always particular about teeth, my master. It was too late to save hers so the barber pulled out the broken stumps. That was a prodigious act of Christian charity from a man whose home was overrun by witches. I only know what he did on account of the mistress finding the bill among his papers, prying where she shouldn't have been. She was puzzled by his interest in Margaret Mitchell, but seemed inclined to praise him. He wouldn't hear tell of any compliments. Indeed, he seemed un'asied.

◖@ ◖@ ◖@

"James! My best gown! It's riddled with holes!" The mistress's screeches were enough to raise the dead.

"Ach, dear me, Isabel! It's too bad. The moths have nibbled away your lovely green frock."

"Moths? You think moths did this? My gown was ripped to pieces deliberately. And I know who's responsible."

"Hush now, Isabel, you don't know what you're saying."

"Don't I? It would take a moth the size of a bullock to make a hole this big. You could put your fist through it."

"There, there, dear heart. We'll buy you the cloth for a new gown, twice as fine as this one."

"I don't want a new gown, James, I want a new home. I can't bear this house. It's all the fault of Knowehead. It's oozing with poison!"

"Settle the head, now, woman. You're upset, but that's no excuse."

"I've every right to be upset when Hamilton Lock tears my clothes to shreds."

"Don't be daft. You're seizing on unnatural explanations when there's a perfectly natural one."

"What's natural about only one gown being wrecked? All the other garments in the chest are untouched. This one was chosen to teach me a lesson. It's malice, deliberate malice, that's what it is. I can't bear it!" Her wails rang out over the house.

"Daddy, why's Mama weeping? Has the bad man hurt her?" Wee Sarah was drawn to her daddy's side.

"Hush, sweetheart, Mama's got a headache. She'll be right as rain after she has a lie-down.'

My master billed and cooed over his lady, and made promises about taking her to Dublin for a spree. Finally, he had Noah harness up the ass and cart and drive her to Carrickfergus with Jamesey and Sarah for the day. She needed some hustle and bustle round her, he said – the house was too melancholy. He'd ride into town and join them later, after attending to some letters which could be posted in the town.

I went off to the dairy, mulling over the damage to the gown. Only a few days previously, the mistress took it into her head to store some of her things in the great chest in Mary Dunbar's chamber. The green gown was among the clothes she had me put into it. I always liked the dress, and took particular care with it as I folded it away. I knowed for a fact there was nothing wrong with it then.

Hand and mind churning, I didn't hear my master come up behind me. Next thing I knowed, my cap was wheeked off.

"Master, stop that!"

"I can't stop, Ellen. I can't stop thinking about you. I can't stop watching you. I can't stop wanting to be near you. Have pity on me."

Tell him to go, I urged myself. But I was weak and the words wouldn't come. When I said nothing, he took it I was willing. His fingers fumbled to unpin my plait, working at it until the hair was spread out over my shoulders.

"Your hair changes in the light: it's like fire. I saw a man eat fire in Edinburgh once. A crowd gathered to watch."

I did not altogether believe him about the fire-eater. He had seen spectacles, my master, but he was a man who liked to tease as well. You could never be sure with him.

"You're funnin' with me, master. You know right well how little I've seen."

"I've seen plenty, but I've never seen anything to match the sight of you this day. You're so steady and calm, Ellen. Isabel's antics would drive a man to distraction. Just being near you soothes me."

I turned away from him, trying to resist, but he put his arms round my waist, leaned in and buried his face in my hair. As his body pushed against mine, the edge of the wooden table dug into my belly, and I cared nothing about the sharp corner.

His words filled my ears. "I think about you all the time. You gave yourself to me so sweetly before. I burn for you, Ellen. Burn for us to be close like that again."

I tried to think of the danger. I groped for the memory of that potion I had to take, and my fears I might be carrying a child. But it was useless. My master wanted me. I was seduced by pleasure. A contented clucking came from the hens outside, a beam of sunlight stole through the door, and I closed my eyes as his hands roamed my body: ready to yield to him again, come what may, without another word said between us.

He turned me back towards him, and took my face between his hands, leaning towards my lips. They parted for him, and I could almost taste him on my mouth.

But first, he spoke. I daresay he thought they were words such as might appeal to a maid you were courting. "You are the master, and I am the servant," he said.

And at that, as sudden as a summer shower, I was filled with rage. It came gushing out of me, like a river overrunning its banks, and I put my two hands on his chest and pushed him away. He lost his footing and fell on his backside on the ground, shock causing his handsome face to gape.

"Aye, I gave myself to you. An' I wound up expectin' your child. Not that you'd know the first thing about it. Because you took your pleasure, and rode away without a backward glance. Never even troubled yourself to ask me about it when you came home. Not so much as a care for me, or what I might have dealt with. You want to be free to take what you want, when you want, no matter what price I might have to pay. I gave you the best of myself, and you took it for granted. You're doin' it again now. Well, you'll never have me again, James Haltridge. You're my master and I'm your servant, that's the way it is. But know this. If you lay another finger on me so long as you live, I'll open my mouth and I'll outroar Mary Dunbar, so I will."

His face was stiff with shock. "Christ above, are you still with child?"

I stamped my foot to release some of the fury coursing through me, before charging into the house. Up to my bed in the attic I went, and in I climbed with all my clothes on. Then I pressed my face against the lumpy pillow that held my head at night. And I wept, oh aye, I wept. Every tear I ever kept in check on his account emptied out of me.

Because I understood how it was between us. So much for me thinking he saw something special in me. It was no more than nonsense, and a gentleman's knack for fancy words. My master was only ever aping the lover with me. What meant poverty and dishonour to me was playacting to him.

⟨⟨ ⟨⟨ ⟨⟨

The first chance he got, Master Haltridge pressed me again as to whether I was with child. This time, I took pity on him, and said my courses had washed away what he planted in me. He couldn't hide his relief. And because he never liked anybody in his household to be out of sorts, he made his peace with me with a silk rose to pin on my shawl, along with some coins. I longed to throw them back at him, but could not, because Da was out of work again and Ma couldn't make ends meet. For my mistress, he arranged that trip to Dublin. He warned her he had business to attend to there, on account of being called away suddenly before, but said time would be spared for amusements. Meanwhile, I was to be left in charge of Master Jamesey and the wee missie.

This plan put my back up. Who wouldn't be unhappy about staying in Knowehead on their own, with only childer for company? So it was proposed that Noah Spears should sleep over, resting his old bones on a pallet on the kitchen floor. "His white beard will halt any wagging tongues about the proprieties," said the mistress. Remembering how I once thought about offering myself to him in exchange for marriage, I resisted their scheme. After all, December and May matings were not unknown. I had no anxieties about Noah creeping into the attic – but grave anxieties about folk saying it of us. Having risked my good name with my master, and got away with it by the skin of my teeth, it was more important than ever to guard my reputation.

The Haltridges bargained with me, saying I should sleep in the nursery, where the childer could preserve my good name and, for my trouble, I would have the job of cook as soon as a new girl could be found to train up as maid-of-all work. At that I agreed – despite my nerves.

"How about takin' on Ruth Graham, if she can be tracked down?" I was chancing my arm, but the mistress gave me a look fit to sour milk and I backed off.

I was surprised they went, in the end. The night before they were due to leave, the household was wakened to the sound of a shovel in the earth. Nothing was found to account for the noise, but the mistress screeched about it being a grave dug, till the master shouted at her to hold her whisht or she'd scare the living daylights out of the childer. I thought they'd cancel their plans, for sure. But with him doing the convincing, and her wanting to be convinced, they made ready to set off to be gay and take their ease.

It was Master Jamesey rather than his sister who clung to his parents when the time came to bid them farewell, begging not to be left behind. The mistress was sorely torn, but my master told Jamesey he was too old to turn cry-baby. I stroked his hair, as we waved them off, thinking how peaky he was again already. The bloom from his stay in Belfast at his grandparents' house was faded. At least Missie still had roses in her cheeks.

"We'll have a nice time, just the three of us," I said, when their parents were out of sight.

"Don't forget Noah," piped up Sarah.

"Aye, there's Noah. But he has his work to do during the day."

"I wish Noah could sleep with us," said Jamesey.

"It would'n be fittin', Master Jamesey. Noah's to bed down in the kitchen."

"But you're sleeping with us, Ellen. What's the difference?"

This was no time to explain about good names. "I daresay you could lie in Mary Dunbar's chamber, if you prefer. Maybes you're gettin' too old to sleep with lassies. Only the other day, the mistress said she planned on movin' you into a room of your own shortly."

"No!" he howled. "Don't make me sleep on my own. I'll stay with you and Sarah. Please, Ellen!"

Well, of course I said he could, wide-eyed at his panic. Wondering, too, whether it was quite wise for my master and his lady to leave the bairns – even though they put it over as a compliment to me, because they had faith in my abilities.

When bedtime came, the childer asked for a candle to be left burning, and pressed me to promise I wouldn't be long going up after them. As far as I knowed, we all slept sound.

But the next morning, Master Jamesey wasn't in his bed. Such a fright it gave me. I ran through the house calling his name, while Noah searched the outhouses and found him in the barn, sound asleep. His nightshirt was soaked through, and his feet were filthy and covered in cuts. Taking off the nightshirt to wash him, I spotted patches of dry skin flaming on his body, like a heat rash. They were inside his elbows, at the backs of his knees, and inside his armpits. It puzzled me not to have noticed them before. Master Jamesey always had smooth, unbroken skin, like his father.

After rubbing in some salve, I tucked him into bed with warm milk. He was drowsy, but I lingered to put some questions to him.

"Jamesey, what made you go wanderin' about at night?"

"The black-haired man."

"What black-haired man?"

"Hamilton Lock."

I didn't like what I heard, but I can't pretend I was surprised. Mary Dunbar's leave-taking had made no difference – Lock came and went as he pleased. "Does he talk to you?"

"He's always on at me. I try to stop my ears but he keeps at me. I can't help hearing him."

"Does he appear to you?"

"No, I only hear him."

"What does he say?"

"Tells me to do things."

"Like what?"

"Don't want to say."

"Tell me."

"Last night, he said he was going for a swim in Donaldsons' pond, and I should go with him. I said I didn't want to and he called me a lily-livered lassie. Then I said I could only swim a few strokes, but he promised to look after me."

My mouth went dry and I tried to swallow, but my throat was full of pebbles. Lock had evil planned for Master Jamesey – and with his parents away, there was only me standing between the lad and that fiend.

"Why did you go with him, chicken?"

Jamesey pulled the sheet tight under his chin, bunching his knees against his chest. "He makes you want to do things. Things you know you shouldn't. He used to talk to me before, when Granny was sick. But then Cousin Mary came to stay, and he stopped. He's back talking to me now."

"Why did'n you tell anybody? You should a said somethin' to your mama and daddy before they went away."

"He told me if I said a word, he'd lock Sarah in the chest in Granny's room. And by the time we found her she'd be nothing but a skeleton." He began sobbing, loud, hiccupping wails, and between them he gulped out, "Ellen, I tried not to say anything. Honest I did. But I'm too scared to keep it in."

I sat on the bed, rocking his trembling wee body against mine until the storm eased. But the storm in my own mind continued to rage. Hamilton Lock wasn't satisfied with the mischief he made over the witch trial. Now he was latching on to the young master, biding his time till the Haltridges were far from home. He'd not let go of his own accord – his kind of trouble wasn't the sort to pass over of itself, like clouds.

Something needed to be done about Hamilton Lock. But could I be the one to do it? He was a formidable enemy.

All day long I didn't dare let either child out of my sight. That night, Noah Spears pulled his pallet against the kitchen door to block anybody going out that way. "Call me any time if you're worried, lassie. A full night's sleep is ne'ther here nor there at my age. Have you locked the front door an' bolted the casements in case the laddie goes sleepwalkin' again? Good.

I'll double-check after you go up."

"I locked an' bolted everything last night but the young master still got out."

"We'll have to see to it he stays in his bed the-night. I'll keep my axe near-hand, just in case."

"It's not axes we need. What we're fightin' does'n bleed."

"Aye, I hear what you're sayin', lassie. I have the Good Book, an' all. I cannae read it too well, but it gives me comfort."

"Noah, you've never slept inside Knowehead, have you?" He shook his head. "Did you notice anythin' last night? Did you sleep right through?"

"I slept fair. Except –"

"Except what?" I gave myself a stabbing pain in the neck, so sharply did I twist my head to look at him.

"Except the pillow kep' fallin' on the floor. Half a dozen times, I woke when my head bumped agin the pallet. You'd nearly think somebody was wheekin' it out from under me for the fun of it. But sure, who'd do that?"

Who indeed, I thought, making my way upstairs to the nursery. The door had no lock, so I pushed a chair against it when I went in, Jamesey watching me while his sister slept.

I kissed him. "If Hamilton Lock talks to you, call out to me at once."

"Even if he says I mustn't?"

"Yes," I said, with more confidence than I felt. In truth, my heart was fluttering round my chest, like a bird banging against the bars of a cage. But it relieved Jamesey, because he closed his eyes and fell asleep.

I had no intention of sleeping, and sat on another chair in the nursery, watching the childer. I brought no Bible with me, since I had no faith in a book – even a holy book – as a weapon against Hamilton Lock. Not after what I saw when Robert Sinclair was called to pray over Mary Dunbar. All I could trust to was the love I felt for those bairns.

Convinced though I was that I wouldn't sleep a wink, I must have dropped off at some point, because an almighty bang woke me. My eyes flew to the bed, and I saw to my horror that the counterpane was thrown back, the chair blocking the door moved, and the door lying open.

I clattered downstairs, shrieking, and found Jamesey in his father's study, sitting among a pile of papers tipping out from a drawer. The drawer falling on the floor must have been the crash I heard. Jamesey had a key in his hand, and was crying his eyes out. Noah wasn't far behind, axe gripped between both hands and a fierce look on his whiskery old chops. Whiles I petted the young master, I sent Noah up to sit with the wee missie. Imagine if something happened to her when we were both busy with Jamesey.

When Jamesey was more settled, I led him out to my cosy perch in the kitchen, and folded my shawl round him. Down I crouched beside him, my face level with his.

"Chicken, what were you at in your daddy's study that couldn't keep till morning?"

His eyes were ancient in that eight-year-old's face. "Hamilton Lock whispered to me."

"What did he want you to do?"

"Find Father's pistol."

A shiver tiptoed along my spine. "But you know you're forbidden to touch your daddy's pistol, Jamesey. He's told you it's not a toy. That's why he keeps it locked away."

"Hamilton Lock told me where to find the key. He said he'd show me how to fire the pistol. He told me I was a big boy now, and it was time I knew how to do it."

At that, my blood ran cold. "Wait here. Don't budge." I raced back to the study, hoaked among the papers spilling from the drawer on the floor, and found the pistol. "Noah!" When I went into the hallway, he was standing at the top of the stairs. "Can you take this and put it someplace till my master comes home? I don't want it in the house."

He creaked down towards me and took the gun.

"How's Sarah?" I asked.

"A right bit un'asied, tell you no lie. The wee visog on her would make you powerful sorry." Out in the yard, the rooster let out a throaty crow. "Listen to your man – it's daytime now. Everythin' looks better in the light o' day."

I went back to the kitchen, climbing over Noah's bed to unbolt the top of the half-door. The sky had torn patches in it, pink splashes showing through. It was a new day, and important work lay ahead of me.

But first, I needed to gather together my courage, and keep a tight hold of it, because right now it was running through my fingers, the way a handful of sand does. I lifted Jamesey onto my lap, his legs dangling, wrapped my shawl about both of us, and stared at the wall while the lad dozed. Reminding myself why I had to succeed where the kirk, the law and the plain folk of Islandmagee had failed.

There were reasons to do nothing, chief among them the desire to save my own skin. But I had just cause to try and put a halt to Hamilton Lock's gallop. What waited to be done was not just for Jamesey and Sarah's sake, but for others caught fast in Hamilton Lock's web of wickedness. Lizzie Cellar and the women in Carrickfergus Gaol came to mind. But other voices called out to me, even louder than those eight.

An entire clan, near enough, murdered at one man's conniving. Without him, talk of revenge against the Irish might have been no more than that – talk. But he hatched a plot, working the militia into a frenzy till no quarter was given. And now that he was a spirit, Hamilton Lock was just as bloodthirsty and twice as dangerous. Terrified though I was of taking him on, I understood that Lock's ghost had to be laid before it did any further harm. Nursing Jamesey in my arms, listening to his ragged breathing, I made up my mind to it. I would gamble my life to put paid to Lock's evil.

It was fitting, after all. If not me, then who?

You see, the name I go by is not the one that's my birthright. They call me Ellen Hill on the island. But Hill is just a name my grandfather took to avoid notice. It was unwise to use our real name. Safety in numbers: there were plenty of Hills.

My grandfather was the only one of his family left alive after Hamilton Lock led that raid on the island. He was six years old when his father lifted him into a hidey-hole in the roof. He lay on his belly and watched through the rafters as his father and three brothers were slain, his mother and sister herded outside. After the soldiers left, my granda crawled out and looked at their handiwork. His da's head was a foot away from its body. His two wee brothers were twined so close in death, you couldn't tell whose limbs were whose. But the one he wept sorest over was his older brother Philip, the ten-year-old boy who had been hidden in a chest – until Hamilton Lock arrived.

My granda managed to get away to join his mother's people in the Glens of Antrim. It was arranged by his sixteen-year-old cousin, Brian Boy Magee, who lay outside in the long grass while the soldiers swung their axes. He put my granda on a boat at the Gobbins Head, saying he'd join him in a day or two. First, he wanted to go to Carrickfergus Castle and appeal to the commander for justice. But Brian Boy Magee, with his beardless cheeks and faith in foreign laws, was held by the long golden hair by one man, his throat cut by another – without ever getting to see the colonel he thought could be trusted.

My grandfather, Donal Magee, returned to Islandmagee when he was a grown man. His land was taken by then, and others lived in his family's house. But he settled as close to his father's land as he could, down Carnspindle way, using the name Donald Hill to fit in. His heart remained a Magee's heart, while the blood running through his veins was Magee blood. And he told the tale to his childer, making them promise to pass it on to theirs. "Keep the story alive," he said.

"Memory cheats death."

My grandfather was not free to claim his name, no more than I am. But I spoke it then, sitting in the kitchen with Jamesey heavy on my lap. Out loud, I said it.

"Ellen Magee is my name. I am a Magee of Islandmagee. Do you hear me, Hamilton Lock? I'm Ellen Magee an' I'm comin' after you."

Tick-tock, went the landing clock.

Wound tight as a bowstring, I listened.

Tick-tock.

"Were you callin' me, lassie?" Noah's arrival was noiseless in his stockings.

I started, and the young master grumbled in his sleep. "Talkin' to myself, Noah. Tryin' to ready myself to do somethin' I'm dreadin'." He raised his eyebrows, and I nodded towards the boy. "Hamilton Lock is up to no good where the childer are concerned. I believe he meant to have the lad turn the pistol on hisself, or his sister – or both."

Noah scratched his beard. "It does'n look good," he allowed.

"He has to be stopped. I'm goin' to stop him."

"Oh aye. Where's your army?"

"I know what I have to do. It should a been done a long time ago. I'm goin' to Lock's Cave to find his skull an' destroy it, once an' for all."

He spat into the ashes. "That'll be some handlin'."

"It has to be attempted. If I duck it, this wee fellow here will end up in a bed of clay before his next birthday. And then maybe it'll be his sister's turn." My words were fiery, but my voice was far from steady. After all, Hamilton Lock was the ringleader of the crew that stamped out my kith and kin. Chances were, he could crush me as easily. In a rush, I begged, "Come with me, Noah. I won't be able for this alone."

"My aul' legs would'n carry me down the path to them caves."

"We could get the loan of a boat and go to them that way."

Still, he shook his head. "You must be off your bap, lassie. You might get witched yourself, or never come back. You're on'y a servant in this house, when all's said and done. Why put your neck in the noose? I keep me head down an' mind me own business. That's our way on Islandmagee. You'd do well to remember it."

"The childer are my business, Noah. I could be sittin' here with a dead child in my arms instead of a live one, if he'd put his hands on thon pistol."

"Aye, I hear what you're sayin'. None of this is the bairns' fault." He sucked the few teeth left in his head. "What will you do if you find the skull?"

"I'm not sure. Bury it, I suppose – maybes stake it to the ground, the way the rest of him was staked."

"Getting' a stake through a skull is no handy matter. You're a strong lass, I'll grant you that, but it'll take some doin'. Forbye that, what if somebody comes along after you and takes out the stake? He'd be off again, bad as ever."

I hadn't considered that, and it pulled me up short. But I wasn't ready to give in. "There has to be a way of layin' his ghost, Noah. I know the skull is the key to it."

He looked me over, taking my measure. "Here's what I'll do for you, Ellen Hill. I'll tell you how to get rid of Lock's skull, if you find it. If he does'n find you first. There's some right big ifs in there. But supposin' you do get your hands on it, I ken what you need to do. Smash it in. Take up a lump o' rock and batter it in. Hamilton Lock's head was the on'y bit of him left unbroken after he was killed. I doubt if there was a bone in his body still in one piece, but the head had har'ly a mark on it. I allus thought that odd, on account of what he done to his da's skull."

"Did you see him die, Noah?"

He glared, hands balled into fists, and for a moment I thought he meant to strike me. "Aye, I see'd it. I see'd enough to know Hamilton Lock was a man to have no truck wi', whether livin' or dead. But you're a daughter of Eve. I daresay you're as thran as all your breed. So if you're bent on chasin' off to the caves, bear in mind what I tould you. The skull cannae be left unbroken. There's power in things that are whole."

Chapter 17

Noah agreed to stay with Jamesey and Sarah while I went to Lock's Cave. Luckily the tide was out, so I could reach the caves by foot. As I took candles and a flint from the drawer in the kitchen table, it occurred to me that I could stop by Frazer Bell's house, and ask for his help. But I was afraid he might point out the drawbacks of my plan, and I would lose heart for going through with it. So I struck out for the Gobbins on my own.

Picking my steps downhill from the cliffs, I tried to figure out why Bob Holmes's search uncovered nothing. He said the skull must have been taken away by the coven, but I wasn't certain the women were witches – let alone that they used the cave. In which case, it must still be there. I had no reason to believe I would find it when Holmes and his men had failed.

But I had to give it a try.

Once or twice, I stopped and looked behind, my nerves quivering. It felt as if somebody was following me. But I saw nobody. You're jumpy, I told myself. Still, I couldn't shake off the feeling. Even at the mouth of the cave, I paused, still with the sense of being watched. It added to my foreboding as I lit a candle, and stepped into the cave.

Even in broad daylight, it was dim inside, though some

weak light crept in from the seaward side. Still, I was prepared for darkness – it couldn't be any worse than the gaol in Carrickfergus. What I wasn't prepared for was my own voice, inside my head, making me doubt myself as soon as I was in the cave. "You're in Hamilton Lock's lair!" it jeered, and at once my teeth began to chatter. But I took hold of myself and advanced a couple of steps. I must have sent a loose stone flying, because an echo started up, bouncing off the cave's walls and shooting back from all sides. I nearly turned back then, fancying it was the cave's way of showing it knowed it had an intruder. Somehow, I summoned up the willpower to stay.

I raised the candle high, and looked about. I had been in other caves beneath the Gobbins, but never Lock's Cave – our mothers had us too well warned, as childer. At first sight, it wasn't so different from the others, except it was taller. The ceiling reached up to a dome high above, like the bell-tower of a church. Its insides were jagged with rocks, and pools of water gathered on the floor. The cave was shaped like a triangle, one side open to the elements and its two walls meeting at a point deep inside the cliff. Shelves made of rock climbed these two walls.

Where to start searching? I took another step forward, and turned on my ankle. Naturally, I put out my hand to steady myself. That was a mistake. It touched a wall, damp and slimy, the way you'd imagine a snail's belly would feel. "Remember Jamesey huntin' for his da's pistol," I braced myself. It helped me to squash the longing to turn tail and flee. "Now, Ellen, use your wits," I muttered. Rather than dig willy-nilly, like the team led by Bob Holmes, I had to think about where the skull might be hidden. I kicked my foot against the ground, and wondered if it had even been buried, or whether it might have been put somewhere. Burial may not have fitted the purpose. After all, the floor of a cave that's regularly flooded by seawater gets worn away.

Peering right and left, I picked my way onward, trying not to slip on seaweed. All at once, a noise came roaring at me – from in front, behind, above. I was at the centre of a deafening ball of clamour. Shaking all over, I sank to my knees, dropping the candle in a pool of water. I clamped my arms over my head, but nothing could block out this ear-splitting sound. It was the din of men shouting and horses whinnying, screams piercing it all – shrieks that sounded as if folk were being torn limb from limb.

Heart hammering, too trapped by fear to think of running away, I gazed wildly about, trying to make out where the rumpus was coming from, but I could see barely anything without the candle. The taste of metal flooded my mouth, spilled over and tickled my chin. Cornered, I knelt there, waiting to be cut to ribbons under those thundering hooves. A sheet of ice travelled through me from tip to toe, my heartbeat slowed right down and missed some beats, my body grew rigid.

I closed my eyes against the darkness, turning misty red now, but the redness was inside my head. And pictures were crashing through it.

Men on horseback. Moonlight glancing off blades. Metal dipped in blood. Women and childer pushing, tumbling, desperate to escape. The Gobbins reached. Nowhere left to run. The soldiers press forward: laughing, cursing, out of control. Here and there, a child collapses. The flight has exhausted them. Or perhaps fear is making their legs give way. They are trampled or run through where they lie, death delivered casually. A few women kneel. "Mercy!" they cry. These women are bayoneted, their bodies tossed over the cliffs. Others look behind – and jump. One woman kisses her baby as she takes flight. Another grabs two wee ones by the hands and leaps with them. Skirts billow. Limbs flap in mid-air. Rocks poke through flesh. The foam turns red. Wails rise up to the heavens: a howling outburst of fright, panic, despair.

An infant is found where its mother left it, pushed to the side, half-hidden by a bush. Hoping it might pass unnoticed in the confusion. A soldier picks it up. "Nits grow into lice," he says, and throws it over the Gobbins. The child's thin bleat sails back on the wind.

And then silence. Even the beasts are still, while the men seem dazed by what they have done. A few go to the edge and gaze into the chaos below. Nobody says anything, until the soldier who spoke before tugs on his horse's bridle, causing it to rear up. "May they rot in hell, along with all their seed and breed." Horses snort, someone drinks from a bottle, burps, passes it on.

And then the soldier cocks his head on the side and looks directly at me. "Another Magee," he says. His smile lights up his face. "Why not join your sisters? They're calling to you. Can't you hear them?"

I am pinned on the end of Hamilton Lock's handsome, black eyes. His voice fills my head. Drowning out everything. It takes on a cozening quality.

"Climb back up the cliff path, Ellen. Stand at the edge of the Gobbins – and jump. You know you want to."

He's right. I do want to jump. I want to open my arms wide, and let myself be lifted by the winds of Islandmagee – flying away from all my cares. I'll spread my wings and soar to freedom. I scramble to my feet. I'll do it at once.

"Ellen!" Another voice hooks me. I shake my head, trying to get rid of this rival voice. I prefer listening to the first one. "Ellen!" The word rushes here, there, and everywhere, booming. "Ellen-Ellen-*Ellen! It's me – Sarah.*"

I blinked. My head pounded, and I felt as if I was woken too soon. There was a sense of loss, as if a dream I wanted to keep dreaming was snatched from me. What was it? I strained my memory. At first, my mind was a blank, until in a flash I remembered. With the memory came bile, rising in my throat. Gagging, I leaned over, boking up my fear and the near-miss I had. Even after nothing was left in my stomach, I retched on, heaving out sour juices.

When the dizziness passed, I became aware of Sarah patting my back. The relief was overpowering. Bless the wee lassie, she saved me from Hamilton Lock. Gasping, I wiped my hand along my mouth, the taste of terror of my lips still.

"Who were you talking to, Ellen?"

"Could'n you see him? A man on horseback?"

"The candle went out. I was trying to catch up with you, and then I couldn't see where you were. But I heard you saying you were going to fly. You said you couldn't wait. You nearly knocked me down."

I reached out my hands, feeling for the top of her head. "You have to go home right away, Sarah. Take to your heels and run like the wind. This place is too dangerous for you. What are you doin' here anyhow?"

"I heard what you said to Noah, and I followed you. He's been teaching me and Jamesey how to track animals. I've come to help."

I hugged her, proud of her bravery though she had to be frightened. It gave me heart.

"Ach, Sarah darlin', you're the best of girls. But Noah'll be half-mad with worry about you by now. You have to go home right away – and don't look back. I'm afeared of somethin' happenin' to you here. Somethin' I bain't able to protect you from."

"We'll protect each other, Ellen."

I sighed. Bless her heart, she was no match for Hamilton Lock. No more than I was, in truth.

She went on, "I told Noah I was going to the Widow Patterson's. I said Mama promised I'd keep her company. I know it's wrong to tell lies. But please, Ellen, let me help. I want to. I know the bad man means to hurt Jamesey."

I wrestled with my judgment and lost. By rights, I shouldn't listen to the child, but Hamilton Lock's trick had come close to shipwrecking me. The temptation to have somebody beside me won out.

"All right, chicken, you can stay for now. God alone knows what we might be gettin' ourselves into, though, so you need to take a care and do everythin' I say. Agreed?"

"Agreed."

"If I tell you to run outside, do you promise you'll do it at once? Without lookin' back – no matter what you hear?"

"I promise."

"And if anybody else speaks to you, pay them no heed. Listen only to me. Do you promise?"

"You mean the bad man, don't you? I promise."

"Good lass. Now, first things first. I have spare candles in my pocket – let's get another one lit." As soon as that was done, I fished out the dropped candle from the pool of water, and dried the wick as best I could. It might yet be needed. That done, I walked round the cave with the second candle, Sarah holding the edge of my skirt. We tried pushing at some large rocks, in case the skull might be lodged in a hole underneath, but we couldn't move them. Besides, the bigger ones looked as if they had been pushed aside already. I could make out the tracks left from rolling them.

"Shouldn't we be digging?" asked Sarah.

I studied the ground, clearly dug over lately by searchers. "I doubt if that'll do much good." Then it struck me a bairn might have more of a notion about hidey-holes than grown-ups. "Tell me, Sarah, where would you hide something in here?"

Her eyes flicked round. "On one of the rock ledges, high up out of sight."

"But how would a body reach it?"

"Climb up – it can't be any harder than climbing the apple tree in the garden. Those bits that stick out give your fingers and toes somewhere to grip. Jamesey and me, we're good at climbing."

"If I hold the candle up, do you think you could take a look?"

She nodded.

"We'll take off your frock in case it catches on the rocks. You'll do it handier in your drawers."

When she was ready I gave her a leg-up to the first ledge, and she was as nimble as a chimney sweep. At each rock-shelf she stopped and ran her hand along, without success. When the first wall was searched, we tried the second wall, again without luck.

"Well done, you did your best," I said. "*Your best, your best!*" mocked the echo.

I was at a loss as to what to try next. Both of us were chilled and shivering, and Missie was worn out, between climbing and crawling. Disappointing though it was, I felt inclined to call it a day.

I did one last sweep with the candle. Then something caught the corner of my eye, and I pushed further into the cave. Right at the back, where I thought the two walls met, there was an alcove with more ledges growing from the rock.

"Do you feel able to try one last time?" I asked, and bless the bairn, she scaled up without a word of complaint.

"There's something here – I can't see what it is," she called back. "It feels like a hard ball. It's very cold."

"Can you carry it down?"

"I think I can hold it under my arm." One-handed, she began to climb down.

I held the candle above my head to light her way. "Take your time, Sarah. Make sure you feel something under your foot each time afore you let go."

Maybes it was all the shouting we were doing that caused them to loosen, or maybes it was no accident. But a shower of rocks from the cave's ceiling rained down on the lassie, and she lost her grip. First to drop was the thing she held – I ducked as it bounced at my feet. She scrabbled to keep from falling, feet going every which way, but it was no good. Down she plunged. I rushed to catch her, or at least break her fall – losing this candle, too, in my headlong rush. Once again, we were in darkness. But at least I had her safe in my arms, flat on my back though I was.

"Are you all right, Sarah?" I rubbed my head, banged off the ground.

"Where is it? Is it lost?"

I knelt up, groping at my feet. My fingers touched a smooth, round object, and my stomach flipped over. But I swallowed down my loathing, and took a hold. I didn't care to think about why it was easy to grip, with a number of holes in one side of it. Then I grabbed Sarah's hand and we went crashing outside.

The light hurt my eyes and I closed them briefly, hearing the tide rush in.

"Ellen, look, it's the skull!"

My eyes fell open on what remained of Hamilton Lock. Though I had gone to the Gobbins to find it, holding it – him – in my hand was a shock. My fingers twitched, ready to drop it. But I didn't let go. I wasn't about to lose this thing so hard found. Carefully, I pulled my fingers out of the eye-holes, cupping my hand loosely round the back of the head. The skull grinned up at me with headstone teeth. Three or four lengths of black hair stuck to it. The bone was the colour of clotted cream, and shone the way a door-handle does in sunlight. I looked away. Those empty eye-holes gave me the heeby-jeebies. No iron spike could hold that thing down, I thought, but there was a surer way to put paid to Hamilton Lock.

"What do we do now, Ellen?"

"We get rid of it."

"In a fire?"

"A fire isn't hot enough to burn it. We have to find a big rock and use that to smash it."

Sarah found me a rock. I set down the skull and looked it over for a weak point on the bone. A shudder ran through me as Hamilton Lock, or what remained of him, looked back. 'I still have the upper hand,' the skull seemed to say. I took a deep breath, juked down beside it, and started hammering. The bone was hard: it wasn't like cracking an egg. But I kept going.

"What do you think, Sarah? Is it broken yet?"

"It's not in bits. But it's bashed in."

The nose and eye holes were one gaping emptiness now, splinters inside the skull and a few scattered near-hand.

"It's certainly not whole," I said.

"Is it time to go home now, Ellen?"

"Not yet." I kicked the gritty sand, but burying it didn't seem like much of an answer. What was buried oftentimes came to the surface again. Like secrets. "Put your frock back on, while I think."

I was buttoning her up when she pointed towards the water. "It's the Nelson brothers."

A boat was rowing not far from us, carrying two fishermen with their catch. They waved, and we waved back. Watching them steer a path through the rocks gave me an idea. I stepped out of my petticoat, and scooped the skull, along with the splinters, into it. Bone was slippery and I was afraid of dropping and maybes losing it. Then I took Ellen by the hand and led her up the cliff path.

At the top of the Gobbins, I went right to the edge, so close a gust of wind would have blown me to kingdom come. I was standing on the spot where the women and childer were driven over. I strained to listen, superstitious enough to think I might hear an echo of their cries, but the only sound was the seagulls quarrelling in their ill-bred way. I took a deep breath, planted my feet wide, and lifted the skull wrapped in my petticoat high above my head between both hands.

"Mind you don't fall, Ellen!"

"Stand back, chicken."

Gathering together every bit of strength I possessed, I flung my bundle as far as I could. It sailed through the air and fell, crashing against the rocks. It bounced back off, landing in the water with a splash. I watched it bobbing below, and noticed how the Nelsons rested on their oars and looked over towards it.

"Sink, please sink," I prayed beneath my breath, afraid Billy and Adam might decide to row over, to find out what was there.

Still, the bundle floated. The petticoat came away from the skull and formed a white, spreading patch on the water. Now the brothers would see what was hidden inside. They might even fish it out.

I shaded my eyes, staring at Hamilton Lock's skull. It was laughing at me. Refusing to go under. No more willing to disappear than he was.

"Take him, he's yours now," I begged, aloud this time – not to God, but to the ghosts of the Magees.

And at that, a wave flicked up, caught the skull and tossed it, before sucking it in.

It was gone.

꧁ ꧁ ꧁

Knowehead House was never what you'd call a merry place afterwards – the most I can say is it was back to that manageable twisty I remembered from first going to work there. Hamilton Lock was no longer under our roof. There was no more witching, no more whispering, no more wandering on Master Jamesey's part, and no more feeling as if somebody was watching you. In time, neighbours took to calling on the Haltridges again, although nobody would ever stay the night. They'd always find some excuse to be on their way.

Now and again the house reminded us that we only lived there on its say-so. Odd things continued to happen. Sometimes you'd hear feet pattering across the floor and think it was mice, but a search for mouseholes would turn up nothing. Other times, a cold wind would rip through the house when there wasn't a casement or door open – and if you tried to walk contrary to that wind, you'd be hard pressed to make headway against it. Once in a while, there'd be something more vexatious, as if to put manners on us. Like the time the blankets on my master's bed were found made up in the shape of a corpse, and we feared it was an omen of a death in the family.

Which it turned out to be.

Something in Knowehead could never abide hymn-singing. If any started up, such a creaking of floorboards and tapping on ceilings you never did hear in all your live-long days. In the kitchen, the pots and beakers would rattle on their shelves, and in the bedrooms, the beds would shake on their legs and the water jugs clatter against the basins they stood in.

The minister came over and tried to settle it. "Hymns keep Christians steadfast," he insisted. "We must not lose our hymns." But the Haltridges had to do their hymn-singing in the meeting-house because none was tolerated in Knowehead House.

I suppose when I list it out like that, it sounds hard to live with. Yet we did.

Even when the wee missie grew clumsy, forever falling down. At first, we put it down to growing pains. She'd come in to me with her totie knees all smarting from nettles, and I'd have to send Jamesey out for a docken to rub away the sting. "Nettle, nettle, go away – docken, docken come again," we'd chant, and I'd give her a kiss. This falling over was something she'd grow out of, everyone agreed. But it got so she couldn't take two or three steps without tripping. And then she couldn't leave her bed at all.

The mistress tried everything to save her, bringing in the doctor, who said it was the falling down sickness – as if we couldn't see that for ourselves – and the barber, with his jar of leeches to set to work on her flesh. "Her blood is boiling. Bleeding her will cool it," he said.

But none of their physick worked. Finally, the mistress sent me to fetch water from the chapel well in Brown's Bay, a cure folk travelled from far and wide to try. But the wee lass faded before our eyes.

One clammy night I sat with Sarah, on account of the mistress being worn to a thread with nursing her chick. Suddenly, the wee lassie was at her last gasp. I should have run to fetch the mistress, but I didn't want to leave her. It was over in a flash. There was a rattle in Sarah's throat, and I felt the spirit leave her body. I opened the casement to let it pass, before closing her eyelids over them blue eyes. I thought I should find some words of scripture to say over her, but all I could bring to mind were the nursery rhymes she loved. "Mary Mary Quite Contrary" and "Hey Diddle Diddle". The best I was able to manage was, "God bless you, best and bravest girl".

Then I called the mistress and she fell to caterwauling – who can blame a mother? – and the next thing you know she had me by the throat, screaming, "Did she say anything? Answer me! Did she speak?"

"She said nothin', mistress."

"Nothing?"

"Not a word. She slipped away quiet, into the arms of Jesus."

"Pray God it was into His arms she went. Pray God that fiend left her alone at the end."

"He has no more power in this house, mistress. Wee Sarah helped see to that."

But in her grief, she never noticed my slip.

Of course, the lassie being taken so early set tongues

clacking again. Grief turned the mistress's hair white overnight, and she took to wearing a yellow wig. As for my master, he was never himself afterwards. Oftentimes, he shut himself into his study and drank steadily till morning. I used to find him passed out in the easy chair by the fire, and put a blanket over him. But don't think he was drunk – holding his liquor is the mark of a gentleman. It was his way of dealing with his daughter's loss.

Wee Sarah died round about the time the witches' sentence was up, although only five of the eight women found guilty of witchcraft left their prison. Gaol fever took Jane Miller and she went into a pauper's grave. Janet Liston could thole neither the cell nor the starvation rations – I daresay Lizzie wasn't able to look about her ma any more, on account of being blind. Maybes what happened to a good girl like Lizzie broke Janet, as much as being in gaol. Before long, Janet thought she was a witch. She yammered about losing a dead man's hand she used for a charm, and was powerful worked up about it, accusing her cell mates of thieving it. Mister Sinclair went in to wrestle with her, threatening to have her flogged if she didn't repent, but he could get no sense out of her. Sure her wits were scattered to the four winds. Lucky for her she was at death's door, otherwise she might never have been let out. How and ever, she had her release by a different way. Janet Liston left the cell feet first.

As for Lizzie Cellar, she bought her freedom in her own way.

It happened the final time Lizzie and the others were taken to the stocks. Mercy Hunter went in to watch – anything for a day out. She couldn't wait to tell me, coming hotfoot from Carrickfergus. It was news I could have done without. But I suppose I had to hear it from somebody.

"The women were brought out in manacles, and –"

"Manacled? But why, Mercy?" I butted in.

"Did'n you know? It happened all the other times. It's in case the prisoners make a run for it."

"Sure how far would their legs carry them after nearly a year in gaol, half-starved?"

"Would you quit interruptin' an' listen to what I have to tell you? Some forward rascals could'n wait for them to go in the stocks afore the peltin' started, and the lieutenant in charge caught a rotten potato in the back of his fine red jacket. He was turnin' the key in the prisoners' chains when he took the blow, and was none too pleased. Then and there, he stopped what he was at and ordered folk to leave off their disorderly ways, or else. He had already unlocked Lizzie's shackles to put her in the stocks when he turned away to warn the crowd off, because all at once she seemed to understand her hands were free. She lifted up her arms, and the iron cuffs slipped off her wrists, and she gave her leg a shake and stepped out of the one on her ankle. Sure she was skin an' bone, a breath of wind would a blowed her over. She tipped her head back on her neck, searchin' the sky for somethin' – blind an' all as she was. Maybe it was just to feel the air on her face again. The lieutenant never noticed, too busy argufyin' with a brute of a fellow who had a handful of wormy apples he was dyin' to let rip with.

"Lizzie stood swayin', free as a bird, an' a lock of folk near the front started hootin'. At that, the lieutenant spotted her, and he must a thought she was set on makin' a holy show out of him. He was on'y young, barely old enough to shave, and he panicked. He grabbed his sergeant's musket off him and pointed it at her, yellin' his head off.

"Lizze could'n see him, but she could hear him. She turned to the officer. He guldered again, tellin' her not to move. An' if I had'n seen what happened next with my own two eyes, I'd be hard pushed to believe it. Lizzie swung her lame leg, an' took a lop-sided step towards him. Then another. And she walked onto the bayonet of his rifle. The blade went into her breast, and she shuffled forward and reached for the butt of the gun to push the point in deeper. All the whiles, the lieutenant jus' stood there with his jaw flappin' open.

"Next thing, he let go his musket as if it burned his hands. Lizzie Cellar dropped to her knees with the blade still inside. As she fell, the wind took her bonnet, and you could see her hair had growed back a fair bit. There was another gust, and her hair floated out behind. Her head nodded once, twice, and the third time her chin touched her chest and rested there. Lizzie died in front of us, on the wooden platform where the stocks were set. Not a sound did she make. And I'll tell you somethin' better. There was'n a peep out of the crowd, either. Not the tearaways. Nor the ministers. They watched, and they hung their heads, and they tiptoed away."

"Ach Lizzie, Lizzie," I said, my eyes welling up. "I should a made you get clear away from Islandmagee while you had the chance. Instead, I put a cattle halter roun' your neck an' led you to that."

"Don't blame yourself," said Mercy.

But I did.

I do.

ᘰᕽ   ᘰᕽ   ᘰᕽ

I saw Margaret Mitchell again once or twice. She set herself up, same as before, trading chickens in the market square in Carrickfergus – looking folk in the eye and gurning at them out of her toothless gob. Gaol didn't knock the stuffing out of her. While Margaret Mitchell didn't prosper, neither did she starve. My memory was jogged when I spotted her there, surrounded by fowl, and I minded my master bought our rooster off her. He came back with the bird under his arm, highly amused by the big woman who looked like a man, arms to match a butcher's and chicken feathers in her hair.

I mentioned it to my master.

"You're mistaken," says he, looking anywhere but at me.

"But she saw you had warts on your thumb, master. She

told you they'd be cured if you bathed them in water from the forge. You did as she bid, and it worked – just as she said."

"That was another woman."

"I could swear it was the same one sold you the rooster."

"You are wrong. Don't you dare repeat it to another soul. I never saw Margaret Mitchell before."

So I never said a word. Not even to Mercy Hunter, who was always niggling for gossip. In fact, she was worse than ever, because she had time on her hands, heavy with child. She had a new master by now, in a smallholding hard-by Portmuck – and ran rings round him, same as the minister, until he took her to wife in the end. Though not before she had a swollen belly. It raised no eyebrows on Islandmagee – most women had their babbies started before the minister was called on to tie the knot.

When first I saw her condition, I whispered to her about the herbs the Irish wise woman told me about, but she said there was no need. Her master had vowed to make an honest woman of her. I felt myself shrink, comparing him with my master. Of course, Mercy's man was no gentleman like Master Haltridge – who could not have made me his wife, even if he was unwed. Still, he did to me what the seventh commandment says a man must only do to his wife and none other.

And I was a willing partner.

I never even shared the gossip I heard about Mary Dunbar with Mercy. Mary Dunbar's name was rarely spoken in Islandmagee afterwards, except once in a while when folk fell to wondering what became of her.

"I hear she sailed to the West Indies to marry a plantation owner, an' lives like the Queen of Sheba there with servants to dress her, wash her and hould the spoon to her mouth if she cannae be bothered doin' it herself," said Mercy.

"She wed a minister an' moved to Scotland," said Noah.

At the meeting-house one Sabbath, after the praying was

over and folk lingered to chat, all the talk was of how she took herself off to Virginia and passed her days teaching the word of God to the natives in deerskins. By way of remorse for all the trouble she caused, I daresay, though folk never could agree if she was more sinned against than sinning.

But I heard a tale about her. Frazer Bell told it to me, making me swear to hold my tongue as soon as he shared the secret. I always suspected I was the first and last soul ever he spoke to about it. He said Mary Dunbar was put in a madhouse in London-town. He had it off an officer passing through Larne to join his regiment, who shared a table at an inn with him. The officer said she was wed to a doctor in a place called York, a match made by her parents, but after less than a year the doctor decided she couldn't be sane. Seemingly she made accusations against his sister, saying she was a witch and turned herself into a she-goat to go cavorting, and before Mary Dunbar knowed day was night he had the papers signed and her locked away in an asylum.

Frazer Bell seemed to take it to heart. Them lunatic places are meant to be a living hell. If you weren't mad going into one, you'd be mad by the time they carried you out.

But who knows? Maybes she sailed to the West Indies and lives in the lap of luxury after all. The one thing I can say for sure about Mary Dunbar is that she was never seen about these parts again.

※　　※　　※

When I study on those events, I think about how neighbours turned their backs on neighbours. How the few were thrown to the wolves by the many. I don't just mean during the witch trial, though they did it then as well. The Judas kiss I'm talking about was given earlier, in 1641, when the Magees were wiped out by Scotch soldiers bent on revenge. Blood was spilled while neighbours looked the other way.

What happened on Islandmagee, I've turned over in my mind, and it's my belief something evil was born out of it. Not so much from the butchery – one side or the other was always doing violence – but because nobody tried to warn the victims, or prevent the soldiers from killing all round them, or save even one Magee child. The planters closed their eyes and ears and waited for murder to be done in their names.

Maybes they felt they had no choice, if they were to put down roots in this country where they never felt completely safe. Always, always, they were watching the horizon. Aye, and their backs, forbye. Even the friendly Irish resented them, and the Scotch never knowed how far they could trust them. But to my mind, that act of looking away at the time of the Magee killings gave birth to the corrupt seed. And the hush that followed – denying the truth – allowed it to grow.

I've turned it back and forth, like the wheelings of the tide, and this is how I see it. Knowehead is a house apart because it belongs to the land, not to them that raised it up or them that live in it. It was built in a place held sacred by a people who lived here long before Gael or planter. We call them pagans and think ourselves better than them, but they grasped how everything comes from the land and sinks back into the land. Aye, and they understood how folk serve the land, rather than the other way round.

Knowehead was using Hamilton Lock, using Mary Dunbar – just like I doubt maybes it used me. I wouldn't be surprised if it was the house sent me to Lock's Cave.

Lately, I've found myself dwelling on the manner of Lizzie Cellar's death. I can no more undo what she did than store clouds in my pocket, nor do I seek to try. But the choice she made fills my mind. I can't stop wondering if she thought about the Magee women and childer at all when she did it. I know there's no reason to believe she did – and yet, could she have been influenced by the stories of how they met their end?

Her dying pops into my head when I'm instructing the new

maid in her duties, or when I'm collecting speckled eggs, or when I'm plucking a chicken, saving the feathers for a pillow. Out of the blue, I see her last moments as clearly as if I stood below the stocks in Carrickfergus market square that morning: watching her press her flesh against the cold metal of the lieutenant's bayonet, embracing it like a lover. Mister Sinclair says it's perpetual darkness for any that die by their own hand. He preached a sermon about it: "Woe to them that share the fate of Judas."

But is it possible that, just for a few seconds, Lizze felt free? So deliberate were her actions, she must have knowed what she was about. There's freedom of sorts in that. In facing two evils and making a choice. It might have been the same for those women with their babbies, chased by soldiers at the Gobbins. They might have felt free too, as they flew through the air, before meeting the rocks below. There was something appalling behind them, something no less terrible in front – but for the space of a heartbeat, there might have been release.

Oftentimes, my feet take me to the cliffs and I stand looking over them, silence hanging like an anchor. I can no longer hear the tide or the gulls, or see anything beyond grey sea reaching up to grey sky. All I can think about is how it might have felt to step off, as Hamilton Lock urged me to do, into the arms of the wind that blows about Islandmagee. To let go at last.

And then I step away from the edge and turn my feet for home. Drawn back, always, to Knowehead House.

THE END

BRIAN BOY MAGEE
by Ethna Carbery (1866-1902)

I am Brian Boy Magee–
My father was Eoghain Bán–
I was wakened from happy dreams
By the shouts of my startled clan;
And I saw through the leaping glare
That marked where our homestead stood,
My mother swing by her hair –
And my brothers lie in their blood.
In the creepy cold of the night
The pitiless wolves came down–
Scotch troops from that Castle grim
Guarding Knockfergus Town
And they hacked and lashed and hewed
With musket and rope and sword,
Till my murdered kin lay thick
In pools by the Slaughter Ford.
I fought by my father's side,
And when we were fighting sore
We saw a line of their steel
With our shrieking women before;
The red-coats drove them on
To the verge of the Gobbins gray,
Hurried them – God! the sight!
As the sea foamed up for its prey.
Oh, tall were the Gobbins cliffs,
And sharp were the rocks, my woe!
And tender the limbs that met
Such terrible death below;
Mother and babe and maid
They clutched at the empty air,
With eyeballs widened in fright,
That hour of despair.

(Sleep soft in your heaving bed,
O little fair love of my heart!
The bitter oath I have sworn
Shall be of my life a part;
And for every piteous prayer
You prayed on your way to die,
May I hear an enemy plead
While I laugh and deny.)
In the dawn that was gold and red,
Ay, red as the blood-choked stream,
I crept to the perilous brink–
Great Christ! was the night a dream ?
In all the Island of Gloom
I only had life that day–
Death covered the green hill-sides,
And tossed in the Bay.
I have vowed by the pride of my sires–
By my mother's wandering ghost–
By my kinsfolk's shattered bones
Hurled on the cruel coast–
By the sweet dead face of my love,
And the wound in her gentle breast–
To follow that murderous band,
A sleuth-hound who knows no rest.
I shall go to Phelim O'Neill
With my sorrowful tale, and crave
A blue-bright blade of Spain,
In the ranks of his soldiers brave.
And God grant me the strength to wield
That shining avenger well –
When the Gael shall sweep his foe
Through the yawning gates of Hell.
I am Brian Boy Magee!
And my creed is a creed of hate;
Love, Peace, I have cast aside–

But Vengeance, Vengeance I wait!
Till I pay back the four-fold debt
For the horrors I witnessed there,
When my brothers moaned in their blood,
And my mother swung by her hair.

[Taken from *The Four Winds of Erinn: Poems by Ethna Carbery*. Edited by Seumas MacManus (her husband). Dublin, Ireland: M. H. Gill and Son Ltd 1906]

AUTHOR'S NOTE:

"It were better that Ten Suspected Witches should escape, than that one Innocent Person should be Condemned." Increase Mather, Puritan minister in Salem.

The last conviction for witchcraft in Ireland happened in County Antrim on March 31st, 1711. In the same year that Massachusetts repented of its notorious Salem Witch Trials, reinstating the rights and good names of those who were condemned for witchcraft nineteen years earlier, a version of witch fever broke out in Ireland.

A group trial involving eight women accused as witches was held at the Assizes in Carrickfergus. The eight were named by a girl of eighteen called Mary Dunbar, who claimed they used their evil arts to torment her. This was said to have taken place on nearby Islandmagee, where Mary Dunbar was staying with relatives. She was described by the Vicar of Belfast, Dr William Tisdall, who attended the trial, as "having an open and innocent countenance, and being a very intelligent young person".

A swarm of neighbours and local clergymen told the court they witnessed the victim thrown into convulsions and attacked by invisible hands. They also said they saw her regurgitate objects ranging from pins to waistcoat buttons, which were shown in evidence to the jury of twelve men. In the absence of a natural explanation, the gap was filled with a supernatural one: witchcraft was blamed.

All of the defendants maintained their innocence. Some had alibis, while others were known to be regular churchgoers. None of the eight had a lawyer. Nor was there any medical evidence regarding the state of the accuser's health. It was a case of Mary Dunbar's words against theirs – and the jury unanimously believed the pretty young woman.

The eight were found guilty and sentenced to a year and a day in prison, with four turns in the pillory on fair day: the standard term for non-lethal witchcraft. The crowd was worked up into such a rage against them that one of the convicted women had her eye put out by a missile thrown while she was in the stocks.

Just twenty-five years later, the crime of witchcraft was removed from the statute books. After the court case in Carrickfergus, accuser and accused alike faded from history. But on Islandmagee, the 300-year-old story has not been forgotten – though it is not much talked about. A local farmer has a rock on his land called "the witch's stone" where legend has it one of the accused dragged her nails along its surface as she was carried off to prison. Descendants of the eight women convicted of witchcraft still live in the area. And Knowehead House, where Mary Dunbar claimed to have fallen under the spell of a witches' coven, remains occupied to this day.

This novel is inspired by a true story, although I have taken liberties with some of the facts – especially in relation to the haunting of Knowehead House, which I imagined, by Hamilton Lock, a fictional character. There was a massacre of Magees in Islandmagee by Scottish troops in 1641, but it is disputed whether women and children were driven over the cliffs. (I invented the letter in the prologue; no such document is held in Belfast's excellent Linen Hall Library. The pedlar's ballad is also a piece of fiction, although modelled on ballads of the period.) Eye-witness accounts of events in Islandmagee make for chilling reading, however. A raid was carried out with the intention of eliminating the Magees, as reprisal for the killing of settlers by native Irish elsewhere. A small number of Magees escaped, and a few neighbours made efforts to shelter them. But I played this down for narrative purposes. Instead, I attributed some of the documented actions of other solders during the massacre to my fictional character, Hamilton Lock. There was a woman called Annie McGill, not Bridget McGill, who survived a bullet wound to the neck during a raid on Eiver Magee's house. I changed her name because of the potential for muddling her with Mistress Anne. I also changed two of the accused women's first names, from Janet Carson to Becky Carson and from Janet Mean to Bessie Mean – four of the women tried for witchcraft were called Janet or Jane, a popular name at this time and place, but confusing for readers.

As for Mary Dunbar, she was real enough, and lived in Knockbreda, now part of Belfast. I relocated her to Armagh. She was observed to vomit up the items mentioned in the story. This was taken as proof of her being witched. But the ability to swallow and regurgitate small objects at will is not unknown. Indeed, it was later used in vaudeville acts and is still performed by entertainers today. Nobody knows her motivation for making the accusations, so I have speculated on possibilities.

A stone, known as the Rocking Stone does stand on Islandmagee, and tradition holds that it was used as a seat of judgment in pre-Christian times. It was said to rock if a wrongdoer approached it. But it was not pulled down on the orders of the minister, and it is situated near Brown's Bay rather than in Kilcoan More. It is one of a number of boulders left behind by the retreating glacier that carved out the territory. But I prefer the idea of a pagan people putting the boulder in place deliberately for ceremonial use – a Celtic shock-and-awe tactic.

Finally, unlike Salem, and other witchcraft trials, the eight women convicted of diabolical practices in Antrim in 1711 escaped execution. But while Salem subsequently tried to do justice by those it wronged, the same cannot be said for Islandmagee's so-called witches. They never had their convictions overturned by the authorities, nor their reputations restored to them. The taint remains.

GLOSSARY

A-coorse – of course
Afore – before
Agin – against
Bairn – child
Bap – head
Barge – scold (noun and verb)
Bate – beaten
Bawbee – halfpenny
Bide – stay
Birl – twist
Blether – gossip/nonsense
Boke – vomit
Bogging – dirty
Brae – hillside
Brave – very
Braw – handsome
Burn – stream
Cauld – cold
Clabber – mud
Clatter – pile
Clatty/clattery – dirty and untidy
Clocks – black beetles
Codding – fooling
Collops – bacon slices topped with fried egg
Cow claps – cow pats
Cowp over/up – turn over
Cozen – deceive
Crabbit – bad-tempered
Crawley-boy – runt of the litter
Cub – boy
Cuddy – girl
Dander – stroll
Darsent – dare not

Dirk – dagger

Docken – dock leaf, a traditional remedy for nettle stings

Dose of – lot of

Dulse – dried seaweed

Dunder – thump

Dunderhead – stupid person

Fash – worry

Fly – cunning

Footer with – fiddle with

Forbye – besides/as well

Fornenst – in front of, opposite

Founder – freeze

Gabbon hawks – goshawks, gabbon is another version of gobbins

Gawp – stare

Give someone the time of day – say hello

Graylords – pollock

Gulder – shout

Gulpin – ignorant, uncouth person

Gurn – frown, pull a face

Gurney – frowning

Haet – scrap

Haggery duff – a type of bread made from potatoes and oatmeal

Handling – business

Hap up – tuck in

Hard-by – near

Hidin' – beating

Hirple – limp

Hoak – poke about

Juke – duck/dodge/crouch down

Junketing - merrymaking

Keek – peep

Kehoe – making a loud noise

Kitling – kitten

Lock of – several
Maither – complain
Megrum - migraine
Mind – remember
Mizzle – drizzle
Nar – than
Near – mean
No call – no need
Oxters – armpits
Piece – slice of bread, sandwich
Ploughter – traipse
Pockle – fool/Pockling – messing, fooling
Pother – trouble and worry
Quare – very
Rare – odd
Redd up – cleared up
Riz – risen
Scaldies – baby birds
Scrab – scratch
Screek of day – daybreak
Scundered – sickened
Sea-pig – porpoise
Shebeen – unlicensed pub
Shimmy – petticoat
Shoon – shoes
Shuck – ditch
Skelp – slap
Skite – go quickly
Skitter – unpleasant person
Skittery – small, inconsequential
Skitter-jabs – freckles
Snatters – snot
Soldiers – soldiers
Sonsey – buxom
Stoor – dust

Streeling – dragging

Striddle – dawdle

Targe – battleaxe

Terrible – very

Thatch – hair

The-day – today

The-morrow – tomorrow

The-gether – together

Thole/tholing – endure/enduring

Thon/thonder – that/there

Thran – stubborn

Thrapple – choke

Through-other – disorganized

Titter – bit

Totie – tiny

Un'asied – troubled

Visog – face

Wee'an – child (wee one)

Wee drap – something to drink

Wheek – snatch

Wheen – some

Whisht – hush

Wile – very

Yammer – cry

ACKNOWLEDGEMENTS

Many people helped me with this project along the way. I'd like to acknowledge them here, in no particular order:

My agent Lucy Luck, who believed in the book when I was plugging away at it – and whose faith bolstered mine.

George Rutherford of Islandmagee, an extremely knowledgeable local historian who could not have been more courteous when I visited, and who was kind enough to guide me round the area, offering valuable insights.

Dr Stiofán Ó'Direáin who read an early draft and made insightful suggestions, especially in relation to historical accuracy. I am particularly grateful for his kind permission to use an Islandmagee map at the beginning of this novel, borrowed from his own co-authored book, Islandmagee and *Templecorran – A Postcard History*.

Joe Graham of the magazine *Rushlight*, a helpful local historian in Belfast.

Sharon McQuillan of Libraries NI, who gave me a list containing a treasure trove of historical books on the subject.

Jane Alger, director, Dublin UNESCO City of Literature, who pointed me towards useful references to the trial and to the period generally in Dublin's Pearse Library.

Gaye Shortland, stellar editor, whose eagle eye caught anachronisms, among other improvements and contributions.

Paula Campbell, Ward River Press publisher, for imagining the imprint and having the enthusiasm and commitment to act as its midwife.

My loyal and talented writing friends living 'near-hand' (as

Ellen would say) – who go for walks and drink coffee with me, and keep me motivated to persevere with the storytelling.

David Collins of Samson Films for believing there might be something to this yarn of mine.

The Princess Grace Irish Library in Monaco, where I was fortunate enough to spend a month as writer-in-residence – lending space and distance to work on the project. Those associated with the library were welcoming and accommodating, and I remember my stay with affection.

DISCUSSION TOPICS FOR BOOK CLUBS

1. This story is told through the perspective of Ellen, a female servant. Why do you think the author chose Ellen to be her narrator?

2. How would the story have differed if told through the eyes of:
   Mary Dunbar
   Isabel Haltridge
   One of the women accused of being a witch
   One of the ministers
   Constable Blan, the witchfinder
   Frazer Bell

3. Is this a traditional 'haunted house' narrative?

4. Does the fact that the story is based on true events influence your reading of it? If so why?

5. Hamilton Lock is a fictional character (though the actions the author attributes to him during the Magee massacre are documented facts). Why do you think the author has created this character?

6. What factors appeared to influence Mary Dunbar when she began making her accusations?

7. What does the use of dialect contribute to the story?

8. What do you make of the fact that a woman is accusing other women of witchcraft?

9. Discuss the handling of the Ulster-Scots versus the native Irish in the story.

10. How does the Islandmagee community self-regulate (i.e. enforce or uphold its own rules and laws without external intervention) and why?

11. Discuss the importance of the following elements in the plot:
 Land ownership
 Memory
 Superstition and legend

12. Discuss the public entertainment element of the Islandmagee witchcraft trial.

13. What do you think happened to Mary Dunbar after she left Islandmagee?

14. Do you think the author intends us to feel any sympathy for Mary Dunbar?

15. Is there anything quintessentially Irish about the story or is it universal?

 WARD RIVER PRESS

Novels that demand to be read,
not just talked about.

NOW AVAILABLE

The Friday Tree by Sophia Hillan

Ruby's Tuesday by Gillian Binchy

Sing Me to Sleep by Helen Moorhouse

The Last Goodbye by Caroline Finnerty

Into the Night Sky by Caroline Finnerty

Levi's Gift by Jennifer Burke

Kingdom of Scars by Eoin Macken

A Shadow in the Yard by Liz McManus

The Curtain Falls by Carole Gurnett

If you enjoyed this book from
Poolbeg why not visit our website:

www.poolbeg.com

and get another book delivered straight
to your home or to a friend's home.

All books despatched within 24 hours.

POOLBEG

Why not join our mailing list at
www.poolbeg.com and get some
fantastic offers, competitions,
author interviews and much more?

@PoolbegBooks